MW01167485

UPTOWN

a novel by

Jack Gardner

MINT HILL BOOKS
MAIN STREET RAG PUBLISHING COMPANY
CHARLOTTE, NORTH CAROLINA

Copyright © 2011 Jack Gardner

Cover Art and design by M. Scott Douglass

Library of Congress Control Number: 2011943052

ISBN: 978-1-59948-323-8

Produced in the United States of America

Mint Hill Books
Main Street Rag Publishing Company
PO Box 690100
Charlotte, NC 28227
www.MainStreetRag.com

To Amy Shaw Gardner and Dr. Cullen Ruff,
for love and lessons learned

CONTENTS

PART 1

CHAPTER ONE
MORROCROFT

May 2005

The insulated splendor of Morrocroft Estates had a certain artificial exclusiveness, but was no less compelling for that fact. In the absence of any natural distinction, Morrocroft was, much like the city of Charlotte itself, entirely dependent upon the creation of a fabricated one.

As Dr. Stephen Rayfield was waved through the iron gate by the unsmiling security guard, he was struck by the sheer opulent audacity of the place. Many of the city's power brokers, including the chancellor of Stephen's university, resided in enormous homes behind the sturdy brick wall that encircled Morrocroft, an otherwise flat, nondescript tract of land near the SouthPark shopping mall. Some of these luxe pioneers had migrated from the more sedate neighborhood of Myers Park, whose majestic old homes still maintained a historic cachet. Indeed, many of the residents of Myers Park still effected an upward tilt of their noses whenever the vulgar name of Morrocroft was uttered in their presence.

While the oak-shaded streets of Myers Park remained a sanctuary of money and privilege, its antique charm was deficient in one crucial regard. Unlike the fortress that was Morrocroft, it lacked a wall, that tangible assurance of bricks and mortar that said clearly and decisively to all intruders, social or criminal, Keep Out.

Although Stephen had moved to Charlotte almost a year ago, this was his first visit to his aunt and uncle's home. It was an ornate Italian Renaissance concoction and was surrounded by a tall iron fence. That Edward and Missy Harrison required such fortification, in addition to the guarded entrance of Morrocroft itself, only hinted at the treasures within. Stephen drove through the open gate into the circular driveway, which was bordered with boxwoods and a profusion of red and white begonias.

As Stephen ascended the stone steps, his curly brown hair was still wet, looking as if he had just showered. He had the high cheekbones and broad forehead of the Scots-Irish Harrisons, heightened by judicious, though no doubt clandestine, mixing with Cherokee blood some generations back.

The sun was setting, as if on cue. A softening pinkish glow graced the entry terrace. Stephen studied the carved panels of the double-sided front doors, which were supposed to be reminiscent of the Ghiberti doors in Florence, Italy. Rumor had it that his aunt had the sculpted panels specially commissioned by a Florentine artisan. Missy was known for a dedication to all things Italian. Such a sensibility for Anglophilic Charlotteans, where references to Florence typically led to the town in South Carolina, bordered on the exotic.

He tapped the green lion's head door knocker. The massive door was promptly opened by two attendants, a portly man in black tie and a young woman in a black dress. "Welcome," the young woman said, "Mr. and Mrs. Harrison are in the library."

Stephen smiled at Aunt Missy's latest affectation, intrigued, impressed even, by the shameless overreaching of a woman who would actually employ uniformed attendants for a dinner for ten. He stepped inside a cavernous foyer and hall. The white marble floors were so gleaming that he could almost see his reflection as he walked by heavy oak-paneled walls. He proceeded past the grim portraits of various Harrisons and Gilmores, reverently framed in gilt.

Gilt surpasses guilt, he thought, mindful of the more unsavory histories of both clans.

Mr. and Mrs. Edward Harrison stood side by side in the library, in front of the elaborate stone fireplace. Above the mantel, a portrait of Missy holding a bouquet of roses loomed in serene contemplation. The room was furnished in a brown sea of leather chairs and sofas. The walls were lined with shelves crowded with immaculate boxed sets of books, which were distinctive for, if not their actual use, their remarkable color coordination. No doubt mindful of Charlotte's reputation as a cultural wasteland, Missy had deposited a string quartet in a corner, conveniently next to the bar. The strains of Puccini wafted unobtrusively about the room as guests sipped obligatory cocktails.

Missy, smiling effusively, whispered something to her husband as Stephen paused somewhat hesitantly at the door. Missy looked the picture of regal comfort in her green silk cocktail dress, which was cut low to highlight the diamond necklace nestled securely in the crevice of her firmly augmented breasts.

"Stephen! How wonderful to see you," Missy exclaimed, rushing over to the door and hugging him with an enthusiasm notable for its force if not its sincerity. She took him by the arm and guided him into the room like a pet of whom she was fond, but not yet decided on keeping. "Edward, look who's here," she called out to her husband, who was talking now to an attractive young couple.

"Hey there, pardner," Edward said, taking Stephen's hand in a firm, assertive grip. "We finally got you over here." Edward Harrison effected a patient and stoic forbearance, smiling good-naturedly in his well tailored, but still somehow ill-fitting suit. Next to the shimmery, textured blondeness of his wife, his shock of white, wavy hair hinted at a sort of virginal innocence. Given Stephen's limited but telling education in the randy nature of southern men, he could only conclude that such a semblance of purity was surely an illusion.

Edward turned to the couple beside him. "Alice. Bill. I'd like you to meet my nephew, Dr. Stephen Rayfield. He's a history professor out at UNCC."

"Assistant professor. Call me Stephen," he said.

"Oh, he's just being modest," Missy interjected. Then, with a proprietary tone of a satisfied hostess comparing one ornament to another, Missy added, "Alice and Bill here are transplants from San

Francisco. Alice is a doctor and Bill works for Bank of America."
Missy smiled broadly as she and Edward left to continue their orbit
about the room.

"So. History," Alice said. "How do you manage to get those kids
to pay attention? Aren't they all just glued to MTV these days?"

"Oh, absolutely," he replied, "All of my lectures are given in
music video format. I film them the night before."

"Wow," Bill said, "so you can sing too?"

"Sing? No. I can't carry a tune, but neither can anyone on MTV,
can they? An actual melody would only confuse them. I have worked
out some fabulous dance moves though. You should see my Jefferson
tango."

One of those awkward, silent intervals ensued, as the newly
introduced trio glanced appraisingly at one another. Stephen assumed
that Alice and Bill Owens were still, as he was, relatively new to the
bumpy terrain of social life in Charlotte. They probably approached
events at homes such as the Harrisons' with the curious gaze, if not
attire, of a couple on safari. Fortyish looking, each retained a lean
and athletic form that more than hinted at their enduring, vaguely
sensual, capability for all sorts of exploration. Given their still
youthful attractiveness, not to mention their esoteric backgrounds,
Stephen suspected that they were greatly in demand, if slightly
suspect, among Charlotte hostesses.

Dinner consisted of overcooked seafood risotto and the
compensation of a delightful Vernaccia di San Gimignano. The
wine was of an impeccable vintage and was in no way diminished by
Aunt Missy's doomed efforts to correctly pronounce it.

The guests, reduced to nine as a result of the much commented
on absence of the husband of Frances Bulwark, the textile heiress,
earnestly discussed banking mergers, the athletic struggles of the
Panthers, and, in somewhat more muted tones, escalating crime.
There had been another carjacking just the other day in Providence
Plantation, in the very bosom of affluent southeast Charlotte.

"Do you share your aunt's fondness for Italy?" Dr. Alice Owens
whispered to Stephen, lightly touching his hand with her own.

"Oh yes, of course, but not like Aunt Missy. She has, I would say, a more elevated appreciation for the Italians. My preference is for the earthier variety. I was just there last summer, backpacking, after finishing up my dissertation."

"Did you go by yourself?" Alice asked.

"Yes," Stephen said, then winked, "part of the time." He noticed that her eyes, like his own, were a dark shade of blue.

Alice smiled. "I would guess you don't lack for company for long."

Stephen was about to reply when there was the faint tinkling of a wine glass, an exquisite blue Murano goblet with a gold stem. Missy, her blond highlights pulled tight into a helmeted pile, smiled with equal tautness and rose from her seat. In the Harrison household, one of the modest gestures to feminism was that Missy always gave the toasts at their parties.

Edward Harrison, with the affected and vacant pose of a campaign wife, glanced across the table as Missy began to speak, carefully modulating the deep tones of her menopausal voice. "Everyone, I can't let this evening go by without thanking you, each and every one of you, for being here with us tonight, and so I must propose a toast."

She paused a moment, frozen in misty-eyed nostalgia, as if she were already remembering this evening as a particularly treasured occasion. "A home is only bricks and mortar and bits of wood. Well, okay, and Brunswig and Fils fabrics! No offense, Frances," she said, glancing at Frances Bulwark, whose beleaguered textile empire produced simpler cloth.

"None taken," Mrs. Bulwark said, waving her bejeweled fingers, no doubt wanting to add that the 'l' in Fils was silent.

"Those are just things," Missy continued, "It is friendship and family that we treasure. And that is what you all mean to us."

Just as Missy sat down, Mrs. Laura Caldwell raised her glass. Mrs. Caldwell had the oddly delicate look of a plump Lladro figurine. Everything about her seemed soft, yet somehow precise and tapered, from the gentle waves of her jet black hair to the manicured opal smoothness of her fingernails. She appeared to be a woman for whom nothing, not even her own expanding girth, should ever be out of its appointed place.

"I would like to thank Missy and Edward for this lovely dinner," Laura began. Her husband Andrew, whose resigned slouch and insistent paunch were his most assertive attributes, stared at the centerpiece of towering orchids. "They make the world," Laura continued, "which can be so discouraging these days, a brighter place. Generous. Compassionate..."

She hesitated, searching without success for another adjective. Her somber expression caused her chin to collapse into multiple waves of doughy flesh. Then, her expression settled into a resolute smile, tensing the flabbiness of her face into something perhaps more solid, but, Stephen observed, infinitely more discouraging. Finally, she concluded, "They enrich our lives every day. God has blessed us with these dear friends, and we thank Him. Here's to Missy and Edward."

Stephen lifted his glass along with the others. He tried not to wince at Mrs. Caldwell's convivial reference to God. He glanced at Alice and Bill, and was impressed by their noncommittal, but reverent, expression. Stephen reminded himself that most of the people at the Harrison table shared, or at least pretended to share, Laura Caldwell's fervent bond with Jesus. At the end of the day, Charlotte was still a city of banks and churches. Praise the Lord.

Tiramisu, inevitably, was served for dessert, along with cappuccinos. Alice Owens nudged Stephen and said, with just a slight nod to southern womanhood, "Goodness, I can't tell you how glad I am you were here tonight. It's such a pleasure meeting you."

"The pleasure is mine," Stephen said, his blue eyes gazing mischievously at her. He thought he saw Missy glaring at them from her perch at the head of the table, but decided she was just displeased with the tiramisu. It probably wasn't a bit like what she had enjoyed in Milan last year.

Stephen would look back at the end of that unforgiving summer and recall the odd number of guests seated at the enormous mahogany table that evening in May. Nine. An uneven number.

But, there had been another, unseen guest. A final visitor, heedless of glistening sunsets or Murano glass, oblivious to ambition or regret, and notable not so much for entrance as for exit. The spectral presence that eventually arrives unbidden and unwanted in every life was there that evening at the Harrison home. And it was quietly, patiently waiting, knowing that the walled fortress of Morrocroft Estates was not so impregnable after all.

CHAPTER TWO
PIPER GLEN

T hank goodness that's over," Andrew Caldwell said to his wife, as they were driving home. "Why does she always have those Italian desserts? Just once I would like to have a decent piece of apple pie."

"Well, I will just have to get you some apple pie when we get home, sweetie," Laura said, patting his hand as though consoling a recalcitrant child. Her friendship with Missy Harrison exceeded by some years her marriage to Andrew Caldwell. It was unfortunate that Andrew and Missy disliked each other, always circling each other with amiable contempt. This was a challenge to Laura's considerable diplomatic skills, and usually accomplished with diversionary tactics. In that regard she was exceedingly grateful that both her friend and her husband were so easily distracted.

In the many years that she had known Missy, since their days at Queens College, their lives had run parallel, but at varying altitudes. Missy had ascended to ever loftier heights on the wave of Edward Harrison's genius for making money. Meanwhile, Laura had to reckon with the subordinate success of her husband, who was a partner with Harrison Associates, and with her widowed mother, whose control of what was left of the family fortune was predicated on an insistent desire to keep it to herself.

Laura's family was Old Charlotte and among the first residents of Myers Park, when it was developed as a suburb on the streetcar line in the early years of the 20th century. In her home in Piper Glen, a decidedly new suburb with decidedly new money, there was a photo of her grandmother Soames as a child. Her grandmother used to entertain Laura with tales of tea parties at the legendary Duke Mansion. "Such a sweet child," her grandmother would say, studiously avoiding any mention of Doris Duke's sordid escapades as an adult.

The Soames family was a member of that insular group that at one time controlled the city with gentlemanly agreements over poker tables, or in quiet chats after church. Those benign gatherings were supplanted now by a gaggle of lawyers and accountants scurrying along the chilly corridors of the Bank of America Plaza.

The Charlotte of Laura's childhood was as frozen in time now as the golden statue of crazy old Hugh McManahan, still waving his towel at the confusing intersection of Queens and Providence, where Queens Road continues in two directions and Providence Road does likewise. Mr. McManahan used to direct traffic with a white towel and go roller skating through Myers Park with only one skate. "Can't find the other one. Can't find the other one," he would cackle as he rolled lopsidedly by.

Laura sighed. In those days, a neighborhood eccentric like Mr. McManahan, and perhaps the occasional morphine addicted aunt locked discreetly in the attic, was the extent of exotic lifestyles. No more. Times had changed in that regard as well. Now it was drag queens on parade and noisy celebrity occupants of the Betty Ford Center.

"Wasn't that kind of them to invite the nephew?" Laura asked her husband, in a doubtful tone that suggested it was neither kind nor wise to have done so.

"Who? That guy Stephen? Oh, he seems okay," Andrew answered. "And wasn't he just the hit with Alice Owens? But, that kind of figures, don't you think?"

"Yes. He seems like a fine young man, but..." Laura paused, uncertain as to any further speculation, and then commented, "They certainly kept the wine flowing tonight, didn't they? I thought Frances was drunk before the soup arrived. Really sad." Poor Frances, Laura thought, besieged on all fronts by a declining market for domestic linens as well as an unreliable husband.

"When did Missy and Edward become so liberal?" Andrew asked. "If you ask me, it's their church. Way too tolerant. A lot can happen if you just keep looking the other way."

"That's true, hon. So true." Laura agreed with her husband that the Harrisons' church, Myers Park Presbyterian, which Laura had herself attended as a child, had drifted away from Biblical teachings. On the other hand, it was difficult to see how it could have much influence on the Harrisons, given that their visits to the church were so infrequent and grudging.

"Missy has always been so headstrong," Andrew said vaguely, as if an inherent stubbornness was somehow fatal to Missy Harrison's spiritual well-being, not to mention the basis for her more earthbound imperfections.

"I wish I could persuade her to come hear Reverend Dunlap." Laura said. Laura and Andrew attended Central Galilee Church and were undisturbed by the condescension that the evangelical church aroused in the more sophisticated circles of Charlotte. The grandness of the church, its towering chapel visible from miles away, was a comforting beacon.

"Is Reverend Dunlap preaching this Sunday?" Andrew asked anxiously, having recently developed an uneasiness for the assistant minister, Reverend Tensile, whose bouncy red curls and exaggerated laughter hinted at decadent tendencies.

"Yes, he is. His sermon is going to address the Internet, or as he calls it 'Smut Highway.'"

"Great," Andrew said. Quickly changing the subject, he asked, "Did you make the reservations at the Palm?"

"Yes, I did, hon, for seven o'clock. Plenty of time to get there after the ceremony." They were planning on having dinner there after their son Ben's graduation from Charlotte Latin in two weeks. Andrew was inordinately fond of the Palm's chocolate cake.

"And is her majesty going to join us?"

"No, she has other plans," Laura said, acutely aware that, by mutual assent, her mother most often did have other plans.

Laura banished thoughts of her mother from her mind as she and Andrew entered Piper Glen Estates. Like most of Charlotte's upscale neighborhoods, it was a parade of colonial or continental homage. Occasionally, they would pass a contemporary home, usually adjacent to the pond, with defiant posts and beams, ablaze with lights from floor to ceiling windows. The winding streets were lined with carefully spaced dogwoods and Bradford pears and neatly curbed and rarely used sidewalks. Piper Glen may have lacked the pedigree of Myers Park or the exclusionary wall of Morrocroft, but it did boast an undulating carpet of a Robert Trent Jones golf course. Its enviable hills, on which some of the grandest homes in Charlotte were perched around groves of trees, were suggestive of Tuscan vistas. Laura suspected that this distinction was not lost on Missy's Italian sensibilities.

Andrew pulled the car into the garage, one of those ubiquitous three-car side entry garages designed to accommodate large SUVs and the inevitable acquisitions they transported. The Caldwell garage was as neat as the house within, with not a rake or flower pot out of place. It was, for Laura, as welcoming and calm as an oasis, so long as the oasis remained pristine. Toward that end, the Caldwell home was perhaps one of the few in Piper Glen, if not Charlotte at large, where the housekeeper was under clear instructions to thoroughly mop the concrete floor of the garage once a week. If it was not the grandest home in Piper Glen, and it wasn't, it certainly could be regarded as the cleanest.

They walked into the equally immaculate kitchen and Andrew switched on the lights. "I'm going on up, honey. You coming?" Andrew asked, looking at her with unmistakable anticipation. She noticed that, under the glare of the kitchen lights, gray roots were usurping his thinning, combed over thatch of black hair. She had gently suggested, to no avail, that he go with a lighter shade.

"No," she said, noticing the dirty dishes that their daughter, Debra, had left in the sink. "I'll just straighten things up down here. How about your apple pie?"

He paused a moment, disappointed. "That's all right. I'll have some tomorrow. Good night, then. See you in the morning."

Laura began rinsing the dishes in the sink and then placed them in the dishwasher. Bits of lasagne, singed and crusty, clung to a pale blue plate. She decided to let it soak in the sink overnight.

Her work completed, she turned out the light and made her way quietly upstairs. In the landing above the stairs, she looked out the window toward the street, motionless under a cloudless sky. The night was so quiet, so still, Laura felt almost suspended in time. Then, she noticed the gentle flickering of a streetlamp and felt oddly reassured.

CHAPTER THREE
BLUE MARBLE

Missy Harrison awoke to the sound of a ticking clock, annoyed by the sing song, explosive rhythm. The golden timepiece sat on a blue marble base, beside which there was a bronze sculpture of a recumbent woman reading a book. Missy, appreciative of the clock's form, if not its function, reached over and irritably unplugged it.

The morning light filtered through her enormous bedroom window, as she lay in bed, swathed under a 600-thread count Egyptian cotton sheet and a yellow silk comforter. The colors of her room, without exception, were yellow and blue. Even the floor was of a pale blue marble. The floor had evoked mystified comment among some of her more inelastic friends, which only improved its value to her.

She gazed out at her emerald lawn, considered to be one of the most spectacular in Morrocroft Estates. Purple flowering azaleas glistened from the earlier exertions of the sprinkler system. Missy Harrison had always imagined living in such a splendid home. While she had not been born into upper class comfort, she viewed that as an error inevitably and long since corrected.

She and Edward were among the first arrivals in this synthetic Eden, where their social life consisted primarily of people to whom Missy was studiously gracious, but for whom she had minimal affection. Indeed, Missy viewed most of them as necessary players in her husband's career as a real estate developer. Her friendship with Laura Caldwell was the emotional exception to a social life almost exclusively orchestrated by more material considerations. In that regard, their enduring bond was a singular triumph of personal history over social dictate.

Most of the women, in particular, seemed to Missy like aging dinosaurs, frozen in time, paralytic matrons unable to move beyond Charlotte's conventional borders. These women, many of whom were housewives, were resigned to, though not always content with, their elegant homes, furnished with impeccable, if uninspired, Ethan Allen taste. They catered to their husbands and children, undeterred by the boorishness of the former, the ingratitude of the latter, and the betrayals of both. They danced at the Myers Park Country Club and flirted with their friends' husbands. They raised money for the Mint Museum and dutifully patronized, though only occasionally attended, the Blumenthal's Broadway series. They believed in a demanding God and, if they were somewhat inhibited in unlocking their souls, they were steadfast in opening their checkbooks every Sunday, usually at Myers Park Presbyterian Church.

These women stumbled along a familiar, comfortable path, while Missy, a newcomer among their ranks and unconstrained by their history, briskly searched other avenues. That such a disparity of vision was not fatal to their friendship with Missy was due to two things. One, her husband was a titan of the New Charlotte, expertly riding a wave of metastasizing, unstoppable growth. And two, Missy's command of passive-aggressive maneuvers, which she accepted was the requisite quality of any successful southern woman, was unimpaired by her more cosmopolitan ambitions.

Missy was openly ravenous to explore other worlds, but she had no intention of leaving the still-nourishing old one behind. If her friends were somewhat perplexed by the former aim, they were reassured by the latter. They viewed her, in a word, as an amusing gourmand whose variable appetites far exceeded their own. And, to be fair, she did bring them the most marvelous little things from her travels.

She smiled, as she invariably did whenever she contemplated her meteoric rise and the considerable dust she had kicked into the eyes of the people whom she had left behind. She threw the silk comforter off her taut body, and lazily walked into her dressing room. She wore an abbreviated white silk negligee, which accentuated her tanned, Pilates-toned legs. Her wardrobe was carefully organized, and she efficiently selected a grey Donna Karan tank dress.

Missy was fastidious about her weight, which had not varied by more than a pound or two in the quarter century since college. Her enduring youthfulness was enhanced by the attentions of an excellent stylist, who colored her hair to a blond perfection, and a certain physician, whose more intrusive ministrations with a scalpel insured that her celebrated high cheekbones remained aloft.

Missy walked downstairs to the columned, light-filled breakfast room, which was in the design of a Victorian conservatory. Her daughter, Andrea, was sitting glumly at the table, concentrating with the focus of a samurai warrior on devouring the blueberry pancakes stacked in front of her. Missy watched the stack slowly disappear and sighed.

No one, with the possible exception of Missy's pedestrian mother-in-law, could provoke Missy quite like Andrea. The morose child had continued to gain weight throughout high school. Now, about to begin her junior year, she was at least fifty pounds overweight. Andrea had beautiful auburn hair that fell below her shoulders in lovely ringlets, like a Botticelli vision. Missy tried, without success, to focus on the luxuriant hair, but was quickly distracted by the white doughy legs inadequately obscured by Andrea's baggy pink shorts. Andrea had also lately developed an unfortunate case of acne, for which she only sporadically remembered to take medication.

"Good morning," Missy said, resignedly. "Those look good." She had been urgently advised by Andrea's most recent therapist that it was more helpful to affirm than castigate Andrea's appetite.

Andrea briefly put down her fork and looked at her mother. "Yeah. They're okay. I added walnuts." Noting her mother's doubtful expression, she said petulantly, "Walnuts are good for you, Mom.

They have lots of anti-oxidants! Want some?" Andrea was an excellent cook, unlike her mother, who relied on a part-time cook and the deli at Dean and Deluca. That this particular skill only exacerbated Andrea's expanding girth was not a consolation to Missy.

"No," Missy said, "I'll just have my cottage cheese." She sat down, with perfect posture, at the massive travertine table, as Andrea defiantly poured more syrup over a replenished stack of pancakes.

Missy gazed out the paned windows of the breakfast room, which opened to a balustrade-lined terrace. All along the terrace were precisely spaced urns, overflowing with impatiens, their violet blossoms like clustered butterflies. She looked up as her son, John, came into the room.

"Morning," he said, "any pancakes left?" He smiled, revealing a perfect line of impossibly white teeth. "Can you spare just a couple, F.B.?" F.B. was short for Fat Baby, a nickname he had bestowed upon his corpulent sister ever since she had waddled into an overweight adolescence. That Andrea did not object to this was a measure of the grudging affection she felt for her brother. While she may have been resentful of her mother and indifferent to her father, she sought her brother's approval with a fervor that no amount of derision on his part could diminish.

Johnny Harrison had been blessed with the best features of both his parents. His complexion was smooth and tanned. He was tall and square-jawed like his father, and blond and supple like his mother. To most observers, he seemed a potent blend of curving muscles and exacting angularity. He had a sort of anticipatory glow, eagerly counting down his last few days at Charlotte Latin, and looking forward to a lazy and sundrenched summer before going off to Vanderbilt in the fall. And if his parents might insist on other, more productive plans for his summer, that was only a minor and distant irritation.

Sinking into the deeply cushioned chair, he effected a languid and virile pose, waiting for Andrea to serve him breakfast, and enjoying the undisturbed composure of one who had always, for the most part, gotten whatever he wanted. This was an attribute he shared with his mother. The assured satisfaction of his desires had only increased them, and his appetite for diverse pleasures was easily the equal of his sister's singular one for food.

"Juanita will get dinner for you tonight," Missy said, referring to their marginally competent cook. "Remember, your father and I have the symphony thing tonight."

"Oh, great," Andrea replied, pouring another handful of walnuts over her pancakes, "I'll help her make burritos."

Missy grimaced, averting her gaze from her daughter's double chin, and said firmly, therapist be damned, "No. No, you won't. She has already prepared a salmon. Don't make a face. Salmon is good for you."

Andrea slumped further into her chair and then, drawing on some reserve of defiance, stood up and walked over to the stove, where she began pouring a fresh batch of pancakes. John, enjoying the ongoing dietary battle between his mother and sister, smiled placidly, and asked, "Who were your victims last night, Mom?"

"Victims! Listen to you," Missy said, laughing. "Just the usual." She delicately spooned a small cluster of cottage cheese, then added, "And your cousin, Stephen."

"Stephen? Professor Stephen? Here?" John asked. "Well, that must have been fun," he said, flicking his wrist lightly in the air, "just *fabulous.*"

CHAPTER FOUR
GOLDEN BOYS

"**B**en? Are you having breakfast today?" The soft but insistent voice of Laura Caldwell ascended up the stairs, down the hall, and into her son's room.

Ben had long marveled that his mother possessed such a mild, yet pervasive voice. But, that was just one of the many paradoxes involving his parents which he chose not to dwell on too long. He was only eighteen and already aware of an insistent introspection. If life was a stage, he was in the front row, always observing, assessing, critiquing. This was his preferred means of making sense of the world from the time he had conscious memory. He was an exceptionally cautious youth. If this did not reward him with a carefree childhood, it did provide a relatively stable one.

"Yes. I'm getting up," he answered. In contrast to his mother, his voice was melodious, lilting, with a deep post-adolescent timbre, but one sensed that each note of every syllable was calculated. Dissonance was not in Ben's repertoire. Nor was a sense of hurry. He was enjoying the lazy ambience of his Saturday morning, basking in the last nostalgic days, the sort of quiet pause that occurs leading up to graduation.

He reached for a pair of faded Levis and a blue tee-shirt. During the past year, it seemed that every muscle of his six foot frame had suddenly expanded. Although he was not a gifted athlete, he was a tenacious one, and his exertions on the football field and in the weight room had paid off handsomely. He gazed intently at his reflection in the mirror, pleased with the padded rise and curve of his pectoral muscles against the soft blue cotton and his smooth thighs thick beneath the denim pants.

"Ben! Your breakfast is getting cold," said the kindly, yet emphatic maternal voice again wafting up the stairs. He ran his hands through his wavy black hair, in a losing battle to bring it under some kind of control, and hurried downstairs.

"Good morning, sleepy head," his mother said, smiling. She looked wistfully at him. Each passing day now brought his move to Duke University closer to fruition. His mother had prepared French toast for breakfast. This had been his favorite for as long as he could remember, though his appetite was basically conducive to anything edible. His sister Debra, who slouched in her seat, silently devouring the latest *Vogue*, was the exact opposite. For a while she wanted only sausage biscuits. Then she insisted on omelets, but only with gouda cheese. Eventually, she raced through breakfast with a simple bowl of Total, although preferably with raisins. But, not too many. Unlike Ben's steadfastness, Debra's tastes and preferences were as changeable as the fashion magazines that she constantly studied. And Ben knew that their mother fervently prayed, with good reason, that this fluidity did not extend to Deb's moral standards as well.

His sister possessed the height of a fashion model, but not the posture or poise, and was only two years older than Ben. She attended Wingate University, a small Baptist school twenty-five miles away, just outside the town of Monroe. Under the strenuous promotion of loyal alumnus, Senator Jesse Helms, the modest college had become a university, in name if not in fact. It was an undemanding, conventional institution, and the ideal school for Debra. Wingate accommodated her limited academic gifts, but presumably restricted her more amatory pursuits. Not surprisingly, she remained at the school with considerable ambivalence.

"So, what's on the agenda for you two today?" his mother asked, as she served Ben another piece of toast.

"I'm going to the pool with John," Ben said.

Debra continued poring over her magazine, and then looked up at her brother. "Oh, really? I might like to go too."

"Nah. Just us guys today," he replied. "But I'll be sure and tell Johnny that you send your love." His sister's crush on his best friend, who was young in years but precocious in appeal, was as longstanding as it was unrequited. John Harrison, as dazzling a personage as Ben had ever known, preferred buxom blonde cheerleader types and Debra was a lean brunette with minimal cleavage.

"Don't you dare!" she shrieked. "Mom, tell him. John already thinks I'm a freak!"

"Ben, don't tease," his mother pleaded. "Why can't you two get along?"

"I was just kidding," he said, lightly punching his sister's shoulder. Ben laughed, in the engaging, disarming way that softened, but never quite extinguished, any resentment his less gifted sister might have for him.

His mother paused, and then busied herself with clearing the table. Ben knew that she worried about him. If there seemed lately to be an edge of sorrow to his laughter, it was simply the prospect of pending goodbyes. And yet, whatever his surface ebullience and the mature appearance he had only recently acquired, he was still mindful of more ominous depths. In that regard, he was very much like his mother. Just as surely as their dark, wavy hair would always shadow their inviting smiles, they shared a knowing and anxious love.

"Great breakfast, Mom," he said, giving her a hug. Then, ever judicious, he hugged his sister. "Seriously, Deb. Don't fret about Johnny. Your secret is safe with me."

The tranquil blue water of the Piper Glen swimming pool rested on a bluff adjacent to the pro shop. The golf course, in waves of green, stretched out below. Ben had driven his mother's Mercedes to the pool, although it was less than a mile from the Caldwell home. While his parents viewed the current generation as spoiled, overly indulged, and generally a deviant flock from God's demanding love, they would not compel their son to actually walk the uninviting sidewalks of Charlotte. A firm parental hand, not to mention Christian forbearance, was not incompatible with the realities of suburban sprawl.

Ben lay on a chaise lounge and contentedly looked out toward the tree-shaded hills. His friend John Harrison rolled over on his side in a chair next to Ben. "Oh, wow, look at that one!" John said, nodding appreciatively toward a young woman, barely covered by a pink string bikini, wading into the pool. He leaned in closer toward Ben and whispered, "She looks like your mom."

"Gross!" Ben said, laughing. "And how would you know anyway?"

"Haven't you ever looked at their creepy old yearbook from Queens. God, what a parade of skanks. But, your mom looked like Julia Roberts." Considering the alterations of time, he added, "Well, she did then, anyway."

"Who did your mom look like?" Ben asked.

"No one. She pretty much was the same." John sat up, brushing away beads of sweat coursing along the smooth, undulating ridges of his browned abdomen, and gestured toward two young women. "Okay, Ben, which one do you want? Mama look-alike or the one by the umbrella?"

"Neither, I love another," he said with mock drama, tilting his head back sighing, "and I must be true." He grabbed John from behind, and maneuvered him toward the swimming pool, pushing him in.

"Jeez, you're such a homo." John laughed, splashing around in the water, his blond hair flattened like silk. "Donna? Still? She's too old for you and she wouldn't get you off if you put a gun...or, whatever...to her head."

Ben floated on his back in the cool water, soft against his smooth skin. He got out of the pool and stretched out on a deck chair. He shifted his weight, recalling those knotted up evenings with Donna Fleischmann. She was a year older than Ben. She had entered the University of North Carolina the previous year. In the beginning, they had managed to see each other at least every two weeks. She would come to Charlotte or he would visit her in Chapel Hill and stay in the dorm room of one of her friends.

Gradually, the weekends turned into months, and one day she told him that she had met someone else. In truth, he did not really mind. In the intervening months, Donna had become a comfortable memory. Indeed, it sometimes seemed to Ben that the memory of love was easier, and far simpler, than the actuality of it.

Donna was beautiful though, and Ben had relished the envious glances of his friends, including John's. John had even once said to him, "Come on, Benny, we could share. Just the three of us. How 'bout it?" It was an entangled image that Ben had more than once thought about since, but Johnny Harrison was forever serving up enigmatic smiles and provocative suggestions, endlessly entertained by Ben's prudishness.

There were times when Ben sensed that Donna Fleischmann wanted him more than he wanted her. This excited him, knowing that she wanted him so badly. What could be more appetizing than someone else's hunger?

Usually, after they went to see a movie or had dinner, they would go back to her house in the Medearis neighborhood. The Fleischmanns were not as affluent as Ben's family, but they lived in a pleasant two-story cape cod home. It had a white picket fence around a courtyard in front of the house, and Mrs. Fleischmann had planted roses all along its border. It was beautiful when the roses were in bloom, but slightly forbidding in winter. For two years, Ben had walked past those tangled vines to the green front door, and rang the bell with such anticipation and longing.

The Fleishmann's living room was exquisitely furnished and rarely used. It was thus the perfect, isolated room for Ben and Donna to be alone in. They could be secure in their privacy so long as they could hear the television in the den, far down the hall of the house, where the rest of the family sat in rapt attention. Like many homes of fairly recent construction, the hastily installed floorboards of the house creaked with a warning insistence that older homes had taken many more years to acquire.

Ben's church was clear in its prohibition of pre-marital sex, though more subtle in its disparagement of Jews. He strenuously adhered to the dictates of his faith, embodied every day of his life in the caring but expectant glances of his mother and father. But, Ben allowed a guarded latitude as to what constituted sex, not to mention salvation, with Donna. He knew that many of his classmates, including John, were far more promiscuous, engaging in oral sex, and more, as cavalierly as sneezing.

After the Fleischmanns went to bed, Ben and Donna would continue making out on the Victorian sofa in the living room. "Ben... Ben... " she would whisper, almost chanting his name, wrapping her arms and legs around him. He raised himself up on his straining biceps and, as if on cue, she would slip her hands underneath his jeans, underneath the tight band of his briefs. The touch of her hands on his naked skin was overpowering. He stood up, and slowly unbuttoned his shirt and then slid his pants off, leaving only his pendulous underwear on. He stood there, teasing, tantalizing, as she stretched out languorously on the sofa. Waiting. Waiting for him.

Well, that was past, Ben thought. He dived back into the pool, erupting in a rush of water around John. And, suddenly, he felt his best friend's heavy arm around his shoulder, pulling him close. John paused a moment and, as he always did, playfully punched Ben's shoulder. John squinted into the sun, his blue eyes gazing challengingly at Ben, his full lips pursed into an enticing half-smile. And Ben felt the resurgence of an overwhelming heat, buried far below his conscious thought. There was a profound mystery in that desire, as alternately drenched and parched as the rivulets of water that splashed along the pool's hard, hot asphalt.

"We got to find a honey for you," John said, his hand gently resting on Ben's shoulder. "Look at that one. Oh, baby. What about her?"

CHAPTER FIVE
GO 49ERS!

D r. Stephen Rayfield sat at a table outside the student union cafe, debating whether or not to finish a stale croissant. Deciding against the croissant, he got up from the table and began briskly walking—there being minimal appeal to linger— across the charmless, if neatly shrubbed, campus of the University of North Carolina at Charlotte.

UNC-Charlotte was located so far up the northern edge of Charlotte's suburban sprawl that some acid tongues called it UNC-Concord, referring to the old mill town next door. If Charlotte had long labored under the shadow of Atlanta, its largest university had similarly languished under the daunting stature, and antiquity, of the university at Chapel Hill. Like its municipal namesake, UNCC had grown dramatically during the past twenty years, aided in no small measure by the prodigious fundraising efforts of Edward and Missy Harrison, each of whom had served as energetic members of the UNCC board of trustees.

UNCC was not Stephen's first choice—a fate he suspected he shared with many of his students—but, given the dearth of teaching opportunities, he had eagerly accepted the appointment. History was an alluring doctorate, but not a practical one. Many of his fellow graduates were still looking for jobs, while a few were languishing, gratefully, in small colleges in the desert of Arizona or the frozen tundra of Minnesota. Comparatively speaking, UNCC had been a plum assignment, and one that Stephen had managed to secure without the assistance of his aunt and uncle.

Stephen noticed the dinosaur-like building cranes that hovered over the ever expanding campus. But, this impressive size seemed at odds with a relative lack of stature. Acres of pavement without any nuance or context. For, whatever it was, it could never be Chapel Hill or State or even UNC-Greensboro, which had began as the Woman's College in the 19th century and at least enjoyed some historic pedigree. If Americans love that which is big, they secretly admire that which is old, and the charms of antiquity were a decidedly limited commodity in Charlotte and its namesake university. Both tried to make up in concrete what they lacked in nostalgia.

Stephen approached Garinger Hall, one of the older cement block boxes on campus, and marveled again at the astonishing lack of imagination in its utilitarian design. The building was all straight lines and narrow floor to ceiling windows with metal beams down the center of them. The hallways were yellowish cinder block and tan vinyl floors. The rooms smelled of disinfectant and new polish. Clean, antiseptic, and utterly bland.

As he walked toward his classroom, where he had begun teaching a summer session class called Democracy in America, a janitor was vigorously, yet haphazardly, mopping the floor. The janitor, who appeared to be middle-aged, had balding hair and a slight paunch, and a back that was already slightly stooped from so many years of pushing brooms and mops. Hunched over, he glanced up as Stephen went by.

"Good morning," Stephen said, as the janitor grunted some unintelligible greeting, and continued his violent exertions with the mop.

Although Stephen's students were only a few years younger than he was, he viewed them, as they assembled in their seats, as the members of a related but alien tribe. Their proximity only exacerbated their mystery. Surprisingly, they were dressed much like their parents might have been dressed back in the 1970s, in varying

ensembles of blue jeans and tee-shirts. The only deviations appeared
to be an inclination of the women to bare their midriffs and of the
men to wear a cap.

Stephen lamented that he had yet to find only a handful of their
number who had an original thought or, alternatively, a willingness
to express it. They possessed the formless imaginations, and fatally
limited attention spans, shaped by countless hours of music video
bombardment. It was a generation that seemed bereft of all but the
most egotistical curiosity.

Undeterred, he resolved yet again to try to engage them, and
he had determined that direct, provocative questions were essential.
"Good morning," he began. "Today, we will be continuing our
discussion of race in America. Miss Baker, let's begin with you. Is
America a racist society?"

Miss Baker was one of the more enthusiastic students in his
class. He imagined her growing up in some small North Carolina
town, not at the top of her class, but a hardworking Honor Society
member, diligent, earnest, and conventional.

"I'm not sure if it is or not," she began hesitantly. "I mean,
like, sure, it used to be. But, now, like, I don't know." She looked
nervously at the cluster of black students who always sat together in
the back of the class.

"Okay, that's honest enough," Stephen said, silently cursing the
day that the word 'like' subverted a pause. He directed his attention
to Chris Denton, one of the black students. "Mr. Denton. What are
your thoughts?"

The young man looked at him warily. "Racist?" he asked sullenly.
"Everybody knows nothing has really changed. If I'm walking into
the Blockbuster with a bunch of white guys, who do you think they're
going to be coming after?"

"Dr. Rayfield?" Tom Jarrett, the squeaky-voiced president of the
Young Republicans, had raised his hand.

"Yes, Mr. Jarrett. Do you have a comment?"

The young man paused, then said, "Yes, sir. I do." Several students
shifted nervously in their seats and looked at him as if he were about
to put his hand on a very hot stove. "If most of the shoplifting that

occurs in stores like Blockbuster is committed by bla…by African-Americans…is it still racist if I look more closely when a, ahm, a person of color comes in?"

"It's still racist," Chris replied, glaring at his classmate. "It's still white people beating down black people. A brother picks up a video. Big deal. White people do that all the time. They just steal the whole company. Like Enron."

Tom waved his hand, "But, I don't think that…"

"Except, most times white people don't get caught," Chris interrupted. "Just like with drugs. It's the brothers that go to jail, not the white people at their parties downtown."

"But, if we could go back for a moment to the guy who's managing the Blockbuster store," Stephen said, "all he knows is that crime is inordinately high among young black males. One can speculate as to why, but it is indeed the reality. So, is the store manager making a logical, defensible assumption, or is he still a racist?"

"Racist," Chris argued. "Black people have been beat on for four hundred years in this country. We were slaves and we're still at the bottom of the rung. The system is oppressive. You can't expect a starving man to use the right fork at dinner. He just wants some of the food from the table."

"Then he should work for it like everybody else," Tom Jarrett said, trying without success to summon up a conciliatory tone. "I would like to know when, if ever, are people blamed for *anything*? If everything is okay because I am a victim, when is it *not* okay? Can I steal and murder and not work and that's all right because my great-great- grandfather was a slave? I'm sorry, but, I just don't get that."

"Nobody asks you to get it," Chris said, pounding his fist on the desk. "Blacks were brought here against their will, packed into slave ships like animals. White people never understand what it means to be black."

"Mr. Denton raises an interesting question," Stephen said. "Here we are, in the early years of the twenty-first century, forty years after the passage of the Civil Rights Act of 1964, and do the races understand each other any better now than they did then?"

"But, Dr. Rayfield," Tom said, "this isn't about understanding. It's about responsibility for my own actions. My own behavior. And if I am never responsible, then is anybody else?"

Miss Baker raised her hand, emboldened by the debate. "I agree with Tom," she said. "I mean, like, is it okay for an ignorant white person to join the Klan because he was raised to hate black people? Can he say, 'Don't blame me for being such a bigot because my daddy and my granddaddy were bigots too'? No. He is, like, responsible for that. Why should a minority be any different? And, well, what about immigrants? They come here and manage to work hard and, you know, they save their money and get ahead."

"Is she for real?" Chris asked, glancing warily at the several Hispanic students who were so far quietly observing the debate. "Same tired old story. They just want black folks to be nice and mow the lawn and clean the toilets. Just want us to play by the rules made up by white folks. That's all. Just be quiet and play by the rules."

"All right, you have made excellent points," Stephen said. "What can we learn here? Democracy is an ideal, a great, profoundly important ideal. But, its application in the rough and tumble of history is something else entirely, and far from ideal. And nowhere is this more true than in the tortuous history of race relations in this country."

"That said," he continued, "the condition of many blacks in America, despite civil rights legislation, despite affirmative action programs, despite all the things that government can do to improve the lives of its citizens, is still deplorable. Why? It is true that there is a stronger black middle class. But, it is also true that four out of ten young black men are in prison, with most of the violent crime against other blacks. The majority of black families are headed by a single parent—usually, the mother or grandmother. This is highly correlated to poverty. To illustrate, in 1890, according to the census data, 80 percent of black families were headed by husbands and wives. That percentage was mostly unchanged until 1970, when it had decreased to 64 percent. Can anyone tell me what the percentage is now?"

Silence. Even Chris Denton appeared to be biding his time. "Anyone? Well, according to the 2000 census, only 38 percent of black families were headed by married couples. By comparison, it was 65 percent for Hispanics, and 77 percent for whites."

Chris, still seething, erupted. "Who cares? Lots of people do just fine being raised by their mom. Like President Clinton."

"Actually, that is not correct," Stephen said. "President Clinton was raised by his mother and a stepfather. A reportedly abusive stepfather, but one who did nonetheless help to provide for the family. But, that is beside the point. No one is arguing that all single mothers are failures. Some of the most inspiring, hardworking, dedicated people in this country are single mothers. And single fathers. But, the correlation between single parent families and poverty is indisputable. For every race and ethnicity."

"There is an epidemic of crime in black communities. This country does not honestly talk about these things. And the victims, time and again, are so often other blacks, including, I might add, the innocent young black man who walks in to the Blockbuster store and is immediately suspect. He too is being punished for this state of affairs. So, my question for this class is, as Mr. Jarrett asked, who *is* responsible? Who *is* accountable? And why is the answer to that question so important?"

CHAPTER SIX
HONOR THY MOTHER

E dward Harrison, as was his custom after a long workday, was enjoying his Macallan scotch, alone, on his back porch. Missy insisted on calling it a terrace or, in her more overblown moments, a terrazzo, but to Edward it would always be simply the back porch.

The porch of his Morrocroft mansion was the only instance of real estate in which he did not assess value in monetary terms. It reminded him of his grandmother Rose. He remembered, though he could not duplicate, the front porch of her plain wood frame house at Centerpoint, just outside Chesterfield, South Carolina. It had spanned the length of the house, and was supported by smooth white columns on top of aged brick bases.

The last time he saw his grandmother, just a week before she died, she was sitting on that porch, waving goodbye. Such a tiny woman, barely five feet tall, with a hunched back, yet able to always welcome the hordes of family who trekked to her modest home year after year. When he was a child, she always greeted him with a hug and a conspiratorial whisper, telling him, "There's cookies in the pantry."

His own porch, as was typical of a world that had come to value seclusion over sociability, was relegated to the rear of the property. It had yet to witness the laughter of children playing kick the can on firefly-lit nights, or the lively gossip of inventive aunts, or, God forbid, neighbors stopping by unannounced. It was lined with elegant, corinthian columns, which Missy had imported from Tuscany. Missy loathed the unadorned white columns that held up the roofs of most of the porches in Morrocroft and Myers Park. Such columns bespoke of the ordinary taste of the undiscriminating herd, a herd from which she was determined to break. Edward, to his great surprise, actually liked the columns. While they were indeed the conventional bright white, they had distinctive handcarved leaves at the top, and delicate vertical fluting.

That however was Edward's single concession to his wife's continental pretensions. He had insisted that the decorator provide simple, thickly cushioned white rattan seating and, to Missy's horror, four caneback rocking chairs.

"It looks like a country store," she had shrieked when she saw the rocking chairs. "Why don't you just put a spittoon in the corner?" He gave her an antique snuff box for Christmas that year. She was not amused.

Missy deviously managed to place silk cushions, obtained in bulk from some little shop in Ravello, whenever they had company over, but he was willing to allow her that. He was not oblivious to the fact that many of the things that impressed Missy also impressed their guests. And that was good for business. He would have agreed to an Egyptian barge in the pool, with Missy dolled up as Cleopatra, if it were good for business.

He smiled ruefully at the image of his wife as Cleopatra. Her exoticism extended no further than the borders of Italy and rarely breached the strict confines of their marital bed, where he was allowed to indulge his husbandly prerogatives no more than once a month. Not that he really wanted more. Passion had long since breathed its last gasp between the two of them. Lovemaking, like so much of their life together, was more a matter of keeping up appearances, even if, in this case, it was only with each other.

On reflection though, he did not blame his wife. Boredom and complacency seemed to be the lot of many long-term marriages. Theirs was no exception. He could not fault Missy for human nature. What he resented was her chilly acceptance of it. Where she seemed sanguine, almost relieved, to apparently be beyond the tumult of lust, he was perplexed and embittered.

Such frustrations aside, Edward savored his solitary cocktail hour on the palm-fronded, corinthian-columned porch. It was a breezy evening, and he quietly surveyed the splash of pink and white dogwoods that gently sloped down to a sparkling blue pool.

His respite was, he well understood, temporary. Edward called his mother every Tuesday night, almost without fail. And, once a month, he drove the twenty miles to Monroe, where Myrtle Harrison still lived in a nondescript brick rambler on Durant Street. Edward and his sister, who had long since fled to New York, had grown up in that house. If not an affectionate son, he was at least a dutiful one.

He followed a careful ritual prior to telephoning Myrtle. Once he finished his drink, Edward fortified himself with a cup of coffee, with just the slightest infusion of brandy, and dialed his mother's number. Taking a deep breath, preparing to be submerged under a torrent of chatter, he listened to the phone ring. Possibly she would be at Applebee's, where her elderly boyfriend, Fred, took her to dinner several times a week.

"Hello," she answered on the third ring, "Edward! Is that you?"

He managed a "Yes, it's me. Hi, Mom..." before the flood waters opened up.

"I was just telling Fred that it was about time for you to call. Thank the Lord for my Edward. Your sister never calls. Well, hardly ever. Now and then she calls. I spoke with her last Sunday. But, you know how busy that girl is. Always up to something. I said to Fred, 'Fred, the only one I can count on to see if I'm even still breathing is Edward.' Well, and Stephen. Bless his heart, he does try to see me now and then, but I know he's young and busy with his new job. I never thought we'd have no professor in the family. But, there he is, as good as any of 'em!"

Not waiting for her to pause, which would be an exercise in futility, Edward blurted out, "Yes. Stephen's doing very well. He had dinner with us last Friday."

No doubt grievously reflecting on her own very infrequent invitations to Edward's home, Myrtle sighed, "Oh...well, I'll bet that was fun. I bet Missy had everything just beautiful. Why didn't you invite your poor old mom? I get so bored here in Monroe sometimes. There's just nothing to do. I said to Fred the other day, 'Fred, there just ain't anything to do in this old town.' Sometimes we go to the senior center, but you know I don't want to hang around with a bunch of old folks. The last time we went there, they was playing bingo, and I could barely hear them calling out the numbers. I said to Fred, 'Fred, I can't hear a thing that woman's saying. She needs to speak up. Good Lord, us old folks need somebody we can hear..."

Edward held the phone away from his ear, knowing that she would now speak for a good five minutes on the theme of Monroe's unrelenting dullness, all of which would find its way back to her resentment that he had not invited her to dinner along with Stephen. Edward periodically lifted the phone to his ear. "...and I said, Fred... Myrtle Beach...your father never...highway robbery..."

His efforts to direct the discussion, a maneuver of which he was singularly brilliant in conference rooms throughout Charlotte, were doomed to further fan the monologistic flames. It was as if he would stamp out one fire, only to have another flare up in its place. And yet, he tried nonetheless, abruptly interrupting her and asking, "Did you see Dr. Ross? How did that go?"

"Well, I went to see him last week. And he didn't do a dern thing except check my blood pressure and thump my chest. My blood pressure was up. I only take those pills every other day. They cost me $80 a month! So, I told Ross, I said 'Dr. Ross, I will take them every day from now on.' He wants me to come back in two months. But, now, Edward, let me ask you, why should I do that, just to pay him another $150 to get my blood pressure checked? I can go to Wal-Mart and check it myself, or I thought about getting one of those home checkers."

Edward jumped in. "If all he is going to do is check your blood pressure again, and it reads normal when you check it, I don't see the need for you to go back. If that is all he wants to do. *Is* it?"

"Yes. $150 just to do my blood pressure again. I tell you, if it reads normal at Wal-Mart, I am not going to do it. Us old folks on Medicare and fixed incomes..."

Edward once again lowered the receiver. Her litany of the impoverishment of retirees was good for at least another five minutes. "...barely get by...gas is sky high...and ride a bike if I could...doesn't pay nothing..."

The currents were now swirling around Edward's head, and he felt himself going under. With one last effort, he said, "Mom, listen, I need to get ready for dinner. Good talking to you. Have a good week."

"You too, honey. Oh, before you go, guess who called me last week? Go ahead, you'll never guess."

"Who?" he asked, trying not to sound too impatient.

"Evelyn," she said.

Evelyn was the widow, since remarried and predictably divorced, of Edward's cousin Jerry. Born on the wrong side of the tracks, she had, in any objective estimation, managed to stay there. Edward saw her once a year, as briefly as possible, at the Harrison family reunion. "What in the heck did she want?"

"Hah!" Myrtle said. "She wanted my Cadillac! The nerve of that woman. Said that her old Chrysler was about to break down and she had heard I might be interested in selling mine. Well, I told her right straight, I said 'Evelyn, I already traded it in for a new one.' Course I didn't tell her you paid for it. That's none of her business!"

"I never could understand what cousin Jerry saw in her," Edward said.

"Well, your dad sure did. He used to look at her—and you know she never was very attractive—and say, 'Well, Myrtle, that Evelyn must be something else between the sheets.'"

"Well, all right then, Mom, take care. Don't forget John's graduation is two weeks from this Saturday. I'll talk with you again next week."

"You better, youngin'. And give Missy and the kids a big hug from your old mom. Did Missy get that recipe I sent her? It's the peach cobbler recipe that Mama used. I sent it to Missy before, don't know what happened to it. Tell her to be sure and use one stick of butter. You have to..."

Drowning by now, Edward managed to mumble, "Right. Will do. Gotta go."

"Don't work too hard," she said. "Remember to drink plenty of green tea. It's good for you! I drink it every morning. E-mail me tomorrow! Love you!"

CHAPTER SEVEN
TRYON STREET

E velyn Harrison Peck lay stretched out on the checkerboard sofa, with one pale, mottled arm flung over her head, and the other arm clutching the *Charlotte Observer* as if it had just sprouted fangs. Her red hair was a frizzy, flaming thatchwork over the brown woolen pillow. Her black spandex pants tightly encased, but did not secure, her fleshy legs, and accentuated the insistent arc of her stomach.

"Miss high and mighty," Evelyn bellowed, as she stared at a photograph of Missy Harrison. "Says here she's the chairwoman. Hah! I knew her when she didn't have a pot to piss in. Always putting on airs. God, that two-faced bitch..."

Her son, Keith, ignored Evelyn as she furiously tossed the newspaper on the floor. "Turn up the damn t.v.," she commanded. "Put it on the weather."

Keith wearily clicked through the channels. His mother began mumbling bitterly about some man named Arnie. "That bastard... what does he take me for? Wouldn't even drive me home...son of a bitch." She dropped the offending paper to the floor and closed her eyes. Evelyn had been out late the night before, and soon her son could hear her sporadic snores.

Keith shifted uncomfortably in the old recliner, staring at the television, and tried to ignore the gurgling eruptions of his mother.

He considered for a moment which was worse, the screaming tourists excited to be seen with some chubby weatherman on television or the choppy honks of Evelyn.

Their two-bedroom home on Tryon Street was only a few blocks away from the luxurious new condo buildings in South End and Uptown that were soaring skyward, piloted by developers like his father's cousin Edward Harrison. It was an irony that neither mother nor son was inclined to dwell upon.

Occasionally they would read something in the paper about Edward and Missy, a woman whom Evelyn rarely saw and greatly despised. The distance between them and cousin Edward, usually minus his two-faced wife, narrowed exactly once a year at the annual Harrison family reunion. On such occasions, Edward offered effusive but brief greetings, and there was something in his tone that did not encourage further engagement.

Nevertheless, Keith was proud that a man like Edward Harrison always spoke so fondly of Keith's father. "Son, your dad and I had a heck of a time back in the day," Edward had once said to Keith. 'Yep, Jerry was the real deal."

The Peck's gray frame house, with its peeling paint and sagging front porch, had a small front yard, which Evelyn and Keith had long neglected. The spindly shrubs that survived the relentless exhaust of the cars were pitiful, scraggly things, naked in winter and bereft of blooms in spring. The only improvement to the property, borne of grim necessity, had been the installation of bars on the windows.

The house had seemed larger when Keith was a child. But, he was now six feet two inches tall, with an oversized body reminiscent of the old-time wrestlers, who made up in bloated cunning what they lacked in fitness. With each passing year, he had felt more and more caved in by the shabby little house. Cracked plaster walls. Dust balls floating along the floor. Old newspapers and magazines stacked in a corner. His mother was loath to throw anything out. Every few months he managed to gather up the magazines and newspapers, only to see a new stack emerge with each passing day.

His father had died when he was a young boy and then Evelyn had briefly married a man named Peck. Since then, his mother had only grown noisier and heavier and had easily transferred her disdain for both of her husbands on to her only son. Most of their neighbors had either died or moved away as the neighborhood, modest to begin with, had withered under a barrage of neglect and crime. The homes around them were now filled with Hispanic immigrants and blacks, all of whom Keith and his mother regarded with a gratifying contempt.

Three blocks away, at the corner of Tryon and Camden, where the new light rail line was to be built, art galleries and chic clothing stores were sprouting up. This newly appointed Promised Land, for which cousin Edward was a sort of Moses, extended further to South Boulevard and then into the long-blessed dwellings of Dilworth itself. Someday, this renaissance might reach the dilapidated homes at Tryon and Park, but for now it might as well have been on the Upper East Side of Manhattan. Places like the Canine Cafe, Renegade— where a pair of New Religion jeans could set you back $200—and the Phat Burrito were already catering to the residents of new condo buildings like Park Avenue 115.

Keith Peck had recently walked over to the Phat Burrito on a Friday evening for one, solitary beer. A large blue banner on the side of the Charlotte Arts League Gallery proclaimed 'Gallery Crawl Starts Here Every First Friday'. Young men and women, all polished and primped and gleaming with promise, moved up and down the street, sipping wine, munching on cheese blocks on toothpicks. He noticed a couple of black guys, dressed in the classic baggy jeans and droopy tank tops, studiously ignored by the young professionals, and as out of place as Keith himself. By the time he glanced up at a store called Vertically Integrated Manufacturing, which for some reason was very proud of itself for selling clothes all made in the same building in Los Angeles, he had turned bewilderingly home.

As Evelyn continued her rhythmic snores, Keith got up from his chair and walked into the kitchen. The small refrigerator was well-stocked with beer, and, despite the early hour, he reached for a Budweiser. He went back into the living room and noticed that his mother had one leg resting on the sofa and one on the floor. Suddenly, she shifted and kicked one leg in the air, calling out "Henry! Henry!"

As she was flailing her arms at some imaginary presence, while still kicking up her leg and calling for Henry, Keith shook her and said, "Wake up, goddamnit."

"What the hell?" she barked. "Let go of me! What you doing? I'm asleep!" She looked at him, dazed, and accusingly raised herself up on one elbow.

"Who is Henry? You were calling somebody named Henry."

"I don't know no Henry," she said dismissively. "I guess now you just got to be in charge of who's in my dreams, that about right?" She laughed at her own joke, laughed so much that her jiggly basketball of a belly began to shake. Then she got up and walked into the bathroom across the hall and slammed the door.

Keith sat back down in the recliner, looked out the window at the overcast sky, and listened to the traffic surging by. He hated the purposeful hum of those cars, the busy, rich people like cousin Edward, headed Uptown to fancy offices in those gleaming new buildings. He had no place to go. And so he sat there behind the barred windows.

Keith's grandfather, Walker, was forever known as the Harrison family's only *convicted* felon. The family, conveniently, argued that Walker came back from the slaughters of World War II a different man. Family lore further insisted, only somewhat tongue in cheek, that he had robbed the bank in Florence, South Carolina, simply to get away from Cora, his plain, nagging wife. Support for this theory included the fact that the getaway car, a 1943 Ford, would not start on the morning of the robbery. Several of Walker's brothers had to give him a push and a running start, down the long dirt driveway from the house. In the family's view, Walker had decided, not unreasonably, that prison would be preferable to further confinement with Cora.

Keith's father was the only child of Walker and Cora. He had been a quiet, unassuming man. And yet, when Keith was only five years old, his gentle, congenial father had managed to exit a rather dull existence in spectacular fashion by crashing down head first from high atop a construction crane.

The family was living in Kinston, North Carolina, when Keith was called out of kindergarten one Monday morning. Mrs. Clark, the obese widow who lived next door to the Harrisons was in the principal's office, waiting for him. "Oh, come here, poor child," she said, drawing him into her enveloping breasts, "I'm going to take you home, honey."

"Everything will be okay, darling," she said, tears streaming down her face, as she drove him home. "Just trust in Jesus, honey."

Why? he wondered. What for? When they arrived at the little cinder block house his parents were renting, he saw his mother crumpled on the sofa, wailing hysterically.

"Oh, no. Oh, God no. It can't be! It can't be!" She ignored Keith and kept repeating her shock as if this might reverse the reality of it. "What will we do? What?"

Keith stood quietly in a corner of the living room, and finally his Aunt Sally told him that his father was in heaven. He learned later that his father had been working on a crane that morning. A cable had given way and Jerry Harrison grabbed it for an instant, but was unable to hold on to it. He plunged forty feet, landing head first.

The funeral was the following Wednesday afternoon, on a spring day when the dogwoods were at the height of their blooms. Amidst a profusion of pink and white blossoms, Keith Harrison bid goodbye to his father. His mother, accustomed to blaming Jerry Harrison for misfortune in life, now inevitably blamed him for further misfortune in death.

"I don't know how we gonna make the rent," she said to young Keith as soon as they got home from the funeral and out of earshot of the Harrison clan. "How we gonna eat? Your father! Your father! He shoulda been more careful. He always was a daredevil. Always showing off!"

Widow's reeds did not become Evelyn. Within a month, she had met a man named William Peck at a local bar. Mr. Peck, ten years Evelyn's senior and safely employed as a stock clerk at Winn-Dixie, was a steady, though not overbearing, suitor. Six months later, Keith was told that William Peck was "your new daddy" and they were moving to Charlotte. "It's a big ole city," she had told him, "but you'll get used to it."

Keith's adoptive father, while not particularly interested in Keith, did at least serve the valuable purpose of distracting Evelyn.

Unfortunately, after six arduous years, having apparently decided that neither Evelyn nor Charlotte was adequate to his needs, he got on the train to New Orleans one day and never came back. It was rumored that he was not traveling alone.

While Evelyn did not marry again, she did maintain a steady stream of boyfriends and, except for the annual reunions, detached herself from the watchful and disapproving glares of the Harrisons. It did not help matters that, at every family reunion after Jerry's death, she had flirted with any second, and some first, cousins she could grab on to. Her marriage to William Peck had surprised no one. Nor did the subsequent divorce.

Keith still sometimes had nightmares of his real father, suspended in mid-air, clutching against an empty blue sky.

Evelyn returned to the living room, ignored her son, and redeposited herself on the sofa. She reminded him of an overweight alligator, sidling back up to shore. She began filing her toenails, which were dark and uneven, rife with an unyielding fungus. Evelyn was surprisingly agile in this effort, managing to pull her leg up toward her chest and continue filing with considerable concentration. The large toenail was the worst, its top having grown thick and resistant as a ragged plexiglas. By the time she had finished, she was gasping for breath and glaring at her son.

"See what else is on," she hissed.

"See for yourself," he said, tossing the remote to her.

He wondered if his mother had a date later in the evening. Although she did not go out as often as she used to, she still managed to latch onto a few strays, the occasional hound dog in a pickup truck sniffing around. She had been pretty when she was younger, with a sort of overripe quality, if the photos were any indication. A lifetime of trading on her looks could not be altered, even if that currency had long since lost most of its value. He suspected she relied heavily on dim lighting and even dimmer boyfriends. He despised all of them.

Evelyn grunted irritably with each click of the remote, finally settling on *The Price is Right*. "Hah!" she guffawed, "That Bob Barker. He must be a hundred by now."

CHAPTER EIGHT
HIGHWAY TO HEAVEN

Wednesday morning, Andrew Caldwell, after a hearty breakfast of grits and eggs and link sausage, was delighted to see apple pie waiting for him in a tupperware dish on the kitchen island. "I put two pieces in for you," Laura said, smiling. "You need to keep up your strength." She handed him the pie. "Do you want another cup of coffee?" she asked.

"Nah. No time," he said, kissing her on the cheek. Laura stood by the door, waving him goodbye as he hurried out to the garage. She wore a royal blue satin nightgown, tied securely at the waist and trimmed with white lace stars, like snowflakes along her ample bosom. As was her custom, she had swept her hair up into a sort of dark, cushioning halo.

"Have a good day. You be careful out there," she said, no doubt mindful of car crashes and armed robbers preying upon Charlotte. Every morning, her breakfast prayer, in a sort of divine repetition, always concluded with *Dear Lord, keep us safe in your guidance and mercy.* Laura continued waving as Andrew backed out of the driveway. He lingered on the still remarkable sweetness of her smile, and tried not to notice the jiggling flesh of her arms.

Andrew hurried along Rea Road, glancing at occasional solitary walkers, ghostly, vaguely subversive figures, on the lonely sidewalk that ran the entire length of the road. The vast parking lot of Calvary

Church to his left sat vacant and quiet, but he could already see the stalled traffic on Highway 51, with steam rising in a golden haze off the hot asphalt. As Andrew waited at the light, he put on his sunglasses to shield his eyes from the glare, and wiped away small beads of perspiration from his forehead.

Highway 51, on Sundays, was a convergent and well-worn path to Charlotte's massive evangelical churches. Christ Covenant, Carmel Baptist. The towers of Calvary Church. It was ridiculed by the sophisticated as the highway to heaven. Well, it was the highway to heaven, Andrew thought.

The light turned green, and Andrew crossed Highway 51, with traffic on either side parted like the Red Sea. He continued on Rea Road, cautiously following its two-lane curve, and passed by a succession of newer neighborhoods. The parade of cars began to slow and hesitate, as he listened to the aggravating but profitable hum of another hectic, grasping, traffic clogged day in Charlotte, North Carolina.

Andrew shifted irritably in his seat. The thickness of his belly, straining against pinpoint cotton, was a lava-like surge over his belt. This flurry of sweaty softness was, he feared, somehow unmanly. There was something vaguely effeminate in the flabby descent of middle-aged men, but also in their vain self-consciousness of it. He reached to loosen his belt, feeling for all the world like a woman adjusting a merciless girdle.

Andrew followed the convoy of traffic onto Providence Road, which now stretched as far as the eye could see in either direction. Where once there had been small farms, redolent of cow manure, squawking chickens, and rows of summer corn, now these rolling hills of southeast Charlotte were tracked by a convergence of commuter traffic, like an endless line of monotonous ants. As he inched his way along the clogged road, his frustration was tempered by the dictates of a real estate developer's reverence for the bottom line.

Harrison Associates, led with commanding, and some said overbearing, vision by Edward Harrison, had created and sold many of the mushrooming communities that now lined Providence Road. In Andrew's view, any attendant growing pains were a necessary price to pay. Charlotte had been a malnourished child, subsisting on the scraps thrown from the table of its far more illustrious and ambitious sibling Atlanta. But, that was past now, mere prologue to the new Charlotte, a sprawling banquet of a city, cresting on the determination of robust bankers, conservative churches, and reliable police. Andrew would no more question the rightness of all this feverish enterprise than cast doubt on the Virgin Birth.

Nevertheless, he was unnerved by the kamikaze maneuvers of some of his fellow commuters. The huge Suburban following behind him was way too close. Every lurch in the flow of traffic brought the behemoth inches within his very polished Lexus bumper. Bumper. Ass. Kiss my ass, he muttered. Yeah, kiss my ass, the scumbag. He thought of Laura and quickly regretted his obscenity. Not becoming. No, not becoming at all.

He sometimes blamed this lapse of civility on the influx of northerners. No one called them *yankees* anymore. That would betray a certain Old South backwardness. A dreaded provincialism that would be the death knell of continued growth and prosperity. No, they were northerners, in theory just a necessary spice in the rich, savory Charlotte stew, involving no more historic distaste than any of the other thousands of newcomers that arrived each year. History was out. Banking was in. And God was in charge.

He was openly disdainful of the avalanche of Mexican laborers, all of whom seemed to congregate at McDonald's these days, but more subtly resentful of the wave of professionals from places like New York and New Jersey and, most radically, California. And yet he grudgingly accepted that Charlotte's future depended on this invasion of outsiders who arrived every month, some with shovels, some with calculators, but almost all with ambition and a willingness to work. Whether from Hoboken or Tijuana or New Delhi, this combustible mix fueled Charlotte's prosperity, but complicated its identity. It was a city forever unsure of itself and now, gorging on growth, struggling to make sense of a cacophony of Spanish and Yankee voices. It would all work out eventually, he was certain of that. As Edward Harrison had recently said at a meeting of the board, "Nothing profitable is alien to me."

But, those grating *accents*. The unshaven rabble of day laborers at the 7-Eleven. The clipped commands of Jersey money men. The impatient, frantic pace they seemed to always maintain, whether Mexicans running stoplights in pickup trucks or New York lawyers barking into cell phones in their BMWs. This swarm, buzzing about with even less sensibility, or understanding, of Charlotte than its natives. It had nothing to do with rivalry or religion, though many of the Yankee heathens were, admittedly, Jewish. It was just the strangeness of a suddenly unfamiliar terrain.

"Well, that's life, isn't it?" he thought. Faith was the only certainty, the only answer to questions we cannot even begin to understand. He passed the gleaming white Temple Israel. Unlike the soaring, hopeful spires of Calvary Church, the synagogue was a squat, round fortress with abbreviated, uninviting windows. Well…The ways of God were mysterious, and Andrew Caldwell had no pressing inclination to pass judgment. That was God's territory, not his. Even Billy Graham, on *Larry King*, had said so.

The mysteries of God. Andrew Caldwell was acutely aware of his own imperfections, and likely to be gently reminded of them by Laura Caldwell should his memory ever falter. He deferred on questions of eternal damnation, confident that the one true God most certainly did not.

CHAPTER NINE
QUEENS COLLEGE

Missy Harrison was not by nature a nostalgic individual. Her interest in the passage of time was primarily confined to an acute assessment of its effect on the state of her porcelain complexion. She had almost decided against attending the class reunion, but Laura Caldwell had practically begged her to come. Since conscious memory, Missy's focus had always been on something up ahead and very little left behind. This point of view afforded her an exciting, and some said calculating, air. If anything, her thoughts were centered not on her four undistinguished years at Queens College, but on savoring the ravages of twenty-five years later on her former classmates.

Most of those girls, like Missy, had been from, and remained, in the Charlotte area. She was familiar with the declining fortunes of many of them since their graduation from Queens. And, since no one could appreciate the reversals of others quite like one who had avoided such losses herself, Missy was agreeable to rekindle the warming collegial circle, at least for this one day.

Her smile bordered on the charitable as she drove into the parking lot beside Belk Hall. Noting the phalanx of Accords and Camrys and Jettas and even, good Lord, Buicks, Missy emerged confidently from her Mercedes and quickened her Gucci clad step as she walked toward the red-tiled hulk of Burwell Hall.

Missy saw a group of women on the porch, none of whom she recognized. They were laughing and hugging each other with the strained and manic style of reunions, as if mimicking their departure so many years before. The world had changed a great deal since then and, to Missy's observant eyes, so had her classmates. Most had assumed the mantle of middle-aged frumpiness, with varying degrees of youthful counterattack, girdled in regrettable Ann Taylor pantsuits, their hair bottle-dyed and whipped into compliant waves, framing faces that suffered under the glaze of too much foundation and eyes overly decorated with too much mascara. And then there were the grim few who appeared to throw in the towel altogether and looked as if they had just casually stopped by in between shopping expeditions to Costco.

Missy smoothed the gold trim of her Chanel suit, suddenly annoyed to detect an errant thread. She clutched her black beaded handbag, which nicely complemented the gleaming diamonds of her watch. As she walked up the steps alone among the throng of women, she felt a momentary hesitation. Then she saw Laura Caldwell's plump figure, oddly dwarfed by the tall black doors under Burwell Hall's massive stone arch.

Laura rushed toward her, arms outstretched. "Missy, you scamp. I was wondering if you were coming!" she said, hugging her.

"Not coming?" Missy laughed. "Are you kidding? No way would I miss this."

"Did you get stuck in traffic, hon?" Laura asked, as they walked inside.

"No, not at all," Missy replied. "Just got a late start."

As they stood in the entry foyer, Missy scanned the parlor for any familiar faces. She saw none, with the exception of the portrait of one of the school's ancient educators, Mary Anna Burwell, which hung above a gold-lettered marble plaque. The plaque read *This hall is erected to the glory of God...It is dedicated to Mary Anna Burwell.* The old crone was posed in a dark unisex robe, with a black veil that covered her judicial looking white curls and eternally perplexed expression. Mary Burwell, who had gazed down on Queens students for so many years, would forever maintain that severe and somewhat mannish visage. She always seemed to Missy to slightly resemble Franklin D. Roosevelt.

Missy noticed that the lower portion of the inscription on the plaque pledged to perpetuate Mary Burwell's work in the education of *women*. A porcelain bowl had been placed on the foyer table in front of the plaque and obscured the word 'women'. Given the now coed population of Queens University, this was perhaps by design.

"Burwell looks as mean as ever," Missy said to Laura.

"Well, at least she hasn't changed. That's something," Laura said consolingly, taking Missy's arm as they walked inside. "Goodness, Miss, doesn't everyone just look wonderful?"

I n Missy's opinion, the years had not been kind to Laura in either circumstance or demeanor. Had Laura allowed herself the indulgence of vanity, she might have languished over, and perhaps resisted, the betrayal of her softening body. Instead, she constantly seemed to have a tray of Godiva chocolates in front of her. Her enduring sense of style did enable her to somewhat obscure the growing folds of flesh that protruded from her waist. She artfully wore loose silken fabrics, including Hermes scarves draped around her shoulders and just over the crest of her corpulent, sagging breasts. But, there was little she could do to disguise the bags under her eyes. Laura was not a drinker and her sense of revelry was generally confined to an extra glass of champagne on New Year's eve. Her body's decay was not due to ribald excess or to a surfeit of vanity, but rather a fondness for all things sugary and a loathing, unlike Missy, for all things surgical.

They had met in the freshman literature course. An aversion to Shakespeare and to their mothers was their initial bond. Neither had traveled particularly far to get to Queens College. Missy had come by way of a modest tract house in Rock Hill, and Laura by way of a Georgian mansion in Myers Park. They had arrived on campus that hot August day with the usual fervor of emancipated teenagers. If some of the girls came to feel that they had left one prison for another, most enjoyed the expansive and secure red brick lanes of Queens College. It was a quiet, defiantly sedate quarter, completely

at odds with the era of protest that had washed over most campuses
as the Vietnam War had festered and bled. If the 70's had emerged as
an aimless decade, during which swirling disco balls had supplanted
angry peace signs, Queens College was a comfortable setting in
which to linger.

Missy lived in Belk dormitory as did Laura. The official
explanation was that Laura's father and mother wanted her to have a
complete college experience, even if they did live in baronial splendor
on Sherwood Street just four blocks away. However, as Missy learned
later, there were other, more complicated, considerations.

Missy's first introduction to the Soames family was not an
unqualified success. Laura had relocated to her parents' home for the
summer, and invited Missy to come by one Saturday for lunch.

"You have to come," she pleaded. "They'll both drive me crazy
inside of a week if I don't have reinforcements!"

As Missy walked up the immaculate drive that long ago summer
day, lined with the most precisely trimmed boxwoods she had ever
seen, she felt a slight annoyance with her friend. *How can she have so
much and appreciate so little?*

She rang the bell, and waited a bit nervously on the grand
columned front porch. An attractive woman, who appeared to be in
the nether regions of early middle age, opened the door.

"Mrs. Soames, I'm Missy. Laura's friend? Thank you for inviting
me!"

The elegant woman looked at her quizzically for an instant
and laughed. "Oh, no, mademoiselle. I am Helene, Mrs. Soames'
secretary. Won't you follow me? They are waiting for you in the
morning room."

"Oh, gosh. Sorry!" Missy said, and meekly followed her along
a black and white tiled corridor, past dark paneled rooms, into the
morning room at the rear of the house. Laura and her mother were
seated on a pale green velvet sofa, with darker green fringes bordering
the marble floor. The entire back wall of the room was lined with
three French doors that opened to the verandah. The effect was a
stunning blend of shadow and sunlight, silhouetting them in a sort

of emerald glow. Missy decided it was the most beautiful room she had ever seen.

Mrs. Soames rose to greet her. "Hello. A pleasure to meet you. It is so nice of you to join us, Missy." Mrs. Soames was still a beautiful woman. She had jet black hair, and that day had pulled it back tight into a pony tail. This accentuated her high cheekbones, and the remarkable angularity of her face. She was elegant, but hard-edged. Her voice was crisp, with barely a hint of warmth.

In this somewhat chilly formality, Laura also seemed surprisingly remote and tentative. "Hi, Missy," she said, with exaggerated politeness, "thanks so much for coming."

"Oh, thanks for having me. You have a beautiful home. It's just so gorgeous. Why, I don't think I have ever seen such a beautiful room. Why..."

Mrs. Soames interrupted her. "Yes, it is a wonderful home. My husband's grandfather built this home, so it has been in the family for many years."

The three of them stood there for an awkward moment when, as if on cue, Helene reappeared. "Madame, will you have lunch in the dining room?" she asked.

"No, I think we girls will be casual," Mrs. Soames replied, gracefully flicking the ashes of her cigarette into a crystal ashtray. The three of them sat at the antique mahogany table beside a large arched window. Lunch was prepared by the cook, Brenda. My God, Missy thought, how many servants do they have? Brenda was ironically thin, almost emaciated, with a pinched, unfriendly face. She methodically brought them some sort of salad with onions and potatoes.

"This is just delicious," Missy lied, secretly craving a cheeseburger.

Mrs. Soames smiled with the patience of one who has checked the time remaining and resolved to endure it. "Laura tells me that you are from Rock Hill. Were you born there?"

"Oh, no ma'am," Missy said. "My family is originally from Winston-Salem. That's where my mother is from. We moved to Rock Hill when I was in fourth grade."

"Rock Hill is a lovely town. Our friends the Thompsons live there. Are you acquainted with Jerry and Polly Thompson?"

"No ma'am. We have never met. But I know of them. Mr. Thompson is a deacon in our church."

"Missy lived in Florida!" Laura volunteered, as her mother looked at her stonily.

"Florida! Well, that must have been nice for you," Mrs. Soames said, with just a hint of derision in her steely voice. "More tea, dear?"

"Yes, thank you. This is all just so delicious," she repeated, aware now of the quivering of her upper lip, always a consequence of her nervousness, and of a growing resentment toward this icy woman.

"Mother," Laura commented, "Missy got an A in our freshman lit class. Isn't that great?"

"Yes, congratulations." Mrs. Soames paused, as if trying to locate the source of a recent wound and looked at her daughter with cold and unforgiving eyes. "I only wish that Laura could have done as well. You received a B- if I recall."

"Yes. Just a B-," Laura said forlornly. "I really loved Scott Fitzgerald. He's my favorite writer. But, I just couldn't get into Shakespeare."

"That is no excuse," Mrs.Soames said, hurling these harsh words at the downcast girl. "Life will be full of things that you cannot, as you say, 'get into', but that is no excuse. You still must try to do your best."

"Ma'am?" Missy said timidly, sitting up straight in her seat. "Laura did work really hard and I think she did try to do her best."

"Really?" Mrs. Soames asked, arching her precise eyebrows, and directing her lethal smile toward Missy. "Is that right? Well, I think I am a better judge of my daughter's efforts than you are, my dear."

"Oh, I don't mean anything by it, ma'am. But, I *was* in the class with her, and I just think that she worked very hard. Her essay on *The Great Gatsby* was the best in the class. We can't always get A's."

"Is that right?" Mrs. Soames asked, staring at her with utter contempt.

"Well, yes. It is. I mean, I only got a C+ in biology, and I never worked so hard in my life."

"Thanks, Miss," Laura said, suddenly emboldened.

"To B or not to B," Missy said, laughing as Mrs. Soames stood.

Mrs. Soames' dismissive smile was set in stone, and she effected a greater interest in the rounded perfection of her ivory toned manicure. Missy had never seen such polished and smooth nails.

"Well, in any event," Mrs. Soames said, lighting another cigarette. She pushed a button underneath the table, and almost immediately the somber cook appeared. "Brenda, yes, I think we will have dessert in the living room."

Mrs. Soames motioned for Laura and Missy to follow her into the living room. She looked again at Missy, studying her, but now with an expression that suggested a sort of irritated admiration. "You have lovely hair, Missy. But, have you thought of wearing it up? That would help accentuate your cheekbones, which, if you don't mind my saying so, are a little weak."

Not so weak, Missy decided, not so weak after all. Jewel Soames lived now in lonely elegance in her Myers Park condominium, minus the servants, getting by on the last dregs of the Soames estate. She was rarely seen these days, and her vibrant good looks had surely long since vanished. Missy suddenly had images of rusting steel.

The gathering in Burwell Hall was predictably interminable. Missy wondered how much longer she would have to feign some meager enthusiasm for this faded assemblage. Laura, though, seemed to relish every greeting, every moment of shared laughter. Her green, billowy dress from Talbots failed to disguise her girth, but did accentuate her emerald eyes.

Laura had once been so beautiful. The one remaining compensation, a sort of stylistic mercy, was Laura's resilient hair. She had it colored once a month, and her stylist at Euphoria salon had created a lustrous dark wave, shadowing over an eroding landscape. While the effect was incongruous, it at least afforded her a degree of mystique. This was no small matter, given that Laura, of all Missy's friends, had always been the most transparent. It was the one quality that in fact had, for so many years, cemented and sustained their friendship. Missy was as secretive of her own motives as she was suspicious of the motives of others, and Laura had always seemed incapable of subterfuge or caution. Whatever she could not bring herself to reveal, her face inevitably betrayed, one trembling lip worth a thousand words.

How much longer? Missy wondered. How much longer before she could make a graceful exit? The gathering was nothing more than a fundraiser disguised as a nostalgic reunion. Missy was more inclined to write a check than suffer the soggy canapes arrayed on tables set up in the parlor or endure one more gushing eruption from people she could barely remember. She noted with derision the Oriental rugs and matching antiques crowded into the cavernous room. The design was so rigidly symmetrical that even the throw pillows on the sofas on either side of the fireplace were of the exact number, size and design. The pillows even had a floral design similar to the obscuring bowl hovering below Anna Burwell's ancient portrait in the foyer.

Missy glanced at her diamond-studded watch, both to monitor the time and to reassure herself—and others—of the opulent distance she had traveled since graduation. That distance, judging by the still upturned noses and dismissive expressions of her former classmates, was not quite so far as Missy had imagined. For this brief afternoon, Missy was, with mounting irritation, once again relegated to the role of the poor relation. It was a group that, solely due to Laura, then and now, only afforded the most limited entree to Missy Gilmore Harrison and, to Missy's surprise, their condescension still grated. She felt an enduring resentment not only toward these ripened snobs, but even, unexpectedly, toward Laura herself, who still glided so serenely in their midst.

CHAPTER TEN
THE ARBORETUM

I t had been an unexpected pleasure—the most exemplary kind in Dr. Alice Owens' view—to meet the handsome young professor at the Harrison dinner. And so she had eagerly invited Stephen to join her for lunch following a doctor's appointment that she had near the Arboretum shopping center.

They agreed to meet at Abilene's American Cuisine, which offered a reliable, if unspectacular, menu. Alice slowly circled through the cramped parking lots of the serpentine Arboretum, which her husband Bill called the *Carboretum*. She found a spot near Abilene's and edged into the stingy space just before an enormous Hummer was about to squeeze in ahead of her. Victorious, she walked into Abilene's and requested a table near the window.

Waiting for Stephen, she enjoyed the stillness. Long inured to an incessantly demanding life, Alice had come to enjoy the occasional silences, the exquisite in-between time, when she could allow herself, alone and content, to just be.

W hen she had first learned that Bank of America was assigning Bill to Charlotte, she was horrified. And her friends, perhaps overly empathetic to her plight, could offer nothing more than a consoling sigh, tempered by an obvious gratitude that it was she who was moving to the wilds of North Carolina and not them. Comfortably ensconced on hilltops throughout San Francisco above the glistening bay, they imagined a move to Charlotte, North Carolina, as the transitional equivalent of a dive off of the Golden Gate Bridge.

Those consoling friends regarded her and Bill much as ancient Romans must have viewed the poor souls who were exiled to a remote and barren Mediterranean island. "You'll get used to it," they would sympathize, with visions of her and Bill pacing in despair across some forlorn southern rock, with the only distractions being a bank, a Baptist church, and a strip mall. A strip mall no doubt very much like the one where she now sat waiting for Stephen Rayfield.

Alice had taken a position as an obstetrician/gynecologist at Carolinas Medical Center. "But what will you do?" one of her more acerbic friends had asked. "Don't they still have babies at home there?"

During the long drive from San Francisco to Charlotte, as Alice watched the flat American landscape take her farther and farther away from California, she marveled at their fate. How could a bank in a little noticed backwater like Charlotte take over the Bank of America? Laura recalled the smirks and laughter at their going away party.

"Just remember," one of her Pacific Heights neighbors advised, "everything there is *world class*. I'm told that you can't buy a turnip at the grocery store without commenting, 'goodness, this is world class!'"

As the endless miles accumulated, she and Bill endeavored to make an adventure of it, and were grateful for the excited anticipation of the children.

"Are we there yet?" Taite or Devon, their eleven-year old twins, would periodically ask.

"No, not yet," Alice would answer, and then whisper to Bill, "thank God."

They had purchased a beautiful old Tudor house in Myers Park. She loved her home, which had been renovated and enlarged by the previous owners, and Bill loved that it had cost so much less than their place in Pacific Heights. That house had small, cramped rooms, albeit with its irreplaceable view of the bay, and was wedged into a sliver of grass between two imposing mansions. That one of their neighbors was a Getty did not ameliorate the minimal space of her kitchen.

Bill's commute to his office downtown—in private, they refused to refer to it as Uptown—was brief and the envy of acquaintances who lived in one of those outlying, luxurious suburbs like Seven Eagles or Piper Glen. She and Bill laughingly, but very discreetly, referred to their new city as Car Lot. The latter reference was reinforced every day that she braved traffic to get her girls to Country Day, a school that they predictably loved. Alice often wondered how she had raised such uncomplaining, well-adjusted children. With typical, if not entirely unjustified, modesty, she gave considerable credit to the unerring assistance of Aurelia, their au pair. Aurelia, a beautiful, shy young woman from Brazil, had begun working for the Owens shortly after they arrived in Charlotte. The young woman's adjustment to the South was even more stark than their own, and this had an oddly soothing effect on whatever tumult they encountered.

In time, they had come to appreciate the friendliness of their neighbors and the lush charm of Myers Park. But, the meager cultural life of Charlotte was still unnerving. And Alice Owens understood that, for all their 'hi darlin' good humor, Charlotteans were wary of her. Her presumed San Francisco sophistication. Her polished finishing school diction. Even, perhaps, her career as a physician. And, most definitely, her inadvertent wounds to the delicate sensibility of Charlotteans.

And what a sensibility it *was*. Charlotte, growing at the seams and wildly energetic, was like a teenager, all dressed up with no place to go. Charlotte's boosters, who were legion, were ever alert to any unfavorable comparison involving their *world class* city. Alice discovered early on that her friend in San Francisco was right—they really never did tire of trotting out that designation. This did result in rather farcical efforts at distinction, whether inexplicably referring to their downtown as Uptown or, her personal favorite, the feeble boast of the Charlotte Visitors Bureau that some magazine named

Nations Restaurant News had designated Charlotte one of the "Top 50 Cities that Sizzle." As Alice quietly surveyed the beige blandness of Abilene's, she could only wonder about the other forty-nine.

Stephen Rayfield entered the restaurant with the aggressive gait of a former rugby player and waved to Alice. She hugged him warmly, and laughed, "I'm so glad you could have lunch with me. What a treat."

"My pleasure," he said. "Everything okay with the doctor?"

"Oh, fine. Just a routine check-up. I'm not a very good patient though. I always imagine the worst."

"Isn't that sort of expected when you work with sick people all the time?" he asked.

"Yes, I suppose so," she said, "but I also worry because there is a history of breast cancer in my family. My mom was diagnosed four years ago. She's doing well, thank God." Alice glanced at the menu, and then sighed, "Anyway, I'm clean as a whistle. But, you have to deal with the hand they give you, right?"

"Absolutely," he agreed. "That's what my grandfather said when he was told he had terminal liver cancer. He knew it was hopeless and, on the way home from the oncologist's, he said to Grandmom and Uncle Edward, 'When I have a losing hand, I usually get out of the game.'"

Alice smiled. "That's marvelous. Well, aren't we a grim pair? I *knew* I would like you."

Their waitress, a dazzling blonde dynamo, with the precise gait of a beauty queen, approached their table. "Good afternoon," she beamed, "My name is Jessica, and I will be your server today. Would you care for something to drink?" Stephen ordered a Corona, while Alice asked for the house chardonnay.

As the beauty queen waitress waltzed away, Stephen said, "House chardonnay? I thought all Californians were wine snobs."

"Really? Well, it is my considered belief that everybody is a snob about *something*. Wine seems pretty benign, don't you think?"

Jessica returned with their wine, the glasses teetering precariously on a small tray, as she balanced expertly on her exacting heels.

"Here you are. Have you decided what you would like?" Alice ordered the caesar salad, and wanted to add 'good luck in the talent competition.'

"I'll have the chicken salad sandwich," Stephen said, "I'm saving room for dessert."

"My, you plan ahead, don't you?" Alice asked.

"Only if it's something unimportant, like dessert," he said. "The cake is pure defiance on my part. I got on the Lifecycle this morning for thirty minutes, and then weighed myself. I had gained two pounds overnight. So...cake is the only sensible option!"

"Very logical," she said. She moved her chair in closer and whispered, "Isn't this shopping center just hideous? It's like Jurassic Park, except instead of dinosaurs there are those huge SUVs."

"Think of all you will learn and discover, then," he said, cupping his hand over his mouth, going along with her conspiratorial tone. "For example, did you know that—and I have this on good authority, my Grandmom Myrtle in fact—when the Arboretum was first proposed, the plan was to bring in a store like Lord and Taylor. Well, as you can imagine, the anticipation in Providence Plantation was palpable. Alas, it was not to be. Instead, well..." He motioned outside toward the huge Wal-Mart.

"You're kidding, right?" It was the ultimate retail nightmare of status-conscious suburbanites.

"Oh, no. True story. Happy ending, though. Grandmom says that the Wal-Mart packs 'em in. In heavy disguise, of course."

"Does your grandmother live in Charlotte?" Alice inquired.

"God, no," he said. "She would say that Charlotte is way too, quote, 'highfalutin'. No, she lives in the same house where my mother and Uncle Edward grew up in just down the road in Monroe."

"Are you close to your aunt and uncle?"

Stephen considered the question, cupping his chin in his thick hands, and then said, "Well, they kind of keep to themselves. I mean, they wouldn't want me to say this, but they are, let's just say, a little higher on the social scale than the rest of the family. But, they have been really kind to me since I moved to Charlotte, probably because Uncle Edward and Mom have always been close, and I guess I present reasonably well at parties."

"That you do," Alice agreed. "I must say, they are an intriguing couple. Your uncle, I think, has unexamined depths. And he seems more, how should I put this, more down to earth than Missy."

"You noticed, huh? Well, let me just say that *everybody* seems more down to earth than Missy. I should get her an embroidered pillow with that quote from Montaigne. You know the one? 'No matter how high the throne, you always sit on your own rear end.' She probably would not see the humor in that. I like her though. She means well."

"Does she?" Alice asked, slightly challenging the assertion, then said, "So, getting back to Wal-Mart, sometimes I think that Charlotte has some kind of retail curse on it. For example, have you noticed that the restaurant at Morrocroft shopping center is Ruby Tuesdays? And, my personal favorite, the hotel right next door to the Palm restaurant at Phillips Place is a Hampton Inn? I mean, it's a *nice* Hampton Inn, but still…"

"And they say Charlotte has no sense of humor," Stephen replied. "Where else can you have a Hampton Inn on one block and a Via Veneto that sells $1000 pocketbooks on the other? Trust me, my friend, this place is not for the faint of heart."

"Well, maybe the curse is broken," Alice said hopefully. "We do have Nieman-Marcus now out at SouthPark."

"And you are an optimist," Stephen said, admiringly. "They must teach that out in California. Do you miss San Francisco?"

"Yes and no," she said evasively, mindful of the flammability of such an inquiry in Charlotte. "Like most people in California, I came from somewhere else. I grew up in Lake Forest, Illinois, just outside Chicago, and moved to California to go to college at Berkeley, and then stayed for medical school and residency at UCSF. That's where I met Bill. He had gone to Stanford Business School, and was already in mid-climb at Bank of America when we met."

By the time dessert arrived—both of them decided on the peach cobbler, but only after Stephen had confirmed that, in classic Old South fashion, it was prepared in an iron skillet—Alice had asked Stephen, "What about you? Don't tell me a good-looking guy like you is single."

"You are a flatterer," he said, laughing. "That is my primary requirement in any friend. How did you know? But, to answer your question, I am currently single."

"And before?"

"Before? Well, I pretty much managed to ruin a perfectly wonderful relationship. He was in medical school, and I was completing my doctorate."

"What happened?" she asked, not in the slightest surprised by the pronoun. She looked at him intently. She had the rare gift of showing genuine interest, and acceptance, without seeming too prying or cloying.

"Well, you know the old poem—two roads diverged in the wood? Everything was fine, but, always on the horizon, getting closer day by day, were our respective graduations. And what then? Dylan had requested UNC as his first choice for his residency. But, he matched at Georgetown instead. We tried things long distance, and managed to make it work for a while. Then, one weekend, he came down to Durham and...well...it went badly." He took a sip of his wine, and then added, wearily, "It was all my fault."

"Fault is a complicated thing," she said. "Most relationships are just dumb luck, with a little extra effort. That's all. Honestly, it's amazing to me that anyone stays together."

"That's pretty cynical," he said.

"No, just realistic," she said. "People are never so imperfect as they are with the person they marry. I have been very lucky with Bill. Of course, we do not have what might be called a typical marriage..." She noticed his questioning expression, and paused, wondering if she could confide further in this engaging young man, and decided, for now, no. Alice believed that one of the greatest virtues was candor, but only when it was tempered by discretion, so she simply said, "Stephen, romance, much like comedy, depends on timing. The two of you just met at the wrong time. Bad luck."

"How do you know when it is the right time?"

"Oh, you just do. Even it if is just for a little while."

"I'll have to take your word for it," Stephen said. "Anyway...how do you like the cobbler?"

"It's delicious," she answered. "Crusty on the edge, bubbling in the middle. Thank the Lord for those iron skillets."

CHAPTER ELEVEN
WIFELY DUTY

I have to replace this comforter, Laura thought. Its heavy brocade was a nightly source of regret to her even during the winter, when the price of its warmth was a burdensome weight. It was covered with a very fine silk and, when unencumbered by actual bodies in the bed, it was lovely. Atop the comforter rested a half dozen silk pillows, all in burgundy shades. She abhorred rooms that were too busy and contentious with a mishmash of styles, colors and patterns. Her bedroom was a tribute to a linear and symmetrical order. The ornately carved mahogany bed was new, but its style was soothingly historic.

Laura was a light and uneasy sleeper, in contrast to her husband, who usually fell asleep within seconds of resting his head on his pillow. As a result, she routinely approached her bed, with its weighty, ironic comforter, with apprehension. Sleep was a sometime victory in her nightly combat with insomnia. And it was usually a battle that she waged alone, while Andrew snored in tranquil slumber beside her.

Her children were not yet home. Ben was at yet another graduation party. And Deb, always vague with regard to her Saturday night plans, had called to say that she was "with friends" and would be home later. Laura listened uneasily to the rain. She had not yet acquired the sort of nonchalant equilibrium of other mothers, who typically viewed their children with amusement or derision, but seldom with any discernible anxiety. Laura realized that, at bottom, her fears were not a reflection on her children, whom she fundamentally trusted. Well, she tried to, at least. It was the frenetic, slippery society into which they were now plunging alone that aroused her darker fears.

She could hear her husband in the bathroom. Surely a shared bathroom, with its revelatory potential, was the death knell for marital passion. Andrew had a surprisingly prim quality, such as when he was careful to urinate above the water line of the toilet, so as to minimize any sound. He was also fastidious about first brushing, then flossing, and then a thorough Waterpik cleansing. Although he had suffered through two root canals in the past year, he was undeterred in his rigorous dental hygiene. As she heard the usual whooshing and clicking, it occurred to her that he might want to make love. Laura never referred to marital relations in any way other than making love. On this particular evening though, she had no interest in making love or anything else. Her only desire was restful darkness and sleep.

Andrew Caldwell was a good husband and a good father. Laura knew that she could rely on him. And yet, her confidence in her husband's fidelity had not always been so strong. She was all too aware of the proclivities of weak men and the eager women waiting in the wings to indulge them. She did not believe the popular notion that the more tempered sensibilities of women could reign in masculine lust. It was faith, and faith alone, that had saved her marriage. While Andrew continued to steal glances at attractive women, and he on occasion sat a little too close to some of them, Laura regarded him as no more culpable than a mischievous child. While he might go near the stove, he would never touch the burner.

Laura waited, listening as Andrew gargled noisily. Tawdriness was nothing new, she realized, only more prevalent now. Her mother had taught her that.

Mother. Laura wondered how a word so fraught with complication can still roll off the tongue so simply. Her mother, the former Jewel May, had been working as a sales clerk in ladies' lingerie at Belk's when Tom Soames walked in one day. On that propitious day, Laura's father was fifty-five years old, rich, and hopeful that just the right lingerie might strike a spark in the frigid woman to whom he had then been wed for thirty long and desolate years. He reminded Jewel of Cary Grant, and she practically ran over the other salesgirl to get to him first.

"May I help you?" she asked breathlessly, her bosom heaving under her snug cashmere sweater.

"Yes," he replied, looking at her for a pivotal and telling second too long, "I was hoping to purchase a nightgown for my wife. It's for her birthday next week."

"Oh, well isn't that just the sweetest thing." She paused a moment, and added, "Your wife is a lucky woman. Come with me. I have a few things you might like to see."

Liking very much what he saw, Tom soon began an affair with Jewel, thrillingly under the radar of the ever watchful and suspicious eyes of Charlotte society. Tom's wife, Mary, finally and conveniently died three years later, and he played the sedate widower for one year before he began publicly squiring the radiant Jewel around Myers Park. Their first date was a joint appearance at Sunday school at Myers Park Presbyterian. Jewel wore a gray wool dress and a devout demeanor.

She was viewed, inevitably, as a gold digger by some, in particular by the substantial cadre of hopeful widows who had dreamed of reeling Tom in for themselves. Yet, the prevailing view was that Jewel was a burst of sunshine in the grieving world of poor Tom Soames.

The first Mrs. Soames had, from a distance, been universally admired. It was simply a given that he had been devastated by her loss. If anyone suspected that the bright light that was Jewel had been lit a little prematurely, such heresy was never uttered. Whatever their pecuniary misgivings, the matrons of Charlotte society were as one in their romantic view of the Soames union. Their husbands, perhaps for reasons of their own, encouraged such soft focus illusions and volunteered no contrary, lusty speculations.

When Laura arrived a scant eight months after the wedding, "just a little early", her parents imbued in her a worship of conformity and old-fashioned morality, with a fervor typically found among reformed sinners. No one can appreciate the risks of a fall as fully as those who have themselves experienced the weightless plunge.

Weightless plunge…Laura rubbed her eyes, welcoming the drowsiness enveloping her. She turned out her light, assumed her preferred fetal position, and pushed the comforter over toward her husband's side of the bed. As she heard Andrew getting into bed, she muttered, "Good night, honey, pleasant dreams." He crawled into bed close beside her and hugged her tightly. Thus bidden, she turned toward him to offer an affectionate farewell of a kiss, as a weary traveler might bestow just before setting sail.

"Lauro, baby," he cooed, "You are my baby girl." As he spoke, his hand began a familiar route from her face to her shoulder, briefly idling on her breast, then, with a calculated detour around her expansive stomach, continuing down to the relative hardness of the small of her back. "Please, Laur, okay baby doll?" She felt the palm of his hand pushing her next to him. If his arousal was still pending, his intent was clear.

"I'm awfully tired, honey," she said, gently pulling away from him. "How about tomorrow morning? How about then?"

"Aw, come on, sweetheart, I can't wait till then. You are just too gorgeous," he said, his hand resolutely in place on her back.

"Okay," she said quietly. "Okay."

"Thanks, baby," he said, leaning into her with his entire body. "Would you touch me too? Remember I told you I need to be touched a little more…You know…down there."

"Honey…I'm really tired."

"Well, then, how about a nice, slow kiss?" he said, slightly irritated and commanding, turning his face, rough with stubble, to hers. She kissed him, and he took her hand and gradually drew it down lower. Slowly, she felt the familiar hardening of him in her hand. He rolled over on his back, and she continued her ministrations. It didn't take long. He gasped. She sighed.

Wifely duty, she thought, wifely duty. She silently recited it like a mantra, or a prayer.

CHAPTER TWELVE
SATURDAY NIGHT DANCING

The annual benefit for the Mint Museum promised to be the sort of formal, choreographed assemblage that Bill and Alice Owens had experienced many times. As they walked arm in arm into the cavernous Hyatt ballroom, Alice felt a wave of affection for her husband's enduring discomfort with such starchy, but necessary, theatrical evenings.

They proceeded toward their table, located near the dais, and were welcomed by a sea of smiling faces. At Bill's insistent pleading, citing the unyielding social demands of corporate life, she had really tried to take these well-meaning, well-connected southerners as they were. And, having grown up in suburban Chicago, she was not exactly in alien territory. A matter of style and accents, not of substance. She accepted that axiom intellectually. But each time she had a honey-dipped conversation with the likes of Missy Gilmore Harrison, waving at them now from the table, she bristled at the surreal quality, the strange blend of sugar cut with vinegar.

In one of those arrangements where it is rightly assumed that conversation will flow more freely if spouses do not sit together, Alice found herself seated next to Edward Harrison. Alice had initially viewed Edward and Missy Harrison as she viewed most of the corporate couples of Charlotte—conventional, polite, and, in their own rigid predictability, oddly mysterious. Like most stereotypes, she knew that this one was mere surface, but it helped her in the beginning to secure some kind of perspective of the new tableau in which she found herself. She rarely thought of Edward independent of the formidable, if somewhat brittle, woman who was now holding court at their table.

"I just think it is shameful that Charlotte does not get more of that homeland security money," Missy was saying, as the other occupants at the table nodded in agreement. "Why, we are just as important as Houston or Atlanta. Just as big a target as they are. Probably bigger. But, as usual, we don't get our fair share. I was talking to Congresswoman Toller about this just the other day, and she said…"

Alice's thoughts drifted as this familiar grievance circulated around the table. She had heard it, or some variation of it, many times before. Glancing at Edward Harrison, who quietly sipped a scotch as his wife led the resentful chorus about Atlanta, she was reminded that some men exude a magnetism that requires close proximity for full effect. Edward was one of those men.

"I had lunch with your young nephew today," she said, turning to Edward.

"Stephen? Well, lucky him," Edward replied. "I noticed that the two of you seemed to hit it off at our house."

"Well, I have a weakness for young southern men," she said, almost whispering this confessional information, then quickly added, "but not just the young ones."

"Oh, well, lucky me then."

"Close your eyes," she said to him.

"Say what?"

"Close your eyes," she repeated. "I am conducting a serious experiment!"

He closed his eyes, suddenly aware of the cacophony of mundane chatter and the roar it created across the room. "Now," he heard her say, in a light, whispery voice, a voice that hinted at frothy, conspiratorial intrigues, "tell me what color is the carpet and the flowers on the table."

"The carpet is blue, and the flowers are violet," he answered confidently, opening his eyes.

"My God," she said, briefly touching his hand, "you're right. You are one of the few men who's ever gotten it right. My theory is that most men don't pay any attention to decor. You're not gay are you?"

"Certainly not," he huffed, but not too energetically. He did not want to offend the liberal sensibilities of this exotic San Francisco transplant. "But, I'm glad I passed. It's good to be a credit to straight men. We need all the help we can get."

"Oh, you are. Definitely." She laughed, again just briefly touching his hand. "You are."

"Thanks," he said appreciatively. "Don't be *too* surprised." He was entranced by her laugh, which had a lilting, yet slightly raucous quality. Her laugh hinted at a lusty nature beneath that elegant facade, or was he reading too much into it? He tended to do that, imagining that most of the attractive women whom he knew were, despite their varying degrees of refinement, fountains of hidden sensuality. This fantasy of urgent moans, of silky legs straddling him and perfectly coiffed hair falling messily over supple breasts, was in stark contrast to his cosseted wife.

Edward, emboldened by a long delayed, and desperately longed for, resolve, took another sip of his scotch. He furtively looked about the table, then returned his gaze to the inviting blue eyes of Dr. Alice Owens. "Would you like to dance?" he asked her, reasonably certain that she would.

Evelyn Peck stared into the medicine cabinet mirror in the bathroom and carefully applied blue eyeliner. The mirror had a jagged crack which created an uneven divide down her heavily rouged face. She was getting ready for a dance, and it was by no means certain that she would have sufficient time. She walked into the living room. "Keith," she yelled, "How does this dress look?"

The fact that her son had no expertise in womanly fashion, and even less interest, did not in the slightest deter Evelyn from seeking his opinion. Her need for attention was ravenous and, if starved enough, she was not above relying on the meager offerings of her son. "Looks fine," he mumbled, not even bothering to look up from his *Star* magazine.

"Well, look! Does it or don't it? You ain't even looking!" She was wearing a red, skin tight polyester dress that was glued to her skin, ending about six inches above her knees.

"It looks like a miracle you can still breathe. Can you?"

"Oh, shut up. You don't know nothing about anything. Who cares what you think, anyway?" She smoothed the wrinkles down the front of her dress, and then adjusted the low-cut bodice, attempting to plump up her breasts, which were already overflowing the black bow fastened to the sea of red.

"Where you going?" he asked.

"The dance at the Hometown Inn. I'm going to meet Clara there. And Gene. He's gonna be there. To see yours truly."

He ignored her boasting and asked, "Well, what am I supposed to do? Just sit here like a knot on a log?" Keith's driver's license had been suspended for multiple DUIs. The judge had told him last time that one more DUI and he would send Keith to jail, no questions asked. "You know damn well that I can't drive nowhere on my own."

Evelyn sat down on the sofa and began squeezing her plump feet into tight black heels. "Shoulda thought about that before, buster brown. I sure as hell ain't taking you to the Hometown Inn."

"That's the *last* place I want to go. How 'bout you drop me off at the East Tavern?" he said, with a tight, forced grin.

His expression reminded her of her long-vanished second husband. Any reminder of Fred Peck was a source of alarm to Evelyn. "Wipe that grin off your face," she shrieked. "Listen, I will take you to the bar, but how you gonna get home, smartass? You don't have no money for no taxi."

Keith rose from his chair, and began combing his thinning hair. "You can stop there on your way back. That won't kill you, will it?"

The Hometown Inn was located among the outer reaches of South Boulevard, a dreary procession of industrial warehouses and dilapidated old apartment buildings. The portion of South Boulevard that was closer to Uptown was bursting with development, its sidewalks newly curbed and lined with elegant new streetlamps, all in anticipation of the new light rail. But, this more distant area was like a gangrenous afterthought, neglected and forgotten.

The Hometown Inn had once been a place where middle class families stayed when they visited Charlotte. Now, many of its residents were more or less permanent, with housing vouchers from the Mecklenburg County Department of Social Services.

The parking lot of the Hometown Inn was only half full. As Evelyn parked her car, a drunk man staggered by, clutching a beer in a paper sack. It had begun drizzling rain, and she walked briskly toward the lights and music of the dance, which was held in the inn's squat main building. The brick walls were painted white some years before and were thick with soot and grime, smudged now by the increasing rain.

Evelyn opened the heavy metallic door. A disco light was casting out rainbow colors over the dance floor, where a solitary couple swayed to an old Donna Summer tune. Most of the patrons remained at their tables, drinks firmly in hand. Evelyn scanned the shadowy room for sight of her friend, Clara. Suddenly, she heard the high-pitched voice of Gene Johnson.

"Hey good lookin'. Whatcha got cookin'?" Gene was a big Hank Williams fan, and even looked somewhat like the legendary singer. He was a tall man with a tendency to slouch. The latter attribute made him always slightly importuning in his air, a quality that fueled the amorous designs of Evelyn Peck.

"Gene! Well, hello there honey. I weren't sure if you'd be here tonight. Have you seen my friend Clara? Remember her? She was here with me last week."

"Naw. Ain't seen no Clara," he said gruffly, "but, I got a table over here. Come have a drink with me."

Evelyn sat down beside him, and he quickly placed his long, thin arm around her shoulder. "This place is pretty dead tonight, ain't it?"

"Where you wanna go, baby?" he asked, as he leaned toward her so that every possible part of his body would have contact with hers.

"Wherever *you* wanna go, honey," she leered. "How 'bout the moon and back?"

In response, he squeezed her shoulder a little tighter, and let his hand drift ever so slightly southward. Evelyn turned toward him, exposing the unfortunate folds of her double chin, and kissed him hungrily.

"Where you all live, anyway?" she asked. "You ain't got a wife at home, do you?"

"Hell, no," he exclaimed. "I ain't got no wife. Used to. Four times, used to. Good riddance though."

Evelyn laughed. "Listen to you. Where do you live?"

"I got a mobile home just outside Concord. I got a pickup truck. I got a $25,000 boat. And all the young girls just wanna run with the niggers!"

"Got any kids?" she asked, snuggling closer to his slight and oddly soft body.

"Six of 'em. Only one lives with me though. He can't find no work. Rest of 'em gen'ly on their own. How 'bout you?"

"I got one boy," Evelyn said. "And that's a plenty." By now, Gene Johnson's hand was firmly on Evelyn's generous breast. Stationary though. She could tell he was at heart a gentleman.

"Why don't we go to your place?" he whispered.

The evening was growing late, and Missy glanced suspiciously at her husband and his prolonged, and by all appearances very enjoyable, attentions to Alice Owens. As she was considering a polite, but decisive, interruption of their little waltz, the table was suddenly commanded by the silky smooth voice of Janey Burroughs.

"I saw the Hinkles at Morton's last month and never would have guessed. Just a shame about them, isn't it?" Janey commented with a somber enthusiasm regarding the recent separation of the Hinkles. "Such a lovely couple," she gleefully continued, "and haven't they been together for almost thirty years?" Mrs. Burroughs served up that query with a compassionate shudder. Indeed, dramatic shudders, usually accompanied with a violent quiver of false eyelashes, were her signature gesture.

"I always felt that Don Hinkle wasn't good enough to shine that woman's shoes," her husband said. "He should've held on to her." Adam Burroughs was rich enough and powerful enough to, almost, say whatever he wanted. While such a freedom of expression would be somewhat dizzying for a white man in the rigorous conformity of Charlotte, it was positively intoxicating for a black one.

"Yes, well, perhaps," Missy said, her eyes downcast in contemplation of human folly, sexual or otherwise, "but, I understand that Gloria is just torn up about it."

Janey Burroughs, following Missy's lead, assumed a similar stricken and philosophical air. She possessed an unfailing empathic radar, which was invaluable for anyone tilling the fertile soil of insufficiently flattered Charlotte matrons. "How could he abandon such a wonderful woman, and the *mother* of his children?" she asked, then added knowingly, "And for, well, I hate to say it, for that dime store bimbo?"

As the women at Missy's table exchanged uniformly grim assents, and the men, looking furtively away, discovered a sudden fascination for strawberry shortcake, Alice Owens said, "Well, she may be a wonderful woman, certainly. But, maybe she wasn't so wonderful for *him*."

Forks dropped in unison in the wake of this heresy, and Bill Owens quickly poured himself another glass of merlot. "I'm not criticizing Gloria," Alice clarified, "I'm just saying none of us has walked in their moccasins."

"Alice," Missy said, managing to smile and smirk at the same time, "That's kind of you. Very *charitable*. But, what about the sanctity of marriage? That still counts for something. Here. In Charlotte...well, so long as it is between a man and a woman."

Edward, who typically avoided such discussions with the agility of a born diplomat, blurted out, "I agree with Alice." Heads suddenly turned in his direction, anticipating a rare oracular pronouncement. He noticed, with some discomfort, that no one looked more expectant in this regard than his wife. "I mean, well, of course, Missy is right. About marriage and all. But, well, we don't...none of us can honestly say...Hell, they've got to live their own lives." Edward looked nervously about the table, embarrassed now by his outburst. And yet, while Missy seemed perplexed and slightly annoyed with him, he was consoled and, he had to admit, palpably excited, by the appreciative gaze of Alice Owens.

"I know what you mean," Adam Burroughs interjected. "But, people throw in the towel too quickly. I say, 'bring back hypocrisy.' That system kept a whole lot more marriages together than this let it all hang out world we live in now." He paused a moment, glancing at the suddenly more attentive gaze of his own wife. "And, speaking hypothetically, of course, a man doesn't have to tear up the whole field to sow a few wild oats."

"Adam, what a curious fellow you are," Missy laughed, smiling at him. "And Janey, how on earth do you put up with him?"

"That's easy," Mrs. Burroughs said. "My mama, rest her soul, she always used to say, 'girl, you need *high* expectations to get a man, and *low* expectations to keep him.' Believe me, ladies, it works every time."

"Well, okay, then," Edward said, smiling, pleasantly aware that Alice Owens had moved perceptibly closer to him, and was watching him with increased interest. Of course, Missy was watching him too, but, he well understood, with considerably less regard.

Keith Peck sat by himself at the bar of the East Tavern, nursing the single beer that he could afford for the evening. It was nearly one a.m. and the bar was almost empty. One tired looking redheaded woman was at the opposite end of the bar. Her hair was kinky and reminded Keith of a brillo pad. She stared at her gin and tonic, and occasionally glanced over at Keith.

Finally, she came over and sat beside him. "Howya doin'? This place sure is dead tonight," she said slowly. She had a hard, lean look, all angles, no curves. Even her fatigue seemed sharp, jagged, in the harsh and spidery lines that creased around her mouth and forehead. "Looks like we're 'bout the only ones left." She attempted a feeble smile and looked vacantly over his shoulder.

Keith never knew what to say to women, especially tired, brillo-padded women whom he sensed, rightly, would have very little to say in return. The woman's comment about the bar indeed probably did exhaust her store of conversation. Without enthusiasm, he said, "Yeah, guess so."

The inevitable silence ensued. Both of them stared at the row of bottles behind the bar, as if there were some secret labeling mystery to Johnny Walker or Cuervo Gold that would momentarily be revealed.

"You staring at that beer like it's your best friend. Looks like you need a new friend. I might could use another one myself."

"Naw, I'm good," he mumbled, and then, fatally, volunteered "left my extra cash at home."

"Oh, that right? Well, no harm there." Her thin lips had by now disappeared into two small apathetic lines. She waited for a few moments before getting up from her stool. "Well, take care," she said, and walked to the back of the bar, where she began talking to an old man who was seated at one of the rickety little tables they kept near the pinball machines.

She just wants a free drink, Keith thought. Trash. Women are such trash. He wondered why he never was able to meet a nice girl. He had gone to church a few times, but all the women there just wanted to deprive him of the few pleasures he could still imagine in his life. Plus they were not friendly. They always seemed to glance at him, disapproval or disappointment quickly registering in their eyes, and then look just as quickly away.

In the back of the bar, the brillo-haired woman was still talking to the old man, who was slumped over the table. She had gotten her drink, and was now twirling her bony fingers around grandpa's limp gray hair. Some guy was playing the pinball machine, leaping and thrusting his body in time with the gyrations of the machine.

Keith Peck was not a philosophical man, but as he sat there in the deserted bar, looking at the girl playing with the hair of an old man and the guy dancing with a pinball machine, it did occur to him for a moment that perhaps his life was not quite as he had intended.

Suddenly, he heard the unmistakable sound of his mother entering the bar. "Keith," she yelled across the room, "drink that beer. It's time to go! I'm double parked." Without so much as a nod in her direction, in the faint hope that no one would think she was in any way related to him, he got up and quickly walked toward the bathroom.

"Where the hell you going?" she screeched, now in hot pursuit. "Get back here. Don't make me follow you into the goddamn john. Get over here. " By now she had caught up to him, and was grabbing the sleeve of his shirt. The brillo girl, and the old man, and the pinball guy were all looking at him and Evelyn, and laughing as if they were in on the joke too.

"All right. I'm coming. Jesus Christ, calm down," he hissed at her. He pushed her hand off of him, turned around, and stalked out of the bar in a rage. It was still raining, and he felt the humid wetness soaking him as he walked outside.

She was right behind him, scowling. "Get in the damn car. Some thanks, after I go out of my way to come get you. You think I like coming into this rat hole? Well, do you? I was nearly attacked by some wino on the corner. Thank the Lord I had Gene following me in his car." Then, suddenly, she waved daintily at a man in the truck behind them, ignoring Keith.

"Don't you spoil this for me," Evelyn said, as they drove along the darkened, eerily quiet street toward their house. Keith regarded his mother, from whose mouth a cigarette precariously dangled, and said contemptuously, "No problem. Hope you'll invite me to the wedding."

"Grow up," she screamed. "At least I have someone who wants to see me. When's the last time anybody bothered to come see *you*? Huh? Answer me that, smartass. You're just jealous. Jealous of your own mother." She began to laugh, that awful razor sharp laugh.

When they pulled into their driveway, Keith got out of the car and stormed into the house, not waiting for any introductions to Mr. Gene Johnson. He timed the slamming of his bedroom door just as Evelyn and her new boyfriend walked inside the living room.

"What's the matter with him?" the man asked.

"What ain't?" his mother said, giggling.

He heard her door close, and Keith Peck tried to sleep through a drizzly night of muffled sighs and abbreviated moans, trying not to remember something that he had tried for a very long time to forget.

CHAPTER THIRTEEN
IN THE GARDEN

Y ou, my friend, are drunk," John muttered, slumped beside Ben in the car. They were parked in the empty lot next to the Piper Glen Clubhouse, above the lake and golf course. A steady rain splashed against the windshield. "Saturday night and our good little Benjie is smashed."

"Guilty as charged," Ben said, turning toward John and folding his hands into a prayerful gesture. "Beg your pardon. Not worthy, no, not worthy to call you my friend."

"Too late," John said, pushing Ben's hands away. "The damage has been done. And I always thought you were so good. So good."

They had been to a graduation party at the home of a classmate who lived in Providence Plantation nearby. Beer had been liberally consumed, even by Ben, who tended toward soft drinks. The golf course below them was in wet, spongy darkness, except for the shadowy glow of the moon, which glided in and out of the clouds.

John slumped further down into the seat of the Oldsmobile, his thick legs splayed out in front of him. He shifted his weight and lifted his arms behind his head, exposing the ridged hardness of his abdomen. John was the better athlete, and was varsity in football, basketball, and baseball. Having enjoyed a youth steeped in athletic triumph, he had a complete lack of self-consciousness of his body, except in its undeniable and democratic power to entice.

"Look at you," Ben said, noting John's naked stomach. "No beer belly for ole Johnny." Ben reclined and lifted his own tee-shirt. "But, I still got you beat," he muttered, rubbing his hands up and down his smooth as vinyl stomach.

"You're so *good*," John mumbled. "Always the good boy."

Ben glanced at his friend, at the slight tufts of blond hair against John's bronzed skin, just below his navel, slowly rising and falling with each lazy breath. His baggy shorts had slid lower, exposing the angled thickness of his torso. John's eyes were closed, and his arms remained behind his head, as if making an offering of biceps that curved in a perfect, bulging arc to his shoulders. "So *good*," he repeated drowsily.

John remained in his reclining position and looked at Ben. "Still can't believe we'll be graduating week after next," he said. "Trashville, here I come. Vanderbilt is a long way from here, that's for sure."

"Yeah, it is...long way..." Ben said, returning John's gaze, and then staring out toward the downpour, listening to the rain's rhythmic drumbeat against the car.

"You should have applied there," John said, punching Ben's shoulder. "You and me, bud. The next Brooks and Dunn."

"But, you can't sing, moron. Remember, even the church chorus wouldn't take you."

"Yeah, well, whatever. I wish we could just hang out this summer." John paused, his face darkening with an expression that seemed a mix of disappointment and resentment.

"What?" Ben asked, turning toward John. "Why can't we?"

"Didn't I tell you? Mom and Dad want me to intern with Congresswoman Toller. God, that fat-ass dweeb. You ever met her? Looked in those beady little eyes?"

"No, haven't had the pleasure. My dad loves her though," Ben said, and then asked, "So, are you going to do it?"

"Yeah, I guess so. If they sweeten the pot."

"How so?"

"You remember that BMW convertible I wanted?"

"Sure. You got it?"

"Not yet, but I will. It's simple, bro. They give me stuff, and then I do what they want."

Ben looked at John and wondered again at the languid, easy self-confidence encased in that hard, voluptuous body, and then said, almost in a whisper, "I'm going to miss you."

John smiled and again closed his eyes. His legs were almost touching Ben's. His breathing was slow and deep, as if he were drifting off to sleep. Ben looked out toward the moonlit pond below them, its smooth surface punctured by the falling rain. He felt the touch of his friend's leg, and it suddenly seemed as if the world had become microscopic, with a laser focus on the intersection of his skin to John's.

Half asleep, he felt a growing pressure in John's leg against his own. Aware now only of the sound of their breathing and the rain against the window, Ben shifted in his seat, and allowed his massive thigh to rest against John's knee, falling into a warm, intoxicating mix of softness and hardness. John moaned, as if in a dream, and placed his hands just above his still naked waist, and began to lightly move his hands up and down, his elbow just grazing Ben's thigh. And then, for just an instant, Johnny Harrison opened his eyes, glancing at Ben, and smiled.

Ben knew that he should sit up, laugh this off as drunken fantasy. But, he could not move. He felt a straining confinement, bound to John as if an invisible cloak, enveloping and seductive, had been wrapped around them. He felt the hypnotic comfort of an inevitable, unwanted recognition, and powerless to withdraw from the heat of John's insistent body. And so, desperate and somehow elated at the same time, he surrendered himself to John's caressing hand, not in opposition, but in a kind of bewildered communion and promise.

Sunday morning, the rain of the night before had almost stopped, capable now of only modest droplets on the windowpane outside Ben's bedroom. There was no other sound in the room, or the house for that matter, except the ticking of the alarm clock beside his bed. It occurred to him what a quiet house he lived in. Their house was as silent as a church, as tranquil as a sanctuary. And yet, Ben no longer felt safe in this peaceful home. His heart was pounding, almost in a bizarre duet with the minimal raindrops or the ticking clock. When he had arrived home the night before, that irretrievable, irrevocable night by the lake with John, his parents were already in bed, and he went up to his room immediately.

Ben was certain that if his mother or father had seen him last night, they would have immediately marked the shame on his face. He could not endure looking at them. Or, more precisely, their looking at him. And he could not stop thinking of the exact ejaculatory moment, in his frenzied, desperate intertwining with John, when the intensity vanished in an instant, and he was left only with a gelatinous feeling of revulsion and regret.

John had laughed it off. "Man," he said, quickly zipping his pants up. "Whew! We just needed to get off. No biggie."

Ben recoiled from John's touch, but assumed the same casual air. "Okay." He could find no other words, and managed a tentative, uncertain grin.

He could faintly hear his mother and father down the hall, getting ready for church. He would be expected to go with them, as he always had. The rest of the world was proceeding on schedule. It was this surface normalcy, this ironic calm, that he found most unsettling of all.

"Ben, are you up?" His father called to him. "Let's get going, son."

"I'll be ready in a minute, Dad," he answered, hearing his own voice with a sort of surprised recognition. The voice he heard was controlled, even, but without a hint of its usual melody.

Ben quickly dressed and went downstairs. He avoided the studied glances of his parents. Even Deb seemed to regard him with an unexpected curiosity. For once, he was grateful that, in the Caldwell household, intimate concerns were best disclosed to God and not to each other.

Later, at church, following the usual thunderous exhortations of Reverend Dunlap, the congregation began singing *In the Garden*. Ben reverently listened to the hymn, led by the enormous Galilee Church choir, their voices soaring among the elevated spires of the chapel.

The joy we share as we tarry there... He thought of John. During their frantic fumblings for each other, they had never kissed. It was just sex, Ben thought. Just dirty, animal desire. They were just two animals in heat. That was, at least, he believed, the way John saw it. And yet, even in its revelatory disturbance, even in the unwanted awareness that it forced upon him, it still left Ben breathless to recall it.

None other...has ever...known. For Ben, the memory of his desperate flesh entwined with John's was something more than a drunken stumble and so something far worse. It was a glimpse of himself that he had been conscious of for a long time, and from which he resolved to, once again, look away.

CHAPTER FOURTEEN
WHERE YOUR TREASURE IS

E dward had insisted that his mother be invited. "Will she want to join us at dinner as well?" Missy asked, dreading the answer. She reminded herself that she at least did not have to include her own mother at John's graduation. That would have been, even for Edward, undeniably toxic.

So, Missy had made reservations for five at the Palm at Phillips Place. Her desire to avoid being seen conspicuously with Myrtle Harrison, whom she regarded as the last word in gauche behavior, was outweighed by her determination to provide John with a distinctive evening. No place was more inviting in this instance than the Palm. Such was the celebratory demand for reservations there after Charlotte Latin had made its final adieu that only favored patrons could commandeer a table for dinner. Missy had not only secured a table, but she had specified that it be one of their less visible ones. Insurance against the embarrassing eruptions of Myrtle required careful foresight.

Missy had also made an unsolicited gift to Myrtle of a new outfit for the occasion. When Myrtle had arrived at the house with Edward, she looked almost stylish in the navy blue skirt with matching jacket and white blouse. The jacket and skirt were trimmed with gold lining, and, for added effect, Missy had loaned Myrtle a gold brooch. The brooch, a long ago gift from Edward, was in the form of a peacock. Missy hated it, but thought it was perfect for Myrtle.

"Mama Harrison," Missy had exclaimed, "you look wonderful. Doesn't your grandmom look just perfect, children?"

John, who had long been indifferent to his grandmother, echoed his mother's compliment. "Yeah. Perfect. You'll have to fight the men off with a stick."

Or, barring that, maybe with that hideous gold pin, Missy thought.

Charlotte Latin was a modern red-brick campus carved out over more than one hundred carefully tended acres of suburban woodland. Even at an occasion as fraught with excitement as graduation, the school nurtured a studied air of composure. Nevertheless, as the jubilant graduates crowded into the Beck Center and jostled each other into their seats, their energy, so long controlled by a steady simmer, seemed poised to finally boil over.

The Harrisons found seats near the back of the auditorium, and that was actually to Missy's liking. As much as she enjoyed being front and center, she shuddered at too many awkward introductions of her mother-in-law.

Missy watched as John, his sly vitality undiminished by cap and gown, made his way toward the front with the other graduates. He was surrounded by a throng of classmates, all seemingly hanging on his every word or gesture, all gazing at him, or so it seemed to his mother, with an unconstrained adoration. She noticed that Ben Caldwell seemed to hover uncertainly near John. Missy regarded Ben warily. She sensed that Ben, behind an exterior of congeniality, was, just like his mother, never really at ease. And she did not wish to see this contagion of discomfort extend to her son.

Today, we congratulate these outstanding young men and women for completing their education here at Charlotte Latin. They are our hope, our treasure. And, as the Bible tells us, where your treasure is, there shall your heart be also."

*Where your treasure is...*As Ben Caldwell listened to the dean intone those solemn words, he glanced back at John, who was seated behind him. John's expression was reverent, attentive. And yet, there was just the slightest hint of amusement, as if this were a particular role that John was playing, but hardly embracing. More distressingly, John did not return Ben's gaze, nor even acknowledge him in any particular way.

It had been two weeks since their encounter by the lake at Piper Glen. Since then, at school, at end of year parties, John had behaved as if nothing had happened, and so Ben had acted in a similar fashion. If they could remain as they were before that night, then Ben could almost convince himself that nothing had changed. Time would blur the violent colors of that evening, like a photograph fading in prolonged light, leaving a more obscure, less eruptive memory.

The only alteration to their friendship was a slight distancing on John's part. He was as friendly and approachable as ever, but Ben sensed a chilliness in his demeanor. But, then, perhaps John, with his tentative smile, had always maintained a distance. Ben, feverish now to any hint of rejection, had only begun to notice it.

"And it is with a heavy, but grateful heart..." the dean continued. Ben crossed his arms and assumed a pose of concentration, like John, as if he too were contemplating the words of the dean with the utmost regard.

"So, are you going to D.C.?" he had asked John just before the assembly.

John had put his arm around Ben and smiled. "Probably. Might be fun though," he whispered, his lips lightly touching Ben's ear. "I'm going to miss you, buddy."

The surge of students, followed by their beaming families, poured out of every available door from the Beck Center. Ben stopped in front of the enormous bronze eagle in the courtyard. "You all go ahead," he said to his waiting family, "I want to stay here for just a minute." He looked up at the eagle, which was mounted high above a marble base, its sharp claws clenching the rock on which it perched. Its wings were spread ambiguously wide, either in flight or landing. On this day of beginnings and endings, it seemed to Ben the perfect transitional effect.

On the base was inscribed the Charlotte Latin credo, which had little relevance to predatory eagles, but tended to resonate, fleetingly, with recent graduates. *Excellence. Leadership. Respect. Responsibility. Moral Courage. Honor Above All.* Ben considered those lofty words, momentarily humbled as only an honest judge, even a young one, of human character can be.

He returned his gaze to the eagle, gleaming in the afternoon sun. Its mouth was open in a voracious, crazed expression, the beak sharp and daggerlike. It seemed poised to swoop down in search of prey or perhaps of deliverance. The eagle glared down at him, as if he were its prey, as if with one merciless swipe it could coldly rip him to pieces.

"Ben," he heard someone calling him from a distance. It was his mother. "Come on, honey, it is time to go." He looked one last time at the eagle, hovering violently above him, and then walked over to his mother, waiting patiently. He took her arm, so soft and yielding, and was struck for a moment by her frailty.

"Sure, Mom, let's go," he said. "I was just saying goodbye."

As the Harrisons entered the Palm restaurant, they passed by the bar. Missy glanced at the sketches of noted patrons, famous and otherwise, on the wall. She did not care for hers or Edward's. Their portraits were located just above the bar. She felt that the drawing of Edward exaggerated his jowly cheeks, and the one of her grossly undervalued her chin.

"I don't care if they are caricatures," she said, "they still should be more flattering." Nevertheless, it did please her to be gazing down on her friends, most of whom were not unfamiliar with a seat at the Palm's well-stocked and flirtatious bar.

"Now, John," she said to her son, as she pushed his hair back from his forehead, "order whatever you like, but save room for cake." The chocolate cake at the Palm was enormous, possibly in an effort to be proportionate to the huge steaks. It was a culinary homage to excess, as few people could finish the massive portions on their plates. Missy, observing the fervor with which Andrea was examining the menu, said a silent prayer that her daughter would not be among that corpulent minority.

Meanwhile, Myrtle Harrison surveyed the dining room with a sort of gleeful curiosity. The veneer of money was evident throughout, from the polished mahogany panels to the liposuctioned, face-lifted, botoxed perfection of the women. Good Lord, she thought to herself, it's a roomful of Missys.

She had counted at least three different spas in the vicinity. How ridiculous, she thought. Why do these pampered women need massages and nail polishes? They don't do anything except run up balances on their husbands' charge cards. And their most important work is done flat on their backs anyway. Actually, she realized that wasn't necessarily true either, if her son's frosty relations with Missy were any indication.

Myrtle remembered her mother-in-law's backbreaking, constant labors at the Centerpoint home out in the country near Chesterfield. There was a time when the poor woman had to even wash the laundry down by the stream. Before Laurence Harrison, one of the wealthier sons, bought Rose one of those old rolling pin washing machines and installed it on the back porch, she had to take the dirty clothes, along with her children, down to a stream about a quarter mile from their house. While she scrubbed the clothes in the rushing currents, the older children would watch the younger ones. One day, Doug Harrison, just three years old, fell into the water. Rose heard her daughter, Sue, who had a speech impediment, screaming, "Mama, Doug fell in the 'ping. Doug fell in the 'ping." Rose had calmly fished him out, and continued with her wash. No wonder in later years that kindly old lady had a hunched back. *There* was a woman who could have used a spa, Myrtle reflected. The closest Mrs. Harrison ever got to a spa treatment was an afternoon catnap.

Suddenly, Myrtle heard the syrupy voice of some impostor pretending to be Missy calling her name. "Mom," the voice said sweetly...*Is she really calling me Mom?* Myrtle wondered, almost erupting in laughter..."I would like to introduce you to our friends, Laura and Andrew Caldwell and their daughter, Debra. And this is their son, Ben, who went to school with Johnny."

"Pleased to meet you," Myrtle sputtered. "Lord, this is quite a place. You come here often?"

"Only for special occasions, like today," the woman said, extending a petite hand so at odds with her doughy body. "It's very nice to meet you, Mrs. Harrison. Now we know where Edward gets his good looks."

"Hah! You should've seen his dad. Now, there was a good-looking man. But, thank you. Call me Myrtle! And congratulations, Ben. I know this must be a big day for you, just like for Johnny."

Ben, for all his dark good looks, looked pale and only managed to mumble, "Yes. It is." His lower lip quivered slightly, and he nervously put his hand to his mouth, as if to shield it from further assault. He looked at Myrtle and then, curiously, toward John, then quickly looked away.

Laura Caldwell reached over and gave John a hug. "Congratulations, sweetie. Now, don't be a stranger this summer. We'll see you all soon. It is a pleasure meeting you, Mrs. Harrison. Come and see us sometime." Then, the family walked away to their own table near the opposite side of the room.

"She's a nice lady. You can always tell a lady," Myrtle said, looking askance at Missy. "But, is the boy always so jumpy? He looks like he just lost his best friend."

"He has," John replied smugly. "*Me*. He's a good guy though. Just excited by graduation and all. You know how that is, Grandmom." Actually, having only gotten as far as tenth grade, Myrtle did not know how that was. But, she sensed that there was more to the boy's distress than John allowed.

"Well, he's your friend, but he strikes me as an odd duck. He reminds me of a boy back in Chesterfield. Frankie Shaw. He was a sweet kid, but so quiet, always seemed to be thinking something over. Frankie Shaw. He was always hanging around Centerpoint. Mrs. Harrison practically adopted the poor thing. He and Doug were best friends. Frankie just worshipped your dad, Edward. You remember the Shaw family, don't you? Frankie killed himself just after getting back home from Korea. Can't say any of us was surprised."

"Well, that's ancient history, Mom," Edward said. "I want to propose a toast. To Johnny. We are proud of you, son, and we hope your future will be only good things."

They lifted their champagne glasses for the toast. Out of the corner of her eye, Myrtle saw the Caldwells, seated quietly at a table toward the front of the room. She noticed that Ben was glancing toward them, then quickly looking away. What a sad boy, she thought. What a sad boy.

"Congratulations, son," she said to John. He smiled, accepting this homage as his due. He had such gifts, yet, for all his smooth beauty, for all his charm, he mystified his grandmother. In her experience, any surface that polished was apt to be slippery. "You have a wonderful life ahead of you," she added, "a lot of advantages your mom and dad never had. I hope you make the most of it." It was clear from her wavering voice that she was not at all confident that he would. Myrtle looked away, briefly noticing her seething daughter-in-law.

She thinks I prefer Stephen, Myrtle realized. Well, perhaps I do.

CHAPTER FIFTEEN
POLITICALLY CORRECTED

S tephen Rayfield looked at the scratchy red notations, spreading like a rash on the papers on his desk, as he graded the essay responses of his Democracy in America class. With only a few exceptions, they were abysmal.

An alarming number of his students, though capable of incessant chatter on cell phones, simply could not put a coherent sentence together. He was willing to forgive some of the grammatical and spelling errors, but he could not accept the lazy display of google-searched and often erroneous 'facts'. That most of these students had been in the top 20th percentile of their high school classes was a continual source of wonder to him. Accustomed to effortless As and Bs in the public school swamps from which they had emerged, it was no doubt a shock to them to receive the Cs and Ds that Stephen unceremoniously, and frequently, gave them.

He suspected that in twenty years, with the appalling academic decline now in full gear, all communication would be spoken or filmed. Written English would be as archaic as ancient Hebrew, and commercial advertisement would be the highest form of artistic achievement.

Whatever the sluggish efforts of his students in written composition, a deficiency which apparently was even more pronounced in the heat of summer sessions, they had been brilliantly effective in spreading the word that he was brutal in his evaluations. Already, it was conventional wisdom that his courses were best left to the students who actually intended to apply themselves. Unfortunately, while this discouraged many students from enrolling in his courses, it did not assure the quality of those students who did.

When he had finished grading the essays, Stephen walked over to the student union for coffee. He took a seat in a small lounge area and began reading the campus newspaper. As he scanned the pages in rapid succession, he paused at the opinion page. There was the name of his student, Tom Jarrett, underneath a caption that read "An Immodest Proposal"…

The achievement gap between black and white students is shameful. And nowhere is this outrage more apparent than UNCC athletics. Just look at the appalling under-representation of white males on the basketball team.

It is not a pretty picture, folks.

White males account for over 70 percent of the male student body at UNCC. And how many are on the basketball team's starting line-up? Zero! That's right. Zero! Not…a…single…one. This is unacceptable and yet tragically typical of such programs in colleges throughout our state and nation.

It is time for UNCC to take the lead in ending this bigotry! Now!

Many reasons have been suggested for this unfortunate situation. Some experts suggest that white males are more likely to grow up in environments where they are encouraged to play the country club sports, like tennis or golf or swimming. These sports receive little attention and no one cares about them anyway. White males lack any role models for basketball or football in the big leagues, precisely those sports which society most values and rewards. Once they leave high school, no one expects young white men to succeed. They are written off. Forgotten.

There are, even in these more enlightened times, backward thinking people who suggest that there is a biological difference for these inequities. They point to a similar absence of white males in other sports such as track and field, where almost every member of the U.S. Olympic team is black. These vicious commentators argue that whites are genetically slower and less dexterous than are blacks. That is, of course, a racist effort to blame the victim.

What to do?

I propose that, in an effort to level the playing field, an affirmative action policy should be implemented in the UNCC athletic program, specifically for basketball and football. The representation of our teams should more accurately reflect the racial composition of the student body.

The university has failed miserably in recruiting white players in underserved areas. Arbitrary and punitive measures of athletic ability should be ended at once. What is more important? A winning team or one that respects the diversity of our students?

People, our teams should look like our campus!

A mentoring program should be instituted to encourage these young white men. For too long, our society has been content to leave things as they are, tolerating an inequality between whites and blacks that should shame us all.

The time has come to take a stand! Join me in calling for an end to this injustice!

Later that morning, Stephen stood before his Democracy in America class, wondering if the article would come up in discussion. He did not wonder for long. Miss Baker had her hand in the air, smiling with the anticipation of a mischievous hornet awaiting a disturbance of the nest.

"Dr. Rayfield," she began, "did you read Tom's column in the paper? What did *you* think?"

"Well, I thought it had an interesting Swiftian twist to it," Stephen said. "It was provocative, as all good satire should be. I was struck though by its reduction of the race question to blacks and whites. What about Asian-American students? What about Hispanics? They are underrepresented in the sports that Tom mentioned as well. And there are growing numbers of mixed race individuals. Very little is said about them. We are truly a multi-ethnic culture, but still tend to see the world, if you will pardon the expression, in black and white. But, I would like to know what all of you thought about it."

"It really made me think," Miss Baker answered. "It made me consider, like, how races maybe are different in some ways, and how it's okay in one case to try and change that, but not okay in another. Like it's wrong for the medical school to have so few blacks, but it's okay for the basketball team to have zero whites. And we only talk about racial differences when they're good qualities. Never when it's, you know, maybe bad."

"That's an interesting point, Miss Baker," Stephen said. He then looked about the room and spied Thomas Kim, one of his brightest students. "Mr. Kim, what do you think Miss Baker means when she says it is acceptable to talk about race qualities in some instances but not others?"

Thomas Kim rarely spoke in class. "Well, I guess it is okay to point out, for example, that blacks are better at track and field," he said shyly, "but it is not okay to say that blacks, as a group, are not as good at math. Both are general comparisons, but only the positive one is allowed. Anything negative and people will say you are racist."

"*Are* black students, as a group, as good at math?" Stephen asked, pressing the point.

The young man shifted awkwardly in his seat, mindful that Asians were renowned for remarkable achievements in math and sciences, then said, "Statistically, no, sir, they are not. But, I don't know why that is..."

"I'll tell you why it is," Chris Denton, said, erupting in a barely contained fury. "For three hundred years, blacks were kept out of classrooms. Slave owners knew that knowledge was dangerous. Black students are still encouraged to fail. They are never given a fair chance. All these tests are biased and everyone knows that is true." He glared at Stephen and at Tom Jarrett, and then said, "His article, if you want to even call it an article, is disgusting. How can you act like it's all right?"

"Mr. Denton, I have not said I agree with the article," Stephen replied calmly. "It is a satire. I do feel that if it makes all of us think more honestly about race, then it has served a useful purpose. For example, let's talk a minute about your argument that black students are encouraged to fail. *Who* encourages them to fail? Some prominent members of the black community, such as Bill Cosby, have argued that blacks who succeed are disparaged as 'acting white'. Do you agree?"

"Bill Cosby is just a rich Uncle Tom," the young man countered. "That's all he is. And this so-called article is racist and is offensive to every black person who was ever turned down for a job, or put in prison, or lynched."

"Wait a minute," Tom Jarrett said, "my article was never intended to…"

"Black people were brought here in chains and beaten down for generations," Chris interrupted. "And you compare *that* to a basketball team?" He stood up and walked out of the room. The other black students in the class then grimly followed him.

For a moment, the class was silent. Then Miss Baker, surveying the wreckage, asked, "Dr. Rayfield? Remember when you said that we really don't talk about race in this country? Well, okay, I get it…"

After class, as Stephen walked down the hallway, he saw several students gathered in front of his office. They were whispering, gesturing toward the door.

"Excuse me," Stephen said, as he moved past them.

"Oh, sorry…" one of the young women mumbled. She and her friends quickly walked away.

On the door was scrawled *faggot*. Stephen stared at the defaced door. For a brief moment, he remembered another time, painful voices echoing in his head.

Little baby lost his way? Well? Cat got your tongue, faggot?

Stephen took the red marker from his coat pocket and hastily blotted out the word, then went into his office and quietly shut the door.

CHAPTER SIXTEEN
TURN UP THE LIGHTS

O h, I wouldn't go even if they did ask me to," Myrtle said, as she passed a slice of chocolate pie to her daughter. "What would I have to say to all those snobs? And I don't like that Congresswoman Toller anyway. What a phony. That's what I was just saying to Fred the other day. 'Fred,' I said, 'that woman is such a bag of wind.' She doesn't care about the small fry. That's why she cuddles up to Edward the way she does. *Money.* Money, honey!"

"Well, you can be sure I'm not giving a dime to her," Lynn said. "I'm there for the entertainment, Mom, that's all. And you have to admit, they are pretty entertaining."

Myrtle laughed. "That they are," she said, pouring herself another cup of coffee. "They just don't know it."

Lynn Harrison Rayfield, although she had lived in New York City on the Upper West Side for over twenty years, returned to North Carolina not only to see her family, but also her dentist. Having never quite gotten over a childhood trauma of a bloody tooth extraction by a cigar smoking hack, her reverence for Dr. Crenshaw was unabated by time or distance. She usually was in town for a long weekend, but with her son Stephen now living in Charlotte, she had extended her visit to one week.

Later that evening, she would be attending a fundraising event at her brother's home. Lynn had not actually walked along the marble floors of his home in over three years, and Edward had felt compelled to include her. In addition to an enduring affection between them, there was also the recognition that his sister's New York pedigree was an alluring addition to his table.

Charlotte's clamor to be Atlanta was a plausible ambition. Atlanta, it was generally agreed, could be had. But Charlotte's quivering infatuation with Manhattan remained in the realm of unattainable fantasy. New York was the dazzling society girl by which Charlotte was forever judged and found wanting. It was the dream lover Charlotte would always nervously desire and never acknowledge. Uptown was the *second* largest banking center in the country. There was never any question as to whom was *first*.

Edward, if not Missy, also appreciated that his sister, whatever her Rainbow Room glamour, remained a Tar Heel to her core and possessed a reassuring lack of pretense. One always felt that, while she had no intention of ever again living in Charlotte, she was nonetheless happy to return to it. If Edward was no longer quite as close to his sister as he had once been, he was no less comforted by her steady presence.

"Who all is going to be there besides Toller?" Myrtle asked.

"Oh, well, let's see," Lynn began, "Edward said the mayor would be there. Oh, and Chancellor Dunn from UNCC. Other people I've never heard of."

"A bigwig from the college? Well, put in a good word for our boy."

"Oh, I'd like to, but you know how Stephen is. He told me he doesn't want me to even mention he is working at UNCC. Let's face it, Mom, he likes to do things on his own."

Like mother, like son, Myrtle thought to herself. She had never entirely accepted that Lynn would freely choose, for all intents and purposes, to become a Yankee. She preferred to think of her daughter as a sort of elegant refugee. "Tell him to get on over here and see the old lady," Myrtle implored. "He's still coming for supper tomorrow?"

"Oh, he's coming," Lynn said. "He can't go too long without your peach cobbler. And, frankly, he likes getting away from that depressing apartment." Lynn shuddered. Her esthetic sense was not judgmental, but was acute, and the Edwardian Arms was a dreary outpost. "One of his friends came over to have a drink with us last night though. Interesting woman from San Francisco. Very nice. A doctor."

Myrtle grimaced slightly. She regarded San Francisco almost as alien as New York City. "How's your renovation coming along?" Myrtle asked, changing the subject.

"It's almost done," Lynn said. "I have the best guys working for me. Course every morning I have doughnuts and coffee waiting for them. That helps." She paused, and added, "I'm calling my little condo Centerpoint."

"Well, that is just wonderful," Myrtle said. "Your grandmom would be very happy about that."

"Yes, I think she would be," Lynn agreed. "I have a hand painted sign above the entry foyer that says 'Welcome to Centerpoint North.'"

"You know," Myrtle said, "Grandmom Rose went up to New York City once, for Bradford and Grace's wedding. Once was enough for her, I'll tell you that. They took her to a floor show at one of the clubs, you know with the showgirls and all. So, there they sat, watching these half-naked girls dance and kick. Rose was taking it all in, and she looked at one of them and just said, 'Poor thing, *where* did she go wrong?'"

Lynn smiled, examining the pale blue coffee mug in her hand. "Lord, Mom, do you ever throw anything away? I think I had my first coffee in this cup."

"Well, it's still good," Myrtle said. "If you want new stuff, go on over to your brother's. Everything there is new, honey, including Missy's face."

"No! Really?"

"Well, you tell me, after you see her at dinner tonight. Here's the first clue. Remember how she's always making Edward dim the lights at dinner? Not anymore. Missy is ready for her close-up, and she is very comfortable now with bright lighting. I was telling Fred the other day, I said 'Fred, she's got a new face.'"

"When did she do this?"

"I'm not sure. She turned the lights up about a month ago. Course, last year, she had her eyes done."

"How does she look?"

"Scary. You know, she has always had those strange eyes. Still does, only now her face doesn't move. She reminds me a little of Ruth." Myrtle grimaced as she uttered the name of her despised stepmother. "You know that bitch Ruth always looked at you sideways, which was okay with me. Ruth full on was too much for anybody. I always used to say to your father, I'd say 'Doug, that woman looks like she just broke out of the loony bin.' And I swear if Missy doesn't have those same crazy eyes."

"Well, now I really am looking forward to dinner."

"Just try not to stare," Myrtle replied. "And don't get spoiled over there with the rich folks. Tomorrow night we are having plain fried chicken. Nothing fancy! Of course, I'll make the cobbler for Stephen. And I have a whole batch of peanut butter delights for him to take home with him."

Myrtle had always doted on Stephen. Lynn remembered though how unnerved her mother had been when the family discovered that Stephen was gay. After that disturbing revelation, Myrtle went to the Monroe library to read about homosexuality.

Lynn had been sitting in the den, talking with her father. Myrtle walked in, back from her visit to the library, ashen-faced. "Mom, what's wrong?" Lynn asked.

"I have been to the library, and I read that homosexuals have anal sex. I just can't believe that Stephen would do such a thing," she cried.

Lynn, partly in shock that her mother had actually gone to the library and picked up a book, began to laugh. "Mom, he *doesn't*. Stephen told me he doesn't do that."

Myrtle looked at her with a perplexed expression. "Well, goddamn, then how does he know he's a homosexual?"

CHAPTER SEVENTEEN
SHERMAN'S MARCH

Edward poured himself a bourbon in a crystal tumbler and retreated to the relative quietness of his library, as Missy continued ordering the catering staff around like Sherman getting ready for the march on Atlanta. "No, no, no!" he heard her shriek, "those orchids must be placed on the center table, where the congresswoman will be seated. The smaller arrangements go on the other tables!"

A small platoon of tuxedo clad waiters and attendants had descended upon the house that afternoon to prepare for the arrival of about fifty of Congresswoman Edna Toller's nearest and dearest supporters. Edward viewed the function as a business obligation. He heartily disliked Tough Toller, as Missy, who disliked her even more, derisively called her. But his thoughts were not on the harsh woman who represented Charlotte in Congress. Rather, he contemplated seeing Alice Owens again. Since the fundraiser for the Mint Museum, his thoughts had frequently drifted back to her.

Just as his bourbon was beginning its palliative effect, and Edward was sinking deeper and deeper into the cushioned warmth of his leather armchair and the memory of the touch of Alice's seductive fingers, Missy, like a gust of arctic air, burst into the room. "Edward! Put on your shoes. And not those. You need to wear the black leather ones that I got for you last week. People will be here any minute." Edward dutifully trudged upstairs to put on his shoes.

"And don't forget to talk to her about Johnny," Missy called out to him. Contemplating the prospect of their son lapsing into an idle summer, they had persuaded him to accept an internship with Congresswoman Toller in Washington. A new BMW convertible had convinced John of the value of government service. There remained now the comparatively minor maneuver of persuading Toller to offer the internship.

Missy was swathed in some new concoction that she had ordered directly from a shop in Milan. Lavender colored silk dress, with a low cut bodice trimmed in silver, and a matching turban. It never failed to amuse Edward that she was at her most determinedly exotic in the most conventional of settings. It was as close as Missy came to nonconformity. And, to compensate, every other detail of the evening, including Edward's shoes and the exact placement of flowers, had to be strictly standard.

Congresswoman Edna Toller climbed over the back seat, her ample linen-swathed behind scurrying in mid-flight. She searched angrily through stacks of papers, all the accumulated mobile library that constituted the daily reading material of a member of Congress. "Ken!" she barked at her husband, "Where is the goddamned book?"

"Ahm, it's back there, bunny," he said calmly. He was accustomed to the tantrums of his wife, and in fact enjoyed them. He had always preferred a little spice, which would account for his initial attraction to Edna and his abrupt exit from his first marriage.

After ten years in the House, she and her harried staff, among which there was constant turnover, had yet to develop a more systematic organization except for 'the book.' It was a voluminous, three-ring binder containing her schedule, related speeches, reports, and memos. It was, in short, the Bible of her congressional office.

"Oh, Jesus H. Christ, here it is," she said, falling back into her seat with a slight thud.

"Great, then. I was sure it would be back there. Those kids are scared to death of misplacing it, ever since you fired that last little girl who forgot it." Ken had been especially sorry to see that one go, as she was awfully cute.

"That fucking moron? She didn't know her ass from a hole in the ground. Not a lick of common sense. Kids!" She began reviewing the remarks she wanted to make at the fundraising event being held that evening at the home of Edward and Missy Harrison.

Laura Caldwell loathed politics and, generally, politicians, but Andrew had insisted. He adored Edna Toller. The diminutive congresswoman, a birdlike woman whose most expansive features were a rather inordinately proportioned rear end and a large, usually smirking mouth, was an unseemly creature. The suspense of Congresswoman Toller was that one never knew what she might say and one marveled that usually, somehow, she managed to avoid saying it. She was, in short, a loose cannon that only rarely fired. Laura always noticed that Edna's makeup was rather thickly applied. Too much mascara. Too much blush. Too much hairspray. Too much everything.

Laura's interest in politics was confined by her innate distrust of politicians. The one redeeming feature of Congresswoman Toller was her devout Christian faith, and on that rock Laura established a delicate support for an otherwise thoroughly unimpressive woman.

"Did you read Edna's piece in the paper yesterday about immigration?" Andrew asked, as they slowly made their way along Rea Road. "She really tells it like it is. She says it's time to lock the borders and clamp down on the Mexicans. Great piece. Just great."

Laura did not bother to reply, as she realized his question was solely rhetorical. On the subject of politics, Andrew only desired a listener, not a response. She was usually content to pretend to the former in gratitude for the latter.

"They say she is going to run for governor," he continued. "And she could win, Laur, she could do it. Course, she's got that deadbeat husband of hers to drag around, but she can manage that. She has so far."

Andrew passed a plodding Honda Civic driven by an Asian man, who gripped the steering wheel with both hands and stared ahead with undisturbed concentration. "Chinese drivers," Andrew muttered.

Laura gazed uneasily at the surging traffic on the two narrow lanes of Rea Road, but she had learned not to interrupt Andrew's tirades behind the wheel. As they drove past row after row of grand homes, which seemed so secure, so protected, she recalled reading in the paper that yet another rape had been reported in the area.

The words 'serial rapist' were beginning to be whispered over the dinner tables of southeast Charlotte. The rapist, or rapists, was so brazen now that the break-ins occurred in broad daylight. It was appalling. When she was a child, such a thing would have been unthinkable. She and all her friends ran to and from each other's homes, rode their bikes freely, and complied with the single parental admonition to be home before dark.

Laura shuddered to think that the weekly crime reports in the *Observer* required an entire page, in very small print, just to catalogue the varied litany of homicides, burglaries and assaults. No one was safe or immune from the pack of sociopaths that seemed to prowl the city. Sometimes she couldn't help but wonder a little, whenever she heard the Ednas—and, to be honest about it, the Andrews—of Charlotte boasting about the polished and efficient splendor of the city.

At what exact moment had this Eden reverted to an encroaching jungle? They saw the glory of growing profit margins, but it was the other margins, of crime and displacement, that worried her. When did growth become so cancerous?

Andrew put his hand on hers. His hands were smooth, almost feminine, but long and tapered. When Laura had first met him, one of the things that she noticed was his hands. And his shoes. Her mother had always said that she knew all she needed to know about a man by the condition of his teeth and his shoes. It was one of the few statements Laura's mother had ever uttered that seemed vaguely credible.

Out of the corner of her eye, Laura could see a blue pickup truck about to make a left turn onto Colony Road. She abruptly withdrew her hand.

"Why can't I hold your hand?" Andrew erupted angrily. "Why can't you show me a little affection?"

"Andrew," she said, exasperated, "I just want us to be safe. That truck was about to turn in front of us. I'm sorry. Please don't be upset with me."

They were silent for the rest of the way, both seething with grievances and frustrations that were as trivial as the touch of a hand, and as painful as a festering wound.

M y friends, thank you so much for your support," Congresswoman Toller said, her eyes moving methodically from left to right, affording an attentive glance to each guest. "I need you more than ever." She paused and smiled warmly, her beaming expression as rigidly in place as her hair, which was teased and sprayed into an immovable blond helmet. Before her, seated at round tables in the dining room and, beyond the opened French doors on the Harrison's terrace, were her most fervent, or at least her most generous, supporters.

"And, of course, I must thank Edward and Missy Harrison for making this wonderful evening possible," Toller continued. "I have known Edward and Missy for over twenty years and, in all that time, they have always been there for me. And for Charlotte." She paused a moment, and gazed sweetly in the direction of her host and hostess. They returned her gaze with studied affection. That she knew they held her in utter contempt did not in the least diminish her regard for them.

The congresswoman's eyes began to moisten, and those closest to her could see the frail beginnings of a single, pending teardrop, hanging perilously from a dark, thick eyelash. To veteran observers of the congresswoman, this meant that the conclusion of her remarks was imminent. "I pray to my God every day to help me serve my country," she said, her voice trembling, as if God might answer her at any moment. "To help me serve you, and to always remind me where I come from. That is where I get my strength. From God. And from all of you." She raised her arms in an awkward benediction and smiled victoriously. "Those folks in Washington could use some of the common sense that is out here tonight. They sure as heck could!"

From the time Edna had gotten elected to the Mecklenburg County School Board and then suddenly vaulted to Congress, she had rarely delivered a speech without paying tribute to common sense. And no wonder. It was not in Congresswoman Toller's interest to highlight more academic strains of intelligence. Edna had attended only one year of college back in the little Georgia town where she grew up. She had gotten pregnant and dropped out. Her later meteoric political rise, which had dismayed anyone with a close acquaintance with her very limited gifts, had brought her into contact with many self-made corporate titans, but also with the privileged graduates of Chapel Hill and Duke and Princeton. They had always intimidated her, and with good reason.

The congresswoman and her husband were escorted to the center table with the Harrisons and other distinguished guests. "That was a wonderful speech," Mayor Riggs said, hugging her effusively as she sat down beside him. She returned his hug with equal fervor.

"Thank you, Danny," she said, smiling slyly, as a still very much alive possum might regard a troublesome mouse. It was generally assumed that Mayor Riggs would run for Congress should the great day ever come that Edna relocated to the governor's mansion in Raleigh. She noticed that Mrs. Riggs, as usual, had declined to accompany her husband. It was well known that Mrs. Riggs' affection for politics, not to mention for her husband, was tenuous, and she much preferred to attend to her elaborate ceramic collection. While the mayor's wife's reputation as a hostess was unimpressive, it was said that she did have the most dazzling figurines in Eastover.

Edna contentedly sipped her single malt scotch and noted the opulence of Missy's table. It was covered in a hand embroidered light blue linen cloth, with an enormous assemblage of purple orchids in the center. The flickering lights of the candles, encased in silver candlesticks, illuminated not only the elegant place settings of crystal, china and silver, but also, the congresswoman wryly noted, the enduring angles of Missy Harrison's cheekbones. Toller, after many years of acquaintance, had an experienced appreciation for Missy. It was the recognition of a kindred spirit. Missy Harrison always seemed to get what she wanted. And so did Edna.

Twenty years ago, the people who mattered in Charlotte would not have said hello to Edna Toller on a sinking ship. To them, she simply did not exist. She was just one more fledgling businesswoman, newly arrived in Charlotte, trying to keep an accounting firm afloat.

She had met Ken at a Chamber of Commerce breakfast. Ken Toller was a project manager for a small construction company. After only several business breakfasts, they were having more private culinary experiences in a bedroom at a seedy Ramada Inn on Independence Boulevard. Ted had readily agreed to divorce his wife and marry Edna.

Whatever her somewhat checkered past, Edna adhered to all the pieties that her supporters did, but it was her imperfections that engendered their more abiding trust. Had Edna enjoyed the slightest sense of irony, and she did not, it would have been a paradox to savor.

As for her more prominent supporters, such as those gathered at the Harrison mansion, she reveled in their grudging need and their secret disdain for her. She was accustomed to the condescension of the Harrisons of the world. Their dislike of her personally made their pandering for favors all the more delicious. When certain roads needed paving, or certain tax measures needed passage, Edward Harrison would call her, dripping faux affection. "Edna, Charlotte needs you on this one. If there is anything you can do..."

It didn't matter if she came from the wrong side of the tracks, so long as she helped the train get there on time.

Her career was a monument to the low expectations of others. And few had lower expectations of her limited gifts than Chancellor Dunn, now beaming at her from across the table. He had once indiscreetly speculated as to how Edna had managed to make so very much of so very little. She smiled at him with special malice, anticipating yet another plea this evening for more money for UNCC's new student activity center.

There were exceptions to this condescension, of course, one of them being Andrew Caldwell—though, decidedly, not his wife. "Congresswoman, so great to see you again," he gushed to her, pausing at the table, as dinner was being served. "We are with you all the way. And, if that way leads to Raleigh, you can count on us."

"Andrew. Laura. You're both just, well, precious," she said, smiling broadly, deepening the crevices along the lines of her crinkled mouth. "Your support means the world to me. Do you know that sometimes, up there in Washington, which is just full of weirdos and perverts...well, sometimes, I think of the great folks back home like the two of you. And I ask myself, what the heck would Andrew do? What would Laura do? And that really does help me get through it all and do my best."

Laura smiled politely and said nothing, as Edna endured a rapturous bear hug from Andrew. "Yes, we know that the Lord is guiding you," Andrew said, patting Edna's shoulder as if in benediction. "Oh, and by the way, I read your article on immigration and I just wanted to tell you..."

Missy, who detested bores in general and reserved a special annoyance for Andrew Caldwell in particular, observed his relentless fawning with growing irritation. Andrew paused briefly and Missy interjected, "Congresswoman, the new Bobcat Arena is just stunning. I hear that the Rolling Stones will be performing at the opening next month."

"Oh, yes, it's going to be fabulous," Edna said energetically, grateful to be rescued from Andrew's monologue. "No one can say Charlotte is not on the march now."

"A lot of that is thanks to you," Andrew gushed, eager to regain her wandering attention. Then, remembering the presence of Mayor Riggs, he quickly added, "And you too, Dan, of course."

Missy looked at Laura and subtly motioned toward the table where the Caldwells were to be seated. Laura tapped Andrew's shoulder and said, "Well, speaking of marching, honey, we need to head on over to our table before the chicken gets cold."

It's just amazing how much is happening in Uptown now, Lynn," Missy commented to her sister-in-law. Edward's sister, unlike their verbose mother, was a receptive listener, although Missy had learned long ago that Lynn's reflective quietness hid depths of biting observation. "Lots of people moving into condos there. Of course, it isn't New York. Well, not yet. But, it is getting there. You should go see the Rolling Stones with us…"

As Missy spoke, Lynn was struck by her brother's own silence at the table and, more tellingly, by his furtive, sidelong glances at Dr. Alice Owens. Alice was seated with her good-looking banker husband at the opposite end of the table and Lynn wondered if the ever vigilant Missy, for whom no proprietary suspicion was too minor, had engineered that distance.

Lynn also noticed that Missy's animated face was, under the brilliantly lit chandelier of the dining room, strangely immobile. Emerald earrings, bordered with small diamonds, gleamed as Missy spoke, but it was her eyes to which Lynn was drawn. There was something manic and piercing, yet surprisingly vacant, about those eyes. No amount of plastic surgery will ever soften those eyes, Lynn thought. Or that unfortunate basso voice.

"I never cared much for the Rolling Stones, but I'm sure they will…enliven…the new arena," Lynn replied evenly, as Missy's gaze bore into her. "My favorite was always Bruce Springsteen. Edward, remember when we saw him back in the 70's at the old coliseum? We slipped down from our seats in the balcony to within about ten feet of the stage. He was so great. One of our major volunteers at Lincoln Center is his cousin. She says he is a really sweet guy, but short."

Overhearing this, Alice asked excitedly, "Have you met him? Oh, I just adore him."

"No," Lynn said, "Only in my dreams." She smiled at Alice Owens with encouraging warmth, noticing Missy's annoyance at the woman's intrusion into their conversation.

Edward laughed, as Missy glowered. "That was a great concert, wasn't it? Course Lynn here was hopeless for Bruce after that," he said. "She was convinced he was looking at her while he sang."

"Lynn, you were a groupie? I'm shocked," Missy said derisively.

"Nothing wrong with that," Alice said, looking past the towering orchid centerpiece at Missy. "When my older sister was at Berkeley, she used to wander Haight Ashbury hoping to catch a glimpse of Grace Slick. She idolized the Jefferson Airplane. Then she married her accountant and they moved to Atlanta."

"Atlanta," Mayor Riggs interjected, toying with the sound of Charlotte's archrival. "Such an…intriguing…place. Do you go there often?" he asked Alice.

"Well, I do if I want to see Dee. She hates coming here. She has become such a snob."

"*Hates* Charlotte? Why?" Congresswoman Toller asked, her brittle eyebrows arched in wonder.

Alice felt the unmistakable kick of Bill's foot under the table. "Honestly, I think my sister is jealous," she replied. "She's always bragging about what a great city Atlanta is, and I think that Charlotte's success worries her, like we are catching up or something."

Everyone, with the notable exception of Edward's sister, who had an uncanny intuition for artifice, erupted in laughter. Alice felt Bill's foot under the table again, although this time the contact was of a far more affectionate nature.

"I don't understand all this one-upmanship," Lynn said, regarding Alice with a knowing, but compassionate smile. "Charlotte competes with Atlanta. Atlanta competes with New York. New York with London or Paris. I guess Paris competes with heaven above? Since I am just a poor girl from Monroe, I have never played that game. What would be the point?"

Missy adjusted her emerald earrings, "Well, I guess all those years in New York have just put you above all this silly competition," she said serenely. "When you get to heaven, you will have to give us a full report."

As Edna and Ken were driving home to their ranch style house in Lansdowne, the congresswoman was checking 'the book' with a pen light, and glowering at a mistake that her staff had made. "God, those idiots," she wailed. "Why can't they do the simplest goddamned thing right?"

"Aw, come on now, honey," he said soothingly, placing his hand on her thigh. "You did great, baby. It was a good evening, don't you think?"

"Yeah. It was okay," she answered, shifting her legs slightly to allow his hand an easier progression. "Course, Laura Caldwell still looks at me like I'm there to do the dishes or something. And didn't you just love that bitchy grin Missy Harrison was sporting all evening? Edward's all right though. I almost feel sorry for him, with that Versace shrew he's married to."

"Versace who?"

"Versace, klutz. You know, that fag designer who got shot by some other fag a few years back."

"Right. I remember now. I like Missy, though. You got to hand it to her. She sure knows how to dress up a room."

"Oh, please. With all her money, she just knows all the right people to do it for her. Or she'll ask Laura Caldwell, who, I will admit, has more class in her little finger than a climber like Missy has in her whole body. I did have some fun though. I mentioned to Missy that Edward's cousin keeps sending me letters, bitching about her son's disability. Evelyn somebody."

"How'd they wind up on the dole?" Ken asked.

"Hell's bells," Edna snorted, "She's pure trash. And Missy knows it. Missy looked at me like I had just farted. 'Evelyn?' she asked, all wide-eyed and Lady Bountiful-like. 'Oh, you mean Evelyn Peck? Yes, poor woman. She was married to Edward's cousin. Poor man died in a construction accident. Of course, we rarely see Evelyn. She keeps to herself.' My tail!"

Ken looked at her and licked his lips. "And such a nice tail."

"And now," the congresswoman continued, ignoring his leer, "I'm stuck with the Harrison brat for the summer. My new intern. And watch the road, for Christ's sake!"

"Sorry, baby," Ken purred, still caressing her thigh with his free hand. "Why don't you get a little cat nap, and maybe we can have some fun when we get home. How 'bout that?"

"Jesus H. Christ, you are such a fucking horn dog," Edna said, yawning. She paused for a moment, and then added, "I have to say one thing for Missy Harrison though. That woman could walk into a pile of shit and somehow come back out with a diamond." Edna then tossed 'the book' into the backseat and fell asleep.

CHAPTER EIGHTEEN
A NIGHT AT THE THEATER

G od, do we have to go?" Edward sighed, as he fiddled impatiently with his cufflinks. "*Red River* is on tonight."

"Yes. We do. And straighten your cummerbund," Missy commanded, as she surveyed the tight fit of his tuxedo. "Lord, have you been counting your carbs?" Her hair was pulled back into a severe bun, exposing her long, imperious neck. Edward noticed, with some regard, her strapless white gown, which plunged perilously down her elevated cleavage, where rested a sapphire pendant, encrusted with diamonds.

They had tickets to the gala for *Chicago* at the Blumenthal Center for the Performing Arts. It was an infrequent, but necessary, appearance for the Harrisons. If they were generous with their financial support for the arts, they were correspondingly stingy with their time. In matters of entertainment, Edward watched John Wayne westerns and Missy studied *Vogue*. Any other artistic endeavors in Charlotte were in the realm of obligation, not enjoyment. Such evenings were the cultural equivalent of religious penance, but with more elegant attire and the saving grace of champagne.

When they arrived Uptown, it was evident that many of their friends had chosen this evening for their own pilgrimages for Art. They were faithful if unenthusiastic supporters of the Blumenthal and were dutifully being shepherded into the glass-tiered lobby.

Chicago had won all those awards from People Who Know and the touring production promised to be a relatively painless theatrical experience. At least it wasn't, God forbid, the opera or a bevy of men in tights.

As Edward and Missy walked inside, the enormous theater was humming with the low, expectant murmur of a sold out house. The Belk theater was the Blumenthal's showplace venue. Designed by Cesar Pelli, its acoustics were so refined that performers on stage could be heard clearly to the back of the theater without microphones. It was a sea of lush green seats luminous under a dome ringed with multi-colored lights.

The Blumenthal was a monument to the financial support, and conventional taste, of Charlotte theatergoers. It at least still had a pulse, unlike the ill-fated Charlotte Repertory theater, which had recently expired, weak and anemic, under the deadly weight of controversial offerings. The Rep was always staging bizarre dramas by edgy writers like Sam Shepard or Neil Labute. While it was perfectly acceptable to bore Charlotte audiences, it was fatal to confuse them.

Edward and Missy were ushered to their seats by a surly old woman who looked to Edward as if she had been at Ford's theater the night Lincoln was shot. She handed them programs, mumbling rotely, "Enjoy the show."

Safely deposited into the thickly cushioned seats, Edward sat back, closed his eyes, and took a deep breath, like a man about to be pulled under and forced to swim through the sluggish currents of *culture*. Missy sat beside him, ramrod straight. As the orchestra began playing, Edward looked up at the changing colors of the fiberoptic lights of the dome, which were twinkling softly as in a fluorescent sky. Missy nudged his shoulder and he resignedly sat up. And, just as the lights were turned down, he noticed that Alice Owens and, to his surprise, Stephen, were seated two rows ahead of them, just slightly to their left.

During the first act, he watched her, though careful to effect a sideways glance that would not be evident to the vigilant eyes of his wife. Unlike most of the audience, which was polite if not entirely comfortable with this entertaining but morally inverted depiction of crimes that pay, Alice was unbridled in her enjoyment. In Charlotte, such fervor was usually confined to a Panthers touchdown. He noticed her constant smiling, how her entire body seemed to quiver with laughter, and, enviously, how she leaned into Stephen and grasped his arm.

Squeezed among a sea of tuxedos and waves of blond hair, Edward and Missy slowly made their way upstairs to the lounge. He felt as if they were being slammed by an army of penguins. Edward glanced over his shoulder for a sight of Alice and Stephen. For an instant, he imagined them ensconced in some quiet corner, alone and undisturbed. *What a waste*, he thought.

Once inside the lounge, Edward irritably motioned to an attendant who was carrying a tray of champagne flutes. Edward greedily selected two sparkling glasses and handed one to Missy. "Well, interesting so far," he said mildly. "That lady warden is pretty funny."

Missy was about to reply when suddenly Alice and Stephen appeared beside them. "Well, hello," Alice said, lightly hugging them. "What a nice surprise. And I believe you know my handsome escort."

"Hey there, pardner," Edward said. "Your mom get back to New York okay?"

"Safe and sound, and happy to be back in her little nest," Stephen answered. "You are looking wonderful tonight, Aunt Missy."

"Oh, Stephen, you're so sweet," Missy replied, lightly adjusting the gleaming pendant nestled between her breasts.

"Isn't he?" Alice said. "Bill had to fly out to California at the last minute, and Stephen agreed to come with me." She paused, kissing Stephen's cheek, then added, "I may just have to run away with him."

"Well, don't run too far," Edward said, "we like having you both right here in Charlotte."

"No worries," Alice replied. Her gaze lingered on Edward, or so it seemed to him. "Anyway, what a great show. We saw it on Broadway last year. That was the best, but this is good too. Are you enjoying it?"

Missy idly sipped her champagne. "Not nearly as much as this clicquot," she said serenely.

"I think it's terrific," Edward said, suddenly conscious of the tight fit of his tuxedo. "It is the best thing this theater has trotted out in a long time."

Missy stared at him quizzically and then said, as if to a naive child, "Edward, honey, this is not the Kentucky Derby. Plays are not trotted. They are *mounted*." Then, pleased with her vaguely sexual reference, she bellowed that awful, roller coaster laugh that had grated on his nerves for longer than he cared to remember. Alice and Stephen smiled politely, but Edward detected just a faint note of pity in their expression.

"So, when is Johnny leaving for Washington?" Stephen asked. "Mom said he is interning with Congresswoman Toller this summer."

"Oh, end of next week," Missy said. "He wanted to stay home this summer, but he has a new convertible to ease his way there, and that seems to be helping."

Edward, still vaguely annoyed with both his son's indolence and his wife's lofty brusqueness, said, "Yeah, true enough. I had a convertible when I was in college, but I got it bagging groceries at Food Lion." Missy winced, as Edward knew she would, at this regrettable reference to his humble origins. Certain he would be reprimanded later, and not caring, he added defiantly, "Course, in those days, teenagers did not see work as a four-letter word."

"I hear you, Uncle Edward," Stephen agreed. "I was mowing lawns by the time I was twelve, just to get a new Schwinn bike."

"Heavens," Alice said, "it sounds positively Dickensian, doesn't it Missy?" Alice did not need to add that her own childhood had been considerably more privileged, or that Missy's had not. Diplomatically changing the subject, she asked, "Are you going to visit John in D.C. this summer?"

"Yes, later this month I am," Missy said, emphasizing the singular, "before our vacation at Pawley's Island. Laura and her son, Ben, are going with me. I've already booked a room at the Hay Adams. Do you know that hotel?"

"Only by reputation," Alice replied, "but I hear it is excellent."

"Yes," Missy said confidently, "it is. Right next to the White House."

The bell began to ring, signaling that intermission was ending. As the four of them began returning to their seats, Alice held back slightly with Edward. For a moment she put her arm on his shoulder and gently touched the back of his neck.

"Enjoy the show, it's a derby winner," she said. He felt the brief, light caress of her fingers on his hair, and then heard her whisper, "and so are you."

CHAPTER NINETEEN
FIRST NAMERS

Congresswoman Toller's seniority, as well as her mystifyingly charmed connection with the House leadership, had garnered her a spacious suite in the ornate Longworth building, with a window that looked out toward the Capitol. The reception area boasted a fireplace with an Italian marble mantel. Adjoining that was a staff room, where four young assistants were at her beck and call, and worked slavishly to meet the most mundane needs of her constituents. Their desks were separated by low-rise partitions, but the room was usually a welter of ringing phones and urgent conversations.

She demanded that every phone call and every letter from a North Carolina resident, even if not in her district, be followed up with a letter from the congresswoman. E-mail, the bane of every office on the Hill, was another matter. It was impossible to maintain correspondence with the endless campaigns of mass e-mails. So, her office sent an automatic *'thank you for your views'* e-mail response. Edna's genius was in knowing when she was licked, and then moving on.

Her office was down a short hallway, away from the staff room. Her legislative director, Owen Paine, waited nervously for Edna in his small, cluttered office next to hers. He was a pale, lean man in his late thirties. Like so many other staffers on the Hill he had started as a staff assistant right out of college. The decade and a half had aged him. He already had a slight stoop, and his hair was prematurely graying. He had been Edna's legislative director for three years, which was an eternity for him and a record for her.

"Owen!" she bellowed.

He practically leapt from his chair and quickly went inside her office. "Good morning, ma'am, how was your trip to Charlotte?" As he stood in the doorway—he never sat down until asked—he had the obsequious air of an eager waiter.

"It went well...mostly," she said, pausing, which was always an ominous sign. "But, Owen, let me say this just one more time. I need two copies of that goddamned appointments book when I go home. Not one, goddamnit. Two! And the memo for the Harrison fundraiser. Who put that together?"

"David, ma'am," Owen sputtered, bracing himself for the eruption to come.

"Get...him...in...here!" she said, each word clipped razor sharp.

Owen walked down the hall. David was on the phone.

"Yes, sir. Yes, I am from North Carolina too. Yes, I will let the congresswoman know that you have proof that abortion is murder. Yes. I sure will, sir, yes, thank you for calling. O.k. Yes, I have noted that. Yes. Goodbye."

"Morning, Dave," Owen said. "Ah...the congresswoman wants to see you for a moment." Owen felt protective of his young staff, and of Dave in particular. Dave Brooks was an exceptionally bright fellow, a recent Phi Beta Kappa graduate from Wake Forest. But, Owen realized that Dave's impressive academic record was not an endearment to the college dropout for whom they worked. As they walked down the hall to Edna's office, Owen felt much like the biblical figure of Isaac on his way to sacrifice his son to a spiteful God.

"Sit down," she said, indicating the two overstuffed chairs in front of her desk. She took a memo from the book and handed it to Dave. "Mr. Brooks, I understand you prepared this. I want you to look at it and tell me what is missing. Can you do that?" she asked condescendingly. She wants the best, Owen thought, and then she pummels them.

The young man nervously reviewed the memo. Finally, he shrugged and said, "Ma'am, I'm sorry, but I can't tell what is missing."

"No? Well, keep looking." She paused, tapping her fingernails, letting the awkward silence fill the room.

"Here. Let me see if I can help with this," Owen said, reaching for the paper. It appeared to be complete, listing all the pertinent information regarding the event: time, location, hosts, attendees, and brief remarks. And then it hit him. "Oh…hmmm….Mrs. Harrison's nickname is Missy. She is listed here as Margaret."

The congresswoman smiled grimly. "Mr. Brooks, who is running for election here? I am. Not you. *Me*. If you cannot understand that one basic, simple fact, then you do not belong on my staff. Mrs. Harrison is a first-namer. You would have known that if you had looked at the first-namer book. I assume you have a copy of that book at your desk?"

"Yes, ma'am. All staff have copies," Owen interjected.

"Then…Jesus H. Christ…use…it!" she screamed, throwing the book against the door. Owen stood up, signaling to Dave that the meeting was over and a prompt exit was now in order.

Don't worry about it," Owen reassured Dave later. "She's wigging out lately with all the talk about her running for governor. And, believe me, she would remember Missy Harrison's nickname if she were delirious and on her deathbed. They have known each other ever since the congresswoman asked Missy twenty years ago if she wanted to make some extra cash working part-time in her accounting firm. Can you believe it?"

"True story?" Dave asked. "Did Mrs. Harrison actually take the job?"

"Oh, God, no. Anyway, you will get to know more of the Harrisons this summer. Their son, John, is going to be an intern here starting next week. I was hoping he could work a little with you."

"Sure. No problem," Dave smiled. "Does he have a nickname?"

CHAPTER TWENTY
GOD AND CHEESECAKE

It seemed to Laura Caldwell, as she and her family waited in a line of cars streaming into the huge parking lot of Central Galilee Church, that they were part of a gathering army, ready to do battle for God. Whatever the disappointments of her life, Laura was always grateful to return to the potent embrace of her church. She believed that Central Galilee's virile expansion was a sign of God's pleasure and the rightness of its mission. And Reverend Dunlap was clear about what that mission was. Their sacred obligation was to bring souls to Jesus and, once there, to repent of the twin devils of secular humanism and sexual license.

Central Galilee was not held in esteem among the more sedate attendees of established churches like Myers Park. "That Reverend Dunlap is an embarrassment," her mother had haughtily admonished her recently, during one of Laura's infrequent visits to Jewel Soames' luxurious condominium at the Crillon.

"Mother, you have your church," Laura replied, "and I have mine. I'm sorry if you don't approve."

"Don't approve?" she asked incredulously, lighting yet another cigarette. "Laura, honestly, you can be so naïve. The man is a hack. A charlatan. Now I hear he owes back taxes."

"That story was distorted by the *Observer* which, as usual, got it all wrong. He apologized for any misunderstanding."

"Really? And has he commented on the rumors that he has slept with half the women in his church? And possibly a few of the men? Although, I must say, having seen that lunatic with a mascara brush he married, it is no wonder he would seek comfort elsewhere."

"Mother! I cannot believe you would repeat such filth. Reverend Dunlap would never betray his wife, who is a very sweet woman. Why, if you could only see them, you would know that they are devoted to each other." Then, unable to stop herself, she added, "But, perhaps that is just something you would not understand."

The Galilee chapel could seat well over a thousand people and, as the Caldwells walked inside, most of those soldiers for Jesus had already claimed their seats. The sunlight filtered through stained glass windows, which arched ninety feet high, almost as high as Calvary's just down the road.

Andrew motioned the family to seats on the far right side in the back. This distance would be alleviated however by a concert worthy sound system. A billboard size video screen projected the image of Reverend Dunlap as the choir massed behind him sang *Blessed Redeemer*. The reverend smiled with the grim satisfaction of a man who has acquired a frightful knowledge and now desires only to impose it.

Laura put her arms around both her children, as if to further solidify their solidarity in the faithful confines of the church. And, if her reach did not quite extend to Andrew, that was a regrettable limitation of which she was powerless to change.

"Hon, put your phone away," she whispered to Ben. He had been checking it for messages throughout the morning. It must be some girl, Laura thought, recalling the obsessive, pitiable desires of youth. It was odd, though. She always assumed that Ben, with his shy, dusky allure, would be more pursued than pursuing. Perhaps, heaven forbid, he was getting back together with Donna Fleishmann. She was tempted to ask him whom he was trying to call, but instinctively declined to do so. One of Laura Caldwell's saving graces was that, in a revelatory world, she understood the sanctity of secrets.

Reverend Dunlap was speaking now. He was a short, compact man with a lean body. Neither his face nor his body betrayed, accurately or not, any hint of worldly softness. His was the disciplined visage of an acolyte for Christ. His curly brown hair was tightly coiled and had a swath of gray straight up the middle. Not for Reverend Dunlap the vain corrections of natural, God-given aging. Although many of his flock, particularly the women, were not so circumspect in this regard, he excused this as perhaps justified in their biblical duty to please their husbands. That some of these women occasionally endeavored to please Reverend Dunlap himself was simply an occupational hazard of a charismatic shepherd.

Jesus, it's hot," John Harrison mumbled, loosening his tie. This was his last weekend at home before going to Washington, and he was far more inclined to immersion in the swimming pool than any more spiritual baptism. He refused to wear a jacket to church, and had already rolled up the sleeves of his blue pinpoint Oxford shirt. Beads of sweat began to slide along the muscled cords of his forearms.

At least once a month, the Harrisons attended Myers Park Presbyterian Church. Both God and public rectitude compelled occasional appearances, allowing a sort of monthly payment on a mortgaged salvation. While the vagaries of faith did not unduly perplex Edward or Missy, and their duty to God was at best a sometime thing, they did retain a minimal sense of devotion. If that devotion had more of the aura of an insurance policy than any more pious aims, it was no less compulsory. As Christian soldiers, Edward and Missy were, at best, weekend warriors, and their children were the rawest of recruits.

The four Harrisons marched resignedly across the muggy front lawn. The gothic tower of the church loomed above them. Andrea Harrison, squeezed into a moistening navy blue dress with a scooped collar, suffered in silence, correctly surmising that her overweight presence, in the eyes of her frowning mother, was irritation enough.

John's cell phone buzzed and he quickly glanced at the number. Ben Caldwell again. Fuck, he thought, why can't he give it a rest?

"Turn that damned thing off," Edward ordered, as the surly quartet walked up the church steps. The sanctuary was almost full and humming with low whispers. The permed, waved, and closely cropped heads tilted confidentially in quiet asides, or reverently in contemplation. A few of the heads glanced around in bored appraisal of the new arrivals. Many of those same critical faces would later that afternoon be hungrily eyeing half-naked bodies poolside at Myers Park Country Club and tossing back martinis as effortlessly as pieties.

"There's Alice and Bill," Missy said, motioning toward one of the pews to their right, near the back. She waved to Alice, who smiled and pointed to the empty seats beside them. The Harrisons filed into the pew, briefly exchanging hushed greetings. Edward, the last to enter, sat down beside Alice. He nudged Missy slightly with his shoulder to move over.

"There's no room," she hissed. Andrea was wedged in to the end of the pew as much as possible, but John insisted on slumping into his seat and splaying out his legs.

Edward leaned over and snarled, "John, sit up straight."

Alice, amused, looked at Edward and whispered, "It's popular here today." She wore a white dress, with a simple gold necklace. As the service began, he could feel her breathing, each exhalation like a feathery embrace. She stared straight ahead, politely attentive to every announcement, every hymn, even every word of the interminable sermon.

The congregation rose to sing *God of Our Fathers*. Alice's lilting soprano seemed to hover above the other voices, perfectly in key but apart, and floating above the muted drum of Missy's atonal hum.

They sat back down, and the ushers began passing the communion trays. First the crusts of bread. In a delirium of sacrilege and fantasy, Edward reveled in the warm, breathy closeness of Alice Owens.

This is my body.

Edward glanced at Alice as she handed him the plate. Her expression was pious, tranquil, but in her eyes, for just an instant, he could see an unmistakable invitation. Then the glasses of grape juice.

This is my blood.

The limpid purple glasses sparkled in the light. As Alice passed the communion tray to him, their hands touched and, in mutual assent, lingered in an exquisite, almost imperceptible, caress.

The Caldwells slowly exited Galilee Church, part of the orderly herd spilling out from the churches that lined Highway 51. This mass exodus required multiple police officers, rather like cowboys determined to prevent an unlikely stampede.

Having nourished their souls, the Caldwells typically had lunch at the Cheesecake Factory at SouthPark Mall to nourish their bodies. Andrew loved the desserts there, which were an indulgent counterbalance to the spartan exhortations of Reverend Dunlap.

"Debra, what are you thinking about? You are awfully quiet back there," Laura said as the policeman waved them by.

Debra smiled benignly. "Oh, nothing. I'm just thinking about Reverend Dunlap. I love his new haircut."

"Well, I suggest you think more about his message and less about his hairstyle," Laura replied, alarmed by her daughter's irreverence. In truth, though, she herself had found the reverend to be especially attractive today. That rock-jawed, tightly cropped head, those constraining curls, that hard, devout body under the tailored suit...Laura abruptly halted any further considerations of Reverend Dunlap, God's warrior, and shifted her gaze to her silent husband. Andrew concentrated on driving, maneuvering past the hordes of worshippers now pouring out of the churches along Sardis Road.

The Cheesecake Factory was crowded with the after-church throng, all waiting patiently for enormous platters of food. Just as surely as Nieman Marcus had supplanted Belk as the favored department store of new age Charlotteans, so had the Cheesecake Factory replaced the K and W cafeterias of an older generation.

The Caldwells were escorted to a red booth bordered by a towering brown-veined column. Within seconds an attractive young woman approached them. "Hi, I'm Carla," she said. "What will you all be having today?" She looked at Ben, who was yet again checking his cell phone for messages. "Hey there, Ben. You probably don't remember me."

Ben quickly dropped the phone on the seat beside him and looked at her blankly. "Carla? Carla Martin? Sure, I remember you, we went to Bible camp together last summer. Right?"

"Uh huh," she said, resting one hand on her hip. "How *are* you?"

"Okay. Doing okay," he said unenthusiastically. "Good to see you, Carla." He nervously fidgeted with his water glass, slowly turning it in a circle.

"Well, you too. Gosh, you look great." She paused for a moment and then, flustered by Ben's awkward silence, reverted to her professional role. "Ahm...so can I take your order?"

After the waitress had left, Deb laughed, "Good grief. Was she undressing you with her eyes or what?"

"That is no way to talk," Laura said, admonishing her daughter.

"Yeah, come on Deb, stop it," Ben said, blushing.

"So, why don't you ask her out?" Deb persisted.

"Why don't you mind your own business?" he said, knocking the glass over, its water splashing his cell phone.

"Don't you like her?" she continued, almost prosecutorial in her questioning. "She's practically throwing herself at your feet."

"All right, Deb, that's enough," Andrew Caldwell intervened. "You've had your fun."

Ben said nothing, and a silence as palpable as any accusatory question lingered in the air, each of the family unwilling, or unable, to see it clearly, but conscious of it all the same.

CHAPTER TWENTY-ONE
THIS CROSS OF GOLD

S tephen sat in the overstuffed leather chair opposite the mahogany desk of Dr. Robert, *never* Bob, Williams, and studied the Revolutionary War-era prints on the wall. It was an incongruous office, an unadorned box decorated in classic style. Leather chairs, mahogany furniture, Oriental rug, marble vase, brass-sculpted bookends. All that was missing was a tapestry to mute the unfortunate yellow cinderblock walls. It was as if an Oxford don had stumbled into the cement enclosure of Garinger Hall and brought his furnishings with him.

Dr. Williams, while perhaps not quite Oxford material, was a competent chairman of the UNCC history department. He had graying, neatly combed hair and a gently officious manner. Stephen sometimes wondered how such a docile creature had ascended through the university's shark-infested waters, but remembered that the most agile climbers were of a decidedly more subtle lethality.

Unseen fangs tend to be the sharpest.

Stephen was reminded of the nickname of some long-forgotten television executive—the 'smiling cobra'—as Dr. Williams benignly shuffled through some papers on his desk and rearranged the bronze bust of William Jennings Bryan. Dr. Williams was a recognized authority on that perennial also-ran of American politics. His essay on Bryan's *Cross of Gold* speech was said to be a model of concise scholarship.

"Well, Stephen, let's get this off the table as quickly as we can, shall we?" Dr. Williams said with generous solicitude. "First of all, I want you to know how deeply sorry we all are about the incident last week, the...ahm...the defacing of your door. That sort of thing is not tolerated here, and you can count on the department's support."

"Thank you. I appreciate that, sir, but I realize that these things happen sometimes."

"Yes, *sometimes*," Dr. Williams concurred vacantly. "But, I also need to inform you that several students in your democracy class have lodged a complaint. They accuse you of making racist statements."

"What do they regard as racist statements?" Stephen asked.

"They allege that you referred to blacks as criminals. They say that you accused them of being inferior as a result of single parent families." Dr. Williams paused, studied Stephen's blank reaction, and wearily continued. "I know. It's ridiculous, of course. I wish I had a gold nugget for every time I have had some oversensitive brat come in here and waste my time with these tales. But, in accordance with university policy, I am giving you a written statement of the complaint." He handed the two-page statement to Stephen.

"And how should I respond to this?" Stephen asked.

"I'll need a written response, your comments, by Friday. That will be the end of the matter. And, Stephen, don't worry. You're doing a fine job. We are lucky to have you in this department." Dr. Williams stood, smiled reassuringly, and ushered Stephen to the door.

CHAPTER TWENTY-TWO
THANK YOU FOR YOUR VIEWS

John Harrison was bored. After a couple of weeks in Congresswoman Toller's office, he had grown weary of the mundane errands that were the lot of interns. On his first day, it had all seemed so impressive. The Longworth office building, just across the street from the Capitol itself, had ancient marble corridors, where one felt the footprint of history in every step. And the congresswoman had been so friendly when he first arrived.

"John, it is so good to see you!" she had enthused. "Did you have a good trip?"

"Yes. Thank you, ma'am. It is just great to be here. Thank you for giving me this opportunity."

"Good. That's fine, then. Now, Owen will get you settled here in the office. I have a committee meeting in five minutes, but we will talk more later. So glad you are here with us, John."

"Thank you ma'am. I won't let you down," he said, a little too emphatically.

"Yes, well, thank you then," she replied, ushering him and Owen out of her office. And, somehow, the week had gone by, and they had not had that time to talk further. Since then, he caught fleeting glimpses of her coming and going from the office, and noticed that her interaction with her staff was kept to a minimum. And his primary source of entertainment had become watching the deer in the headlights reactions of the staff whenever they sniffed that Tough Toller was approaching.

Other, more intimate, recreation was also being provided by a legislative aide named Tricia Mitchell. Her long, auburn hair and lean, toned body had immediately attracted John. She was a fanatic about Pilates, and exercised almost every day. After John had been interning for about a week, she approached him and asked, "Do you run?"

They began running together after work. He noticed her clandestine glances at his muscular thighs, and made a point to stretch in ways that would allow his baggy white shorts to ride up his browning legs as far as possible. He was lying on his back, with one leg pulled up and across his chest, when she said, "I live just a few blocks from here."

Since that afternoon, she had been a little too clingy for his taste. But, in the privacy of her Ikea-decor apartment and, once, in the copying room at the office, she was very accommodating in other more immediate regards, though not to the full extent that he desired. While John's eyes continued to wander freely, he had generally managed to confine his hands to her eager embrace.

She was, at twenty-six years old, a veritable, and highly alluring, older woman to John. That she had agreed to go out with him, however, did not surprise him in the least. He had quickly come to the pleasant realization that his golden luster was not confined to the modest environs of his hometown. Not only was he just as appetizing in Washington, D.C., but there were many more people at the table and they seemed noticeably hungrier. Of all he would learn during his summer in the Capitol, and, in truth, he learned very little, this was perhaps his most valued insight.

Meanwhile, his day was filled with interminable printing at the copying machine, helping to answer whiny phone calls from low rent losers back home, and typing out the call sheets to list their concerns. The one black staff assistant, Dave, had given John some form letters to write. Very boiler-plate language...*Appreciate your taking the time to apprise me of your views...will carefully consider...assuring you of my desire to be of service.*

After work, John often contented himself with ferocious drives down Constitution Avenue, speeding past the gaggles of clueless tourists, past the White House and the Washington monument, and then across the Roosevelt Bridge and onto the winding curves of the George Washington Parkway. The top down, his blond hair blowing in the wind, the trees and the river a greenish blur, he felt an exhilarating power.

As the days went by, he decided that there must be some sort of I.Q. criteria that determined who called congressional offices and, for his own amusement, privately began assigning scores to each caller, especially the repetitive callers, the ones the staff ridiculed as 'frequent flyers'.

"I need to speak to the congresswoman," one caller said. "My name is James Fallow. She'll know who I am. I got a problem with my veterans pension. I need help!" Mr. Fallow called at least once a week and was one of the office's well-known 'frequent flyers.' Last week he had called to demand that the VA pay for Viagra. "I really *need* it!" he had shrieked.

"Sir, the congresswoman is in a meeting," John said.

"She's always in a meeting!" Mr. Fallow screamed into the phone. "I need help now. They gonna take my disability away."

"Sir, I understand," John assured him. "If you could give me your phone number, I will make sure the congresswoman gets your message, and someone will call you back."

"Is *she* gonna call me back? She's up there cause I put her there!"

"Sir, let me have your phone number. I have other people waiting on this line."

"Fuck those other people, ass wipe. You talking to *me*! James Fallow!"

"Sir, I am hanging up now." John had been advised by the legislative director, Owen Paine, that it was excusable to terminate a call if the constituent used foul language. Mere verbal abuse was not sufficient cause, but obscenity most definitely was.

"Prick," John muttered. Definitely a sub-100.

In addition to showing John the unexpected thrills to be found in the copying room, Tricia had also taken him under her wing professionally, arranging for him to work with her on several legislative projects and coaching him in navigating the minefield that was Edna Toller. That John was a Harrison insulated him to a degree from the congresswoman's tantrums, but there were occasions when he could feel the lacerating impact of stray shrapnel.

"Kitty has her claws out today," John heard Tricia say. *Bad Kitty* was the code name for Toller that the staffers had come to dread hearing. "Better batten down the hatches."

"How 'bout we go make some...copies...instead," he suggested.

"No, seriously. Dave called me on his cell phone," Tricia whispered to John. "He picked Kitty Cat up this morning to take her to the airport and she started screaming at him about the letters. God, she is a maniac about those stupid letters."

"What's the problem?" John asked.

"Well, apparently, she came into the office over the weekend, and there was a stack of mail over a month old, just sitting in a basket out front. We usually hide it in the desk drawer, but, anyway, somebody forgot to do it Friday evening. Just wait, she'll send the pit bull in." The 'pit bull' was Faye Hart, Congresswoman Toller's greatly feared and minimally respected chief of staff.

A door down the hall opened and slammed shut. "Oh, Jesus, she's here," Tricia moaned.

About ten minutes later, Owen Paine called the staff together. "Faye wants everyone at the conference table. Now!"

John had on more than one occasion marveled at how a woman such as Faye Hart, with weary folds of milky white flesh spilling out in every possible direction, with a burdened and bowlegged walk beneath that bulbous carriage of a body, could exude such sharp and daggerlike venom. And, yet, exude she did. He noticed early on that the entire staff always stepped carefully around this tightly fanged lump, who seemed ever ready to strike at anyone who crossed her path.

Inevitably, the forbidding and reptilian chief of staff softened her tone on the few occasions when she slithered toward him. While she appeared to be deficient in any genuine affection for anyone, John included, Faye was obsequious in the extreme to the congresswoman and to V.I.P.s, the hallowed First Namers. John was the beneficiary of such deference, while the rest of the staff were not so fortunate. Whatever sugary deposits of pleasantries Faye grudgingly afforded to the congresswoman or to people like the Harrisons, she always replenished her emotional coffers with venomous attacks on the staff. Indeed, it was an axiom in the office that any meeting that Faye had with Congresswoman Toller would be followed by the ritual skewering of some helpless underling. She was a sort of vampire, dependent on drawing fresh blood from powerless staffers.

In truth, even the congresswoman was somewhat intimidated by the foaming and curdled manner of her chief of staff. There was something so faintly sinister about Faye Hart that even Tough Toller felt obliged to carefully take her measure and to keep Faye tightly leashed and generally out of view. But, Faye Hart, who had begun working for the congresswoman as a receptionist, was, like her employer, an uneducated and brutal force. Having worked her way up, step by step, Faye had collected a number of secrets along the way, secrets that ensured her continued employment with Edna Toller.

And so, as they had on so many occasions in the past, the aides gathered anxiously at the conference table, waiting for the latest explosion from the chief of staff. They were not disappointed. They could see, and hear, her rumbling approach, her close-cropped gray hair hovering over pale flesh and dark eyes, like a thunderclap on an overcast day. Faye stopped at the table, not bothering to take a seat, frowning and grimly bemused, as if the staff were an assortment of unappetizing bon bons that she would, nonetheless, enjoy munching on.

"People," she said, with her exaggerated, brittle enunciation, "we have a problem." In contrast to her bulgy and pliant body, stuffed today into a dark blue sack-like dress, she was stiff and formal, with a resentful smile that was as devious as it was unnatural.

She paused for an agitated moment, and then gathered up a stack of mail about a foot high, squishing the flesh of her exposed arms, and dramatically threw all the letters down on the table. A number of the letters slid off the table, landing softly at the feet of the hapless staffers.

"This mail is over a month old! Fix it!" She then looked stonily around the room at each staffer, as if each and every one was guilty of the most heinous crimes. "Fix it!" she screamed, "And if you can't do it, I will find someone who can."

The staffers returned quietly to their desks, as Faye stormed back into her office. John nudged Tricia, who seemed slightly shell shocked from Faye's latest outburst, and laughed, "God, she's hot."

CHAPTER TWENTY-THREE
UPTOWN

Edward Harrison carefully reviewed the plans for the renewed development of Kannapolis. A new and stunning town would literally rise from the ashes of the dying mill community. It would be a legacy that any developer would treasure. And yet, on this quiet Saturday afternoon, as he looked out his window and saw the thin trail of a jet streaking across the sky, his mind was elsewhere.

Since his encounter with Alice Owens at church, he could not stop thinking of the feathery touch of her fingers briefly wrapped around his own. With Missy in Washington visiting John, every indecisive moment seemed a squandered opportunity to finally see Alice alone.

For a man who had recently begun taking Viagra just to fulfill his infrequent couplings with his wife, this tidal surge of longing was unexpected and overwhelming. And if Alice, always so cool, so composed, was not similarly drenched, this only excited him more.

He remembered that Alice had mentioned to him that she and Bill had actually considered purchasing a condo when they moved to Charlotte. In the end, they had decided that the oak canopy of Myers Park was more enticing than the clouds of Uptown. He knew that Bill Owens was often in New York or San Francisco for the bank and, on a chance, as nervous as a schoolboy, Edward dialed Alice's cell phone.

"Edward, what a nice surprise," she said in a soft, unhurried tone that suggested she was not in the least surprised. "How are you?" She paused and then asked, "Did you need to speak with Bill? He's in New York till this evening."

"Oh, no problem, it can wait." *But, I can't, not anymore…* he thought to himself. "Actually, I'm just sitting here in my office in Uptown. Didn't you all look at living down here? How would you like to take a look at what you missed?"

"I really can't imagine, at this point, what that could possibly be," she replied serenely, "but do go on."

She agreed to meet him at the Wellington Tower nearby, one of the signature developments of Harrison Associates currently under construction, at one o'clock. "My girls are at a play date until four. Do I need to bring anything?"

"No. Don't worry, I'll lend you my hard hat," he said.

A lice moved to a chaise lounge and slowly stretched out on the dark green cushion. She looked up at the white boulders of clouds slowly drifting over a canvas of powder blue. She had known that Edward Harrison would call. The only question in her mind was *when*. Having observed his frosty exchanges with the imperious Missy, it was her considered judgment that his call would come sooner than later.

Given the twists and turns of her own marriage, Alice was invariably prone to speculate about the marriages of others. She smiled when she thought of her husband. Bill. Charming Billy. That was what she had always called him. Alice loved her husband, and she was confident of his love for her. After seventeen years of marriage, she had no reason to doubt their bond. But, her view of marriage was more elastic, more European than American, and in ways that her Charlotte friends would not condone.

Alice contemplated an affair with Edward Harrison as one might wander into a peripheral, only occasionally used room. A lovely space to be sure, with silk cushions and thickly carved moldings, aromatic of roses, but not central in a very well-appointed home. A home that she still comfortably shared with her husband.

She and Bill had been married for nine years when he slept with her friend Sara. She found out when Sara, triumphant with guilt, had confessed to her one day at lunch.

"It's *my* fault, Alice, not his," Sara had sobbed, as the waiter hovered nearby, like a Greek chorus, waiting to take their order. "I pursued him. Relentlessly. I wouldn't leave him alone. I'm so ashamed. It was like I was possessed or something. I don't expect you to forgive me, but I just had to tell you."

As much as Alice was devastated by her husband's betrayal, she hated even more that it came in the form of a woman like Sara Brooks. Sara, who sat across the table from her with a look of pious anguish, was consumed not by lust or regret, but by melodrama, an insatiable craving for center stage. Alice refused to become a hysterical supporting player in Sara's latest careless spectacle.

"Sara, please," Alice said dismissively, "this isn't necessary." She motioned for the intimidated waiter and calmly ordered a salade nicoise.

Sara, known for her epic appetite on all fronts, ordered the quail and a bottle of chardonnay. "You mean you don't *care*?" she asked, shock having magically curtailed her tears.

"Well, I care, of course I do," Alice said. "But more in an abstract sense. Bill and I have an understanding. Each of us is free to see other people, so long as we're discreet. I know he pretends otherwise. He seems to think that the back alley drama excites some women more than the it's-okay-with-my-wife approach." She looked at Sara knowingly and added, "And I suppose it does."

"Well, do you want me to stop seeing him?" Sara asked, desperately trying to shift the focus back to herself.

"That's entirely up to you. And Bill." Alice smiled, enjoying this sabotage of Sara's latest histrionics. "I just don't want to know about it. I mean, I know the movie is playing somewhere, but I don't want to see it."

"Really? You are an amazing woman," Sara sighed, dramatically reaching across the table and taking Alice's hand in hers. "I don't deserve such a friend, such understanding. No, I don't. I..."

Alice withdrew her hand. "Don't worry about it. It is not, if I may put it this way, my affair."

That evening, with tears now of her own, Alice confronted Bill. And as they discussed the tattered state of their marriage, she realized that what had begun as a petulant response to Sara's narcissism was an accurate reflection of Alice's feelings.

Alice had noticed the increasing bitterness of some of their friends, couples who struggled to remain technically faithful but had long since abandoned each other emotionally. Couples who were bored and frustrated, at best, and who loathed each other, at worst.

Perhaps, in the end, it was just a matter of odds. "Men," her mother had once crudely told her, "just want a place to stick it." Alice had come to accept that fidelity, while an admirable ideal, was not a realistic one. In her opinion, virtue was not heightened by the deceptive skirmishes of marriage. She was resigned more to the tenderness of discretion, a human attribute which was, while less rewarding, far more reliable. And, free from wrestling with sexual morality, she had learned to exercise other varieties of virtue. This tenderness for the frailties of others extended not just to humanity at large, but, refreshingly, to her husband as well.

There was, she had to admit, a delicacy to such latitude, and she was prone to a gnawing fear that some day either she or Bill might venture too far away. But, in the meantime, she did not expect perfection in her husband, in the fervent hope that he should certainly not expect it in her.

She and Bill never spoke of it again.

Edward left his office and went downstairs. He nervously glanced about the empty lobby, but assured himself that most of his associates would not be Uptown on a Saturday afternoon. While they were extolling Charlotte's downtown as the new epicenter of Queen City trendiness, they had so far resisted its charms beyond an occasional steak at Morton's. No, they would be among their barbeque pits in Seven Eagles, or their dogwood-shaded terraces in Myers Park, or perhaps golfing at Quail Hollow or mixing martinis in the privacy of their oak-paneled dens. Except for a few token pioneers, his acquaintances would not be in the hip new towers of Uptown. Of that he was certain. They were, arguably, visionaries, and Uptown might indeed be the new Promised Land, but they did not wish to reside there themselves.

One reason for this enduring reticence was apparent when he stopped for the light at the corner of Trade and Tryon. This was the very heart of Uptown, with the Bank of America tower on the corner, a thriving, pulsing artery of commerce and progress, all polished granite and glass, humming with the sound of money and deal-making. On *weekdays.*

Trade and Tryon was where throngs of black-suited bankers and lawyers scurried about in search of points and profits and new angles. It was where the old historic bank building next door that had somehow survived the wrecking ball looked almost quaint in its ornate smallness. And yet, on that corner, on any given Saturday afternoon or weekday evening, while the Bank of America tower was as silent and eerie as an Egyptian tomb, one could see a congregation of homeless people. Most of them were black, many of them seemingly deranged, slouching at the small tables and chairs, clutching bottles of cheap wine in brown sacks.

Homeless. Edward derided the very term. They were *bums,* he thought, wading in a sea of booze and drugs. Others were just plain crazy. And, along with the menacing teenage gangs that prowled Uptown, they were the one forbidding roadblock in Charlotte's march. Still, the towers did rise, the tourists did venture to Discovery Place, the young and hip, and even celebrated, did crowd into Ra Ri and Aquavina and Capital Grille. But, the shabby, drunken, disturbed, possibly dangerous 'homeless', squatting at Trade and Tryon, staggering along its sidewalks, and passing out on its benches, remained. And millions of dollars in public relations campaigns could not entirely remove this ominous stench of crime and disorder.

And yet, by nightfall the tide would turn and the restaurants and bars would be teeming with youth and vitality. It was as if a slumbering giant, which used to be asleep by 5 p.m. when the bankers returned to their suburban homes, had decided to remain awake well into the night. So it isn't New York, he mused, but at least they don't have to put up a temporary nightlife now like they did when Charlotte had hosted the NCAA basketball tournament barely a decade earlier.

Charlotte had come a long way since that embarrassing experience. In those days, Uptown was so deserted after 5 o'clock, its nightlife was so paltry, that a temporary one had to be erected, like a movie set to be dismantled after the shoot. That had been perhaps the pivotal humiliating moment for the city. Charlotte was never so energized as when the rest of the country was laughing at it or, worse, ignoring it.

Edward walked one block over and stood inside the half-finished lobby of the Wellington Tower. Its thirty floors of luxury condominiums was the crown jewel of Harrison Associates. Wellington Tower was so exclusive that most of the condos had sold before the first brick was laid. Of course, as Edward well knew, many of these eager deposits were placed by institutional investors, buyers with deep pockets and even deeper caution should the market soften.

A crew of drywall workers, all Hispanic, was busily engaged in plastering the walls. When Edward first entered, they were talking and laughing animatedly while they worked, but, sensing that he was a man of importance, a man who had power over their livelihood, they became silent. A couple of the men shyly acknowledged him as he stood there by the front door. "Hello, sir," the supervisor of the crew said.

"Hello," Edward replied stiffly, discouraging any further interaction. After only a few minutes had passed, he saw Alice turn the corner and cross the street. She was wearing blue jeans, a pale blue tee-shirt, and brown work boots, and she was carrying a large tote bag.

"Well, you certainly come prepared, don't you?" he said, giving her a chaste, respectable, just-a-client if anyone was looking, hug.

"That's right," she whispered, "I was a Girl Scout before I drifted." He opened the door for her, and glanced at the contents of the bag. It contained sandwiches, brownies, assorted fruits and nuts, a bottle of red wine and, tantalizingly, a small red and black blanket. "I thought you could use some lunch," she said. "I love picnics, don't you?"

For a moment, he was speechless, and tried not to stare at the inviting, and infinitely compromising, blanket. "Yes, well, sure. Great. I'm starving," he managed to say.

"Yes, I can see that you are," she said. She looked up at the soaring lobby. "So, when will people be calling this place home?"

"Early next year, with any luck. Let's go inside and take a look." He handed her a hard hat, and ushered her toward one of the elevators. "I love buildings when they are like this. Taking shape, but not finished. Roughed in."

"Just like life," she said, laughing.

The Wellington, a partially constructed shell of steel and concrete and glass, had a faint, but pervasive taste of dust. Edward put his arm around Alice as they continued walking around the thirtieth floor.

"It's beautiful, Edward, just beautiful," Alice said. "Like heaven up here." And yet it was difficult to envision the glittery sheen of granite and brass and crystal that would soon adorn these barren spaces. It occurred to her, as Edward proudly showed her the magnificent vistas from each corner, that the Wellington was not so much a place to live as a *way* to live, an *idea* of living.

Among all this mortar and steel and pipes and wiring there was something much less tangible but far more telling. The future. The Wellington was the future, the place to start over, to move up, to move on. It was like Charlotte. Pushing. Overreaching. So hungry for a loftier place in the order of things.

Uptown with no corresponding downtown.

There was only Uptown, emblem of Charlotte's ascendance, and it insisted on its singular primacy. It insisted on being enough, but trembled that it would not be. And so, Alice realized, did the man who was now kissing her with such desperate exploration.

Alice embraced Edward Harrison on the dusty, isolated pinnacle of the Wellington building. She felt his strong, grasping hands roaming urgently along every rise and fall and curve of her body. He dropped to his knees, his arms around her waist, burying his face into her. She gazed out past the humming city below to the tree-lined horizon, suddenly aware of the massive greenery that, from this lonely height, could still effect such a stunning, determined beauty.

She looked down at Edward and smiled and lightly touched his silvery head. Puffs of white clouds drifted by outside the window. Her pliant body, arching to the welcoming touch of his gasping kisses, seemed to almost be floating as well, held aloft by a sort of swelling, bonding heat. She struggled to the floor and pulled Edward down to her, where they lay together on the red and white blanket, their frantic moans echoing in the cavernous space.

Later, Edward looked into the pale blue eyes of Alice Owens, and for a moment he thought he might be dreaming. He started to say something, but then simply rested his hand on her cheek.

"I still cannot get over this view," she sighed. She lay beside Edward on the blanket she had brought for their picnic. Edward, more self-conscious about the betrayals of his middle-aged body, had put his shorts and tee shirt back on and lay on his side, still drinking in the sight of her. From the Wellington's lofty, quiet perch, they could see beyond Uptown, past the Bank of America Plaza, and to the pine-tree laden horizon. "It is the most spectacular sight I have seen since I left San Francisco," Alice said.

"Really?" Edward asked, rolling over onto his back, "I was afraid you might find it a bit of a letdown. It's a nice surprise that you don't."

"Good," she said, lightly kissing his cheek. "My old Aunt Betty used to say 'Better to surprise than to bore.' She lived in an old, decaying house in Lake Forest. Had hardly a cent left by the time she died, but what a character. She used to invite all of her wealthier friends over for afternoon bridge, and served them beer and crackers. They loved it."

"That sounds like something my mother would do," he said. "Is your aunt still in Lake Forest?"

"No, I'm afraid not. She was diabetic and went blind near the end. But, she kept her wits about her. I remember visiting her after she had gone blind. She said to me 'Don't worry. I have seen enough!' She would have appreciated all this."

"Do you think so?" he asked.

"Yes, I know she would. You can really *see* Charlotte."

He kissed her cheek, wanting to say something memorable, but settling instead for the truth. "You always manage to surprise me, Alice. Why is that?"

"Because, you *want* to be. Everyone does. Badly. Once we have it all figured out, then what?" She kissed his shoulder and reached for the remnants of a cinnamon muffin. "Which is why, I might add, your virtue is still relatively intact."

"What about your virtue?" he asked, lightly touching the upper curve of her breast.

"That's another mystery," she said, kissing him, and deftly taking his hand.

"Like your new hometown?" Edward asked.

She sat up, straddling him, and looked out the window. "Yes. But, up here I finally realize something. Charlotte isn't just banks and churches and highways. Look at it," she said, pointing toward the horizon, "all that land, miles and miles of forest. Charlotte rises up in the middle of nowhere, and I wonder how it ever came into being in this exact spot."

"I'm not sure what you mean," Edward said, delirious in the intoxicating weight of her.

"Why *here*? Why not somewhere else?" she asked. "The wonder of Charlotte is that it exists at all. That is its mystery. And no one seems to get that. All those desperate chamber of commerce tag lines to make it distinctive. And here it is in the middle of the woods. Its very existence is a kind of surprise. Isn't that wonder enough?"

"Yes, I guess it is," he said, wrapping her in his arms, feeling the length of her soft and welcoming body against his own. He gently brushed a lock of hair that had fallen across her eye. "I wish we could stay here, just like this. That would be enough for me."

CHAPTER TWENTY-FOUR
MOONGLOW

Missy roared up Interstate 95, singing along with Kitty Wells. She, discreetly, loved the music of the older country singers—Hank Williams, Patsy Cline, even the ancient Carter family—despite the stereotypical image of their fans as hicks crowded around a jukebox. Laura shared her affection, if not her insecurity, regarding those singers. Ben, in the backseat, listened to music on his iPod.

Laura glanced at the odometer. 90 mph. Protest, she realized, would have been pointless, so she said a silent prayer. *Dear Lord, keep us safe.* Even on a Saturday morning, the interstate was crowded with traffic. Huge, belching trucks lumbered past, sometimes two or three at a time. They seemed to Laura like dinosaurs on wheels.

"You're awfully quiet there," Missy said to Laura, turning down the music, as she deftly sped alongside an enormous oil truck.

"Oh, I was just thinking about the article in the paper yesterday about highway 601. Did you read it?"

"Briefly," she replied dismissively, "not much new in it."

"I wouldn't say that. You know they're calling it the Highway of Death now? So many folks get killed out there every year."

"Really?" Missy replied, unconcerned. "Well, they'll be widening it."

"Yes, but that was supposed to happen two years ago. The state says they don't have the money. I'll tell you one thing, if anyone I loved died on that highway, I would sue the state of North Carolina."

"How about if it were someone you didn't love?" Missy asked, as she raced ahead within inches of a sluggish pick-up truck. "Slow drivers in the fast lane. Yeech! Move over, cowpoke."

Laura shuddered and said another silent prayer. "Walmart should have never built that distribution center out there. All those trucks on blind curves on a little two-lane road."

"I suppose not," Missy said, slightly annoyed with Laura's chronic anxieties, "but Laura, I declare if the world ended tomorrow, your first words would be *I told you so.*" Whatever the benefits of Laura's fervent trust in God as to the perfection of the next world, it did not seem to provide any assurances in this one.

"Yes, well..." Laura said, wearily gazing out the window now.

"It is a lousy road," Missy conceded. "But, you worry too much. Relax. What can you do? I just take 74 when we go to Pawleys."

Laura stared out the window at the convoy of trucks. She loathed the directive to 'relax', particularly when uttered by someone as tightly wound as Missy herself. Laura recalled the quiet little lane that traversed Pawleys Island. Her family had a home there when her father was still alive. It was a small cottage on the beach, white clapboard with green shutters, and had survived several hurricanes in Laura's lifetime alone. She remembered a porch swing, facing the ocean, and on sunny days she and her father would sit there for hours, gazing out to sea. The house had to be sold after her father died, and it was later torn down by the new owners. In its place was a sprawling stucco villa, much like Missy's own, though not quite as large.

In the back seat, his iPod securely in place, Ben tapped his hand lazily to the music. He had been so excited about the trip to see John Harrison, but with each approaching mile, he seemed more and more withdrawn, drifting into some private world of his own. Kids, Laura thought, we'll never figure them out.

The Hay-Adams Hotel, located just across Lafayette Park from the White House, was a model of understated elegance. The small lobby and front desk, a simple alcove of oak and brass, was a world away from the cavernous spaces of the Marriott and Hyatt convention hotels. Missy, always determined to avoid the common herd, had selected the hotel. Had she known, and indeed she did not, that the hotel's antecedents were a Secretary of State and a great-grandson of President John Adams, its allure would only have increased.

Missy had specifically requested a room with a view of the White House and was not disappointed. The room had two double beds, with lush Laura Ashley fabrics, and a fireplace with an ornamental marble mantel.

"Oh, look," Laura gushed, pointing to the window, "there's the White House."

Their bellboy, a pleasant young Asian man, placed their luggage beside the beds. "Thank you for staying at the Hay Adams," he said. "Where are you from?"

"Charlotte," Missy said, somewhat grandly.

"Charlotte? Yes. Very good place. They have a great university."

"Oh, why yes, it is. I serve on its board of trustees."

"I was there once," he added, "and also toured Thomas Jefferson's beautiful home."

"No," Missy icily replied, "you are thinking of Charlottesville. The University of Virginia. Charlotte is in North Carolina."

"Oh, pardon me...I thought that...well, I am sure that Charlotte..." he sputtered.

"Thank you," Missy said, handing him a $20 bill.

After he had left, Laura asked, "$20? Isn't that a bit much?"

"No," Missy said, "The next time he hears of Charlotte, he'll know where it is."

As his mother and Missy began to unpack, Ben sat down at a small table by the window and looked across Lafayette Park toward the White House. A throng of war protesters had gathered in front of the statue of Andrew Jackson. They carried a banner that said *U.S. Out of Iraq Now* and screamed in unison, "No more war...no more war...no more war..."

Suddenly, a cell phone began ringing. "Oh, it's mine," Missy said, glancing at the number on the screen. "It's Johnny." She took a seat in one of the chairs, covered in yellow chintz, that faced the fireplace. "Hi," Ben heard her say, "Yes, we are here at the hotel. Beautiful place. Oh, really? Well, are you sure you can't get out of it? No, don't worry about it. We can fend for ourselves." Then, Ben's heart sank as she concluded, "Yes, that's fine. You go ahead. We will see you tomorrow."

"Is there a problem?" Laura asked.

"No, not at all," Missy replied, somewhat defensively, "It's just that Johnny has to go to a get together tonight that his coworkers are having. It's a last minute thing, and he felt obligated to go."

"Well, sure, of course," Laura said doubtfully. "Well, Ben, I guess you will just stay here with us girls tonight. We'll have them bring up a cot."

The next morning, a limousine service had been arranged by the concierge, who made a point of stressing that one of his nephews lived, *very* contentedly, in the Elizabeth neighborhood of Charlotte.

Their driver was an older black man. "It will be my pleasure to assist you," he said pleasantly. "Have you been to our nation's capital before?"

"No," Laura said, "not since college days. And my son—this is Ben—is here for the first time. It is so exciting. Such a beautiful city."

"Yes, wonderful place," Missy added scornfully, seeing the Capitol dome up ahead, but also noting the homeless people sleeping on the sidewalk. "My son is here this summer working for Congresswoman Toller."

"Well, that is something," the driver said. "You must be very proud of him."

Missy smiled. "Yes. Very."

The townhouse where John was staying was located on a historic block of row houses, all beautifully restored, with wrought iron railings leading up steps to paneled oak doors. The street was lined with maple trees, and many of the homes had flower boxes in the front windows, full of impatiens and begonias. And yet, given the district's enduring reputation for crime, Laura suspected that this verdant enclave was merely the neatly tended edge of a far messier, weed-infested expanse beyond. She took Ben's hand as they got out of the car. "Goodness, what a beautiful place," she said.

"I suppose so," Missy said doubtfully. "I wanted John to get something in Georgetown."

John answered the door. "Hey there," he said. He was wearing gray cutoff sweatpants and a Vanderbilt tee-shirt. "Come on in." He ushered them into a living room, its worn sofa and enormous flat screen television somewhat at odds with the elegant building. "Did you have a good trip? I guess you did, since Mom's driving didn't land you in the hospital."

"Not a scratch on them," Missy said, laughing, "although Laura swears she is taking Amtrak back home."

He gave them a quick tour of the townhouse and put Ben's luggage in his room. "We're only three blocks from the Capitol," he said proudly. "Lots of senators and congressmen live around here. Senator Holt is just around the corner. I see her walking her dog most mornings. She's pretty good-looking to be so old!"

Ben allowed himself, for an instant, to admit how happy he was to see his friend again, but uneasily recalled that John had not returned his calls since graduation.

Only the night before John had left for Washington did he finally call. "Hey, dude. Guess what?" he had asked excitedly.

"Okay, what?"

"Guess who has a new BMW convertible?"

"Who?"

"Me. That's who, you fuck."

"You're kidding," Ben said, genuinely impressed, and then added, "Why don't you swing by here and let me see it? Out of pity. I'm still stuck with Mom's Pontiac."

"Sure. I'll be there in about an hour or so."

It was the 'or so' that should have warned Ben. The hour came and went, during which time Ben ran any number of possible fantasies in his mind, picturing himself next to John, the two of them racing along the countryside in that little car, and then, later, saying goodbye in Ben's room. But, John did not come. And did not call.

The next day, Ben had a message on his cell phone. "Hey, it's me," the seductive voice of John Harrison had duly recorded. "Sorry about last night. Mom and Dad crowded in after I called you. Come up to D.C."

Ben tried to put the night at the lake out of his head. It was a stumble, a fluke, just schoolboy playing around. He had asked God to forgive him. Almost every day he had prayed for forgiveness. Johnny Harrison, flawed, never quite within reach with his golden half-smile, was his friend. Nothing more. Nothing abnormal or sinful about it. And when unbidden caresses broke violently through the smooth surface, Ben pushed them just as vigorously away.

They went to the Old Ebbitt Grill for dinner. The restaurant was packed with tourists, many of them waiting impatiently in the foyer or crowded around the massive bar.

"The concierge told me that this would be a fun place," Missy said. "Their steaks are world class."

"Yes, very nice," Laura agreed, "but, it is a little crowded, don't you think?"

"That's what reservations are for," Missy replied, as they were led to a booth trimmed in green velvet cushions.

Ben took a seat, and John slid in beside him. Johnny Harrison seemed more imposing than ever. The booth was small, and his body was crowded next to Ben's. He put his arm around Ben's shoulder. "So, is Ben behaving himself, Mrs. Caldwell?" he asked, his eyes glancing about the room.

"Oh, of course," Laura said. "He has been working very hard helping me with my landscaping project. We have planted a new azalea garden that slopes all the way down to the pond."

"Well, that sounds...exciting," John said, studying the menu now and moving just slightly further away from Ben.

"Do you miss Charlotte?" Laura asked.

"He's loving it here, aren't you, Johnny?" Missy answered for him. "Besides, he was just home a couple weeks ago."

Ben shifted in his seat, pulling himself as far into the corner of the booth as he could. John noticed his discomfort and quickly said, "Yeah, just for the weekend. I was pretty rushed...no time to see anyone, even my best friend here."

"Well, it's nice that you could get home to Charlotte for even a day or two," Laura said diplomatically. "How do you like working for the congresswoman?"

"Very interesting. For one thing, I never knew there were so many crazy people back home. You wouldn't believe the calls we get. They had me answering phones last week, and, Mom, guess who called?"

"Who?" Missy asked.

"Evelyn Peck," John said. "She is known in the office as one of the Frequent Flyers, one of those nutcases who call and write all the time."

"Oh, God," Missy sighed. "Toller mentioned it to me before, something about getting their disability increased."

"Who is Evelyn Peck?" Laura asked.

"A distant relative of Edward's," Missy answered, frowning, "one who lives at the bottom of the Harrison barrel."

"Well," John continued, "I never told her who I was. No way." John tapped his foot, which pressed his leg against Ben's. "So, it has been fun so far. But, I miss everybody." Then he looked at Ben and smiled. "Especially this guy. He's smarter than anybody in this town."

So, where do I sleep?" Ben asked, as he followed John up the stairs, after Laura and Missy had returned to the hotel.

"You're in bed with me," John said, winking. "It was that or put you in my housemates' room. Trust me, you don't want to go in that hell hole without an exterminator."

"And like I don't need to call Orkin in here?" Ben asked as they walked into the bedroom. Dirty clothes littered the floor. A shriveled ficus tree was in the corner by the window, most of its leaves long since perished. The double bed was unmade, the mattress naked save for a tattered fitted sheet clinging to one corner and a Domino's pizza box leaning against a pillow.

"Help me make the bed, will you? And stay on your side, buddy. I'm a light sleeper."

"Where are your roommates?" Ben asked, as he straightened the sheets on the bed. "Are they ever here?"

"Yeah. Some of the time. Both of them have girlfriends, and they kind of go back and forth. Fine by me though." He pulled off his tee-shirt. "Listen, I'm going to take a shower. You need anything?"

"No, I'm good." Ben undressed and got into bed. He pulled the covers up to his waist, and lay there. Waiting. Listening to the sound of the shower down the hall. And then silence, followed by the sound of John's heavy footsteps.

"Okay, I feel better now," John said. He was wearing a towel and tossed it to the floor as he turned the light out and climbed into bed. He lay on his back under the sheet and stretched out in the bed, putting his arms behind his head. His elbows lightly touched Ben's shoulders. "I've missed you. I wish I had a friend like you here."

"Aren't you having a good time?" Ben sat up in bed, carefully arranging the sheet to remain at his waist.

"Oh, yeah. Sure. It's great," John said. "I got a secret to tell you."

"And?"

"Her name is Tricia. Funny name, isn't it? I get excited just thinking about her."

"But, what is the secret part?" Ben asked.

"We work together. She's an L.A. for Toller. And she's twenty-six. An older woman, Ben. A...very...experienced older woman."

"L.A.?"

"Legislative assistant."

"Well, congratulations. She sounds great."

"Oh, she is. Only she hasn't slept with me yet, well, not counting a blow. Drives me crazy. See? Look." He brushed his hand against himself.

"Okay, I get the picture," Ben said, laughing nervously.

"How 'bout you? You nailed anyone this summer?" He yawned lazily and stretched out slowly in the bed.

"Hundreds," Ben said. "I have a harem out back now. It's been a great summer so far."

John took his pillow and hit Ben over the head. "You are so full of it," he said. "Good night, stud."

Ben slid further over to his side of the bed, but facing John, and hoping that his friend could not feel the pounding in his chest. "Okay, see you in the morning," he said.

John turned over onto his stomach, his face toward the wall, and flung the sheet off his naked body. "God, it is hot in here." Ben lay on his side, opening his eyes and mesmerized by the body beside him. A ray of moonlight through the window rested on John's back. John pulled one leg up toward his stomach, tightening his thick body into a smooth, curving mass in the glow of the light.

Ben listened to the clock ticking on the nightstand beside the bed. He turned over to lie on his back, his body next to John's. "John?" Ben whispered, "John, are you awake?"

Silence. As the body beside him rose and fell in a gentle rhythm, Ben cautiously moved his hand to rest on John's back, and began slowly caressing the silky moonglow skin.

John moaned slightly, almost inaudibly, and turned his head toward Ben. He opened his eyes and raised up on his elbows, causing the muscles of his arms and back to expand and tighten. He looked at Ben for an instant, quizzically, and then reached for his hand.

The townhouse was eerily quiet when Ben awoke. John had already left for work. Ben dressed quickly, absently throwing on the clothes he had worn the day before, and walked into the kitchen. "Morning, honey," his mother said, glancing up from the newspaper. "We let ourselves in. Sleep well?"

"Okay, I guess," he mumbled, looking away from her. "You?"

"Oh, wonderful. No complaints," she said cheerily. She crisply surveyed the wrinkled shirt and jeans. "Here, we brought bagels and cream cheese for you."

"No, thanks," he answered. "I'm not hungry. Where is Mrs. Harrison?"

"She's upstairs in the bathroom, just putting the finishing touches on her face before we go over to see the congresswoman." Ben could see her studying him, even as she pretended not to. "Sweetie, you look exhausted. Everything okay?" she asked.

Ben nervously sat down at the table. "Me? Sure, I'm fine, couldn't be better. Say, maybe I will have one of those bagels. How about sesame?"

Missy Harrison appeared in the doorway to the kitchen. She was dressed in a pale blue business suit, and had fastened her hair securely in place with a thin gold band.

"Good morning, Mrs. Harrison," Ben said politely.

"Well, Ben, look at you," she said, laughing. "Why, you look like death warmed over. Did that son of mine keep you up with wild tales of the city? No. Wait. Whatever he told you, I don't want to know."

They walked silently to Toller's office in the Longworth building, as Ben nibbled morosely on the remnants of his bagel. He tossed it into a trash can, just as they were greeted by a hulking woman with a pinched face. "Hi, I'm Faye Hart, the congresswoman's chief of staff," she said with exaggerated formality, attempting a smile and seeming vaguely in pain for the effort. "The congresswoman is so sorry she was not here to greet you, but she has been called to the floor for a vote."

"Oh?" Missy asked, annoyed. "How long do votes usually take? We were planning on meeting with the congresswoman this morning."

"Yes, she is so sorry she could not be here to welcome you. But, she suggested that you take a tour of the Capitol, and then maybe she will be out in time for lunch." The chief of staff clasped her hands together and assumed a grim look not unlike an undertaker pricing coffins for the grieving family.

"Why, we don't want to be any bother, but that is so kind of you to arrange." Laura said, "Thank you so much."

"Not a problem," Faye said, again affecting a strained smile. Her dark, squinting eyes cast a forbidding shadow over the egg white fleshiness of her face.

Goodness, Laura thought, she is like ancient Sisyphus, only instead of endless attempts to push a rock over a hill, she's trying to lift a smile.

"If you will excuse me for just a moment, I will let Joseph, who will be giving the tour, know you are here." She lumbered toward the door, with a cumbersome, bowlegged exit, the folds of fat straining against her dress and strangely complementary to the rigid curls of her close cropped hair.

They sat down on the sofa across from the fireplace, as Faye Hart exited through a side door, which she was careful to close. Unfortunately, while old congressional office buildings were thickly constructed, they were not always soundproof.

Faye's booming voice, its crisp diction rapidly vanishing, could be heard screaming, "Where's Joseph? Joseph? Goddamnit, get over here."

The receptionist, a petite young woman, like a porcelain doll in contrast to the rolling pin chief of staff, looked embarrassed behind her computer. "Can I get you a cup of coffee?" she asked sweetly.

"No, thank you though," Laura said. "We're just fine. This is a lovely office. How long have you worked for the congresswoman?"

"Oh, just for two months now. It's so..." She suddenly stopped speaking, as Faye emerged with the hapless Joseph, a lean, short young man who looked as if he were still in high school. They were followed by John, like a blond Adonis towering over them both.

"This is Joseph Barnes," Faye said, "and of course you know this guy." If precise diction had seemed an acquired trait with Faye, forced collegiality assumed truly schizophrenic heights. "We are so lucky to have him with us," she gushed robotically, while ignoring Joseph, who stood nervously at attention.

"John, you are welcome to go with them on the tour if you want to," Faye said, beaming at him and all but reaching up and pinching his cheeks.

"No, you all go on without me," he said, stepping back slightly. "I need to finish a project I'm working on with Tricia."

"Such a hard worker," Faye said. Then, casting a bitter glance around the room, she added, "I sure wish *everyone* could be like your son, Mrs. Harrison."

"Can you believe Toller?" Missy asked, as they were driving home that afternoon. "I mean, fine, I can understand how things can come up, but what just burns me up is that she did not reschedule."

"I know," Laura said, acutely aware of Missy's tendency to speed even faster when she was upset. "Well, I'm sure she'll call at some point."

"She should have called *before*," Missy thundered, now racing at ninety miles an hour, "instead of bringing in that creepy assistant."

"Oh, she's not so bad," Laura said. "I'm sure she means well. I felt sorry for that little guy, Joseph, though. She shouldn't treat that poor boy like that."

"Laura, please! She's a bitch," Missy said, grimacing, as she deftly maneuvered around an enormous RV. "A grade-A bitch. Such a prickly voice and that odd accent. It's like talking to a human cactus."

"Well, it was an interesting trip anyway," Laura said. "And John seems to really like Washington. Don't you think so, Ben?" She anxiously glanced back at her son. He was staring out the window. "Ben?"

"Yes. Yes. I heard you, Mom. John, I know. He loves it here."

None of it matters anyway, Ben thought, allowing himself to sink into the comfort of that soft, leathery back seat. Away from the haunting eyes of Johnny Harrison. Away from the memory of John's warm, overpowering body the night before, resting beside him, breathing heavily as Ben had touched the glistening skin. So soft to the touch, yet rock hard, like velvet over oak. John looking pensively at Ben through the moonlit night, taking his hand. And then roughly pushing it away.

"What are you doing?" John had asked. "What the fuck are you doing?"

"I thought...you seemed...didn't you...?" Ben stuttered, searching for the right words when he knew there were none.

"You thought wrong," John murmured, his voice grotesquely soft and vicious. "Jesus, Ben, you really are such a fag."

John got up from the bed. "You thought wrong, bud," he repeated, as he grabbed a blanket and backed up toward the door. At that moment, all that was solid and vanishing for Ben was the golden form of John Harrison, beyond Ben's grasp as surely as any fading sun when darkness falls. And at the last moment, just before he disappeared behind the closing door, John Harrison laughed. An odd, strangely victorious laugh.

CHAPTER TWENTY-FIVE
THE EDWARDIAN ARMS

Stephen sat on the balcony of his apartment, sipping a cup of lukewarm coffee. He watched the frenzied suspended animation of a hummingbird that was hovering just above the feeder hanging over the railing. While it was somewhat sobering that signs of life at the Edwardian Arms had been reduced to the humble exertions of a midget bird, the fluttering wings were a riveting performance all the same.

In any event, he preferred the balcony to the awkward beginnings of a morning with a stranger in his home, a young man named Barry currently snoring peacefully in Stephen's bed. For a moment, Stephen recollected flutterings the night before of a far more carnal nature. It was not a memory that he savored.

They had met at a bar optimistically called Liaisons. The bar was in an old Victorian house, painted an evocative pinkish hue, in the historic Dilworth neighborhood. When Stephen arrived there the place was half empty, as the Friday night bar scene did not really get going until after midnight. Small clusters of men, and a few women, were assembled at the upstairs and the surrounding tables.

"What can I do you for, honey?" the bartender had asked, as Stephen sat down on a bar stool painted bright purple.

"I'll have a Corona," he said, trying not to stare at the silver ball embedded in her tongue.

"You got it," she said. "Be right back." She was a wiry looking woman and wore a white tank top and black jeans. Her almond brown hair was spiked into a spearlike sharpness.

Stephen pretended to watch the baseball game on the television as he surveyed the crowd. Not encouraging, he thought. Two older lesbians sat at a table to his right, avidly watching the game. One of them, with coiffed, wavy white hair and wearing a blue shirtwaist dress, reminded him of his Aunt Mildred. Her friend, somewhat younger looking, but heavier and with a vaguely menacing buzz cut, snarled at the television when the batter fouled out. "Hit it! Hit it!" she yelled.

"Here you go," the bartender said, sliding the Corona over to him. She leaned against the counter, one hand on her hip, and one steely elbow on the counter, her hand resting under her square jaw. "Haven't seen you here before. What's your name?"

"Stephen," he answered shyly. "How are you doing tonight?"

"Oh, fine. Can't complain. Enjoying the quiet. More folks'll be comin' in about an hour."

"That's an interesting jewel in your tongue," Stephen said, careful to convey a nonjudgmental tone. "Did it hurt to have it put there?"

"Naw," she exclaimed. "Well, maybe a little. But, I tell you, the girls like it, if you know what I mean."

"Yes, well, I guess so," Stephen stammered. He took a sip of the cool beer and began to relax, even while slyly looking about the room to see who might be looking at him. Beside the fireplace, which was tucked into a corner and boasted an antique oak mantel, a slight young man with sandy blond hair was talking quietly with a friend, while glancing at Stephen. He smiled. Stephen smiled back. It appealed to him that the young man looked so average. So ordinary.

Stephen walked outside to the deck, facing the lights of Uptown. The soaring, diadem studded Bank of America tower seemed engorged against the night sky. After a couple of minutes, he heard the door behind him open and close. An hour later, Barry with the sandy hair accompanied Stephen back to the Edwardian Arms.

Now, the morning after—there was always a morning after, Stephen mused—the hummingbird finally abandoned the feeder and darted off to a more relaxing destination. Stephen walked inside the apartment to get another cup of coffee. The rhythmic snoring continued, a steady and complacent contrast to the lusty gasps of the night before.

Stephen stirred some cream into his coffee and sat down at the kitchen counter, facing the living room. He had only lived at the Edwardian Arms since moving to Charlotte the previous August, arriving amidst a blaze of crape myrtles. It was a sterile complex of redundant brick boxes, but he had quickly discovered that escape was not an easy task. He loathed the impersonal strip malls that dotted the landscape of University City. And he had no desire to venture farther north into the chaotic waves of Lake Norman, where the automotive herd left their cars and regrouped in a stampede of speedboats.

Suddenly, Stephen heard the sound of Barry urinating in the bathroom. "Hey there," Barry drawled, as he walked into the living room and gave Stephen a hug. "Howya doing?" He wore white boxers, a smooth counterpoint to the rampant hair that covered not only his head, but, as Stephen had discovered during their languorous undressing the night before, most of the rest of his body as well.

"Good," Stephen answered, noticing the dark lines of hair on Barry's back. "Would you like some coffee, or something to eat?"

"No, thanks. I need to get going. I have to get over to the Cheesecake Factory." Barry worked part-time there and was taking classes at Central Piedmont Community College. He walked back into the bedroom, and began dressing. "Let's get together again sometime," Stephen heard him call out.

"Sure, that would be great," Stephen called back enthusiastically, fulfilling an etiquette of casual encounters, and making a mental note not to dine anytime soon at the Cheesecake Factory.

After Barry left, Stephen glanced out at the balcony, wondering if the frantic hummingbird had returned. It had not, although a blue jay had now briefly landed on the dogwood nearby. Stephen sat down on the living room sofa, alone now, and conscious once again of the mournful space that followed such rubbery collisions. He considered driving back over to Dilworth for coffee and perhaps a morning of reading at Freedom Park, but suddenly he felt very tired.

The black students in his democracy class had not only persisted with their complaint, they were still refusing to attend the class, daring him to fail them. And since the word *boycott* was journalistic catnip, even for a student newspaper, there had now been two articles in the campus paper. It was only a matter of time before the *Observer* would pick up the story.

He glanced at the print on the wall of Monet's *Girl with an umbrella facing right*. It was one of his favorite paintings, so evocative that one could almost feel the breeze blowing the auburn hair of that pensive young woman, standing on a hillside, a bright blue and white sky looming up behind her. She seemed so luminous as she stared into the distance.

Was she waiting? Or remembering?

He had first seen that painting in Paris. Stephen, reluctantly, thought of France. And then, of course, Dylan. Always Dylan.

Dylan had been taking a semester off from medical school at UNC and planning a trip to Europe. Stephen was working on his dissertation at Duke, and in the most impetuous decision of his life, flew to Paris to be with Dylan.

They had only met a few weeks earlier in Chapel Hill at a Labor Day cookout given by a mutual friend. Stephen was with a group of people on the deck of their host's townhouse. Suddenly, a tall and lean young man joined them. Stephen would always remember the way he entered, and commanded, a room.

"Hi everyone, I'm Dylan." His brown hair hung about his shoulders and had a silky reflection under the light on the deck. Stephen was immediately struck by the man's unusual grace. Even when he was standing still, there was a liquid, supple motion about him. His long legs were accentuated by snug black jeans. He smiled serenely and asked each and every one of them, individually, their names, and bestowed a beaming greeting on each. Stephen was awed by the performance.

A year later, when Paris was still a fresh, sweet memory, Stephen met Dylan's mother. She was a corporate attorney every bit as dynamic as her son and she told him that Dylan had actually been an extremely shy child.

"But I encouraged him," she had explained, "and he just totally came out of his shell. Of course, his sisters have said to me more than once, 'Mom, you created a monster!'"

No, you didn't, Stephen thought bitterly, glancing again at Monet's girl waiting on that lonely hillside. Dylan was an angel. The monster was me.

PART 2

CHAPTER TWENTY-SIX
LIKE A ROLLING STONE

The Rolling Stones?" Laura had looked at Andrew incredulously when he informed her of their upcoming concert date.

"I know," Andrew conceded, "but we have to be there, at least to put in an appearance." The selection of the Rolling Stones was a regrettable opening act for the new Bobcats Arena, but it was not an event that the Caldwells could easily decline. The new arena would stimulate continued growth Uptown, much of which would be developed by Harrison Associates.

Laura had agreed, under protest, and only if they could take Ben along. She hoped that the concert might cheer him up. But, now, as they sat in the luxurious private suite, Mick Jagger pranced onstage and reminded Laura nothing so much as an aged lizard.

"Laura," she heard Alice Owens calling her over to the bar. "Isn't this fun?" Alice was wearing white jeans, a V-necked aqua pullover, and gold earrings. Laura envied Alice's lean, simple elegance.

"Yeah. Fun," Laura said flatly. "I guess the Grateful Dead were booked?"

"Oh, come on. It's the Stones! They won't bite you," Alice said. "Okay. Keith Richards might, but you got your booster shot, didn't you?"

The vast arena stretched out before them, a roar of noise rising up to their box. The Stones seemed frozen in time, and the middle-aged

crowd was entranced by some collective memory of wilder, and long
gone, days. It was an odd reunion of sorts, a feeble connection with
the dim past. Those college days when so many, but not Laura, had
smoked pot and went streaking across college lawns. When Saturday
night disco was a dance and not a punch line.

And now? The men in their suite wore Dockers slacks and polo
shirts, as if they were on their way to a tailgate party in Chapel Hill.
The women, martinis in hand, swayed to the music in cocktail dresses
with slightly shorter hems, their one concession to a more raucous
history.

Across the room, Alice spied Missy sitting at a small table, talking
quietly with, of all people, Reverend Parks. Pale and almost ghostly,
he hovered above Missy. He would be ministering to this gang of
sedate renegades tomorrow morning.

"Laura, look," Alice said, nudging her in the direction of the
bar. "There's Reverend Parks. See, you're not surrounded by satanic
worshippers after all."

Laura laughed. "Well, I feel a little better," she said, as Mick
Jagger's ragged, and now absurd, lament for satisfaction echoed in
the new arena.

Stephen loved the Rolling Stones and he was pleased when Aunt
Missy had invited him to attend the concert at the new arena. He
welcomed the distraction from his growing problems at UNCC, and
was reassured that Missy still regarded him as an asset to her social
ambitions.

He understood that his aunt trusted him. He was subtle, never
garish or intrusive with regard to his personal life. This was not
difficult, given that his personal life was so minimal since Dylan.
There were no awkward allusions to partners or 'friends'. He realized,
with some regret, that he was as appealing, and unobjectionable, as a
sitcom player and that he had tacitly complied with this expectation.
Such was the price of a box seat at the Bobcats Arena.

Stephen parked his car and walked toward the new arena. The
enormous structure was a cluttered mix of brick and glass and aimless
curves. He went inside and ascended an escalator above the frenetic
crowd, higher and higher toward the private suite.

As he was ushered inside, it occurred to Stephen that this was what privilege felt like. To his surprise, he rather liked the feeling. But, the cacophony of noise, punctuated by Mick Jagger's irrepressible lewdness, propelled Stephen, forever inclined toward balance, to a soft leather seat near the back of the suite. Glancing toward the bar, he spotted Aunt Missy ensconced on a bar stool. Holding a martini glass in her hand, she was a tangle of purple chiffon, in a billowing dress that hearkened back to the early sixties. With her legs crossed, she looked like an escapee from the Moulin Rouge. Edward Harrison stood awkwardly beside her, as they chatted with Laura and Andrew Caldwell.

As Stephen was pondering Missy's studied bohemianism and his Uncle Edward's surprising look of discomfort, a tall young man with wavy black hair sat down beside him. The young man seemed almost too imposing for the space, stretching his long, thick legs to the edge of the railing in front of them. He briefly acknowledged Stephen and stared off into the arena. He folded his arms and looked up absently at the ceiling.

"Not a big fan?" Stephen asked.

"They're okay," he replied, shyly looking down toward the stage and pushing several wayward strands of dark hair over his forehead.

"How'd you wind up here in the land of rock and roll antiques?" Stephen asked.

"My parents wanted me to come," he said, somewhat defensively.

"Oh, right," Stephen said, extending his hand. "I'm Stephen Rayfield."

"Ben Caldwell. Good to meet you." The boy looked intently at Stephen, as if awakening from a reverie.

"Laura and Andrew Caldwell's son?" Stephen asked. "So, were you really brought here against your will?"

"No, not exactly. My parents thought I might enjoy it."

"Well, the night is still young. I've met your parents at my aunt and uncle's house. The Harrisons," Stephen said, and then, in a conspiratorial whisper, added, "that's my Aunt Missy, the purple peacock, perched over there by the bar."

The boy anxiously looked in Missy Harrison's direction. "I know. She's talking to my mom. I go to school with John. Well, that is, I used to. We just graduated." Ben paused, his eyes dimly scanning the suite, "Is John here tonight?"

"No, I don't think so. I hear he's having a great time up in D.C. And, of course, he would," Stephen said, arching his brow in some hinted at disapproval. "D.C. is a terrific city."

"We visited him a couple weeks ago," Ben said, gazing out across the arena, as if looking for someone, or something, that was no longer there.

"Everything all right?" Stephen asked.

"What? Oh, yeah, sure...Sorry, just tired," he said, appearing more like a penitent at church than a fan at a concert.

Suddenly, they were joined by Alice and Bill Owens. Bill, looking very fit in blue jeans and a blue polo shirt, grabbed Alice from behind, and began singing into her ear. "And I tried. And I tried. I can't get no..."

"Stephen, you have to rescue me from this bizarre man," Alice exclaimed, and then sat down on Stephen's lap, her arms dramatically around his neck. This occasioned the slight, but unmistakable nod of several disapproving faces, including Edward Harrison's, discreetly looking their way.

"Good thing I am not a jealous husband," Bill said. "First those weekly lunches you two have, and now this…"

Alice, with mock contrition, reached for her husband's hand.

"Oh, no," Stephen protested, "stay where you are. This could do wonders for my reputation. The only thing that would be better is if you were a black woman."

"How *are* things at UNCC?" Bill asked. "Alice mentioned it to me. I hope that's okay."

"Sure. No problem," Stephen said. "The sharks of academe are circling, but it will be okay." Stephen noticed the young man beside him shift nervously in his seat. "Oh, I'm sorry, where are my manners? Alice, Bill, this is Ben Caldwell, Laura and Andrew's son."

"A pleasure to meet you, Ben," Alice said, standing now and assuming a somewhat more maternal tone. "You look very much like your mom. She is such a lovely person."

"Thank you, ma'am. Yes, she is," Ben said, smiling more comfortably now.

"Anyone want anything at the bar?" Bill Owens asked. Stephen was once again struck by Alice's husband's natural ease, his unassuming air of friendliness. But, more intensely, Stephen regarded Ben Caldwell, this brooding, oddly imposing boy, who seemed so unlike the bland, scraggly youths that Stephen was used to seeing on the UNCC campus.

As the concert continued, and the Rolling Stones' geriatric gymnastics dazzled the crowd, the occupants of the suite made their treks back and forth to the bar, or danced in clumsy remembrance, or chatted noisily above the music. But, Stephen kept his seat beside Ben Caldwell, as if the two of them had claimed a quiet space, even as the din of the crowd in the vast arena was rising and falling all around them.

Later in the evening, as the Stones were croaking out yet another nostalgic song to the ecstatic audience, Stephen turned to Ben and said, "Well, guess I better go say hello to the peacock. I wouldn't want to ruffle Aunt Missy's feathers. Who would?"

"Oh, okay, well…thanks," Ben said, shaking Stephen's hand. "This wasn't so bad."

"Great meeting you, Ben. Take care."

"Sure," Ben answered, "good meeting you too, Dr. Rayfield."

"You can call me Stephen. And…" Stephen hesitated, uncertain of what to say. He could see Laura Caldwell waving at her son from across the room. It was clear that the Caldwells were leaving.

Stephen put his hand on Ben's arm and quickly, almost surreptitiously, handed him his card. "Listen," Stephen said, "if you ever need to talk to someone, just give me a call. Will you do that?"

Ben took the card and glanced over at his parents. His mother was motioning, more insistently now, for him to come join them. Ben put his thick fingers, nails bitten to the quick, over his mouth for a moment. "Thanks," he said, and then, smiling just slightly, added, "*Stephen.*"

Stephen watched Ben return to the rather eager fold of Mr. and Mrs. Caldwell. And, over the waning howls of Mick Jagger, past the pulsating noise of the crowd, hovering just beyond the awkward grace of Ben Caldwell, Stephen could almost hear the faint murmur of warning.

CHAPTER TWENTY-SEVEN
BACK TO MONROE

The sky was overcast and threatening as Edward backed his blue Mercedes out of the cobblestone driveway. All of the epic landscaping of his Morrocroft neighbors, the rows of begonias, the orderly boxwoods and towering hollies, the beds of petunias and impatiens, all were obscured by the overwhelming mugginess of this July day. While Edward was not particularly attuned to the lush blooms of a Charlotte morning under a blue sky, he did notice the approaching gloom under a gray one.

Traffic was light. Edward began to relax in the air-conditioned comfort of the Mercedes, gliding him along Sardis Road. The grand homes set back from the road were quiet, their owners just beginning to stir. At such times, Charlotte seemed almost unspoiled in its green expansiveness.

This idyll ended the moment Edward arrived at Independence Boulevard. As he headed east on the boulevard, with the Charlotte skyline receding behind him, Edward was struck, as always, by the decay along this old highway. In his youth, growing up in Monroe, Independence Boulevard had been a vital gateway into Charlotte. To Edward, it had been emblematic of a larger world that he could only imagine in the small confines of Monroe. It led to movie theaters and concerts at the Charlotte Coliseum and dinners in restaurants that had Mexican and Italian food and waiters and live music. Now, it was like a racetrack, with ghostly strip malls dying along its barricaded border.

There were four lanes in each direction. Here was the worship of the automobile at its most basic. Two middle lanes were bordered with concrete girders. Old intersections had been removed, and access to and from the highway was only grudgingly afforded. The gush of traffic which once was the lifeblood of the shopping centers and businesses that lined Independence now indifferently passed them by.

Edward regarded the boarded up shopping centers, the empty parking lots, with resignation. Whatever nostalgia he felt for this anemic stretch of commerce was tempered by a Darwinian sense of survival of the fittest. The herd, for now, had moved on, and was now feeding elsewhere. That was, in Edward's view, inevitable and not to be resisted. And, just as inevitably, he knew that someday the towering construction cranes, which were now grazing Uptown and in SouthPark, would return.

As he continued east, bypassing the hopelessly overrun village of Matthews, development resumed. Intersections reappeared, leading to a new succession of Targets and Sam's Clubs and Exxons and movie theaters, Outback Steakhouses and Comfort Inns and McDonalds. This suburban expansion continued almost unbroken now for the fifteen miles to Monroe on Highway 74. Car dealerships, gas stations, RV dealers, and golf cart sales centers lined the highway.

When he finally arrived in downtown Monroe, Edward was again reminded of the brutal indifference of the bottom line. The eerie silence of Main Street on a Saturday afternoon was in stark contrast to the frenzy of the sprawling development beyond it. Ever since the first mall opened out on Highway 74 when Edward was still in high school, Monroe's historic downtown had become spectral and insignificant. Even the original Belk department store, founded in Monroe, was abandoned.

The Belk mansion, an ante bellum showplace around the corner from the white-steepled First Baptist Church, still stood proudly behind its iron gate, but the mansion was very much an isolated bloom in a long neglected garden. The downtown retained its redbrick Victorian courthouse in the square, and the ugly high-rise county office building, but very little else. It was as if the former heart of Monroe was barely beating, while the steroidal growth along outlying arteries was bursting.

Edward drove slowly toward his mother's modest brick home on Durant Street, at once nostalgic and annoyed by her insistence in remaining there. "Why should I move?" she once asked Edward, who had offered to buy her a condominium in Charlotte. "It's my home."

Most of the homes on the street, which curved back in a circle, were small ranch style homes, with unpainted trim and untended yards. During Edward's youth, the neighborhood had been unimposing but respectable. "We were *solid* lower-middle class," his sister Lynn used to say. But, even then, there was the ominous presence of apartment buildings at the entrance to their circle of houses. Tenants who were schoolteachers and firemen had slowly given way to welfare mothers and disabled elderly. Now the apartments were a mix of black and Hispanic residents, and all poor. Old cars were parked on dirt yards in front of the apartments.

The Harrison home was on a sloping corner lot. Edward's father had added on a family room to the side, and then a garage, on lower elevation, connected to the family room. Later, he built a den downstairs from the kitchen, and a brick enclosed patio. "Come on Eddie, put some muscle into it, boy," his father would order, half amused, as the adolescent Edward struggled to mix the cement.

His mother greeted him at the door. "Hi, youngin'! Come on in!" she said, giving him a big hug. He walked through the small living room, furnished with the same grainy beige sofa that had been there when he was in high school, and into the kitchen. Edward took a seat on one of the hardback chairs at the simple maple table. His mother did not believe in turning in the old for the new unless absolutely necessary. He had offered to replace her furniture, which was threadbare, but she refused. She did let him buy her the new Cadillac, but only after her old one had reached 200,000 carefully tended miles.

"I made you a peach cobbler," she said, motioning to the bubbling pie in the iron skillet on the stove.

"Oh, thanks Mom, but Missy has me on a strict diet. Salads and chicken. I'm about to go crazy just for a baked potato."

"Well, I can rustle up some potatoes too!" she said, serving him a heaping plate of cobbler. "Look at you. You are just the right weight, you don't need to lose a pound! Where does that woman get her ideas from? Your father, bless his soul, he never went on a diet a day in his life. He had cake every day. I know because I made them. And, up till he got sick with the cancer, he did just fine. He was the healthiest man I ever met."

"Okay, but just this one," he said, eagerly taking the plate. "But, don't tell Missy."

"When would I tell her anything? I never see her!"

"Now, Mom, don't start. You know how busy Missy is. She barely has time to see me." He defended his wife out of a halfhearted sense of duty, and, lately perhaps, a moldering sense of guilt. He vaguely felt that a criticism of her was a criticism of him. But, the truth was that Missy rarely spent any time with Myrtle. His mother was invited to their house exactly two times a year, for Thanksgiving and for Christmas, when even Missy deferred to traditional family obligation. On Myrtle's birthday, Edward always took her out to dinner, over her protests that it was far too expensive, to Morton's Steakhouse Uptown. Missy had not once deigned to accompany them.

Edward decided it would be best to change the subject. This was an easy thing to do with Myrtle, so long as the subject was on her rather limited list of topics. If the list was narrow, it was at least consistent, in that it typically revolved around herself. His mother was an odd combination of a generous heart and a voracious ego.

"How's your boyfriend?" he asked.

"Oh, boyfriend! Hah! Fred and me are just good friends. He's visiting Blanche in Greenville. I guess he'll be back home tomorrow, but I really don't give a damn. I told him, 'Go, go and see Blanche if you want to. It doesn't matter one bit to me! I said 'Fred, she's your ex-wife, and if you want to still be friends with her, that's fine with me. Just don't expect me to sit by the phone.' No, I am *not* going to do it! There's plenty of fish..."

Edward settled back and enjoyed his cobbler. One thing about visiting Myrtle, you did not have to work too hard at conversation.

"He says he goes to see her because she isn't well, and he also needs to visit his grandson there," she continued. "I've seen pictures of her. She's not attractive, kind of horse faced if you ask me. And that grandson of his. All he wants is a handout from Fred. He can't keep a job, and always has some scheme for needing money from Fred. He's had enough so-called car repairs to buy a Rolls Royce. I told Fred. I said, 'Fred, he just wants your money. That boy needs to get a job.' Course I might as well have saved my breath."

Edward finished the cobbler, and was tempted to go for seconds, but the fullness in his stomach counseled otherwise. When his mother paused for a brief second, just as she was about to begin her diatribe against the breakdown of civilization in Monroe, he said, "Mom, have you thought anymore about moving to a condominium. If you don't want to move to Charlotte, we could look for something here in Monroe."

"No, honey, I am fine right here." She began clearing the table, and carried the dishes over to the sink. She did not have a dishwasher, viewing that as a silly contraption for anyone who could still use the hands God gave them. "I'll admit, I keep my doors locked and I'm glad to have a burglar alarm, thanks to you. There are some weird characters who live over in those apartments. You just can't go outside anywhere after dark anymore."

"How about Charlotte? There is a beautiful new condo building over in Myers Park."

"Hah! Charlotte is just as bad. And at least here I know some of my neighbors. We look out for each other. I'll stay with what I know. Why, look what happened to my friend Jean. She left her home, moved all the way to Kansas to be with her son and his wife..."

Ah, poor Jean...Edward contentedly sipped his coffee and pretended to listen. There was a comforting rhythm to the steady chatter of his mother. Sometimes when he sat at that maple table, he could still see them all there. Dad, and Lynn, and his mother. They had finally landed in the little house just as Edward was about to start tenth grade at Monroe High.

Myrtle, having finished the saga of Jean in its entirety, paused. This in itself got Edward's attention. A lull in speech, and the deeper reflection of thought that it might entail, was, in his mother's case, the equivalent of dead air time on the radio, and just as rare.

"I got a call the other day from Stephen," she said, as she began washing dishes in the sink. Stephen was her favorite grandchild, as everyone knew, and one of the few people capable of shifting her gaze away from herself.

"Oh? Everything okay?"

"Fine. He seems fine," she replied. "Some trouble with the college, but he says not to worry. What's going on out there?"

"Tempest in a teapot, Mom. A couple of black kids riled up. It will blow over."

"I just wish he would meet a nice friend. Don't you?"

Edward could not have been more uncomfortable if his mother had just asked him if Missy was a screamer. His homosexual nephew's personal life was something that he preferred not to think about. "I suppose so," he said curtly, hoping she would change the subject.

"He just seems so lonely since his friend left," she continued. "And I worry about him out there. I hope he has safe sex. Do you think he is careful?"

"Mom, please. That's Stephen's business. Say, you know what, I think I will have some more cobbler after all."

She really is getting old, Edward thought. Her hair was still Marilyn Monroe blond, she still flirted with every waiter, but her hands were splotched with age spots, her jowls softening in repose. He could see an unfamiliar apprehension that belied her smile. Time, she seemed to say, is a fearful thing. Well, she could still make a damned good cobbler, and, for now, that was reassurance enough for both of them.

CHAPTER TWENTY-EIGHT
SILENT PLEA

Ben lay on his bed, flipping through the pages of the Charlotte Latin yearbook. He turned to the senior class pictures, quickly scanning to John's picture. John's hair was carelessly combed, with one golden layer lightly falling over his forehead, like a caress. His amused pose offered just the hint of a grin. There was infinite promise, or maybe nothing at all, in that cryptic smile.

Ben stared at his cell phone and then quickly dialed. "Hi, John? It's Ben." Silence. "Hello?"

"Yeah, hi. I'm here. What's up?"

"Ahm, not much. I just wanted to call, see how you are." There was no reply, so Ben continued, "I went to the Rolling Stones concert at the Bobcat arena."

"Uh huh. How was that?" John asked indifferently.

"It was okay, I guess. Your mom and dad were there. Oh, and your cousin Stephen, he was there."

John laughed. "Stephen? Well, you know he's a fag?"

"He seemed like a nice guy," Ben said.

"Okay. Whatever."

"John..." Ben said, hesitating.

"Yeah, I'm still here."

"Listen, I just needed to talk to you." Ben continued to look at the photograph in the yearbook. That curious grin John had. Never giving away so much that a person didn't hunger for just a little bit more, whatever *more* turned out to be.

"Now?" John asked impatiently.

"In person. Can we do that? Aren't you coming back in a few weeks?"

"Talk about what?" he asked, ignoring the question.

"I need to talk to you about that night...I thought we were friends. I'm still not sure what happened. And if I did something wrong, it was only because..."

"Oh, jeez. Come on, lighten up," John said.

"The thing is...I don't know, I just can't get clear lately. I..." Ben thought he heard someone laughing, there with John. "Why did you walk out like that? I don't understand..."

"Look, you need to leave me alone. Okay? I gotta go."

Ben hung up the phone and closed the yearbook, then threw the book on the floor. It landed with a thud on top of his Nikes, and slid across the room toward the door. As he lay in his bed, staring at the ceiling, he suddenly thought of Donna Fleishmann, the way she used to look at him from the sofa in her parents' living room. Waiting for him. He remembered how she would roll on her side, her naked breast like an offering, and then on to her stomach, and all the time her eyes never left him, never stopped wanting him.

Only now, as he thought of her, vulnerable and inviting, her lips mouthing his name in a silent plea, she was not looking at him. She was looking at John. The floorboards creaked with John's naked, inexorable approach. Then, she lay on her back and continued to mouth Ben's name in a kind of litany of seduction and sorrow, all the while reaching out for the hard, cruel body of John Harrison.

Laura waited until Andrew and Deb had gone upstairs. Ben was sitting in the den, watching television. "It's getting late, sleepyhead," she said. "About time for bed, isn't it?"

Ben remained silent. Laura sat down in the rocking chair by the fireplace. "Is something wrong? You know you can talk to me, hon. You know that, don't you?"

He looked at her sleepily, with locks of hair dangling in front of his forehead, reminding her of when he was just a little boy. "I'm fine," he said softly, looking out at the fountain behind their house. The clusters of impatiens that they had planted were a blur now of red and purple and white under the full moon.

"Okay, sweetie. Okay." She began straightening the clutter of magazines on the coffee table. "So, what are your plans for tomorrow?"

"I don't know," he said, distracted now by the brightness of the moon, the way its light trailed down to the edge of the smooth lawn and then like a skipping caress across the silvery water. "Nothing, really. Just thought I'd hang out. Or maybe help you with weeding by the driveway."

"Honey, that's sweet of you," she said, "and I appreciate all your help. But, you have been moping around this house now for weeks. Why don't you get out with some of your friends? You could go back up to Washington to visit John."

"No!" he said angrily. "No. Please, just leave me alone."

"John is your best friend. What's wrong with you?"

"Mom, just drop it, okay," he said, calm again.

She regarded Ben with her curious mixture of kindness and judgment, and then softly replied, "You can always talk to me, son. I'm always here for you. You know that, don't you?"

He looked at her for a moment, as if waiting for the necessary words to complete a long and delayed journey. But, once again, the words, hovering just at the opening of a door, could go no further. "I'm fine," he mumbled. "Good night, Mom."

CHAPTER TWENTY-NINE
THE MAGNOLIA COURT

D r. Alice Owens studied the chart on her desk. Thirty-four year old female. Mother of two. Ovarian cancer. Stage four. *Death.* That was what those numbers were really saying. Death. She had first met this patient during the woman's second pregnancy. A new life. And now…thank God it won't take too long, she thought. That is a mercy of sorts.

She began to dial the number of the oncologist who would manage the woman's treatment when another call came in. It was Edward. "Alice, I'm sorry to call you at work," he whispered, "but, Missy has a trustee meeting out at UNCC tonight, so I thought… maybe…"

"It's okay," Alice answered. "I want to see you too. Where?"

"Well, you know this is a small town, so we have to be careful. But, I know a place. Never been there before—believe me, that is the God's truth. Not the sort of place you are used to, but no one would see us there."

"Don't worry," she said, then gently added, "I'll bring my little blanket." She jotted down the directions to the motel. It was outside Gastonia, so would take at least a half hour to get there. Such was the price of discretion.

Alice called to let the au pair, Aurelia, know that she would be home late. "I have a couple of emergencies to deal with here and may not get home for a few hours."

"Oh, don't worry, Dr. Owens," the young woman said reassuringly. "I will let Mr. Owens know. The girls still want to go see that new movie about the princess. Maybe we could do that this evening? It's Friday, but I don't think the earlier show will be too crowded."

"Sure, they would enjoy that," Alice said. "And I imagine Mr. Owens might like to go too." She paused for a moment, uneasily considering *that* scenario. "Okay then. I have my pager on, so call me if you need to, and give the girls a hug for me."

Alice hung up the phone, and looked somewhat forlornly at the photograph on her desk of her daughters. They were her greatest treasure, and the one for which she feared she was least responsible. Her work consumed so much of her time and energy. And then there were the more personal diversions which sometimes, though not frequently, precipitated her absence as well.

With a twinge of guilt, an emotion she usually managed to elude, she resolved to spend the entire day tomorrow with the girls. And with Bill, if his own schedule allowed. She would not push though. Alice had long accepted that the precise equilibrium of their life together depended on not pushing.

Evelyn Peck did not read the newspaper. Or magazines. Or books. However, she was an avid viewer of television news, so long as it did not conflict with her afternoon soap operas. Her favorite program though was *The Jerry Springer Show*, which presented a menage of trash to which even Evelyn Peck could feel superior.

"Look at that slut!" she shouted to Keith. "Fat as a cow, and you practically see her ass underneath that dress. No wonder her daughter's shacked up with a black guy." As the Springer combatants assaulted each other, Evelyn squealed with delight and her son retreated to the relative quietness of the kitchen to read the paper.

She heard the phone ringing. With the anticipation that it might, finally, be Gene Johnson, Evelyn felt a surge of energy, and leapt from the sofa. He had not called in several weeks. In her considerable experience, that was not a good sign.

"Yeah, who is it?" she asked breathlessly.

"Evelyn, hey girl. This is Gene. You remember me?"

"Gene!" she squealed, "How the hell you been? *Where* the hell you been? I thought you had just up and forgot about old Evelyn."

"Nah. No way," he assured her. "I been on a run to Kentucky. Had to deliver an RV to some farmer out there. I never knew farmers made so much dough. But, I'm back now. How 'bout we get together for a drink?"

"Well," she paused, "I reckon that might be all right. What you got in mind?"

"I got to go over to Gastonia tomorrow. Got to settle a little business over at the courthouse. My ex is making trouble for me again. How 'bout you meet me at the Detour? You know that bar? Say around five?"

Evelyn knew that she should say no. Already, ever since their night at her house, she had made herself too available to him. Always ready to go whenever he called, even if she did have to brave rush hour traffic. But, she figured, when there's only one fish on the line, no point in waiting to reel him back in. "I'll be there," she said, "but don't you be late."

O ne more for the road, Evelyn?" the cute bartender asked, smiling at her. He had a chipped front tooth and his hair was thinning on top, but he seemed to like her. Given that there was at present only one other customer, a sleepy old woman slouching at the other end of the bar, the bartender had plenty of time to pay attention to Evelyn.

"Well, what do you recommend? Should I or shouldn't I?" Evelyn tilted her head to one side and opened her sluggish eyes as wide and flirtatiously as possible.

"I think you should," he said. "You're a big girl. You can take it."

She ordered another gin and tonic, and glanced at the clock. 6:25. That creep, she thought. Suddenly, the door opened, letting in a swath of sunlight and just as suddenly closing it out, and Gene Johnson walked in. He made a show of walking hurriedly toward Evelyn.

"Hey, Evvie. How you doing girl?"

"How'm I doing? Well, *Gene*, I been waiting here for 'bout an hour for an asshole. Who just walked in."

"Aw, don't be mad," he said, taking a seat beside her. "I couldn't tell the judge to hurry things up. He hates my guts already."

"Tell him to join the club," she snarled.

Gene ordered a tequila and moved with Evelyn to a more private booth. Less than fifteen minutes later, after a series of progressively more intimate hugs and caresses, he said, "Let's go somewhere more quiet."

"What's quieter than this?" she asked. "We're the only ones here except for Miss Rip Van what's her name over there."

"You know what I mean. Come on. Let's go."

Someplace quieter turned out to be the Magnolia Court motel, located on the outskirts of Gastonia. Evelyn waited in the truck while Gene went inside the little office to get a room. She could see the clerk—Indian, as usual, these days—completing the paperwork. He had the studied focus of the discreet innkeeper, such discretion being the one essential attribute for an employee of the Magnolia Court.

The motel was two stories, with dingy white brick. A walkway ran along the front of the rooms and was covered by a tin awning supported by rusting poles. Cheap Indian bastards, Evelyn thought. Probably illegals too. She had a good mind to tell Gene just to forget it, the nerve of that man bringing her to such a dump. What did he take her for, anyway?

However, Gene turned out to be an especially attentive lover at the seedy motel, exhibiting a stamina for calculated delay that both thrilled and impressed Evelyn. In her experience, men could basically be divided into two categories. There were those who waited and those who kept her waiting. In the matter of sex at least, Gene was definitely the former. However, whatever her enthusiasm for his talents, she judged that it was in her interest to mute her praise in that regard.

After he completed his ministrations with an ear piercing rebel yell, he rolled over and fell asleep. It isn't even dark out yet, she thought. He did not bother to cover himself with a sheet, much to Evelyn's chagrin. Gene was best observed under urgent and distracting conditions, preferably involving heavy breathing. A more protracted and sober view did not lend favorable impressions.

Sprawled on his back next to her, snoring contentedly, his mouth was open, like those pictures of dead people on television crime dramas. He seemed all elbows and shins, all angles, and yet with a soft belly with splotchy, almost hairless skin. Well, it could be worse, she thought, as she gave a silent prayer of thanks for the shaded windows, and avoided looking at his now conquered and receded manhood, limp and leaking.

Aside from mild contempt for the post coital indifference typical of men like Gene Johnson, his withdrawal was of little concern to Evelyn. It was the act itself that she valued. The rest was just window dressing. Evelyn lacked interest in, or expectation of, any romantic notions of lingering embraces or assurances of undying love. She regarded sexual encounters with the efficient precision of close order drills. Her goal, much like that of most of her partners, was satisfaction of a primal urge, nothing more, nothing less. She did not begrudge the snoring, withering figure beside her.

Nonetheless, bored and spent, Evelyn had no inclination to remain in bed. She sat up and looked about the room. There was little to be said for it, even by her own modest standards. The walls were a tired beige, either from ancient paint or accumulated grime. The woolen blanket on their bed was watermelon red, with countless picks across its surface and its faux satin lining ripped in several places along the border. She stood up, careful to watch for roaches as she walked across the orange shag carpet. Her clothes were tossed on the floor by the window, where a used condom now lay perilously close to her blouse. She quickly dressed and walked outside.

Even though the sun was going down, there was still a heavy, scratchy heat, reminding Evelyn of that tattered red blanket that was bunched up at the sweating feet of a snoring Gene Johnson.

She sat down on the rusting green lawn chair, after first removing the mildewed cushion. She could hear the occasional chirping of crickets, some of whom she had already become acquainted with in her room, and the rumble of the trucks racing by on the adjacent highway. A large gnat hurled itself mindlessly against the single naked bulb above the door. It was not a place to linger. In this respect, the Magnolia Court's location was part of its appeal, accommodating as it was for its clientele's desire for both privacy and for rapid exits.

The gravelly parking lot was empty, except for Gene's truck and one other car, a late model Buick with a broken headlight and dented chrome. The Magnolia Court was located behind the Carolina Court, which appeared only marginally better. However, the Carolina Court was of a sufficient superiority for its back to be turned toward the Magnolia. There was an almost claustrophobic proximity between the two motels, their parking spaces separated by a mottled strip of asphalt.

Evelyn noticed that two cars parked by the back rooms of the Carolina Court were a Mercedes and a BMW, both the more expensive higher numbered series. She had made a bit of a study of luxury cars in her spare time, one more measure of what she most wanted and did not have. Some rich folks doing the secret nasty, she thought. God, they must be desperate to come to a dump like this.

"Evvie! Evvie, where the hell did you go, girl?" She heard the now awake and agitated voice of Gene. He was standing in the doorway, wearing only his shorts, which drooped low on his bony hips. How can a man be such skin and bones and still sport that spongy belly, she wondered.

"Oh, good God, put on some clothes," she answered.

He leered at her for a moment. "Sure? Might have a little traction left. How 'bout it? One more ride?"

She slouched provocatively in her chair. "Oh, hell's bells. Why not?"

About thirty minutes later, Evelyn reached over the recumbent form of her lover and looked at her watch on the single nightstand. "Lord, look at the time," Evelyn said, yawning. "I got to go. It's getting late for this old girl."

Gene was, once again, barely awake, but raised himself to bestow upon her a parting grin, his pale arm propped over a pillow. "You go ahead. I think I'll rest here a while. You done gone and wore poor old Gene out."

"Hah! I'm the one who can barely walk," she said, as she staggered out of bed. "Close your eyes, I got to turn on the light." He closed his eyes and lazily pulled the sheet up. Thank God for small favors, Evelyn thought.

Evelyn dressed quickly. "You be good, hon," she called out as she opened the door, "and if you can't be good, be careful." She saw his skinny arm waving a feeble goodbye from the bed.

Outside, the corridor was brightly lit now, in almost blinding contrast to the tawdry shadows of the rooms. A single scraggly azalea, with garish red leaves, wilted under the fluorescent glare. As Evelyn was getting into her car, she heard a door opening in the room across from her at the Carolina Court. A tall, distinguished looking man with a wavy shock of graying hair walked outside. Beside him was a slim, elegant woman. The man seemed very nervous, looking left and right, as if to assure himself that they were not being observed.

When he looked toward her car, she realized with a shock that it was Edward Harrison. I'll be damned, she gasped, that snooty britches got somebody on the sly. For an instant, he saw her, and then quickly got into his car and drove away. The woman, who was wearing blue shorts and a white blouse, had thick brown hair, which she had tied with a burgundy scarf. Her face was half turned away from Evelyn. Unlike Edward, she seemed unhurried as she went to her own car.

Well, Evelyn thought, recalling her own few, unpleasant memories of Missy, who can blame him?

No one was home when Edward returned from Gastonia. He was certain that Evelyn had seen him, but consoled himself with the thought that, if there were one person in the whole world whose path would not likely cross Missy's, it had to be Evelyn Peck.

He walked inside the empty, quiet house. For all its grandeur, the house seemed too out of scale to ordinary life on the occasions when he was the only life present. He stopped in the front gallery, with its formal portraits of Harrison ancestors.

It had been Missy's idea to have the portraits done, based on old photographs of his great-great grandparents. Certain liberties had been taken with grooming and costuming. Lottie Harrison was presented in an elaborate royal blue taffeta gown, trimmed in a white lace collar. Her lustrous auburn hair was coiffed with pearls. James Harrison was decked out in the uniform of a Confederate colonel. While the suggestion was of an epic and patrician lineage, Edward of course knew otherwise. No Harrison had ever risen above the rank of corporal, in any war, although they had fought in most of them. They were small-time landowners and farmers, and then later construction workers. Not distinguished, but respectable. Industrious. God-fearing. Ordinary. No one wanted to be ordinary anymore, he reflected. Why was that?

He went into the kitchen. He had asked the cook, Juanita, to prepare a chocolate pecan cake the day before. "Okay, Mr. Harrison, you're the boss," Juanita had said, as she glanced uneasily toward the door, perhaps expecting a protesting Missy to storm through at any moment. The cake was under a glass dome on the counter, untouched. He felt an almost sensuous exhilaration as he removed a large portion, and licked the soft, buttery icing from the knife.

Edward poured himself a glass of milk and took his cake into the library. He sat down on the leather sofa that faced the fireplace, ignoring the portrait of Missy that hovered above him, and began greedily devouring the cake.

The appearance of Evelyn had been the only blemish on a perfect day. Somewhat to his surprise, Edward did not feel recrimination or guilt. Possibly that was due to the complacency of his marriage. He had grown so accustomed to gazing at the surface that one more disruption below, even an adulterous one, was a benign undercurrent and of no consequence. But his calmness was also a reflection of the serene Alice Owens. If such a remarkable creature could be so embracing of the sweaty passion that had earlier consumed them, then he reasoned that perhaps he could be as well. While he doubted that such equanimity could be maintained, he was grateful for it nonetheless.

Alice had been very much in command, directing Edward with such assurance and tenderness that any of the tentative fumblings that might characterize other, tawdrier assignations at the Carolina Court were avoided. While he was appalled when he first realized just how faded the motel really was, Alice seemed to regard even that bleak place as a lark. Surveying their room, its musky-smelling furnishings, the stained gray carpet, she laughed. "Oh, Edward. Call room service. Let's have their best champagne!"

It occurred to him now, back in the undisturbed luxury of his own home, that he had *wanted* to see Alice's reaction to such low-rent accommodations. It was a departure from his current life, but was a defiant connection to his old one.

Edward swept away chocolate crumbs that had fallen onto his pants. He closed his eyes and recalled the glorious image of Alice, naked in his frantic arms, tossing the red and black blanket onto the dingy carpet. She had gasped his name over and over. *Edward, Edward, Edward...*

His reverie was interrupted by the sound of the front door. It was Missy's habit to park her car in the circular drive, and enter through the front. "I want to enjoy these beautiful doors every time I come in," she said on the day when the doors arrived from Florence. She does have a passion for those doors, he thought ruefully.

"Fix me a gin and tonic, would you?" he heard Missy saying as she entered the library. "Well, you didn't miss much. Those fools at UNCC have worked my very last nerve." She collapsed upon the other sofa, her arms thrown back behind her head, her legs ajar, recalling to Edward the image of Alice, slyly smiling, on that creaky motel bed.

"It can't be that bad," Edward said consolingly.

"No?" she asked, looking contemptuously at the dessert plate on the sofa beside him. "Well, how about this? Tough Toller is saying she isn't sure she can get the money for the student center, but the chances might improve if it is named after her. Half of the trustees are gagging at the thought, and the other half are already painting the sign. And of course there was the usual bitching about Chapel Hill and State lording it over Charlotte."

"I know," Edward said indifferently, "same old same old." As a graduate of Chapel Hill himself, he had decidedly mixed feelings about the ceaseless aspirations of UNCC.

"Well, what do they expect? If I've said it once, I've said it a hundred times, they never should have stuck that campus out there in the boondocks." She looked at him a moment, as he distractedly mixed a gin and tonic for her. "What's with you?"

"What do you mean? I'm fine. Here," he said, handing her the drink. "I'm just a little tired, busy day."

"No, that isn't it. I didn't mean you look tired. I just had the strangest image of you. Like a little boy."

"That right?" Edward got up from his chair, avoiding Missy's gaze, aware that he was being studied now. "Well, thanks, I guess. I'm going to head on up to bed. I really am tired as a dog." It was one of those comments that had been uttered so many times in truth, it was easily credible in deception.

"Sleep tight, then," Missy said, "I'm going to stay up a while."

Edward walked back into the gallery, and bid a wary goodnight to the fraudulent portraits. He ascended the thickly carpeted stairs, under the dimmed but glittering light of the chandelier, and entered the blue tinted marble glow of the bedroom. He lay down on the huge mahogany bed, felt the satiny touch of the embroidered comforter, and thought of Alice, as smooth as ivory amid the coarse sheets of the Carolina Court.

Keith Peck was sitting in the living room, in the sagging recliner that he favored. Given that he had been sitting there when she left, Evelyn momentarily wondered if he had ever actually gotten up in the course of the day. The television was on, with a young couple earnestly talking about how they earned $200,000 buying rundown houses. An empty bag of Cheetohs was crumpled at his feet, sharing the cluttered floor with several tossed Budweisers.

"Where you been at?" he asked, yawning lazily. His voice was groggy, causing him to run his words together in one long drawl. He stretched back in the chair, briefly causing his tee-shirt to rise up above his belly.

"Gene," she said, smiling, knowing that her son detested him. "Looks like you been tied to that chair all day. I told you to clean this place up."

"I did. But, it got dirty again. Ain't that the funniest?"

"Yeah. Real funny, Jack Benny. Real funny." She considered picking up the beer bottles, but decided that would be sending the wrong message. Let him pick up his own junk, she thought. She grabbed the bag of Cheetohs and sat down on the sofa. "Looks like maybe somebody didn't take his medicine today. That about right?"

"How's Gene the Bean?" he asked, smirking, ignoring her question.

"Oh, a lot you care. I got some funny news though."

Keith effected another yawn, as if to signal that he was not particularly interested. "Yeah, what's that?"

"You'll never guess who I saw coming out of a motel."

"I give up. Who?" he asked, reaching for the Cheetohs and stuffing a handful into his mouth. "And what were you doing there?"

"I was driving by, smartass. Go ahead. Guess!" She walked into the kitchen to get a beer.

"Okay, let's see…ahm, Bob Hope," he called out to her. "Am I right?"

"He's dead, moron," she said, coming back into the room, a Michelob in one hand and a bag of Doritos in the other. "Oh, forget it. Let's just say it was somebody important. With some woman who weren't his wife, that's for sure."

Keith sat up in his chair. "Aw, come on. Who was it?"

"Never you mind. And I think he saw me too. Looked like a deer in the headlights. I nearly busted a gut, watching him scurry away with his tail between his legs." Evelyn Peck rolled back onto the couch, her body shaking with laughter.

The young couple on the television continued to boast of their newfound fortunes. "Look at 'em," Keith said, "maybe they could buy this dump."

"Maybe," Evelyn replied. "But, if not, you never know who might want to. I got some ideas."

CHAPTER THIRTY
BOXES IN THE BASEMENT

S tephen Rayfield was not a confrontational person. Indeed, his natural impulse at the first sign of discord was to retreat to the nearest library or quiet coffee shop. As the summer session at UNCC progressed, it might have been prudent for the young professor to change the subject or at least the tone of his class.

Racial politics and political correctness were volatile ground in academia, and alternate routes were highly advised. And yet, Stephen persisted. In his view, the failure to honestly address the train wreck of the black underclass was a national scandal. Half of the black males in Charlotte's schools would never graduate, and too many of them would in fact go on to lives of crime and incarceration. It was a disaster abetted by silence and platitudes. He could not accept that, and he would expect no less of his students. Climbing over wreckage, of course, one was more apt to stumble.

His expectations of his students were a complicated matter of late, since all but one of the black students were, noisily, boycotting his class. The somnolent days of a Charlotte summer were punctuated now by the vigorous protest, and accompanying media reports, of those students. Each morning before class, the media kite was ascending ever higher and ever farther. First the *Niner,* then the *Observer* and, this morning, local television, were in attendance.

As Stephen approached the class, Chris Denton and a half dozen others were waiting, a veritable gauntlet at the entrance to Garinger Hall, waving placards and shrieking insults at him.

Chris Denton held a placard that said "Racist Rayfield" and glared at him as he walked by. Two young black women held a banner that read "*What* Democracy in America?" Stephen's favorite thought was the slight young man with the sign that read "Welcome to Rayfield Plantation." Stephen smiled and calculated the number of steps remaining to the relative sanctity of his classroom.

The television reporter, as earnest as her helmeted bouffant would allow, thrust a microphone into his face. "Dr. Rayfield, any comments?"

He was momentarily distracted by the extraordinarily red luster of her lips, a crimson shade that would shame any drag queen, but quickly recovered to say, "Yes. I commend these students for expressing their views. They are what democracy in America is all about."

Not remotely satisfied with his generous response, she tried again, red lips pursed for attack, "But, they are saying you are racist. How do you feel about that? Are you a racist, Dr. Rayfield?"

Stephen smiled patiently, and wondered to himself for a moment if it was true that the camera added ten pounds. Such fluffy ruminations always reassured him in times of crisis. "No, that is absurd," he answered, "and I deeply regret that anyone assumes otherwise."

Suddenly, he could feel his heart pounding, as he stared into the bright lights of the cameras. He wanted to tell his smirking inquisitor that they lived in a culture of intellectual bankruptcy, a wink and a nod society that cared only for appearances. The agonies of the least fortunate could be tolerated and prolonged so long as one did not, heaven forbid, point to them and say the impolitic thing. An indelicate remark was the cardinal sin. He wanted to tell her that only honest questions lead to answers worth having. Too often the perceived wisdom is neatly labeled and then packed away, like boxes in the basement. Dusty. Undisturbed. Worthless. *Boxes in the basement, he thought. No, she'll never get that.* This was television, the local news, for God's sake. He knew that her editor would allow at most a five-second sound bite.

"But, of course I respect the concerns of these students," he offered blandly, noticing the collapse of the reporter's ruby red lips into a judicious pout, "and I hope they will return to class and contribute their viewpoints."

Then, in a seamless, defiant choreography, Chris and the other students silently turned to face the wall, their backs to their former professor, and began pounding their chests in unison with their right fists. Sensing more incendiary ground, the reporter moved on to the students, and Stephen continued to his classroom.

The class now consisted of only sixteen students, whose attendance was fueled not so much by an interest in American history as by a fascination for television cameras. Nothing conveyed legitimacy quite like video. This was *real.* They looked expectantly at Stephen, still marveling that their unassuming young instructor was somehow the source of such attention.

"How is everyone this morning?" Stephen began. "I hope you all managed to get here without too much difficulty. Today, we are going to continue our discussion with regard to crime, race, and, just for good, clean fun, the media. Miss Bennett, your thoughts?"

Later that evening, Stephen treated himself to a glass of chardonnay. He sat quietly on the balcony of his apartment, listening to the distant hum of traffic coursing by the Edwardian Arms. Since, in his limited experience the only way to assuage the pangs of one drama was to simply create another one, he decided to call Dylan. They had not talked in over a year. He walked back inside the apartment, poured another fortifying glass of wine, and dialed the number.

A familiar voice answered. "Hello?" Stephen noted that Dylan had retained his energetic urgency, bordering on impatience, no matter what the situation.

"Dylan? Hi. It's Stephen." There was an awkward silence. Clearly, Stephen still had the power, regrettably, to give Dylan pause. "Hello? Anybody there?"

"It's been a while," Dylan finally said.

"I know. I wanted to call you so many times, but I wasn't sure you would want to talk to me." Now it was Stephen's turn to wait, as he recalled that panicked moment last year when Dylan had come to see him in Durham. *Stephen? Are you there? I couldn't stay away any longer.*

"How have you been?" Dylan asked. His good manners never failed him.

"Oh, you know. Busy. Trying to get the hang of this teaching thing. And, let me tell you, Charlotte is definitely an acquired taste."

"A little too quiet?" *Who's this? Dylan had asked, staring in disbelief at the man in Stephen's bed.*

"No, not exactly. They actually have signs of life downtown now. But, self-conscious as ever. They still freak when the newspapers refer to it as Charlotte, North Carolina. 'Nobody says Atlanta, *Georgia!* You never hear them say New York, *New York.*'"

"Jeez, how tiresome," Dylan said.

"So, how's your residency going?" *Please don't go, Stephen had begged.*

"It's going. Honestly, I'd give anything for a full night's sleep." *How could you do this to me? Dylan had asked, and then that wordless, wounded look of betrayal.*

"Oh, you'll be fine," Stephen said. "I never knew anyone who could fall asleep as easily as you. Anyway, I was reading an article today about the riots in Paris. Did you see that on the news?"

"Yeah. Terrible, wasn't it?" *Were there others? I just need to know. Were there others?*

"Just amazing. I still can't imagine that beautiful city in such a state," Stephen said. "You know I always think of you when Paris comes up, Dylan. Our trip there was the happiest time of my life. It was great, wasn't it?" *I was lonely. I'm sorry.*

"Yes. It was. But, well..." *I don't want to hear another word.*

"I know. I miss you. I just wanted to tell you again how sorry..." *Can't you forgive me? Stephen had pleaded.*

"No, stop," Dylan said, "you don't have to do that. Let's just leave it alone, okay?" *I'm going to go now, he had said, and then he had hugged Stephen. Kissed his cheek. I have to go now.*

"Sure. That's fine. I just wanted to say hello."

"No problem," Dylan said. He was strangely as resonant and engaging as that night when they had first met out on the deck, but now there was an unassailable distance. "I'm meeting someone in about thirty minutes, so, listen, thanks for calling. It's good to hear from you, Stephen. Take care."

Stephen sat in the quiet living room, cocooned within the sterile walls of the Edwardian Arms, and, for just a moment, allowed himself to recall their first evening in Paris. They were in his friend Jean-Luc's little car, driving along the Rue de Rivoli. Dylan sat in the front and Stephen in the back. As they followed the bright wave of cars toward the Place de la Concorde, shimmering in crimson and gold, Dylan reached his hand back toward Stephen. And, for a while, in a blaze of lights and beauty, they were so happy.

CHAPTER THIRTY-ONE
LET ME SOW LOVE

Reverend Dunlap did not usually see parishioners individually. His flock had grown far too large to allow for such specific pastoral guidance. And, not coincidentally, his wife had strongly cautioned him that his spiritual effectiveness was perhaps more compelling at a distance than in more intimate encounters. But, for Laura Caldwell, he was willing to make an exception. She seemed so anguished, so desperate for her son, a fine young man for whom she harbored the most disturbing, indeed disgusting, suspicions. Plus, Laura and her husband were among the church's most generous donors. The Caldwell family was a pillar of the church, and such pillars merited any Christian counsel Reverend Dunlap could provide.

"Laura. Andrew. Ben," he said, carefully enunciating each of their names, no doubt in order of their pecuniary significance. "Always a joy to see you."

The three took their seats in front of the reverend's desk. Ben focused his eyes on the floor, and shifted nervously in his seat. Laura looked patiently, imploringly at her son, as Andrew stared out the window of Reverend Dunlap's office. Beyond the window, encircled by tightly clipped boxwoods, was a life-size statue of St. Francis of Assisi, head bowed in an expression of bemused contemplation.

"Thank you, Reverend," Laura began, haltingly. "You are so kind to take the time to see us. I…we…are worried about…" Her eyes filled with tears. She looked at her son with great tenderness, unable to go on.

"I know this is hard for you," the reverend said, "but all things are possible with God. There is no burden that He cannot provide comfort to you. Jesus loves you, whatever your worry." He shifted his gaze, almost accusingly, at Ben, and added, "Whatever your sin."

"He's a good boy," Andrew Caldwell interjected.

"He's just confused," Laura continued. "I'm sorry to say that, Ben, but it is true. You just have not been yourself. So quiet, keeping to yourself. It just isn't like you, son. Whatever is bothering you, you need to tell us."

Ben felt the laser-like gaze of all three adults, the anticipatory hush of their relentless concern. He felt as if they were all poised on a cliff together, catching their collective breath, waiting to plunge. Waiting for him. It seemed that everyone was always waiting for him. Everyone, that is, but Johnny Harrison. Ben searched for the right words to answer them, but none came.

"Ben, this should be a great time in your life," Reverend Dunlap said, his sonorous voice deepening to a more menacing whisper. "God has blessed you with a wonderful family, with a bright future. You have a fine life ahead of you, son. But, you are troubled about something. Let me ask you a question. Is there anyone you are able to confide in, anyone that you can talk to?"

"I talk to people," Ben said lamely. "When I need to."

"What about *Jesus*?" the reverend continued, almost hissing now with each breathy syllable, and his lip curling up in a tentative snarl. "Do you talk to Jesus, Ben? Do you ask our *Savior* to help you? To give you strength?"

"I say my prayers every night, sure," Ben replied.

"That is a pro forma answer, young man," Reverend Dunlap gasped, as if this exhaustive inquiry was taxing the last of his strength. He suddenly raised up in his chair, pointing his finger at Ben menacingly. "Do you really *talk* to Jesus? Because let me tell you right now, and hear me good now, Ben, whether you do or you don't,

Jesus knows *every* thought you have. He knows *every* deed, every hidden act. Every. Single. Thing."

"Well, yes, but..." Ben stumbled.

"You cannot hide from Jesus," Reverend Dunlap bellowed. "Jesus knows *who* you are! Jesus knows *what* you are!" The reverend paused, arching his eyes skyward, then glanced at St. Francis. Calm again, his voice now thick and syrupy as molasses, he cooed, "So, tell us, Ben. Tell us so we can be soldiers for Jesus. So we can help you."

Ben looked at his mother and father, then back to the insistent eyes of Reverend Dunlap. He felt a growing and panicked claustrophobia.

"Confess to Jesus," the reverend whispered, almost caressing Ben with his words. "Jesus already knows all there is to know. Tell us, tell us what is on your heart."

"Mom. Dad." He looked at them with a fearful resolve, edging toward a precipice from which there would be no return. "I think maybe I am gay."

CHAPTER THIRTY-TWO
REUNION

Missy refused to endure the Harrison family reunions. Her disdain for the lower orders of the spindly Harrison family tree, a contempt that she had successfully transmitted to her son, John, had only intensified with the years. She could now dissect its diseased limbs right down to the roots and beyond. "I won't go to their reunions," she once told Edward, "but I might show up at their funerals."

The enforced congeniality that she projected to the Harrison clan on the rare occasions on which she encountered them masked, barely, the disdain with which she viewed them. It was still a source of wonder to her that Edward could have emerged dry and intact from such a swamp of mediocrity.

So, once again Edward found himself asking, "You're sure you don't want to come? Just for the luncheon?"

Missy was seated at the desk in her bedroom, carefully applying her makeup and reviewing her schedule for the weekend. "No. Have a good time. But, no," she answered, studying her appointments book for the inclusion of yet another manicure or seaweed bath. It was Saturday morning, and she wore a sheer flesh-colored negligee, designed to accentuate, yet enticingly obscure, every inch of naked skin underneath. Get a good look, she thought, watching her husband finish dressing.

"Are you in the show this year?" she asked, struggling not to dwell on his unfortunate choice of a dark green, wrinkled polo shirt.

"No. I told them I was too busy to come to the rehearsals," he said, "which is true."

Every year, the Harrisons 'put on a show', a chaotic assembly of skits and mostly lip-synched songs. There was a competition between the North Carolina Harrisons and the Florida Harrisons. This had begun only several years after Rose Harrison's death. With the departure of Edward's grandmother, the matriarchal glue that had held such a disparate family together, other unifying efforts were needed.

"Well, lucky man, then. What is the theme this year, if I may inquire?" Last year, he had reported, they had attempted a cruise ship motif. This overreaching production almost succeeded until the papier mache railings of the 'boat' were tripped over by the too enthusiastic dancing of the irrepressible, and talentless, sextet of female cousins who called themselves the Harrisonellas. But why even think about that now, Missy wondered. Too ghastly.

"Harrisons traveling the globe in search of their roots," he said, smiling. "It has an international theme."

"Oh, that sounds lovely," she said derisively. "Am I correct in assuming there will be no stops in Africa?"

He ignored her question, tired now of her sarcasm. "Missy, I'm not looking forward to it either, but they are family. Right? If your family had a reunion, God forbid, I would go."

"Really?" she asked. "Well, you are welcome to accompany me on my next visit to see Mom and Ellen. I can't promise any formal entertainment, but…"

Edward frowned. He loathed Missy's family easily as much as she loathed his. But, if her own background was dismal, Missy at least was resolute in leaving it behind. She could never understand why Edward insisted on returning to the Harrison's fetid ground every year, so that he could drunkenly splash around once more with the worst of them. The irony of course was that he had absolutely nothing to do with any of them the rest of the year, including the bottom feeders like Evelyn Peck and her son, who actually lived in

Charlotte. If the deep roots of the Harrison clan remained intact, they seemed to endure with only sporadic attention.

Edward had one firm rule regarding the reunions. He always pretended to be glad to see the people there, even if he was not. This resolve was tested almost immediately, and most tellingly, when he and his daughter entered the party room of the Comfort Inn. He glimpsed the determined approach of Evelyn Peck rushing toward him from the buffet table set against the far wall. Her arms were outstretched and her thin lips were puckered in grim assertion, such that he could not be sure if she intended to kiss him or wrestle him to the floor.

"Edward," he heard her shriek, "get over here and give me a big ole hug!" Her son, Keith, towering above her, followed quietly and with evident embarrassment.

Andrea, motivated by hunger as well as an aversion to Evelyn Peck, left her father and headed to the buffet. Edward tried not to recoil as he was encased by Evelyn's pale, fleshy arms, one of which still clutched a greasy chicken wing.

While he endured the annual pudgy embrace of Evelyn and the imminent drip of chicken grease on his shirt, he wondered how Missy would respond to her, in the extremely unlikely event that their paths should ever cross. With some admiration, he imagined Missy demolishing Evelyn with one arched and loaded eyebrow.

"Good to see you, Evelyn," he said, trying to avoid the wiry red hair that brushed against his mouth. "And Keith. How are things, son?"

"Okay, I guess," Keith mumbled. Keith, as always, hung back, an awkward accompaniment to the galloping effusiveness of his mother.

"Good. Good. Good to see you both," Edward stammered, searching the room for a palatable excuse to leave them. "You're looking good Evelyn."

"Thanks! Same back at ya," she said, smiling the gap-toothed smile that had mysteriously hooked poor cousin Jerry. Evelyn was wearing a snug silver lame pantsuit with a barely zipped front.

With each succeeding year, as Evelyn's body had expanded, her attire had correspondingly shrunk, and she was now as securely synched into her shimmering outfit as a link of Jimmy Dean sausage. She excitedly fidgeted with a multi-colored rhinestone cross that lay across her well-padded, uplifted, bosom. "See that man over there?" she asked, pointing toward a portly fellow who was talking to cousin Madge. "I've got my eye on *him*, and he's got his eye on *me!*"

"Well, should be a fun time for you, then," Edward replied, trying not to stare at the slight mustache above her abbreviated lips. Those constricted lips. So incongruous in staking a claim on that wide jello body.

She played idly with the zipper of her pantsuit and smacked her lips lasciviously. "Fun? I reckon so," she said, then, moving in on her prey, whispered, "Course, I guess you been havin' a little fun too. Am I right?"

"Well, I do all right." His baritone voice seemed an octave deeper, with a forced joviality that signaled weakness. This was not a prudent signal to afford Evelyn Peck.

"I heard that," she said, as she pushed her frizzy red hair over her forehead. "Course I never thought I'd see you, you know, *there*."

"There?" he asked innocently. "I don't know..."

"Come on, now," she interrupted, impatient with the deepening timbre of his cheerful voice. "Don't kid a kidder," she said, whispering now with covert animation. "Gastonia? The motel...

"Oh...well, I just wanted to tell you...See, the thing is, the other day...at that...place..."

"Yeah. I thought that was you," she said, her lips stretched to their limit in a triumphant smile. "But, listen, it ain't none of my business."

"Thanks, I appreciate that," Edward mumbled.

"Not a problem. Hey, we are family after all. We stick by each other. And...we *help* each other, right?" Her last comment was equal parts question and conclusion, and seemed to Edward to have the unmistakable tone of a pending request. He was used to hearing that tone in more sedate boardrooms, and was startled for a moment to find it in the fleshy assertions of Evelyn Peck.

"Yes. We do," he said, halfheartedly. "And if there is ever anything I can do for you, well, you just let me know."

"Oh, no, Keith and me is just fine," she said. "Ain't that right, Keith?" She nudged her son, who seemed to be staring off into space, lost in some world of his own.

"Huh?" Keith asked. "Yeah, sure, I guess so. Hey, look, I'm gonna go get a beer."

"Good seeing you, son. Well, thanks again," Edward said, giving Evelyn a hug.

"Right," Evelyn replied, breathing closely into Edward's ear, then adding, "Oh, wait, there is one thing maybe you could help us with."

"Oh?" Edward asked warily.

"Yeah. We need a new roof on our old house something bad. I was wondering maybe if you could help us out with that. I mean, you know lots of contractors and maybe could get someone out there who would give us a pretty good deal?" She put one hand on his shoulder, then added, "A *real* good deal."

"Sure. No problem. Glad to help. And, thanks again for your discretion."

"My what? Oh, right. You bet. After all, I know we can count on each other. That's what family is for, right?"

"Yes, that's for sure. So true. Okay, then. Take care. And let's try and get together real soon."

"That'd be great. Sure enough! And say hello to Missy for me, y'hear?"

"Will do. Oh, there's Mom," he said, spying his mother and easing his way out of the clutches of Evelyn Peck.

Evelyn hugged him again, surprisingly tightly given the flabbiness of her arms. "Don't you worry about a thing, hon." Edward pulled back decisively. She looked at him and twirled her fingers in a dramatic gesture and then cackled loudly, "You can always count on old Evvie! Like a bug on shit!"

Oh Lord, look," Myrtle whispered to her daughter, Lynn, nodding toward Edward across the room, engulfed in the clutches of Evelyn Peck. "Your dad used to say that Evelyn was the trampiest woman he had ever met. And, I hate to say it, but that man knew more than his share of trampy women."

"Grandmom," Stephen said, laughing. "There's a story there, I bet."

"Hah. There might be, but you won't hear it from me. Don't tell all you know. That's what the old folks used to say, 'Don't tell all you know,' and they was right on the money." Then she added mournfully, "Look at that son of hers. I don't think he has ever worked a full day in his life. Well, at least he's calmed down since the doctor put him on some kind of medicine."

"Calm?" Lynn asked. "Mother, he looks as if he's almost catatonic."

"Cata...what? I don't know why my children use such big words!" She looked over at her son, who was now giving Evelyn a parting hug, which apparently was the price of freedom from continued conversation with her. In typical Harrison fashion, he patted her several times on the back. She had to admire her son's style, an unflappable demeanor no doubt honed in all those meetings with bankers. But, Evelyn's pudgy embrace was prolonged and unyielding. She was waving her stubby hand in front of Edward's face and laughing uproariously. "Stephen, go rescue your uncle, honey," Myrtle said. "He's trapped over there."

They watched as Stephen seamlessly integrated himself into that unwieldy group, with Evelyn Peck almost smothering him in her expansive breasts, and Edward just as smoothly slipped away.

"Hi," he said, greeting his mother and sister, and noticing that Andrea was still circling the buffet table. "Well, the gangs all here. What time does the show start?"

"Curtain will be going up in about fifteen minutes," Lynn replied, giving her brother a hug. "Plenty of time to say hello to the rest of the assembled clan, now that you have escaped from the Pecker." Lynn had given that salacious nickname to Evelyn the year after cousin Jerry had died. The newly married Evelyn showed up at the reunion that year in a tight black mini-skirt, possibly her notion of widow's reeds, and spent most of the weekend with one of the husbands of a second cousin.

"What on earth was she holding on to you like that for?" Myrtle asked.

"Mom, please, you have to ask?" he said evasively. "I *am* a man. She *is* Evelyn. Need I say more?"

"No, honey, I know Evelyn," Myrtle said. "If a man is still breathing, he's still fair game. Anyway, we had to send Stephen over to rescue you."

"And I appreciate it, that's for certain," Edward said. "He's a brave man."

"Yes, he is, and he needs to be lately," Lynn said. She had already called Edward on several occasions, concerned with what she viewed as a growing witch hunt against her son. "I am still so angry about that ridiculous television show."

"The one with the Barbie doll?" Myrtle asked. "Oh, I saw it. It just burned me up. My glory, I said to Fred, 'Fred, how can they get away with this?' Saying Stephen doesn't like blacks. Good Lord, he has always been a liberal. Everybody knows that! Those shows are run by a bunch of communists. That's why I only watch Fox…"

"Well, it will all blow over," Edward said, interrupting his mother as she was commenting on how sexy Brit Hume was. "I spoke the other day with Chancellor Dunn."

"You did?" Lynn asked. "Does Stephen know?"

"No, I haven't said anything to him about it."

"That's just as well," Lynn replied. "He didn't ask for help getting the job, and I doubt he will ever ask for help in keeping it. But, I will, Edward. And I really want you to know how grateful I am. I know I can always count on you." She paused, and then added, "And Missy, of course. Missy too."

Just then the noisy laughter of Evelyn Peck, who was apparently amused by something Stephen had said, came blasting across the room like a discordant harmony, overwhelming any tenuous melody lingering below.

CHAPTER THIRTY-THREE
STONEHAVEN RETREAT

The therapist was named Paul Douglas. He was in his forties, but boyish, with thinning brown hair, precisely cut and carefully parted on the right side. Ben sat on a gray, vinyl cushioned sofa, uncertain as to what he should say. Reverend Dunlap had urged that something called reparative therapy was necessary. "Mr. Douglas has helped many young people with this treatment," the reverend had insisted. "He is an expert in his field. You don't *have* to be homosexual, Ben."

You don't have to be...

Mr. Douglas' small office was in his home in the Stonehaven neighborhood. Stonehaven, much like the therapist who lived there, was nondescript, middle class, rigidly traditional. Its well-kept, red brick ranch style homes, bordered by an inexhaustible supply of azaleas and liriope, dated back to the sixties. If Stonehaven lacked the flashy opulence of newer communities, it at least could claim, for Charlotte, a certain age-related deference.

The therapist sat at the other end of the sofa, looking intently at Ben. He continued his studious regard of Ben and then suddenly asked, "When did you realize that you might be homosexual?"

"I'm not sure," Ben said.

"Were you always attracted to other boys?" Mr. Douglas lowered his voice to a conspiratorial tone, as if he were tracking the advent of leprosy or some other hideous affliction. "You can be honest with me, Ben."

"Yes, sir," Ben answered nervously, averting his eyes from the therapist's appraisal. "I think that I have always wondered… But, I thought maybe it was a phase, you know, or that I was just confused."

"I know that must have been difficult for you," he said, as he jotted down notes on a small notebook. "I had to deal with that when I was your age too. So how did you deal with this attraction to other boys."

"I just tried to block it out of my mind. Or, I told myself that, if I seemed to be attracted to a guy, I was just thinking about a *girl* being attracted to him, and it was the idea of the girl that excited me."

"Well, that's a rather inventive strategy," Mr. Douglas said, allowing a brief, furtive smile. "I have to compliment you on your creativity. So when did that stop working for you?"

"When what stopped?"

"Your being able to block those thoughts about other guys out of your mind. When were you unable to do that?"

For a moment, Ben recalled the night by the lake with John, remembering the rain beating down on the car as John slowly unzipped his pants. "I guess…well, I have…I *had* this friend. John. My best friend since junior high. And, well, something happened." Ben paused uncertainly, then added, "It is very hard for me to talk about it."

"I understand, Ben," the therapist said. "I know exactly how you feel."

"Really? You do?"

"Yes, of course. But, if you want it badly enough, you can change. I did, and I have worked with many other men and women who have as well. Reparative therapy has helped all of them lead normal lives. The gay rights people will tell you that you have to be gay. Don't you believe it. You can have a great life with a woman and have children and be the person you want to be. But, it is hard work. You have to want it. Do you?"

"My parents want me to. When I told them I was…well, when I told them about this, Dad just stared out the window and Mom cried. I don't think I have ever seen her so upset. Ever. That was rough."

"But, do *you* want to change?"

"Yes," he said uncertainly. "It's a sin, right? And my mom…seeing her so unhappy and all. But, no, I don't want to be gay. And I don't really think I am. Not really. It isn't me. I *know* that."

"Then you won't be. It's as simple as that," the therapist said. He put down his notebook, pausing for a moment. "Now, if we are going to work together, we need to be very honest with each other, so I will have to ask you some very personal questions, Ben. I don't want you to feel uncomfortable, but this is essential for you to overcome these urges that you have. When you…well, when you, let us say, pleasure yourself, do you think of boys or girls?"

"Boys. Before. And then I try to only think of girls. During."

"How does that work out?"

"Well, sometimes, okay. But, other times, I just can't help it. Like, say, I saw an ad in a magazine of a male model, then I might think of him. What it would be like to be with him. I want to push it out of my mind, but…So, you know, I try not to do *that*…jerking off…at all, but it's hard not to."

"No. Of course not. It is a burden. Testosterone running wild," Mr. Douglas said, allowing himself an abbreviated, high-pitched chuckle. Then, serious again, he continued in his low voice, "But, you have to work on your masculine side. There are scientifically proven methods to help you do this. So, for example, you should avoid magazines that would have those kinds of pictures. You know, fitness magazines and fashion magazines. Those are not the magazines that real men tend to read. Way too feminine! So, here's an assignment for you, Ben. For the next week, I want you to only read *Sports Illustrated* and *Car and Driver*. Okay?"

"Yeah, okay, I can do that."

"And I want you to not, you know, *self*-pleasure at all. That, I suspect, has encouraged your unnatural desires. You are flying with the wrong co-pilot. You have to redirect your focus. So, I want you to think of a girl that you like. And then I want you to picture yourself married to her, and imagine what it would be like to be with her, to have children, in your own home where it's comfortable and safe. Can you do that, Ben?"

"Sure. I think I can."

"You can! You can. Visualize! Visualize what you want! The feelings you sometimes have for other men, like your friend, those feelings are real. I'm not going to tell you they aren't. But, that doesn't condemn you to being homosexual. Those feelings can be controlled."

"I'm sorry, sir. I'm not sure I understand."

"Those feelings for other guys are just weeds, Ben. Crabgrass! Just intrusive thoughts." He glanced at the clock on the wall. "Well, listen, our time is about up. What I want you to get here today is that you can learn to relate to men in a nonsexual way and you can have a normal, loving relationship with a woman. But, that requires confidence in your own maleness and trust in other men."

"Thank you, Mr. Douglas. I appreciate your helping me. I'm going to try. I really will."

"You'll be fine. But, you have to believe that." Ben flinched when the therapist walked over and put his arm around him. Mr. Douglas patted him on the back, a sort of locker room congratulatory gesture that one teammate might give another after a winning game.

CHAPTER THIRTY-FOUR
THE GOOD ROADS GOVERNOR

Missy lay in her bed. It was gray outside, with just a sliver of morning sunlight filtered through the window. She was wearing a new negligee, trimmed in blue silk, and pondering her failure to kindle some last flickering ember in her husband. After so many years, her feelings for Edward were more proprietary than passionate, but when she got into bed the night before he was already asleep, and she was not inclined to rouse him. She was vaguely uneasy though, as she contemplated her upcoming trip to their Pawleys Island vacation home. She would be there for two weeks with Andrea, while John was still in D.C. and Edward would remain at home. Alone, she hoped. Just in case though, she had impressed upon him that several of their matronly neighbors had assured her that they would be happy to look in on him. *Frequently.*

For Missy, physical longing had become something she dimly remembered, sometimes fondly, but strangely in the past now. The middle-aged, gray-haired man snoring faintly in their Venetian bed had once been a blond, lean, square-jawed college tennis player, like a young Robert Redford. When she met him, he was tenaciously hunting for real estate and for women, and not in that order. She was working as an administrative assistant to one of the architects Edward was cultivating for new projects.

Even then, early in their romance, she remembered there was a sort of poetry watching Edward Harrison play tennis. If there was one moment when she realized that she loved him, it was the sight of his determined, sweaty abandon on the court, the light glistening on the golden hair of his legs, his thighs pumping like pistons as he drove himself mercilessly to win. It was clear, she knew, he hated to lose as much as she did. The middle-aged man in her bed had long since given up tennis, not to mention abandon, and his legs, while retaining their general muscular outline, were pale now and softening. But, he retained his relentless drive and will to win. She still held in great esteem that one aspect of her husband, even if she had grown indifferent to the rest.

They had once been so hungry for each other. She had intended to remain, at least in the technical sense, virginal until marriage. In truth, there had been an exquisite pleasure in the nightly drama of Edward's desperate pleading, usually followed by gasping, moaning fumblings of buttons and zippers, and explosive shrieks of relief. Those frantic explorations were eventually followed by a settled, domesticated routine, which was nourishing if not exactly mouthwatering. In time though, even that meager diet had been diminished, a situation to which she was usually reconciled.

The ongoing sexual famine to which she was now subjected had roused her instinctive suspicions as well as her abiding competitiveness. Yet, while she was attuned to the threat of infidelity, she could not quite bring herself to accept its actuality. This hesitation was based not on her faith in her husband's loyalty to her, or in his moral code, but rather in his innate sense of order. He was far too self-contained to admit anyone else into his life. My God, she shuddered, he barely has room for us.

Edward detested clutter and intrusion, either tangible or emotional, and it was highly unlikely that he would endure the general messiness of an affair. But not, Missy realized, impossible. She was not naive. Indeed, she had long been aware of the marital intrigues and betrayals among many of her friends and family. Such knowledge was still imparted in whispers and in arched, disapproving brows, but with a brutal and unforgiving precision. Missy was as cognizant of these connubial train wrecks as she was of the thread counts of the sheets on which the sinners thrashed about with such illicit abandon.

Missy had never felt any serious inclination to stray. Tattered and decrepit as her marriage might be, she expected fidelity. It was in her view the one remaining courtesy, the last measure of respect, in a fading union. She could endure Edward's impatience, petulance, and even condescension over the years, but in this single demand, she would not yield. Her continental pretensions, while allowing free rein in wine and fabrics, did not extend to sex.

Flawed as he was, she still regarded Edward Harrison as one of the more impressive ornaments of her storied life. If she had festering doubts as to his appeal, she had none with regard to his value. She might overlook infidelity on moralistic grounds, but would never deign to do so on egotistical ones. For Missy, the greatest sins would always be the ones that betrayed her vanity.

Missy moved to the divan beside her palladian window and began reading the latest edition of *Charlotte Now,* a periodical that she found particularly soothing. It was a rabidly boosterish publication and an unfailing source of amusement, intentional or not. Acutely aware of the insufficiencies of her own lackluster background, not to mention Edward's, she delighted in feasting on any shortcomings in the pedigrees of others. While comfortable with all manner of pretense on her part, as evidenced by the family portraits that lined her own hallway, she was rarely fooled by the pretensions of others. She had been a scrappy player in the social whirl of Charlotte long enough to quickly note any chinks in the armor of her fellow combatants, most of which could be reliably found between the lines in the puffery of *Charlotte Now.*

She especially relished the historic embarrassments of Charlotte's oldest families, which would be to say the most snobbish and, at least in the beginning, the most resistant to her tenacious climb. Most of them would have ignored her entirely had it not been for her friendship with Laura, a benefit for which Missy still felt a resentful gratitude. And while Missy had studied the old dinosaurs with singular attention, she had always been intrigued by Laura's comparable indifference to them. Missy was not in general a student of history, but she was a devoted scholar of the tortured bloodlines coursing through the native aristocracy.

And so, it was with particular glee that she devoured a glowing profile of former Governor Cameron Morrison. She relished the whitewashing, as it were, of ancient figures like Morrison. Despite a stunning record, even for the 1920s, of racist politicking, he was now, and forever more, to be known simply, reverently, as the "good roads governor."

Missy walked downstairs to the kitchen. She poured herself a cup of coffee and treated herself to one half of a blueberry muffin, as she continued reading every juicy morsel. The article obliquely noted that Governor Morrison was "a bold and crafty politician" but assured the dear reader that such talents had gone to the greater good in his tireless promotion of paving over the state with new roads. Once he was done with his efforts as transportation savior, he lived a life of baronial splendor, thanks to the tobacco wealth of his second wife.

Cameron Morrison's 3000 acre estate, Morrocroft, later afforded his family the opportunity to develop the SouthPark Mall, not to mention the gated refuge where the Harrisons now lived. The governor had died in 1953, at the age of 83, probably still cocooned in a segregated world. Missy guessed that the only blacks he was likely to encounter were the ones who shined his shoes or took care of the thousands of chickens on his property.

Missy was intrigued, impressed even, by the wily old governor, long since gone to his maker, and his still prominent descendants. She was hardly an advocate of retrospective guilt and, indeed, begrudged the governor and his family nothing. What fascinated her though was the evident need to polish him up and make him presentable to latter day Charlotte strivers. The transparently artificial New South, totally dependent on collective amnesia. She loved it. Accustomed as she had become to slogging her way up that hill with them, she was still amused by all the panting deceptions.

The Italians, in her view, were much more sensible. Imagine reading that Lucretia Borgia was the "Good Schools Empress" with careful omission of her unfortunate tendency to disembowel those individuals who impeded her more material ambitions.

Missy nonetheless delighted in the realization that even Charlotte's most distinguished families were apparently not immune to the need to dress up the past. One way or another, they too were forever touching up the family portraits. This was a comforting thought for Missy.

The previous evening, at supper, she had actually offered to take Edward's mother shopping. Determined to placate her increasingly distant husband, she was prepared to endure strolling through the marble halls of Neiman Marcus with Myrtle. Myrtle! A family portrait beyond retouching.

"Should I check for fever?" Edward had asked.

"Don't be silly," Missy said. "I have always been fond of your mom. Maybe we don't have a lot in common, but I've always liked her."

"Who are you?" he asked, laughing. "And what have you done with my wife?"

Missy smiled with the assurance of someone who knew exactly who she was. She was Mrs. Edward Harrison. And she intended to remain so. And the *occasional* sacrifice, such as a brief shopping expedition to SouthPark Mall with her embarrassing mother-in-law, was a fair price to pay.

CHAPTER THIRTY-FIVE
COFFEE AND DESSERT

Hurtling along the mammoth freeway that surrounded Charlotte like an umbilical cord, giving life to ever more sprawling development, Stephen sped past the gleaming Uptown towers and smiled. Having grown up in New York, he was amused by Charlotte's perverse designation of an uptown in the absence of any corresponding *downtown*.

It was with some relief when he entered the Dilworth neighborhood. Dilworth was Charlotte's oldest suburb, had pedestrian friendly sidewalks, and was about ten merciful miles away from the plastic environs of the Edwardian Arms. Its neatly trimmed blocks of historic homes seemed to Stephen to be a journey back to what Charlotte might have once been.

He continued along East Boulevard and parked his car in front of Dilworth Coffee. The coffee shop was an oasis, Stephen suspected, for all of the Charlotte transplants searching for some semblance of what so many of them had left behind elsewhere in other cities. Tranquil, comfortably aged Dilworth was one of the few places in Charlotte that didn't exhaust itself trying too hard to impress. Interestingly, it had become one of the trendiest places in Charlotte. The neighborhood on Saturday mornings was scenic with runners and al fresco diners and mothers pushing strollers to Freedom Park. Secular and leisurely.

Sunday mornings belonged to Charlotte's churches, just as surely as weekdays belonged to the banks, but Saturdays alone were ripe with flexibility.

Stephen ordered a latte and sat down at a brightly painted table by the window. Customers flowed in and out of the little cafe. It reminded Stephen of the Ninth Street Cafe near the Duke campus in Durham, minus the preponderance of students, and had acquired a certain cachet as a hip place to people watch. A *hip* place, Stephen mused. What compliant, trendy cattle we really are, all of us. These Birkenstock-hooved sophisticates would be shocked that, in their flocking together, they were no different than the conclaves of south Georgia rednecks guzzling Buds out at the truck stop.

An elderly couple sat at a table next to Stephen's, and conversed with such tender, solicitous grace, it was like watching a minuet. Stephen enviously regarded the way the man would occasionally reach out and lightly touch the woman's hand, as if the two were on their first date, as if somehow they were still, after so many years, still getting to know one another.

Suddenly, Stephen heard the squeaking of the front door, and felt a blast of hot summer air. He looked up, and saw Ben Caldwell walk inside. Despite the humid day, the young man seemed fresh, unblemished by the slightest hint of sweat or languor. He wore baggy, white shorts, which failed to minimize the thickness of his long legs, and a Duke Blue Devils tee-shirt. As his gaze focused on the room, he squinted for an instant, and then saw Stephen, and just as quickly his crisp assurance seemed to give way to a shadowy discomfort.

Stephen smiled and waved hello. "Ben? Hi. You may not remember, but we met at the Rolling Stones concert last month."

"Dr. Rayfield?" Ben asked, his palm shielded over his forehead now, as if he were surveying an uncertain landscape.

"Good to see you again," Stephen said, rising from the table. "You survived the Stones concert after all. I'm glad."

"Yes, I guess so," Ben replied, crossing his arms against his chest, his pumped muscles a sort of assertion of strength.

"Well, this is a nice surprise. Do you live near here?"

"Here? No. I just finished working out at the Y."

"That's great. I need to get over there myself sometime," Stephen said. "Listen, if you're not in a hurry, can I get you a cup of coffee?"

"No, thanks. I really should get going."

"You sure?" Stephen asked. "Even if I throw in a cookie? You know it is practically an unwritten law that a workout should always be followed by something bad for you."

"No, I didn't know that," Ben said, suppressing a laugh. "But, if it's a rule, okay, one cookie."

Had anyone observed them from a distance, it might be concluded that the two young men were of similar age and background. Each possessed a sort of toned and ripe Abercrombie and Fitch athleticism. Their gradual rapport was a congenial blend of Stephen's natural empathy and Ben's inherent politeness. And yet there remained, always lurking, a resurgent tension between them.

"I shouldn't be here," Ben finally said warily, his unease breaking through the surface. "My therapist wouldn't like it. It's just, you seem like a nice person."

"You see a therapist? God, they're getting a hold of you guys younger and younger, aren't they?" Stephen smiled, undeterred by Ben's perplexed expression. "Hey, listen, we're just having coffee. No crime in that, is there?"

"No. I guess not. But, well, you...your lifestyle and all."

"You mean gay? How do you know that?"

"John mentioned it."

"And?"

"I'm not that way, if you're wondering."

"Okay. What would your therapist say about your having a scandalous cup of coffee with..." Stephen paused and looked around the room dramatically, then whispered, "with a known homosexual."

Ben grinned despite himself. "He says that the easiest way to resist temptation is to avoid it."

"Trust me, no one is tempted by assistant professors at UNCC," Stephen said, wondering what exactly was the nature of Ben's temptations, but suspecting the answer. "Your therapist sounds rather like Oscar Wilde. How surprising."

"Why do you say that?"

"Well, Oscar Wilde was a gay writer well-versed in temptation."

"They don't teach him in my school."

"No, I suppose they wouldn't," Stephen said. "He was a silly man, self-destructive, but a great playwright. Great wit. When he toured America and they asked him if he had anything to declare, he said, 'Only my genius.'"

"That's pretty funny," Ben laughed, revealing a glittering expanse of white teeth.

"You have a great smile," Stephen said, "I was wondering what your smile would be like."

"Well, now you know," he said defensively, his full lips collapsing into a more somber expression.

"Anyway, Oscar Wilde," Stephen continued, "He was a bit of a fool and a *big* old homosexual. Bad combination. It's okay to be a train wreck of infinite vices, but not to love other men."

Ben frowned, tellingly it seemed to Stephen, at the reference to loving men. "Sorry," Stephen said, "I get a little carried away sometimes."

"No, it's fine," Ben said. "You talk a lot though, don't you?" Stephen again glimpsed amusement in those mournful eyes.

"It runs in my family. You should meet my Grandmother Myrtle. Now, there's a pro. I at least try to not talk only about myself. Grandmom hasn't quite mastered that yet. I once clocked her on the phone and she talked—about herself—for forty-five minutes without pausing. I finally said, 'Gran, that's all really interesting, but don't you want to know what's going on with *me*?'"

"What did she say?"

"She said, in all seriousness, 'Well, you haven't given me a *chance*!'"

"Actually, I met her once," Ben said. "When my parents took me to the Palm after graduation. She was there with John. It was funny though, because I remember John's mom doing most of the talking that day."

Stephen laughed. "Aunt Missy? Hah! Clash of the titans! Speaking of John, did you get back up to see him in D.C. again?"

Ben winced and looked away, then shook his head no.

"Ben, can I give you one other quote?"

"Yeah. Sure."

"There was a French writer named Andre Gide. And he said, 'I would rather be hated for who I am than loved for who I am not.'"

Ben looked at Stephen, and was about to say something, but then stopped. "I saw you on TV," he said, changing the subject. "What was that like?"

"Very strange. Like they were having me for breakfast. The media beast has to be constantly fed, but I am hoping that now they will move on to some other tasty morsel."

Ben considered the image for a moment, and then asked, "So, what other dessert are we going to have?"

"I think I will let you decide," Stephen said.

CHAPTER THIRTY-SIX
SHOPPING

Good Lord, would you look at that?" Myrtle Harrison marveled, as she and Missy ascended the escalator at Nieman Marcus. Above them were hundreds of feathery, paper butterflies, revolving slowly on wispy white strands. They were connected by mirrored spangles, sparkling in the bright atrium sunlight. "Ain't that the prettiest thing," she said, reaching up to touch one as they glided toward the second floor. Perhaps even more incredible was that she was in that renowned store with her daughter-in-law. She could not have been more shocked if Neil Armstrong had offered to take her with him to the moon.

"Yes, they are lovely," Missy said, nervously looking up and down the escalator to see if anyone she knew was nearby. When they arrived on the second floor, Missy felt somewhat comforted by the familiar, lofty names, the soft Balenciaga purses, the crisply tailored Chanel suits, the inviting lines of chic Prada skirts.

The walls were adorned with artwork from the Neiman Marcus collection. Next to the Prada room was an abstract work titled *Soft Discovery*. Myrtle looked at it and began to laugh. "Hah! What in the world?" she said, pointing to the pink, purple, and brown streaks of nail polish that dripped down the canvas, pooling at the bottom on a small shelf. "I can't wait to tell Fred about this. He won't believe it."

Missy stopped at the Armani Collezioni. "Oh," she said to Myrtle, reverently running her hand along the elegant folds of an Armani evening jacket. The jacket was a dusky gray and had swirling patterns of black velvet and a satiny, silver flower at its center. "Oh," Missy said again, "this is just gorgeous." She motioned for Myrtle to feel the jacket.

"Yes, it's a beauty," Myrtle agreed. Instinctively, she reached for the price tag, discreetly secured inside the jacket. "Saints alive, Miss, this thing is over $2000. Let's keep moving, honey. They must have something more affordable than that. Now, you know, I'm just a country girl, so we don't have to be too fancy."

They continued and Missy spied an Emilio Pucci silk scarf for a relatively frugal $260. "This would look wonderful on you," Missy said. "Go ahead, try it on. Here, let me help you." She artfully arranged the scarf, which had a shimmery hibiscus print pattern with multiple shades of blue, over Myrtle's shoulders.

"Oh, it is pretty," Myrtle said, looking at herself in the mirror. "But, my glory, you used to be able to buy a dinette set for that much money. I'm almost afraid to touch it. Wonder if they'll have a sale anytime soon?"

"Don't be silly," Missy said. "I promised Edward that we would get you something nice." She effected a grim and determined smile. "Whatever you want," she added, a little too enthusiastically. "Don't worry about the cost. It is our treat."

"Oh, you all are just too good to me. I was just telling Fred the other day, I said 'Fred, my family does everything for me.'" In truth, Myrtle was enjoying herself. After a lifetime of making do with the remainder table at T.J. Maxx, she had suddenly been catapulted into this holy grail of fashion. "What would I wear with it, though? Believe me, Miss, I ain't got nothing that goes with this, that's for sure."

A sales associate, impeccably attired in a soft beige skirt and a white open collar shirt, as taut and graceful as a runway model, quietly approached them. "That looks so lovely on you," she said. "It accents your wonderful complexion."

"Oh, well, thanks," Myrtle said, "but I'd have to take out a new mortgage to pay for it, honey."

Unfazed, the young woman countered, "It's the *best*. And you deserve the best."

"I agree," Missy said, eager to complete the transaction, and the shopping expedition, as quickly as possible. "We'll take it."

"Wonderful," the saleswoman said. "And may I show you a few things that would go well with the scarf?"

Myrtle looked at Missy uncertainly. "Well, I don't know. What do you think, Miss?"

"Oh, of course. Absolutely," she said. "My mother-in-law is looking for something casual, but elegant." Then, noting the anxious look on Myrtle's face, quickly added, "But nothing too fancy."

The young woman ushered them to a grouping of dresses, expertly sifting through them. "Ah, this one," she exclaimed, retrieving a black, scooped neck dress. "It is a Harari, the finest silk, of course, with a marvelous matching jacket. And the scarf would just be the perfect touch."

Myrtle looked at the dress and the jacket. The jacket, also black, had long, sheer sleeves. "How much?" she asked.

Fumbling with the price tags, as if such an inquiry were a new and perplexing endeavor, the young woman finally said, "Let's see. The dress is, ahm, $275, yes, and, ahm, okay, here we go, the jacket is $220."

"Would you take $350 for the set?" Myrtle asked.

Missy cringed. "Oh, for heavens sake, this is Neiman Marcus," she said condescendingly. "We're not haggling over a car, okay?" Edward used to tell the story of watching his mother and father shop for a new Chrysler, and Myrtle's bargaining tactics were so merciless that he actually felt sorry for the car salesman. "So, do you want it or don't you?"

Myrtle looked at her annoyed daughter-in-law and, firmly ignoring her, said to the saleslady, "Honey, I don't think so. You've been so helpful and are cute as a button. But, no, it's a little too steep for an old lady like me." Then, glancing again at Missy, added, "Even if it *is* my son's money."

"Oh, certainly. Do you still want the scarf?"

"No, thanks, honey, but no," Myrtle said, removing the scarf, "not today."

"No problem. Just let me know if I can help you with anything else." The young woman exited as graciously as she had appeared.

"Well, I thought it looked great on you," Missy said. "But, it's up to you, of course. If you don't like it, well..."

"Just not my style, you know? I'm sure I can find something at Dillards. I'll get Fred to run me by there tomorrow."

"Okay. Fine. Whatever you want," Missy replied, as they began walking briskly toward the exit. "Send us the bill."

Outside, in the harsh sunlight, the massive building, a monolith of brown brick and stone, with grudging, minimal slits for windows, seemed like a tomb to Myrtle. "Well," she said, "I thought the butterflies were real nice."

As they drove back to Monroe, with Missy speeding in and out of lanes like a NASCAR driver, Myrtle thought about shopping in the old days with her own mother-in-law. Rose Harrison loved their trips to Moore's Department Store in Chesterfield. Myrtle had heard that the store was closing. Despite the best efforts of Chesterfield to rejuvenate its downtown, the Victorian streetlamps and pots of flowers could not bring enough folks back downtown. Many drove the few extra miles toward Cheraw to the Wal-Mart. If it was sterile and impersonal, she supposed that was a fair trade for working people just desperate for bargains. Myrtle understood that, but she still regretted the loss of Moore's.

"Edward will be so disappointed that you didn't see anything you liked," she heard Missy saying as they approached the outskirts of Monroe.

"Well, I appreciate you taking me there," Myrtle answered. "Really, it was very sweet of you to go to the trouble. But, that place is just too rich for me."

"Is there someplace else you would like to go?" Missy asked, slamming on the brakes as the light on Skyway Boulevard turned red. "I need to get back home before too much longer, but, if you really want to go..."

"No, I've taken too much of your time already." She used to spend the entire afternoon shopping with Rose Harrison. The salesladies at Moore's all knew her mother-in-law. The minute they walked in the door, one of the women would rush over and give Rose a hug. "Mrs. Harrison, what a surprise to see you. Getting some of your Christmas shopping done early this year?"

"Son of a..." Missy cursed, as a green Mustang in front refused to get out of the left lane. "Those slowpokes ought not to be allowed on the highway."

"Oh, I know that's right," Myrtle concurred. "That's why I always drive in the slow lane. Save myself the aggravation." Missy ignored the suggestion, and raced quickly around the Mustang.

"Did you ever go to Moore's in Chesterfield, Miss?" Myrtle asked. "I hear it's closing."

"I went there once. And, believe me, once was enough. Horrid little place. Dust on the floors. Salesladies with the fashion sense of Mamie Eisenhower. Awful!"

"When were you there?"

"Let's see, well, it would have been when Edward and I were still dating. It was the first weekend he took me to Chesterfield to meet Grandmom Harrison."

"Yes, I remember that. I remember Rose telling me how much she liked you."

"Really?" Missy said, surprised. "I never knew that."

"Yes. She did. She said to me, 'Myrtle, that little girl has got spunk.'" Myrtle declined to tell Missy that Rose had added, "I just hope she will use it well."

Missy smiled. "Oh, that's very nice. I mean, she was very sweet to me, but I just figured it was because of Edward."

"No, if she liked you, she liked you," Myrtle said. "She never put on airs. You know, she just loved Edward. She said she didn't have favorites with the grandkids, but we all know she did. It used to really bother some of the other moms. They'd say, 'Mom, you like so and so better than my children,' and she would say, 'No, I don't. He just needs me more.'"

"You're kidding," Missy said, perplexed. "Why on earth would she think Edward needed her more?"

"She just did," Myrtle said, "I never figured out why either. I guess she saw something that we didn't."

CHAPTER THIRTY-SEVEN
BE A MAN

Were you especially close to your mother growing up?" Mr. Douglas was sipping a cup of green tea, and had placed chocolate muffins on the small table.

"Yes, I suppose I was. Am," Ben replied. He wondered if there was anything sexually suspect about a chocolate muffin, and tentatively reached for one.

"And your father?"

"Not as much. Dad's so busy with work, and Mom's at home, so Debra and I just see a lot more of her."

"How is your relationship now with your dad?"

"Okay, I guess. He works so hard to support all of us. We are very lucky."

"It's good that you respect your father, Ben. But, has he ever told you he loves you? Does he ever give you a hug? Even when you were younger? Did he take the time to play sports with you?"

"He did when he could," Ben said, slightly exasperated. "My dad's a good guy, Mr. Douglas."

"I'm not criticizing your dad, Ben. What I am hearing though is that you are closer to your mother. Is that fair?"

"Yeah, I guess so."

"Tell me about your mother."

"Mom? Oh, well, she's a great person. Just great. Always there for me and Deb. I think my mom is probably the kindest person I've ever known."

"But?"

"Well, she just seems so sad to me sometimes. She always does the right thing. Always. You know? Where each fork goes on the table. Taking food to the homeless. She is so good. And she wants us, Deb and me, she wants us to be good too."

"Isn't that admirable in a mother?"

"Yes, well, sure. But, I don't think I have ever seen her really loosen up and just have fun. Just relax. I don't think she has it in her somehow. And that makes me sad for her."

"If you have a problem, who do you go talk to?"

"Oh, Mom, of course. But, she worries about so much as it is."

"Thank you for being honest, Ben," Mr. Douglas said, offering him another muffin. "That is so important. You should know that research has long documented that men who have homosexual feelings are overly close to their mothers. And they never got the love they needed from their fathers. So, they have a greater feminine sensibility and they are constantly looking for a father's love. Do you understand?"

"Well, I'm not sure. Kind of, I guess. But, Deb is closer to our mother too, and she isn't homosexual. Shouldn't she be one too?"

"No, not necessarily. Girls are different. But you, being a boy and all, you are searching for a man to give you the affection that you never got enough of from your father. And the ultimate expression of that takes a sexual form. But, as I told you last week, you have to develop your masculine side and learn to relate to men in a nonsexual way."

"How do I do that?"

"First, you have to be more comfortable with other men, to not think of them sexually, but just as men. Like when we hug at the end of our sessions."

"That's okay."

"Yes, but it is just a start. A baby step, if you will. The important thing is, you may still desire men, but you have to discipline yourself not to panic and, above all, not to give in to it. So, we are going to do an exercise. First, I want you to take your shirt off."

"Why?" Ben asked, alarmed.

"Because I want you to practice being comfortable, but nonsexual, with another man."

Ben removed his shirt. Despite his nervousness, he felt an immediate tug of desire with the exposure of his naked chest.

"Now, I am going to take my shirt off too. And we are going to continue talking, just like we are now. What might be an erotic situation for you will become ordinary and, eventually, unthreatening." Mr. Douglas took his shirt off. The therapist had once been a dancer. As he lifted his shirt, Ben could see the lean biceps and ribbed abdomen of a man who still exercised his body with considerable diligence. There was a heavy coat of hair on Mr. Douglas's chest, but his back was pale and smooth. Ben wondered if he shaved his back.

"If you become excited, don't worry. That is something at this point in time that you cannot control. But, with time, I believe you will be able to. Are you okay with that?"

"Yes. I am fine," Ben mumbled.

"Are you becoming excited?"

Ben shifted nervously in his seat and looked away in embarrassment.

"That's okay, Ben. Don't worry about it," the therapist whispered. "Do you know, after all this time, I even still feel some of that. But, I recognize it for what it is. Just the devil's weakening grip. Remember, Ben, it's just weeds. Crabgrass in the front yard. That's all it is. Now, tell me about your exercises this past week. Did you read *Sports Illustrated*?"

CHAPTER THIRTY-EIGHT
TRUE LOVE

Laura lay quietly in bed, as Andrew engulfed her. She was not so much aware anymore though of the central thrusts of his body, but rather the smaller irritations. The stubble of his unshaved face scratching her naked shoulders. The paunch of his perspiring belly weighing heavily, up and down, protruding into her own. She berated herself for such pettiness and in her lonely recrimination she wondered if it really was her fault, not Andrew's. In her darkest reflections, ones that hovered just at the edge of her conscious thought, she even feared that her failure as a wife had something to do with her son's failure as a man.

God would want her to be more loving. More understanding. The Bible said 'wives submit yourselves to your husbands.' But, she shuddered, as she lay there beneath Andrew's sweating, robotic undulations, then what? She held her breath and turned her head to one side, soft against her pillow, waiting for a conclusion, her own body alert not to her own pleasure but to that one exultant gasp of her husband that would free her and allow a fitful sleep.

That conclusive moment was usually not long in coming. Andrew had long since abandoned any efforts to prolong his own release in the hope that he might occasion his wife's. In that tacit understanding they had arranged the expedient framework of their lovemaking. But, this particular evening, his ardent rise and fall upon her was more prolonged, his agitated breaths not a signal of an approaching release, but rather of a delayed one.

Laura felt pinned to the bed, smothered by the moistening flesh of her husband. Finally, she asked, "Could you raise up, just for a moment?"

He grudgingly lifted himself up on tenuous arms and then said irritably, "You know I can't take much weight on my wrists."

"I'm just asking you to lift up for a minute, honey, for just a few seconds," she said, with rare assertion. "I realize you can't do it for long."

He continued thrusting and then, after a minute or so, lowered himself back down completely on top of her, his arms around her back, and was lost in the convulsions of his own desire.

"Oh...oh...oh..." he cried, and then collapsed, still and spent, over Laura. "I love you, Laur," he said, with a conciliatory sigh. Affection, she thought, had become a luxury only afforded *after* the satisfaction of his hunger, not in feeding it. Only then would he sometimes remember to acknowledge her own needs. "What's wrong?" he asked, daring her to tell him.

"Nothing. Nothing at all," she said, her mouth clenched in a grim smile there in the darkness. She felt imprisoned by his insistent, somehow punitive embrace. "I love you, too," she added, realizing that in fact she did love him. And that love made her sorrow something that was inexpressible and, at times, she felt, unendurable. "I was just thinking about Ben...and his therapy. I hope it's helping."

"Could we *please* not talk about that right now?" He got off of her, and rolled over to his side. Within minutes, Andrew was lightly snoring, contentedly asleep.

Laura, unable to sleep, languished instead in the half-conscious realm of memory, something she seemed to do more and more of late. She saw herself, young and thin and hopeful, walking down the aisle at the small Moravian Church with Andrew. She had refused to have the wedding at Myers Park Presbyterian, a minor rebellion in the eyes of her mother and father, in comparison to the greater offense of Laura's marrying Andrew to begin with. The chapel was so small that, to Laura's delight, they had to carefully restrict their guest list. She was happy to be married only in the presence of the people there for whom she truly cared. Missy had been her maid of honor.

Her mother was true to form right up to the day of the wedding. She had studiously avoided any involvement in the wedding plans, with the exception of constant sniping about every detail from the sidelines. Laura and Missy had planned the entire wedding and simply forwarded the bills to Mr. Soames.

On the morning of the wedding, as Missy was helping Laura get dressed, Mrs. Soames appeared at the door to Laura's room. She was holding two handbags. "Laura," she asked impatiently, "which one of these should I take? The black one or the white one? I can't decide."

"The dark one," Laura replied, seething. "It suits you."

"And black is so slimming," Missy added. In those days, Missy was just an apprentice in the art of the cutting remark, but had discovered a special relish in practicing on the superior bearing of Jewel Soames.

Laura and Andrew spent their honeymoon in Asheville. They stayed at the Grove Park Inn, as a wedding gift from one of Laura's less wealthy, but eminently more generous, aunts. Their room had a view of the surrounding mountains, a view that was at once expansive and yet oddly enclosing, echoing perhaps Laura's own mixed expectations of married life. Under the blue satin comforter of their bed, in the dark room lit only by a sliver of moonlight angling over the hills, Laura endured the hammering, insistent pounding of her new husband.

She had vigilantly guarded her virginity, unperturbed by Andrew's feverish pleading during their courtship. And then, not quite twenty-three years old, she had surrendered it, there in the moonlit room at the Grove Park Inn, not in a soft and yielding embrace, but rather in a painful, bloody penetration. And yet, if these urgent, protracted grapplings did not afford her any real pleasure, there was at least the consolation of her young husband's solicitude. While he, understandably, was intent on completing their union and achieving his own aching release, he repeatedly asked her, "Are you okay, baby?" and expressed a torrent of affection equal to his persistent invasion. "I love you, my beautiful girl. I love you."

Andrew even pretended not to notice the bloodstained sheets the next morning, as he cradled Laura in an oblivious embrace. And so Laura learned that if she could not always depend on desire, she might at least be sustained by tenderness. Andrew would not be dissuaded from the violence of his exertions, but was more than willing to temper it with concern for her comfort.

As the years passed, novelty gave way to routine, and both discomfort and tenderness lessened by degrees. Sometimes she wondered if that accounted for her difficulty in conceiving a child. Eventually, her dutiful acquiescence to Andrew's desires, which had occasioned such gratitude at the Grove Park Inn, had become a source of bitterness for them both. Laura, unable to articulate her own needs, more and more approached their marital bed with a sort of resigned acceptance. What she lacked in lusty relief, she sought to achieve in a more all-encompassing Christian fervor. She consoled herself with the thought that, while she may not be a passionate wife, she was at least an attentive one.

She remembered something her mother had said at the reception. In her dark blue dress, and black handbag, her mother had maintained a dignified, if somewhat funereal, aplomb. Her only, brief betrayal was at the reception, when she proposed an ironic toast to Andrew, her new disappointment of a son-in-law. "Welcome to the family, dear. We never dreamed someone so fabulous would take her off our hands."

Laura had laughed at the joke. How many times had she done that in her life? Smiled and looked the other way. Her stoic sacrifice infused her with an exhausted pride, but was also one more entry in her troubling catalogue of grievances. It had somehow brought her where she was now, lying in bed beside her sleeping husband. She tenderly put her arm on his shoulder, grasping for something that she only dimly remembered and grieving silently for something she had never really had.

CHAPTER THIRTY-NINE
KICK THE CAN

The pecan tree of Edward's grandmother's house was gone. He had heard that it had been struck by lightning several years ago. As he stood there in the front yard with Alice Owens, all that was left was the ground level stump, as smooth and shiny looking as polished stone.

"I used to climb that tree," he said. "Mom has a picture of me sitting up there when I was about six. I was a little guy. You'd get a kick out of my chubby legs, and the sole of my shoe was coming off. I didn't care though."

"How high did you climb?" Alice asked.

"Oh, as close to the top as I could get," he said, still contemplating the vanished tree. "It was a huge tree, at least fifty feet high, and sort of the outdoor entertainment center. All the kids played kick the can out here, hiding behind that tree, dodging fireflies, and crashing there by the porch steps to get the can. And when my dad was a boy, he and his brothers and sisters were so starved for something to do back during the depression —no video arcades then, Alice —that they would join hands and touch the tree during thunderstorms."

"You're kidding. Aren't you?" she asked. "Stephen told me that the Harrisons were wild, but not *that* wild."

"No, true story," Edward replied, ignoring the reference to his nephew. "They had to make their own fun in those days. A few times the lightning did hit the tree and they all say they could feel the current passing through them." Then, before he could stop himself, he added cheerily, "Missy says that explains a lot."

Alice laughed, in that unrestrained, lilting way she had, not at all disturbed by the mention of his wife. Her lack of jealousy or contrition, her defiance of the normal expectations, was refreshing to Edward. One of the burdens of middle age was its bland predictability, and Alice Owens was anything but predictable.

"It's beautiful here," she said. "I love the way that field across the street sort of rises up toward the sky."

"That's kind of you," he said, reaching for her hand. "It's about the only thing left that looks the same." The front porch, with columns resting on crumbling brick bases, spanned the wood frame house with a loosening grasp, affording a feeble welcome to the rare visitor. On the second floor, a double-windowed dormer, its glass panes shattered, was like the broken bow of a listing ship, slowly sinking, beyond saving. "I wish we could have bought the place when Grandmom died, but I could barely afford my own house at the time."

The home, though increasingly uninhabitable, had been rented to a succession of old men, most of whom managed to overlook its obvious lack of amenities through an alcoholic haze. It was currently uninhabited and, needlessly, locked. Edward was relieved in a way that he would not be able to take Alice inside. He had walked through several years ago with his mother, and, decrepit and abysmal as it had been then, it was even worse now. "You should have seen this place in the old days," he said. "You just would not have believed how so many people could fit in here. Easily sixty or seventy at the reunions. That driveway there..." he said, pointing to the gullied, red dirt drive that ran along the side of the house, "would be parked end to end with cars."

"But where did you all sleep?" she asked, incredulously.

"Where *didn't* we? I usually slept in the Boy's Room —that's the room there in the back, on the corner. It had a great old fireplace until Uncle Laurence, the family tycoon, and Aunt Opal insisted on putting in gas heaters. Anyway, the girl cousins were upstairs. And lots of folks on the floor. The rest just pretty much took over the one motel in Chesterfield. Somehow it all worked. Nowadays, if we have more than a couple houseguests in Charlotte, we send 'em over to the Park Hotel."

"And just one bathroom here?"

"Yeah, but that was in the later years. My older cousins used to talk about the outhouse in the back yard. Having to go out there when it was pitch black. And there were spiders. Or worse!"

"Oh," she said, smiling, "now you're just trying to impress me."

In the back yard, a broken clothes line sagged limply toward the ground, between two leaning and rusty poles. The roof of the back porch had now completely collapsed, its asphalt tiles scattered to the ground like black flakes of snow. At the edge of the yard was a small cement block building.

"That's the old pump house," Edward explained, "where we got our water." A rickety door, its wood splintered and faded, leaned against the hinges, and was partially open. "My father and his brothers used to hide their whiskey out here and have a few when they were visiting. It was pretty much 'don't ask, don't tell' with drinking in those days around Grandmom."

"I gather she was pretty old-fashioned," Alice said.

"Well, she was and she wasn't. I mean, there was plenty she didn't approve of, but, good Lord, you can't keep a bunch of sinners together if all you do is condemn them. We've had plenty of divorces in the family, and even back then the ex-spouses liked to keep coming to the reunions. And we've had alcoholics and, at last count, one bank robber."

"How did she deal with all that?" Alice asked, unperturbed by the display of familial embarrassments.

"All I remember is that she was given to sighing quite a bit about one or the other of 'em and saying 'Well, he's a *good* boy.' She believed that a bump in the road should not define the entire trip."

"How often did you used to visit here?" she asked, putting her arm around his waist as they walked back toward the front, past a scraggly row of shrubs that ran along the dirt drive. At least the maple tree on the side of the house was still a tower of leafy green vitality, somehow flourishing amidst the wreckage.

"Oh, quite a bit. Let's see, we all were usually here every year for the family reunion, Christmas and Easter, and I always stayed for at least a couple weeks with Grandmom every summer."

"Well, it sounds wonderful," Alice said. "We visited my grandmother every Christmas. She had a beautiful home. And, don't misunderstand, she was a very nice lady. Perfect manners. But, it was like visiting a museum, and about as appealing."

Edward smiled, but seemed lost in thought, as if he were trying to remember something, or perhaps trying not to. "I did love it here at Centerpoint," he said. "Grandmom never changed, and it seemed really as if her home stayed the same then too. Slow and steady." He pointed to the row of shrubs by the driveway. "I hid in those shrubs once. Must have been about seven years old. Mom and Dad had left me here one weekend, and when they came back, I didn't want to leave. I can still hear them calling, 'Eddie, come on son, time to go.'"

"And did you?"

"Yes," he said sadly, "I did." He didn't tell her that his father was drunk on the front porch, yelling at him, "Boy, you come on now. Get on over here, y'hear?" His father passed out in one of the metal lawn chairs on the porch. And his mother, already exhausted and infuriated with her husband, had little patience left for an errant child. She just marched over and grabbed him by the collar. "Go get your sister and get in the damn car," she said, as she swatted him on the behind. "We're going home."

But I am home, he thought. I *am* home. He had walked back into the house, where his grandmother was in the kitchen. She was hunched over the kitchen table, making sandwiches for them. When she saw Edward, she walked over and hugged him. "Now, don't you worry, honey," she said. "Everything will be fine. You be a good boy, and be sweet to your mom and dad." She reached into the pocket of her housedress and gave him a package of brownies. "These are just for you," she said, smiling.

"Everything okay?" he heard Alice asking, putting her arm around his shoulder.

"Oh, yeah, sure, fine." He looked once more at the sagging front porch, stacked with planks of discarded wood, then said, "The last time I saw Grandmom she was sitting up there. I remember Aunt Lila and cousin Joey were visiting. I was only twenty-seven when she died, and had driven over to see her. Missy and I had just gotten engaged, but she didn't come. She liked Grandmom, but always seemed a little intimidated by her. I couldn't understand that, since Missy is rarely intimidated by anyone and, good Lord, of all people, Grandmom. Anyway, I remember driving away, waving goodbye. She seemed so happy that day, even though her heart condition was, as usual, causing some pain. She was just sitting there, like she always had been, laughing and waving. She died a week later. On a Friday, of course, so no one would have to miss a workday for her funeral."

"You still miss her, don't you?" Alice asked.

"Yes. I guess I do," he said. "When I was just a teenager, we were talking about death one day. She said, 'I won't always be here, but don't you worry, you know I will always look over you.'"

Alice kissed Edward just above his eyes and looked at him for a moment, almost as if she were seeing him for the first time. "I would have liked to have known your grandmother. Gosh, I imagine she would be so impressed with you, with what you have done with your life."

"Maybe," he said uncertainly. "She was so poor for so long, she would be proud of my success. But, that wasn't the main thing with her. She always told us, 'Don't look down on anybody, but don't look up at them either. You're as good as anybody else.' Her whole life was about taking care of other people. That's what she really admired."

"Well, either way, I have a feeling she would understand," Alice assured him. And as they stood there in that all but abandoned yard, she thought of children playing kick the can on firefly nights, of the last embers of a fireplace, and a frightened little boy hiding in the shrubs, and, most of all, of the consoling embrace of a woman like Rose Harrison. Alice looked across the gravelly Angelus Road, toward the unspoiled pasture that rose slowly up to a clear blue sky, and it occurred to her, not for the first time, what a variable and fragile thing the measure of a life could be.

CHAPTER FORTY
MY DADDY LOVES ME

Ben stretched out on the sofa, his head cradled by the therapist. "You have to learn that it's okay to be close to another man," Mr. Douglas said, as he wrapped his arms around Ben's chest and held him tight. "It doesn't have to be sexual. Your fear of men has made you desire them. Don't be afraid."

Ben put his arms around the therapist's waist, resting his head on Mr. Douglas' thigh. "That's fine," the therapist said. "Hold me as tight as you want. Tighter if you like. This is very important for you to do. So, tell me, what are you thinking right now?"

"Well, I'm thinking about someone I saw a couple weeks ago," Ben answered, turning his head slightly upward. "We had coffee. He's gay. Just flat out, 'I'm gay.'"

"Remember, the word gay is a misnomer, Ben," Mr. Douglas cautioned, shifting so that he could stretch out his legs. Ben nestled his head in the therapist's lap. "No, you're fine," he said, with studied nonchalance. "You can stay where you are. So, how do you feel about this man being a homosexual?"

"I don't know. He seems like a nice guy. He's easy to talk to. He makes me laugh."

"Were you attracted to him, Ben?" The therapist softly stroked Ben's hair as he spoke. "Did he excite you? Just a little?"

"No, it isn't like that, not really," Ben answered, his breath moving in rhythm now to the gentle touch of his hair. "I mean, he is, you know, just a regular guy. Rugby player. He teaches at UNCC and is John's cousin. It's strange, but he...well..."

"What?"

"He's so open about it. Like it was no big deal," Ben said, laughing nervously as the therapist moved his caressing hands now to Ben's shoulder.

"I know. It is strange. And sad. I know that type. I used to be that way. Living in New York, partying every night. But, lost. I would wake up in the morning in some strange apartment and have no idea how I got there. What can be worse than being lost and not even knowing it?"

"Yeah, I guess." Ben decided not to tell Mr. Douglas that he had talked with Stephen Rayfield on the phone the night before about the exact nature of his therapy, correctly assuming that the therapist would not be pleased that Stephen had called it 'deranged'.

"Someday, that young man, if he doesn't change, will be old and lonely," Mr. Douglas continued. "He probably he is a very nice person. But, he will be all alone. The homosexual world is heartless to older men when they lose their looks. That's when the party really ends. And by that time, most of them have lost contact with their families, with real people. I have seen this happen so many times."

"I don't want to end up like that." Ben sat up and looked pleadingly at the therapist. "I think I would rather die than end up like that."

"You won't. So, you mentioned that this man is your friend John's cousin. Have you talked anymore to John since you saw him in Washington?"

"No, I tried to," Ben said, wondering if he should tell the therapist about the exact details of that trip. "He doesn't want anything to do with me."

"I'm sorry to hear that. I really am. I know that must hurt. But, you have to put it out of your mind. You are too close to John. I think that is why he is behaving the way he is."

Ben thought of John that afternoon by the pool, the water sparkling in sunlight, John's hand resting on his shoulder, that enigmatic, treacherous grin. *We got to find a honey for you.* But, there was something unstated, more than just teasing, in those words. Ben could not have imagined it. And then, just a couple weeks later, by the lake. *No biggie. We just needed to get off.*

Ben sat up on the sofa, moving away from the therapist. "John was my best friend."

"It's okay, Ben," Mr. Douglas said, hugging him. "Don't worry. You're going to be fine," he said, now holding Ben's face in his hands. "It's all right," he whispered, "trust me."

Ben looked at Mr. Douglas, and then touched his face.

"It's okay," the therapist whispered again, "trust me." He continued moving his hands along the thick waves of Ben's hair.

Ben tilted his head slightly, his trembling hand still on the therapist's face, and then kissed him.

Mr. Douglas paused uncertainly, his lips moist against Ben's, and then jumped up from the sofa. "Whoa, fella! Whoa! That's not okay." His face was flushed and he caught his breath as his arms gestured manically at Ben. "You do not *kiss* other men."

"I'm sorry. I'm sorry." Ben slumped down into the sofa, his hands over his eyes. "I don't know what to believe anymore."

Mr. Douglas sat back down, at the far end of the sofa, and forced himself not to stare at the dejected figure sprawled out in such muscular display. "Ben, you are just beginning a difficult journey. There are roadblocks. Wrong turns. But, I know you can make it. You can."

"How can you be so sure?" Now his arms were behind his head, and the sleeves of his polo shirt slid up the smooth arc of his biceps. Coursing veins curved tightly, snakelike, along his thick forearms.

"Because I did it. Others have too." *My daddy loves me*, Mr. Douglas thought to himself. *My daddy loves me.* "Don't doubt yourself, Ben. You can do this if you want it badly enough."

"But, what if I really am gay?"

"You can still change your behavior. You can still have a normal life. That is why you are still here, talking about it to me." Those legs.

Those massive legs, he sighed, briefly noting the sloping muscles of Ben's tanned thighs. *Daddy. Daddy. Daddy.*

"I hope you are right, Mr. Douglas. I am trying. I really am." Ben sat up abruptly and added, "You won't tell my parents about this, will you?"

"Of course not. Everything between us is confidential. *Everything.*"

"Thank you, Mr. Douglas. That is very important to me."

"I understand," the therapist assured him. "Ben, listen to me. You are going to stumble some times. It's not the end of the world. Believe me, I know. And your mom and dad understand too. We are all here for you. You must remember that one thing. I'm sorry I reacted so strongly. What's important is that you not give up on this. Let's get back to the therapy, okay? Now, have you managed to avoid self-pleasuring yourself?"

"Yes. I have. Except for a couple days ago. I was taking a shower, and started thinking about...well...I need to be honest with you...I started thinking about John. So..."

"Oh. Well, I have been giving this more thought. And there is new research that actually encourages self-pleasuring, under certain circumstances. So, here's what I want you to do..."

Well, are you still gay?" Debra asked Ben, just as Laura was bringing in hot steaming rolls.

Laura put the plate of rolls down with a thud. "Debra, stop. Right now. Your brother is not that way. He is having a difficult time, and the least you can do is respect that."

"Sorry," she chuckled, pausing to reload. "So, Benjie, how's life in the straight lane?" Ben looked stricken, and simply stared at the steaming rolls as if they might afford some projectile for counterattack.

"Debra, that's enough," Andrew said menacingly. "I don't want to hear another word about that out of your mouth. Do you understand me?"

"Geez," she said. "I didn't mean anything by it. Really." Ben glanced at her, then looked away, unable to bear any further scrutiny.

"Your son is trying to find his way," Mr. Douglas had told them. "He will need all the support and guidance you can give him now. But, he can overcome this affliction."

The rationalist in Andrew Caldwell observed the miserable boy sitting there at the dining room table, while Debra ostentatiously suppressed her giggles, and wondered if such a goal was feasible. But, if the reparative therapy for Ben would not necessarily rework the depths, and most likely it wouldn't, then they would have to settle with securing the surface.

Andrew knew there were men who were basically gay who nevertheless managed to live heterosexual lives. And didn't seem all the worse for it, either. At least they had children, stability, and didn't have to worry about catching a fatal disease every time they had sex. And, most importantly, as Laura would insist, those men —and some women too —were obeying God's will.

That such incessant rigor was sometimes a cross to bear was hardly the exclusive domain of reformed homosexuals. Andrew himself felt endless temptations to be with women other than his wife. For example, Miss Parsons in human resources. Every day at work he had occasion to sit across a table from her, and he would have been less than a man not to notice —how could he *not* notice? —the way her skirt rose up her thigh when she crossed those endless legs, the supple, pert breasts that bobbed beneath her blouse when she laughed.

Andrew could tell his son a thing or two about temptation. And repression. And regret. But, he would not. Instead, their conversation dodged all references to sex. When Ben had returned earlier in the week from his latest therapy session, Andrew greeted him as if Ben had just been to Sunday school.

"Hello, son. Good meeting?" he asked, in some strange parody of Ward Cleaver. Ben, attuned to this delicate interplay himself, would reply, much like Wally Cleaver, in general upbeat tones, "Good, Dad. Mr. Douglas is a great guy."

Those sitcom fathers never had to deal with sons being counseled in how to be heterosexual, or in terrifyingly aroused fathers who sometimes had to wait a respectable interval to get up from the table after Miss Parsons had left it. Yes, the Caldwell sitcom was a bit of a departure. They should rename it, he decided bitterly. *My Three Sons, One of Whom Is Gay*. Or, scandalously, he thought, *Leave it to Beaver. Or not*. Among the family, only Debra refused to tread lightly around Ben's situation. It was as if she wandered in from another soundstage entirely.

In the meantime, to be honest, Andrew was grateful for the distractions of the increased demands of his work. The company was involved in a project to redevelop the old mill town of Kannapolis. It would be a historic opportunity to revive a town that was almost dead after the precipitous decline in the textile industry. He felt a special pride in the Kannapolis project. If successful, and he had every reason to believe it would be, a whole new generation of people there would have good jobs and a vital community in which to raise their children. But, the thought of children, and future generations, reminded him of his own children, particularly Ben.

Ben, Andrew thought, he's always the last one to know. And the last one to stop believing. Ben had inherited his mother's piety, and even the normal rebellions of adolescence had not quenched it. When Ben and Debra were in junior high school, Ben went through a phase of such intense faith that he would say a prayer not only before every meal, but before every snack. Laura, incredibly in Andrew's view, had encouraged this manic piety. Debra told them that one day, walking home from school one afternoon, Ben unwrapped a piece of bubble gum, then gazed a moment at it as if were a sacrament, and said his prayer.

"Ben, this is embarrassing," she said. "You don't have to bless bubble gum." Unfortunately, at that moment, two of their school's snootier girls walked by. They were laughing at Ben, and making the sign of the cross.

Ben ignored them, but Debra scowled. "Get over it. He's asking God to pardon you two for being such sluts!" Then, she recalled, Ben looked up at her and admonished, "Deb, you shouldn't use those words."

How could a father not love a son like that? Andrew wondered. And for one candid and sorrowful moment, he allowed himself to concede the unfair afflictions the world might impose on a boy like Ben.

After the family had gone to bed, Ben took the *Playboy* out of his backpack. He had purchased it after the session with Mr. Douglas, as instructed. He flipped the pages to the centerfold. The woman was airbrushed to perfection, with firm, upright breasts. Ben felt nothing. Panicked, he turned to the section with black and white photographs of a man and a woman together, having sex in the kitchen. He was particularly drawn to a photograph that showed the woman sitting on the counter, her legs wrapped around the muscular man, her arms clenching his sinewy back. Well, this will have to do for now, he thought. And I will try to keep my mind on her.

As he continued, images of John filtered in and out of his mind. He recalled that rainy night together by the lake and, later, at the moonlit townhouse before John pushed him away. He even briefly thought of how it felt to kiss Mr. Douglas. And, then, unbidden, with startling clarity, he could see Stephen Rayfield's face, smiling.

Just smiling.

CHAPTER FORTY-ONE
FREEDOM PARK

Y ou don't like Charlotte, do you?" Ben asked Stephen as they walked in Freedom Park. "I mean, you're polite about it, but it's so obvious you would rather be just about anywhere else."

"Is it? Really? I suppose things haven't gone quite the way I expected," he said. "But…well…let's see…I like these crape myrtles. Love the weeping willows. Okay, I confess. Charlotte is a bit of an acquired taste. You've lived here your whole life, right? So, tell me, how long does this acclimation phase usually take?"

"Do you know my vocabulary improves every time I see you? True story. Charlotte's not so bad. Why did you move here?"

"Would you believe it if I said UNCC? It's true. It was either here, Boise, or unemployment. Isn't that sad?"

"No, I don't think so," Ben said. "I think it's pretty cool." Just then, a flock of geese, emerging from the pond, waddled by, quacking in unison. "Just so you know," he said, looking straight ahead, "I'm glad you didn't move to Albuquerque."

"Really? Thanks." Suddenly, Stephen stopped to read a sign posted beside the lake. "Oh, funny. Look at this. Even the birds in Charlotte are out of control."

The sign read: *Due to an overabundance of Canada Geese at Freedom Park, several management strategies are being implemented to reduce the attractiveness of the park to geese.*

The sign showed a picture of a park official with a laser stun gun, directing a *'harmless beam of light'* at the wayward birds. "Now there's the answer to suburban sprawl," Stephen said, "at least for geese."

They walked over to a picnic table, on the lawn that rose up from across the water from the band shell. The table's wood was old, faded and, as they sat down, apparently splintery. "Ouch," Ben said, "watch your butt!"

Stephen laughed. "That's too easy," he said. There were very few people on the lawn. A man and a woman played frisbee. A lesbian couple, each wearing caps, tank tops and baggy shorts, were having a picnic with three puppies. "Wow," Stephen whispered, nodding toward the women, "she's got bigger biceps than I do."

"Are they...you know?" Ben asked.

"Oh yeah, agent Caldwell," Stephen said conspiratorially, "they are very, very...you know. In fact, in my brief time here, I have noticed that Charlotte is chock full of...you know, and a fiercer group of tank-topped ladies I would never hope to encounter."

Ben looked uncertainly at Stephen for a moment. "I kissed my therapist," he said.

"What?"

"I kissed him. Last week. I was getting really upset. So, he hugged me—that's part of the therapy—and then I kissed him."

"What did he do?"

"Before he freaked, or after? First, he kind of kissed me back and, after, he jumped up like his pants were on fire."

"Please tell me you are no longer going to see him."

"What? No. I can't do that, at least not for now. I promised my mom and dad. They all say I'm just confused. It's just a phase. Maybe they're right."

"Can I ask you a question then?"

"Okay," he said warily, his eyes squinting into the sun.

"You don't have to answer this if you don't want to, but what triggered all this? This phase, as you call it?"

Ben stared at a caterpillar slowly crawling across the table, and then kicked it over the edge with a flick of his finger. "A couple of nights, guess that did it. Another guy. It was so dumb. I mean, I know that now. Crazy, right?"

"Was it weird for him?" Stephen asked.

"No, I don't think so. It was…nothing…to him."

"Do you still see him?"

"No." Ben looked toward the pond at the geese, noisily marching out of the water, then said, "He's in Washington this summer."

"I'm sorry, Ben. I really am. You deserve so much better than him. Listen, just do what you feel is best for *you*. That's the only advice I have. And I don't expect anything from you otherwise."

"Really? You don't?" he asked, almost sounding disappointed. "Everybody else does."

"A friend of mine used to say, 'Expectation is the enemy of happiness.'"

"When you say 'friend', do you mean your boyfriend?" Ben asked.

"In this particular case, yes. Ex-boyfriend."

"What happened?"

"Ask me again in about five years. I might have figured it out by then. Let's just say that I'm not very good at relationships."

"Did you ever think about therapy?" Ben asked.

"Sure, lots of times. But, not for being gay. I had a conversation with my father once. He hated that I was gay. Probably still does, though he doesn't care to see me enough one way or the other. Anyway, one time he said to me, 'Stephen, if you just put your mind to it, you can change.' And I said, 'Dad, I'm no more likely to change than you are.' Well, given his epic record of fornications, that ended the conversation pretty fast."

"So, how do you like this park?" Ben asked, changing the subject.

"I love it. It's the first time I have taken a walk in Charlotte without the risk of being run over. Oh, look, here come those damned geese again. They sure know how to follow in a straight line, don't they?"

"That's what they do, isn't it?"

"Yep. It is. They are the great conformists of the animal kingdom. And, if there were any justice, they, not a panther, would be Charlotte's mascot."

"Jeez, doc," Ben said, punching his shoulder.

"Jeez, what?"

"They're just birds!"

CHAPTER FORTY-TWO
HOME IMPROVEMENT

Evelyn Peck stood in her front yard, ignoring the cars rumbling behind her on Tryon Street, and stared proudly at her new roof. The black asphalt shingles almost sparkled in the morning sun.

The roofing crew had come out to her house within a week after her speaking with Edward Harrison at the reunion. "What's it gonna cost me?" she had asked the foreman.

He had smiled, like she had just won the lottery, and said, "It's all taken care of ma'am. Mr. Harrison took care of it."

In the interim, she had convinced herself that this prompt generosity had less to do with her threatening knowledge of Edward's affair than with the bonds of family. She was, after all, still a Harrison, still the widow of Edward's favorite cousin. Why, Edward was probably very happy to have a chance to help her and Keith. And probably would have done so a lot sooner if it weren't for that bitch he was married to.

As she stood there, admiring her new roof, it occurred to Evelyn that she should call Edward and thank him. There might be other ways in which her newfound confidante could assist her in the future. She would assure him of her gratitude and at the same time remind him of the continued value of her ability to, usually, keep her mouth shut. That Edward Harrison would accept her thanks in the spirit in which she intended it, she had no doubt. Unfortunately, in their dealings with each other to this point, he had declined to provide her with his telephone number. Hah, she laughed to herself, he ain't the first man old Evvie has had to track down.

She went back inside the house where, as usual, Keith had the television blaring. He was laughing, a high, strange hyena sort of laugh, at *Judge Judy*. "Sock it to him, Judy," he shrieked, "cut his balls off." He ignored his mother as she walked in to the kitchen.

"Where in hell is the phone book?" she called out angrily, as she began rummaging through drawers and cabinets.

"Haven't seen it," he said, erupting again into a cackling sound as Judge Judy hurled another insult at the hapless witness.

Keith had not been taking his medication the past week, and Evelyn could tell he was becoming more manic. She also knew that this would be followed by depression. Same old roller coaster, she thought, and considered whether she should call his doctor. Mindful of the bother of navigating the mental health system in Charlotte, she decided to cross that particular bridge once it was closer to actually collapsing. Evelyn continued noisily ransacking the kitchen and finally located the phone book in the cabinet above the stove. "Here it is," she muttered angrily, "not that you give a rat's ass." She looked under H for Harrison Associates. Evelyn dialed the number.

"Turn that down in there," she screamed, "I'm on the fucking phone."

"Good morning, Harrison Associates," a soft female voice answered.

"Hey there," Evelyn said. "Lemme speak to Edward."

"Oh, certainly, ma'am," the woman said cheerily. "May I have the last name, please?"

"The last name?" Evelyn repeated, annoyed. "Well, Harrison, of course. Who else? Jeez Louise. Edward Harrison."

"Oh, of course. Thank you ma'am. And may I ask who is calling, please?"

"This is Mrs. Evelyn Harrison," she said, pausing, then added reluctantly, "Peck."

"Thank you, Mrs. Peck, I'll see if Mr. Harrison is in. One moment please."

A moment later, Evelyn heard the young woman say apologetically, "Mrs. Peck, I'm sorry, but Mr. Harrison is in a meeting. Could I ask what this is in regard to?"

"Well, no law against asking, but I really don't see as to how it's any of your business. I just wanted to thank my cousin for a favor. That's all. Can you tell him that? I just called to say thanks for a favor. You *got* that?"

"Yes, Mrs. Peck," the woman said, as calm as ever, "I will make sure that Mr. Harrison gets the message. Thank you for calling, ma'am."

"Uh huh," Evelyn said, slamming down the phone. Well, we got the roof, she mused, who the hell needs that hypocrite? She walked back in to the living room.

Keith, muting the television while a commercial touting the benefits of Viagra came on the screen, looked at her and said accusingly, "You never did say why Uncle Edward gave us that new roof."

"Who wants to know?" she scowled. "Let's just say I did a favor for him, and he did a favor for me. How's that work for you, smartass?" Evelyn smiled ambiguously at her son, knowing that he was suspicious as to what the exact nature of her favors to Edward might have entailed. What the hell, she thought. If she had long since abandoned any inclination to please her son, she retained an unflinching enjoyment in provoking him.

Keith, seething, offered up a vacant, but penetrating glare, as if he could see right through her. He turned the volume of the television up to an ear-piercing level, drowning out the voice of his mother, as a preview of the evening news was breathlessly announced by a white-haired anchorman. "Shooter kills two near Eastland Mall. Details at five." Then the caustic face of Judge Judy appeared back on the screen and Evelyn, trailed by Keith's odd laughter, retreated to her room and locked the door.

CHAPTER FORTY-THREE
UNNECESSARY DISTRESS

Stephen watched the darkening sky, just as the sun was vanishing over the horizon. This was perhaps his favorite time of the day, but a reminder of his solitary state, as the sheet of blue sky faded to black. He took another sip of the merlot, and suddenly felt very tired. The sun having now vanished, he struck a match and lighted the cinnamon jar candle that was on the coffee table.

Earlier that day, he had been summoned by Dr. Robert Williams. "Stephen, first, let me say again," Dr. Williams had begun gently enough, "you have the full support of this department and this university." The chairman's chin jutted forward, solemn and regal, somewhat similar to the William Jennings Bryan bust on the desk. "This is an issue of academic freedom, the defense of which is basic to any great university." Hanging in the air, of course, was just how enduring that defense might be and, also, the rather questionable characterization of UNCC as great.

Feeling obliged to respond in some affirmative way to this tinkling note of support, Stephen said, "Thank you, sir. I appreciate that."

Heading off any further discourse on gratitude, Dr. Williams, looking skyward now, perhaps for divine guidance, raised his hands in a pontifical manner and interjected, "No need to thank me. You are a credit to this institution. And we will not be bullied. However..."

However...It should be banished from the English language, Stephen thought. *However*...That word, so nebulous in itself, was so often the prelude, the warm-up so to speak, to some kind of verbal hit and run. Stephen looked at Dr. Williams and could distinctly hear the gunning of an engine.

"...However, we do have some suggestions that we feel will diffuse this *regrettable* situation," Dr. Williams said casually, glancing at his notes. He then proceeded to outline those suggestions with the precision of an attorney, no doubt the precision of the very same attorney who advised the university in these delicate matters. "First, the department feels that it will be best for you to avoid any future contact with the media. That is in your own best interest, Stephen, and we would *appreciate* your concurrence. Second, we are *advised* that Dr. Meadows should teach the Democracy in America class for the duration of the session. Now, that may *seem* detrimental to you, Stephen, but it is not."

"Seem to be?" Stephen asked incredulously, barely managing to avoid outright laughter. "Seem? Sir, with all due respect, you are telling me that we are bowing to the pressure of a few disgruntled students, students who are being challenged to think, for once, for themselves, and that I am, if I may *phrase* it this way, out on my controversial ass."

Dr. Williams smiled patiently, as if he understood, though could never condone, Stephen's frustration and the unfortunate resort to *unseemly* language. "Stephen, that is not the case. We simply feel that your continued involvement in that class will result in further, unnecessary distress to the students, to the university and..." he paused, allowing the full import of his meaning to gather steam, "to *you*."

To you...

They had parted with an exchange of the usual meaningless pleasantries. *Thanks again...Nothing to worry about...Full support...* But a dagger had been inserted ever so politely into Stephen Rayfield's back and they both knew it.

And so, as Stephen retreated to his balcony, watching the darkening night, he realized that, in the rules of combat, the only way to deflect further injury was to inflict a graver one. Stephen had never disclosed that he was a Harrison. He had resolved that even a second tier prize like UNCC would be attained on his own, or not at all. But, the words 'academic freedom' meant something to Stephen, whatever they were to Dr. Williams. Had the matter been simply about Stephen alone, involving some valid culpability, he might have accepted this demotion masquerading as support. But, it was nothing more than capitulation to a bully. It was simply bowing to the mob.

He remembered once when he was about ten years old and visiting his grandmother in Monroe. He had been riding his bicycle and at some point found himself on an unfamiliar block near Myrtle's house. He stopped for a second and looked up and down the quiet street, lined with scraggly trees and modest cinder block homes set back from the curb. Suddenly, he saw three boys approaching. They were several years older than he was.

"What's the matter, fairy boy?"

"Little baby lost his way?"

"Well? Cat got your tongue, faggot?"

Stephen, who was small for his age at that point, tried to reason with them. "Come on. I haven't done anything to you. Leave me alone." No doubt emboldened by this weak response, they converged on him, throwing him to the ground. He saw his bike topple over, and then he was completely covered by the weighted mass of the three boys. Unable to move, unable even to speak, Stephen, for the first time in his life, knew only panic and impotence. Gasping for breath, struggling to get free, he felt them pinning him to the ground, almost like being buried alive. He finally managed to turn his head just enough to utter a feeble, stricken scream. His scream somehow was more frightening and humiliating than the claustrophobic assault. Then, bored with their conquest, the three got up and, in succession, spat at him.

"Faggot."

"Queer."

"Bye, bye, little fairy."

Stephen had never forgotten that grotesque day and, at times of crisis, no matter what the circumstances, it was those three menacing boys that he felt approaching. It would have been gratifying to believe that he was braver, stronger now. But, the most he could really claim was that he had learned either to flee or land a blow of his own, before, not after, he was thrown to the ground. And, often, it was not until the precise moment of a pending fall that he knew which course he would take.

CHAPTER FORTY-FOUR
DIAMOND GIRL

Y ou've changed your hair," Missy's mother said. "It looks
blonder, don't it, Ellen?" Clara Gilmore was on continuous
oxygen now and, with the ubiquitous tube protruding from
her nose and attached to a portable tank, had finally become the
alien creature that Missy had long regarded her to be.

Missy's sister nodded unenthusiastically. "Yeah. Real blond."
She looked distractedly toward the kitchen and said, "Coffee's ready.
Y'all just keep your seats." Ellen was four years younger than Missy,
but looked older. She also had blond hair, teased back into some
semblance of order, but it was the uniform, brittle work of dye
from a bottle. In contrast to Missy, Ellen had also gained weight,
most of which was concentrated on her bell-shaped thighs. The one
remaining indication of Ellen's status as younger sister was her baby-
faced voice.

"It's the same shade as always," Missy corrected them. "It
must be the light. Could you close the blinds a little? It's awfully
bright in here." Missy regally swept a lustrous blond wave, expertly
highlighted, over her head.

She was a reluctant visitor in her mother's home, and this Friday
evening was no exception. Twice a year, and never on holidays, Missy
drove the twenty miles to Rock Hill, only to find herself confined in
the modest little white frame house where her mother maintained

a limited and tenuous independence. Missy found it ironic that the old woman was tightly leashed to a portable oxygen tank. It was somehow appropriate that a woman of such narrow perspective, bereft of any imagination or curiosity beyond the shabby block she lived on, was now legitimately tied to it.

"We saw your picture in the paper," Ellen said, setting a tray of coffee and a stale looking pound cake on the table. "You looked great, but where was Edward?"

"Oh, he was there," Missy answered. "He's just shy around a camera."

"You got yourself a good man," Clara said in her rasping voice, looking as if, after all these years, she still couldn't quite believe it.

"Yes, I suppose I did," Missy replied coolly, "but, so did you, Mom." Even if you could never calm down long enough to appreciate him, she thought to herself.

Missy studied the photograph of her late father, smiling serenely from the quiet vantage point of the living room wall. It was understood that Missy's presence in the home was due to the most primitive sense of family obligation, without even a hint of affection. After her father's heart attack, as he lay dying in the dingy hospital room in Rock Hill, she had promised him that she would look after her mother. If Missy regretted the commitment, she was resigned to honor it with two brief visits a year and an annual gift to cover the mortgage on the little house. As for the recipient of this generosity, sitting across from Missy in awkward silence, gratitude was neither expected nor offered.

"Well, tell Edward we said hello," her mother continued. "And we hope he and the kids'll come with you next time. Whenever that is."

"Oh, we'll all get together soon," Missy said, glancing at her watch.

On occasion, in her youthful confusion, Missy wondered if perhaps her mother was a witch who had cast a spell on Missy's tranquil, unsuspecting father. She remembered once when they were all watching *The Wizard of Oz* on television, and she kept stealing glances at her mother, assessing any resemblance to the wicked witch of the west.

Missy, on the other hand, wanted to be Samantha, the bewitched housewife with magical powers. Alone, in her room, she would practice wriggling her nose, eager to make her mother disappear and leave her and her father alone. She hadn't yet decided on the fate of her infant sister, Ellen, who was, even then in Missy's view, a virtual nonentity. Ellen's only value was in the distraction she provided in her constant demands for feeding, bathing, and dressing, capped by howls of bloodcurdling ferocity. While Clara Gilmore was not daunted by these outbursts, she was diverted by them, and the more attention required by Ellen meant the greater respite for Missy. But, Missy reasoned, if she could magically cause her mother to vanish, then Ellen's singular worth as a whiny toddler would vanish as well.

Ellen later married her high school sweetheart, Harold, who was an electrician. They, and eventually their three equally nondescript children, lived in a small brick home, perfectly wired, one had to admit, in Rock Hill. They enjoyed the easy contentment of low expectations. And Clara, trailing her oxygen tank from just three houses down the street, was, in a classic reversal of fortune, attended to by Ellen.

"More coffee?" Ellen asked.

"Just a little, thanks," Missy said. "We missed you at Johnny's graduation. He says thanks for your card, Mom, and for the ten dollars."

Clara Gilmore laughed, her close set eyes narrowed in doubt as to her grandson's presumed gratitude. "Shoot, ten dollars ain't nothing to that boy. I know that. You've always spoiled him, given him anything he ever wanted." She paused a moment, catching her breath, and then continued. "How's Andrea? Lost any weight?"

Missy smiled patiently, as if she were humoring a rude child. "She's fine, doing quite well. Edward is taking her to New York this fall for a father and daughter weekend."

Mrs. Gilmore scratched her wispy hair, and said, "New York? Good Lord, you couldn't get me up there for all the tea in China. All those terrorists running around. Why in the world are they going there?"

"It's perfectly safe there," Missy replied. And it ought to be, she thought, with all the money given to New York. It still rankled her that Charlotte was not considered a major target too. The second largest banking center in the country! It was outrageous, but one more instance of Charlotte being overlooked. Of course, that was something her mother would never understand. "Edward is very careful," Missy added.

"Well, if you say so," the old woman said dismissively. "And I reckon Edward still works like a dog. Course *somebody's* got to bring home the bacon to keep a roof over y'alls head, right?"

"Yes, I suppose so," Missy managed lamely. "Edward's so busy with this new project he's developing in Uptown, I barely manage to see him myself." Missy realized at once that this last statement was a mistake, as if it confirmed her mother's merciless calculations as to the fragile state of Missy's marriage.

Missy shifted her gaze from her father's portrait, and from memories of his untimely death, and looked at the clock, encased inside a fake bronze horse, on the mantel. She calculated how much longer she would have to stay chained to the lumpy sofa before she could bolt and speed away. She figured ten more minutes would suffice, five of which could be used up gushing about the bland pound cake her mother had prepared.

"This cake," she began, taking a deep breath, "it's just the best. What is your recipe?"

Missy drove home to Morrocroft, clenching the leather steering wheel of the Mercedes, and bitterly contemplated the latest visit to her mother. Whatever the passage of time or the comfort of distance, Missy Gilmore Harrison held on to her grievances. She could neither forgive nor forget, and if that fomented a certain bitterness of perspective, it also afforded her an embattled vitality. While the finer details of her injuries became obscured by time, the identity of the perpetrators, and the general outline of their crimes, did not.

When Missy was in elementary school in Rock Hill, she recalled waiting nervously at the bus stop with the other children. But, if she was a misfit, she viewed this outlier status as a mark of distinction. Her neighborhood was a club to which she most emphatically did not wish to belong. It was working class, respectable, and dull. One interminable blur of little red brick boxes. Red brick aside, her childhood memories returned not in color, but with a sort of gray and dreary blandness. It was as if the skies were always overcast. Not raining. Not thundering. That would be too vivid. Just overcast and best forgotten.

Ironically, the one virtue she acquired in the pallid and monotonous drone of her childhood was patience. Missy, if nothing else, knew how to wait. It was her great, good fortune that such capability tempered her natural impulsiveness and moderated her inherent vindictiveness. She was detached, cunning, and, when it suited her purposes, charming. In Charlotte, it had suited her purposes, and her husband's as well.

Her mother had regarded her as ordinary, as nothing special. And that, Missy soon determined, was the one unforgivable thing. This maternal dismissal, along with the family's meager circumstances, had fueled Missy's ambition from ember to flame. The one thing she could not tolerate from others, with the chronic exception of her husband, was indifference. She did not wish, necessarily, to be the center of attention. Missy instinctively understood that any egotist worth the name covered her tracks. But, she could not endure a lack of notice or attention altogether. This perspective uniquely qualified her for Charlotte society. However, unlike the grim insecurity of her adopted hometown, Missy possessed a calculated sense of humor.

Early on, beginning with observations of her mother, Missy developed a sense of the ridiculous and an unwillingness to suffer fools gladly. She was encouraged in this amused resistance by her father, who lavished praise and attention on her.

"Missy, you are our diamond girl," he enthused. Indeed, that, and 'Dan', the latter even more inexplicable than the former, were his nicknames for her. Her given name was Margaret.

"Hah!" her mother would scoff, flicking her never extinguished cigarette. "Diamond my ass. Rhinestone's more like it. Maybe you can get her to clean up that pigsty of a room of hers."

Clara was a woman of exceptional homeliness. Nothing seemed to fit that irregular face. Her chin was too big, her flat nose was too small, and her deep set eyes were in a perpetual squint. To Missy, her mother, always smoking, always squinting, seemed to be in a constant state of agitation. In contrast, her father possessed a handsome, unflappable tranquility. She marveled at his equilibrium. Charles Gilmore, drunk or sober, was like a perennial oak in the middle of a storm, solid and unyielding. The union of her parents had long mystified Missy. While opposites may attract, she could not fathom the enduring connection between her easygoing father and the fat-chinned, beady-eyed, shrieking harpy he married. That such a woman happened to be her mother was a further source of wonder.

Her father, who indifferently sold Fords at the local dealership, adored Missy, and saw in her a kindred spirit. This affection from her father only served to fuel her mother's explosive hostility.

When Missy was twelve years old, she began her period. She was too embarrassed to tell her mother. She had learned about menstruation in health class at school, and so she knew that she would have to obtain sanitary napkins. Her only recourse was to ask Mrs. Hurtz next door for some. Mrs. Hurtz was a large, bubbly woman, always smiling, in stark contrast to her skinny, anemic husband who worked as a clerk for the county. She was friendly to Missy, probably because, having observed the frequent tantrums directed at Missy by Clara Gilmore, she felt sorry for her.

Missy walked next door to Mrs. Hurtz's. Mrs. Hurtz came to the door, holding a plate of cherry pie. She smiled, oblivious to a red streak of cherry clinging to her upper lip. "Missy, hello honey," she said. "How are you? Want some pie? It's fresh."

"No, ma'am. No thanks." She hesitated for an instant, and then explained, "We need…I mean, Mom needs…Mom is out of Kotex, and she asked me to see if you could spare one for her."

"Why sure, honey. Wait just one minute, I'll be right back." She returned with an entire box of Kotex, unopened, and discreetly placed it in a Winn-Dixie shopping bag.

"There you go," she said, handing her the bag. "Everything else okay, dear?"

"Oh, yes ma'am. Just fine. Thank you, ma'am." Missy felt so ashamed. Bleeding was bad enough. But, to have to lie to Mrs. Hurtz. At that moment, she hated her mother with an intensity she would not have believed possible.

When Missy got home, she went to the bathroom. The blood had seeped through the tissue paper and soiled her panties. Dried blood was encased on her thighs. She washed herself with a bath cloth. In those days, there were no adhesives, and she did not have a napkin belt, so she had to use safety pins to hook the Kotex to her panties.

A couple of days later, Missy was doing her homework in her room, which was as messy and cluttered as ever. Suddenly, her mother was at the door.

"You little bitch!" Mrs. Gilmore screamed. "I have never been so embarrassed in my life. Why didn't you tell me you got your period?"

Missy was speechless, as she usually was when her mother was in full tirade mode. This only infuriated Clara more. "Answer me! I had to find out from Faye Hurtz! She said to me, 'Is Missy getting her period?' and I said, 'No, of course not.' Why in the hell did you go to that busybody?"

"I didn't want to bother you," Missy stammered. "I didn't know what to…"

"Here," her mother said, throwing a box of Kotex at her. "And when you need more, you can goddamned well march your little ass into Winn-Dixie and get them."

CHAPTER FORTY-FIVE
BEYOND REPAIR

B en sat down on the sofa and waited for the therapist. He noticed again what a spartan room it was, as if any decorative touches would suggest a latent homosexuality. The white walls, worn pea green carpet, and black and white prints of Old Charlotte invoked a manly simplicity. Inexplicably, today there was a gray plastic wastebasket beside the sofa. The only concession to color was the blue cushion on the sofa. Ben held the cushion against his chest.

He could hear Mr. Douglas talking to his wife, through the slightly ajar door. "No, Erma, I *told* you, not *that* one." Mr. Douglas' voice always seemed a notch higher whenever he spoke to his wife. "Honey, did you *listen*? Breyers. Low-fat. Am I being *clear*?"

Mrs. Douglas replied in an indistinct, muffled assent. Ben had never met her, though Mr. Douglas referred frequently to 'my wife.' She seemed a duly noted, if somewhat spectral, presence in the home. He heard the car backing out of the driveway, and then the therapist walked somberly into the room.

Mr. Douglas sat down in the chair across from Ben. With his brown slacks, white button down shirt, and perfectly parted sandy brown hair, he seemed the perfect stylistic match to the room's furnishings. Since the incident of the kiss, the therapist no longer sat on the sofa. Hugs and shirtless sessions had been abandoned. "I think I tried to move you along too fast," he had explained.

Mr. Douglas stared appraisingly at Ben. "Are you still...*friends...* with the professor? Stephen?"

"Well, yeah, I guess we are friends. I mean, I see him and talk with him sometimes." Ben hesitated and then said, "Mr. Douglas, I know you're trying to help me, and I appreciate it. But, well, I don't think I can keep doing...

"Ben, I spoke with your mother and father earlier this week," the therapist interrupted, "and I told them that you are not making the progress I believe you are capable of."

"What did they say?" Ben asked, clutching the pillow more tightly.

"They...your mother especially...begged me not to give up on you. And, of course, I won't. She is still heartbroken about all this. But, you know that, don't you?"

"Yes," Ben said, feeling somehow as if he had just come home with a very bad report card.

Mr. Douglas clasped his hands and brought them to his chin, as if in prayer or contemplation, and then said, "I think you need stronger interventions. Do you know what aversion therapy is?"

"No," Ben answered, relieved that this failure at least was merely one of information.

"Well, in layman's terms, it is a method that teaches you to associate homosexual desire with negative responses. Here's how it works. I will give you a medicine that causes nausea. Then, I will show you images of naked men. You will, literally, want to throw up. Do you want to try this?"

"I'm not sure. How long will I be sick?"

"Not long. About thirty minutes," the therapist said. "Now, you don't have to do this, but I promise you it will help. I still do it sometimes myself to stay strong. But, you have to *want* it."

Ben nodded his head in assent, but felt a growing sense of panic.

The therapist gave Ben a teaspoon of some awful tasting liquid. "Swallow this," he directed. "When you feel sick, you can throw up into the trash can beside you."

Ben nodded as Mr. Douglas handed him a *Playgirl* magazine. The therapist turned to a page that had been dog-eared. The centerfold.

"Now I want you to focus on the pictures. Focus."

A man was pictured in a series of poses in the shower. Standing. Sitting. Sprays of water trickling along supple, hardened muscles. One picture was especially mesmerizing. The man was sitting back in the steam shower, his hands resting on his ridged abdomen, and his massive legs splayed out in a way that reminded Ben of the night by the lake with John.

"Are you okay?" Mr. Douglas asked.

"Yes," Ben muttered. He began to catch his breath, as the first spasms of nausea surged up, like little cascading waves. "Oh. Oh, no..." Ben reached for the wastebasket, watching in humiliation as the undigested remnants of his breakfast splashed onto the plastic liner.

"You're fine. Don't worry," the therapist assured him, briefly touching Ben's shoulder, and taking the magazine from him. "What I'm going to show you now is disgusting, just awful stuff. But, you need to see it."

"Yeah. Okay," Ben gasped, feeling another wave forming in the pit of his stomach. He clutched his side, bent over in pain, as Mr. Douglas put a DVD into the player. Suddenly, the television screen filled with the sight of two men in bed together.

"Oh, I *know*," Mr. Douglas sighed. "Hideous. But, concentrate, Ben. Don't look away. Look closely at the one on top. He is, I'll admit, a good-looking man, but so rough. So dirty." The therapist laughed nervously, then continued, "Those huge arms. Big, sweaty legs. *Dirty.* But, keep looking, Ben. Think of the pain the bottom one must be feeling. Filthy. Think of how disgusted he will feel later."

The bottom one, in fact, did not look to be in any discomfort whatsoever. If anything, he looked anesthetized to any feeling at all. His awkward grunts and moans were certainly not intended to deter the rhythmic pumping to which he was being subjected. The only pain that Ben was aware of was his own, as he again lunged for the wastebasket, and threw up what was surely the last morsel of food in his body.

Ben looked away from the television, but could hear the laughable dialogue of the performers. "Yeah. That's the way. Harder. Harder." It occurred to him that the animalistic coupling was grotesque enough without any induced vomiting. And, just before his third and final eruption, he glanced over at the therapist. Mr. Douglas clenched the arms of his chair, his head tilted back slightly to the side, and was silently mouthing the words 'disgusting', 'filthy', 'dirty'. The therapist gasped for breath, and then slowly slumped further in the chair. "Oh, oh…"

"Turn it off," Ben said. "Please. Turn it off. I think I have seen enough."

Stephen had the air conditioning going full blast, and had aimed a fan directly at his bed. August in Charlotte entailed a particular oppressiveness, like an empty oven that has long since overheated. There was no incentive to venture outside. He lay there in bed, reading a recent and much-heralded biography of George Washington and pondered the freezing, barefoot soldiers at Valley Forge. At first he did not hear the insistent knocking on his door. He lazily got up from bed, threw on a pair of old shorts and a Duke tee-shirt, and walked to the door.

Stephen opened the door and there stood Ben Caldwell. "I'm sorry," Ben said uncertainly, his arms folded against his chest, "I should have called you, but I wasn't sure if you…if it would be okay… but you said I could come by if I needed to, so…"

"Of course it's okay," Stephen assured him. "Please, come inside."

"I'm supposed to be at my therapist's," he said, as they walked inside the apartment. "I'm not going back, and thought I'd come see you instead."

"I'm really glad that you did," Stephen said. "Good for you, Ben. Would you like some lunch? I can heat up some leftover pizza? Do you like pepperoni?"

"Sure. That would be great," Ben answered.

Stephen began taking plates down from the cabinet, as Ben took a seat at the kitchen counter. "So what happened?" Stephen asked.

Ben described the aversion therapy, as Stephen listened with mounting rage. "It was disgusting," Ben concluded. "I thought, of all the places in the world, why am I here? And you know what else?"

Stephen put the pizza on a plate and motioned Ben to the dining table. They sat down and Ben continued, "I thought about you. I thought that if there was one person that I could talk to, it's *you*, not Mr. Douglas."

Stephen impulsively reached out and put his hand on Ben's and smiled. "Thank you."

"This is good pizza," Ben said, eagerly wolfing down a slice. "When I was little, my mom used to take me to Domino's every week. I called it Dommie's pizza and so that's what she began calling it too."

"That's funny. Your mom sounds like such a nice person. I can see why everyone loves her."

Ben looked away for a moment, then reached for another slice of pizza, and asked, "So, do you have a swimming pool?"

"We'll probably melt out there, but, if you want to, sure." Stephen said. "I can lend you a swimsuit."

The swimming pool of the Edwardian Arms was uncrowded. At one end there was a small clubhouse, furnished with upholstered sofas and armchairs, rather like the lobby of an average chain hotel, that was available for residents' parties. Stephen had yet to witness any social gatherings there and it remained as undisturbed as a museum. A gazebo with ornamental white railings and capped with a green metallic roof was at the other end of the pool, and was most often used by mothers imposing timeouts on their unruly children.

On this sticky afternoon, a couple of older residents dozed in their chairs. Several children splashed noisily in the water. A harried woman, squeezed into a one-piece bathing suit that seemed to cut into her pale legs, yelled at her child, "Kevin Lee Burns, get over here right now. I am too tired to come get you. Do you hear me? Don't make me come over there. I mean it." The boy ignored her completely and dove under the water, and Stephen watched as the woman marched by in a sluggish rage.

Stephen and Ben had taken two lounge chairs and Ben promptly fell asleep. It was as if he had run a marathon and, exhausted, had collapsed on Stephen's doorstep. Stephen continued reading about George Washington, but periodically glanced at the sleeping figure beside him. With each breath, Ben's lips parted slightly, in a sort of tranquil sigh. Stephen was struck once again by Ben's dark, pronounced beauty, but also by his sweetness. For, manly or not, that was indeed the word that would describe him. *Sweetness.* And it was probably the one quality that would cause Ben so much distress as he tried to find his way now. That eagerness to please, to not offend or hurt anyone's feelings, would too often be seen as an invitation to intimacies and disclosures that were never intended.

Ben suddenly opened his eyes and turned his head toward Stephen. "Jeez, I was sleepy," he said, grinning. "What time is it, anyway?"

"It's two thirty. When do you have to be back home?"

Ben thought for a moment, as if he had just remembered that there was in fact someplace else where he had to be. "Oh, around five. It's weird, I don't think I ever lied to my mom and dad before. But, I didn't know what else to do. So, I told them that I was going to just hang out at the park for a while." Then, lightly punching Stephen's shoulder, he added, "No rush."

Stephen tried not to notice, as Ben sat up slightly in the chair, the way his abdominal muscles seemed to unfold in hard, tanned ridges. The bathing suit was slightly too large, and its soft cottony band dropped precipitously below the waist. Ben crossed his arms and seemed oblivious to the swelling mounds of his chest or the curving solidity of his biceps. His body seemed almost violent in its chiseled, muscular precision. *But, he's still just a kid,* Stephen thought. *He's so young.*

Ironically, Ben looked at Stephen, and then said. "You must work out. You're in pretty good shape." He laughed and then added, "For an older guy."

"Thank you," Stephen said. "That's very kind. I try and work out when I can, but, actually, I hate to exercise. For me, fitness is a triumph of vanity over laziness."

"So, what's it like being thirty anyway?" Ben asked, punching Stephen again playfully on the shoulder.

"I'm only twenty-seven."

"What's the difference?"

"You'll find out soon enough," Stephen said.

Ben rolled over on his side, propped up on one elbow, so he could look at Stephen more directly. "One thing that Mr. Douglas said that really bothered me was that...ahm...well gay guys," he whispered, conscious of the young woman sitting in a chair near theirs, "it's really sad when they get older. Not older, like you. I mean really older. Seriously. No kids. No family. Do you think that is true?"

"I think what is true is that your therapist is an idiot. Getting older is hard for everybody. Regrets go with the territory, with or without children in the picture."

"Really?" he asked. "Maybe you're right. I mean, my parents have me and Deb, but they aren't happy. They try to be happy, but they aren't. And Mom...She always expects so much."

"Well, don't be too hard on her. Your mom just wants you to have a good life. Parents need a pass sometimes too. That's something else you'll find out."

"So what about older gay men?" Ben asked.

"The truth? A lot of them I've seen are like older straight women. There's just something so frantic about them."

"Being old and ugly?"

"No, trying so hard *not* to be old. A couple years ago I was in Provincetown with my friend, Dylan. It's a very popular place with gay men. One afternoon I was sitting at the beach. Dylan was swimming. And I saw this man. He looked like he was in his late fifties. Short, but very tanned and fit. He was wearing a white thong and he had bleached blond, spiky hair. It was the thong that got me. For all his hours at the gym, his butt had hail damage, you know, cellulite. It was just so desperate somehow."

"That's not so bad," Ben said, with an innocent sympathy that was truly the province of youth. "He just wanted to look good."

"Well, maybe so. But, he was trying way too hard. It was sad."

"Jeez. Sorry I asked," Ben said, falling back against his chair with a dramatic thud.

"Oh, it's not as bad as all that," Stephen said. "Listen, it's an old story. Everybody wants to be beautiful in one way or another. Special. We live in a 'look at me' culture. Everyone tries too hard. Addicts for attention."

"Addicts?"

"Yes, in a way. It's like the 19th century Frenchman who walked his pet lobster through the Palais Royal gardens, babbling about the animal's obedience and knowledge of the sea. Everybody is walking a lobster nowadays."

"Pet lobster, huh? You're a pretty funny guy." Ben shifted on his side and leaned in closer toward Stephen. "This is great…here. I feel like maybe everything is going to be okay," he whispered. He smiled, squinting into the sun, and his green eyes, an emerald glow under thick black lashes, looked at Stephen with an unmistakable longing.

PART 3

CHAPTER FORTY-SIX
BLESS THE SICK AND NEEDY

Laura Caldwell tossed another chicken breast into the frying pan. If a woman of such conventional allegiances could be said to have a rebellious streak, for Laura it would have to be in her defiance of the new dietary regime. She refused to forego the now condemned culinary delights of her youth. Aside from her religious faith, it might be said that her most enduring comfort derived from the sizzling, bubbling, crusted, sugary excess of southern cooking. Her family had learned that one measure of her state of being was the intricacy of her desserts. A simple pound cake indicated an uneventful day, whereas a banana pudding with meringue or a double fudge chocolate layer cake involved more portentous implications.

This particular evening, she was preparing a chocolate raspberry torte with fresh whipped cream. Andrew Caldwell sat in the family room, reading the latest *Kiplingers*. "Supper about ready?" he called out gingerly to his wife.

"Five minutes," she said, as she gently arranged raspberries in a circle on top of the torte's waves of cream.

Deb, wrenched from her e-mail chats, came into the kitchen, and sullenly regarded the feast on the counter. She viewed the simmering, oily chicken and fried okra with distaste, having recently decided that physical ruin was imminent if she adhered to her mother's cooking.

"Oh, thank God," she exclaimed, further surveying the dinner, "we have salad."

"Please take that to the table," Laura instructed, pointing to the mixed green salad, which was resplendent with feta cheese, ripe tomatoes, cucumbers, and walnuts.

"Gladly," Deb replied, grimacing as her mother stirred the buttery mashed potatoes. Deb dramatically grasped the salad, reverently holding it aloft like a sacred icon as she carried it into the dining room.

Ben and Andrew were already seated at the table. It would no more have occurred to either of these masculine products of the south to assist in the kitchen than it would to re-arrange the bouquet of lilies that graced the center of the table. The Caldwell household, under Laura's firm injunctions and Andrew's convenient acquiescence, had no dispute with more traditional domestic arrangements. Indeed, the carefully set table, its crystal glasses and gleaming silverware expertly placed, promised a sort of easy refinement that was in short supply of late in the Caldwell home.

Andrew said grace, a rather extensive oration of thanks for the divine guidance that had, thus far, kept his family safe and well fed. His own father had always said the same blessing, night after night, "Bless the sick and needy, Amen," but Andrew's belief was that God required more fulsome gratitude. The vigorous curl of smoke above the mashed potatoes had dwindled to a feeble blush by the completion of grace.

Laura served each dish from her right. There was a determined formality in her manner this evening. This constricted graciousness, along with the elaborate torte now slowly cooling in the refrigerator, afforded a certain nervous anticipation. Andrew, who had long ago concluded that the only sensible response to his wife's tension was to release it as quickly as possible, began with a conciliatory "Great dinner, honey." He then cautiously inquired, "Everything okay? You look a little flushed."

She silently buttered a biscuit and then poured liberal amounts of gravy over the mashed potatoes on her plate. "This gravy is a little different," she said, ignoring her husband's question. "It's the way

Grandmother Soames' cook, Berniece, made it, but I have added just a little more pepper than Berniece would ever allow."

"It's great, Mom," Ben said. "It's just right."

"Thank you, son. I'm glad you like it," she said, pouring more gravy on his plate. "Why don't you tell us about *your* day?"

"My day?" he asked, as he intently speared a fried okra, savoring its crunchy warmth. "Okay I guess." He looked down at his plate. Like his mother, Ben's face would always betray any subterfuge.

"Just okay? That's all you have to say?" She pushed her plate away, as if all appetites in her had been long extinguished. "I had a call today from Mr. Douglas. He said that you canceled your session with him. He said that you had decided not to see him anymore."

"That's great!" Deb exclaimed. "Finally. I knew you could do it, Benjie."

Andrew pounded his fist on the table. "Deb, be quiet." Then, more calmly, he asked Ben, "Is this true? I thought you liked Mr. Douglas. What happened?"

Before Ben could answer, Laura offered her own weary explanation. "Mr. Douglas said that you don't want to change. He said that you...you are seeing..." She stopped herself, unsure what she might say, and then continued, in a pitiable whimper, "How could you do this? How could you give up so easily?"

"Goddamnit, Laura," Andrew thundered, "would you give the boy a chance to answer my question?"

There followed one of those moments of familial silence, the kind of moment that would be recalled years later, in a sad reflection of grief and regret. Laura put a trembling hand to her face, as if she had been slapped.

"I'm sorry," Andrew said, reaching across the table for her hand. "I shouldn't have said that." Looking at Ben, he again asked, "What happened?"

"I just didn't feel like he was helping me," Ben said, certain that to venture any further into the details of his experience with Mr. Douglas would not be a productive road to travel. "He would tell me one thing one week, and then something completely different the next. It just confused me. I'm sorry."

"Well, then," Andrew said, "there are other therapists."

Laura was silent. She noticed again how morose, how withered Andrew looked in repose. His thin upper lip became something stingy and forbidding and the growing softness of his jowls was more evident. "Your father is right," she said, looking away from those sour, pursed lips. "There are other therapists. Just promise us that you will try. That's all we ask."

"I will do the best I can," he said evasively, then repeated, "the best I can."

Later, after an abbreviated dinner consumed in silence, Ben offered to help his mother clean up the kitchen. While this particular evening was not a propitious time for Ben to assist with feminine duties, she was touched by his solicitude. "That's very sweet of you, honey," she said.

They stood side by side at the sink, Ben rinsing the dishes and then handing them to his mother to place in the dishwasher. "This isn't so hard," he said, laughing.

Laura continued loading the dishwasher in silence. Finally, when they had finished, she stood beside the breakfast table. She looked out the window toward her darkening lawn and the pond, its fountain just visible in the waning light. "Come sit down, would you?" she asked. "I need to talk with you a little more."

"About the therapy?"

"No. Not exactly," she said. Her eyes had the pleading aspect of someone desperately looking for something, but even more desperately afraid of finding it. "I think I know where you were today, Ben. Mr. Douglas told me that you are involved with Stephen Rayfield and that Stephen got you to leave therapy."

"How could he say these things to you?" Ben cried. "Isn't a therapist supposed to not tell other people things?"

"What about Stephen Rayfield?" she reiterated. The therapist had been very clear when he called Laura. *Ben was making such progress... A fellow named Stephen...teaches out at UNCC...He has seduced your son.*

Ben looked accusingly at his mother and said, "He is my friend. Mom, please, I don't want to talk about this any more."

Laura studied her son's face, noticing his downcast eyes and the slight quivering of his lips. The therapist's ugly phrase echoed in her mind. *He has seduced your son.* She was moved by Ben's obvious revulsion for deceit, even as she was confronted with the certainty that Stephen Rayfield was much more than just a friend.

"Do you realize he could have AIDS?" she asked. "Did you know you can get it just from kissing?" She could see his doubtful look and added, "I looked it up. It's a fact. The federal disease center says so. Don't you see the danger?"

"Mom, we're just friends," Ben repeated, knowing even as he said these words that they revealed only a partial truth. "And I'm not suicidal. If you wanted to blame someone, I could give you a much more interesting name." Ben stopped himself, unwilling to further burden his mother. "I'm sorry. I need to go to bed. Goodnight." He hugged her and walked silently away.

"Goodnight," she said. She stood up and began to clear off the center island. She placed a tupperware container of leftover chicken in the refrigerator. There, in undisturbed perfection, sat her chocolate raspberry torte.

CHAPTER FORTY-SEVEN
SAFE HARBOR

Ben was silent, as he and Stephen drove up the long gravel drive toward the home on Lake Norman. He had hesitated to accompany Stephen to the dinner, but finally had agreed to go. In the way that one lie leads to another though, he had been forced to tell his parents that he was going to see a movie with a friend. Given their evident relief that the friend was straight, they did not press him on returning early. Any hint of a resumption of what they considered a normal social life for their son was reward enough.

The driveway was awash in purple crape myrtles, moistened from a light afternoon rain. Stephen's friends, Chuck and Bob, had bought the small Cape Cod style home over twenty years ago and had so far eluded the frenzy of real estate agents who had invaded the shores of Lake Norman since then. Their home, which was now worth a great deal of money just for the water-lapped dirt, had been dwarfed by sprawling mansions. It was like a small jewel surrounded by very large rhinestones.

Chuck and Bob had made few concessions to the monolithic style that had come to dominate the lake. While they kept the house painted and the shrubs trimmed, they much preferred the old comfort to the new opulence. Their one extravagance had been to conveniently, and profitably, purchase the lots on either side of them, fairly certain that two gay men living together on Lake Norman would find optimal privacy a prudent course.

Stephen parked the car and was immediately accosted by Maria, the mutt who seemed almost as old as her owners and still managed a remarkable effervescence in welcoming company. Maria, who was named for the Julie Andrews character in *The Sound of Music*, was rumored to be part golden lab and part collie, but no one knew for sure. She had been rescued from extinction at the pound by Chuck and Bob twelve years ago.

"Hello, baby girl," Stephen exclaimed, as she gave him her paw to shake. "How is my sweet girl?" Maria trotted over to Ben, and began licking his face.

"She always goes for the young ones. Don't encourage her," said a low voice from the front door. It was Chuck. "She has been tearing up my lilies today and we are not on speaking terms. Ignore her, I'm the one who needs a big hug." He waited expectantly as Stephen and Ben walked up the front steps.

"Always wanting the hugs from the youngins'!" Stephen laughed.

"Not so fast," Chuck protested. "You're not that young, and I'm not that old." He looked at Ben briefly. "And you have to be Ben!" he said, taking Ben's hand, smiling, revealing the whitest teeth Ben had ever seen, like the polished grille of an aged Cadillac.

"Come on inside," he said, "Bob is making some weird sort of paella." The living room had a wall of windows with a stunning view of the lake. It was furnished in a rustic, hunting lodge style, which was odd given that neither Chuck nor Bob had ever been hunting a day in their collective lives. The walls were crowded with old prints, watercolors, photographs, oil paintings, even cartoons, each claiming whatever bit of wall space had been available at the time. There was a burgundy leather sofa, with a matching chair, and an Indian throw draped over the back of the sofa. The chair had an embroidered pillow that said *Wear life like a loose garment.*

Bob was in the kitchen, busily shelling shrimp on a cutting board near the sink. Seeing his guests, he put down the shrimp and washed his hands. Then, with a dramatic tilt of his head and a wave of his hand toward the remaining pile of shrimp, he said, "Stephen, thank God. Have you come to take me away from all this? Please say yes. I can be packed in no time flat. And bring this handsome young man with us."

"But what about him?" Stephen said, nodding his head in Chuck's direction.

"*Him*? Oh, goodness, he's just the hired man. I keep him around cause he needs the work and the poor thing has no place else to go."

Bob was only five years younger than Chuck, but considerably more vigorous. It was not uncommon, while Chuck lazily read a book in the hammock in the back yard, Bob would be clearing out underbrush on their property down by the water, or painting the white wood railing on the porch. He still ran three to four miles a day and would not even consider breakfast until he had completed his rigorous sets of crunches.

"You are such a tease," Stephen said. "This is Ben, Maria's new best friend."

"Hey there, young man. Stephen has told us a lot about you. All of it good. Hope you like shrimp."

"I do," Ben said politely. "You have a beautiful home."

"Well, thank you. We like it," Bob said amiably, as he returned to stir the pot on the stove. "Chuck, why don't you take the guys on the tour while I keep the paella steaming?"

As they began walking toward the back deck, Maria ran to Ben, extending her paw. He crouched down to pet her as she rolled on to her back. "Pat tummy?" Ben murmured. "Pat tummy?"

"Watch out for her. She is a total tramp. Like father," Chuck said, nudging his head in the direction of the kitchen, "like daughter."

Stephen shot a warning look to Chuck, as Ben blushed slightly.

D inner was served on the screened porch, the table set with steaming bowls of paella, a mixed green salad, and biscuits. "Now, you all just take as much as you can handle," Chuck said. "No formalities here."

The lake was a placid blue, and the sound of crickets punctuated the darkening sky. Stephen looked out enviously at the view. "I just love this place," he said. "It is really wonderful."

Chuck passed a plate of hot biscuits to Stephen, and laughed. "Thanks. I always say that there is no happiness so great that it cannot be enriched by the envy of others."

"You also always say that there is no difficulty so great that it cannot be alleviated by whining about it," Stephen said.

"*That* one he means," Bob sighed. "And there is some truth to it, I'll admit. Stephen, we have seen those ridiculous stories coming out of UNCC, so if you feel like whining a little tonight, go ahead."

"No, I don't think that will be necessary," Stephen said doubtfully. "Not yet, at least." He had heard unsettling rumors from one of his colleagues. There was talk of a peer review meeting, even possible suspension.

"Well, give it time," Chuck interjected. "You have disturbed the sleeping elephant in the living room. Political correctness…What a tired old bitch, still standing like a two dollar whore on the corner." He paused, glancing at Ben. "Oh, sorry."

Ben laughed. "It's okay, sir, I was hearing much worse by junior high school."

"Thank you," Chuck replied, placing his hand over his forehead in an abbreviated swoon, "I have always depended on the kindness of strangers."

"Oh, God, someone has been on *A Streetcar Named Desire* kick again. Am I right?" Stephen asked.

"Lord," Bob said, "don't encourage him. Any minute he'll start talking about the Napoleonic Code."

"Anyway, dear Stephen," Chuck continued, "your only crime is that you strayed from the acceptable script. Everyone in this country, black, white and turquoise, is a little bit racist, and no one really cares so long as we don't talk about it."

"I agree," Bob said. "It's like the crazy aunt up in the attic. We know she's up there, scratching around, but we ignore her and are offended when someone asks, 'Who's that lunatic up there?' We make assumptions all the time about race but no one will face up to it."

"Maybe I could have handled the situation better than I did," Stephen conceded. "I just wanted my students to think a little more outside the conventional box. It's the dishonesty that galls me. When that blow-dried TV reporter asked me for a comment last month, I wanted to say that nothing ever really is *examined*. All our stale attitudes are just neatly filed away and forgotten, you know, just gathering dust in boxes in the basement."

Ben listened intently to the conversation, somewhat intimidated by these older adults. Then, he said, "My mom once told me that the only black person she knew growing up was the maid. And now, at their parties, usually the only blacks there are Mr. and Mrs. Burroughs. You know, the guy who owns the cell phone company." He paused a moment, shyly glancing about the table, then continued. "And at our church, it's almost all white people. The blacks have their own churches too. Why is that?"

"Well, it's ironic," Chuck answered, "before the civil rights act, blacks and whites were segregated by law. And that was terrible, of course. Now, we all seem to be segregated by choice. I wonder what Dr. King would make of that. And it sure hasn't brought us any closer to judging each other by the content of our character either."

"I guess that's so," Ben said. "I had a friend in school, named Jeremy. Great guy. Very smart. He was black. And nobody really seemed to care that we were friends, but they did notice. Just because it was, you know, different. And whenever he came over to my house in Piper Glen, you could almost see the neighbors peeking through their windows, wondering what is that black boy doing here. That must be awful, to have people looking at you that way, just because you're black."

"Did you ever ask him about it?" Stephen asked.

"Yeah, once I did. And you know what he said? He said that he had gotten used to living in the twilight zone, not black or white, since no one ever really saw him for just himself."

"And that is exactly the point," Bob interjected. "Your friend is no doubt a fine young man. And there are plenty of blacks who will dismiss him, saying he is just acting white, like success is some kind of deviant behavior. And you have whites drawing the curtains and wondering if they need to call the police. That is where we are now, and no one, except maybe for Stephen here, really dares to ask how we got here."

Maria padded over to Ben's chair and sat beside him, immobile, almost frozen like a statue. "Uh oh," Chuck said, laughing, "that's her begging pose. Flawless, isn't it? Don't be taken in, Ben, it will only encourage her." Then, he said, "Well, I have a question. Does anyone at this table think that we will ever be a color blind society, where race does not matter?"

"Yes, someday," Stephen said, "but probably not in any of our lifetimes. But, then, people will beat up on each other for some other reason. Blonds versus brunettes. Who knows? If history teaches us one thing, it is that human beings are not predisposed to harmony."

Chuck laughed at the image. "Blonds versus brunettes? That wouldn't be so bad, so long as there is a plentiful supply of good colorists. Course it wouldn't concern me," he added, pointing to his balding head. "Well, listen, it's time for dessert. I made a banana pudding, so everybody take a breath and get ready to dive in."

"How long have you lived here?" Ben asked, as he hungrily reached for the pudding.

"Twenty-two years," Chuck said. "Before that, we lived for ten years in Ann Arbor, Michigan. That's where we met. We were both teaching there before we wound up at Davidson."

"You have known each other for over thirty years?" Ben asked. "Wow, that's amazing."

"I was in grade school," Bob joked.

"Well, you must pinch yourself, you're like marital marathoners. I know I would," Stephen said.

Bob passed Stephen the pudding. "Honey, no one pinches us anymore, and we certainly don't pinch each other!"

"Not true," Chuck countered. "He still can't keep his hands off me. At my age, it's, to tell the truth, a little embarrassing."

"This pudding is so good, I feel like I have died and gone to heaven," Stephen said. "So, how did you do it? Stay together all these years, I mean. What's the secret?"

"Keep paddling. That and good paella." Chuck answered. "Stephen, boy o' mine, there is no short cut. Just making the effort, sweet as you can, every day. That's the secret. Your generation wants everything quick and easy. Marriage is slow and messy. Do you think either one of us is such a prize? Don't answer that."

"Speak for yourself, gramps," Bob laughed, putting a chokehold around Chuck's head.

"Well," Stephen said, "you do make the best paella in Carolina."

"Just don't expect perfection," Bob said. "There are a lot of lonely people in this world because they wanted perfection, and what they needed was just a little understanding. What they needed was forgiveness." He looked at Chuck with such tenderness as he said this, and Stephen could only wonder at their history together, and the safe harbor into which they had finally sailed.

Stephen would always remember the rest of that evening in shadow. Ben gazing out the window as they drove back to the Edwardian Arms. The lights of passing cars erupting like flashbulbs. The cold gleam of the key unlocking the door to the apartment. Ben's neck soft against his own as they hugged goodbye and Ben's shy smile when he whispered, "I told my parents I was staying at my friend's house tonight." The way those bare and challenging words hung there in the air, suspended between them. And then Ben's feverish mouth on his, insistent and unyielding.

"Ben, you don't..." Stephen protested, as he felt the searching exploration of Ben's hands, of his lips, his entire body a sort of geographic discovery to Stephen's.

"We can't do this, Ben," Stephen said, stepping back. "You know we can't do this."

"Are you sure?"

"Yes, I am...for now."

Ben looked at him, unspeaking, and then suddenly hugged Stephen with a violent force, the dark, wavy hair a wordless, muted caress against Stephen's face. "Please let me stay. We don't have to do anything."

"Ben...Ben," Stephen said faintly, almost capitulating to one last, brief touch of Ben's lips on his. Stephen put his arms around him with an anguished affection, but a no less emphatic, and no less desperate, restraint.

CHAPTER FORTY-EIGHT
OLD FRIENDS

Laura walked into the small foyer of East Bistro in Dilworth, one of those trendy restaurants integrated into the old houses along East Boulevard. A hostess with closely cropped brown hair greeted her. "One?" she asked.

"No, I am waiting for someone. She should be here shortly."

The woman nodded distractedly. "Would you like your table now?"

"I'll wait, thank you."

For as long as Laura had known her, Missy had been notoriously unpunctual. It was one of those small rebellions that Missy, otherwise such a diligent student in social etiquette, allowed herself. In any event, it was no wonder that the leisurely chaos of the Italians appealed to her. Finally, after fifteen minutes had passed, Missy, shimmering in a dark blue linen pantsuit and pearls, appeared in the lobby. She did not effect a frantic air and rush in breathlessly. She never made outlandish claims regarding congested traffic or sudden delays. She always appeared as if she had just come in from a leisurely stroll, and the scenery was simply too delightful to hurry it. If this tranquil demeanor was more surface than depth, as of course Laura knew that it was, it was no less striking, and no less annoying.

"Have you been waiting long?" Missy asked.

"No, not long at all." Laura rose to give Missy a hug.

The hostess reappeared, clutching two menus. "Do you have a booth for two upstairs?" Missy asked, coldly appraising her.

"Yes, ma'am. Certainly. Follow me, please," she sighed, bracing herself for one more martyred trek upstairs.

They were seated at a little table near the old fireplace. "Look, Laur. I love the little track lights on the string down below and the Venetian mirrors. Quirky, isn't it?" Missy smiled, her old, reassuring smile, and, for a brief moment, Laura felt as if they were back at Queens College.

"That's one word for it," Laura replied, neatly folding her linen napkin. "I think this home used to be owned by the Vines. Mr. Vine was daddy's accountant. Dad used to send me over here every April with his tax records. Mrs. Vine was a terrible cook. No wonder the poor man was thin as a rail. He looked like a skinny owl. She used to give me a fudge brownie after I dropped off the papers, and I had to throw it into the bushes. Awful brownies!"

"Well, here's to Mrs. Vine," Missy laughed.

Their waiter, a strikingly handsome young man with light brown, curly hair, approached their table. "Hi, my name is Eric. How are you ladies today?"

Missy studied him appreciatively. "Just fine, thanks. You look Italian. Are you?" she asked.

"On my mother's side. Yes, ma'am."

"Well, Eric," Missy purred, as if she might just dine on the syllables of his name, "I'm going to have that brownie with ice cream and caramel sauce just to celebrate the former owners of this home. But, first, I will have the house salad to balance things a little."

"And I will have the pasta primavera. Thank you," Laura said.

After Eric had walked away, Missy said, "Good-looking fellow, isn't he? What? Oh, don't look so shocked. Edward doesn't pay any attention to me these days. Really. That's the truth. A girl needs a *little* encouragement, don't you think?"

"Miss," Laura said, "don't be silly. You look wonderful."

"Do I?" she asked. "Good. Lately, I just live on the treadmill and lettuce. God, you know I never counted a single calorie till I was past forty." Given that Laura, judging from her still expanding waistline, had not yet begun that count, Missy quickly changed the subject. "How have you been? You look a little tired."

"Me? I'm fine. Did you have a nice time at Pawleys?"

"Oh, same old, same old. It was just Andrea and me. John doesn't get home until next week. And Edward has been consumed with his work, as usual. All those condos Uptown. Lord, he just prattles on and on about them. Swears they're the future of Charlotte. Well, that's one view. I don't think I could get through these hot summers anymore without going to Pawleys. Did I tell you I redecorated the house? It's all in peach and green, and I have some beautiful Mexican antiques there now."

Laura smoothed the napkin on her lap, and nervously looked about the room. "I really don't care for Pawleys much anymore. It has changed so much."

"How so?" Missy asked somewhat resentfully. "You used to love it there."

"Yes, I did," Laura agreed. "But, I don't recognize it anymore."

"It's the same as always."

"Is it?" Laura asked. "Not to me. All those big new homes elbowing the shore, each one trying to outdo the other. I mean, no offense, but it's just...well...too busy."

Missy, annoyed, smiled patiently. "That's silly. Most of those old shacky cottages are still there. Good Lord, our own house is too small if you want to know the truth. The really big homes are on the marsh side. But, then, as you said, you don't go any more...since your mother sold that little house you all had there."

Laura looked away, trying not to dwell on the last time she was in the cottage. She had sat in the swing on the front porch, remembering her father, watching the waves crash ashore. "Yes, I miss our *little* house there," she said. "Just too many memories there for me, I guess."

"Are you all right? You seem out of sorts," Missy said irritably, noticing the slight tremor of Laura's hands.

"Do I? It's always darkest before the dawn, right? Well, anyway, that's what my mother used to say. Of course, she usually had been the one to turn out the lights in the first place, so I guess she would have known." Laura laughed nervously at her little joke.

"What's wrong?" Missy asked, pursing her full lips into a tight line. She had no patience for circuitous routes to any disclosure worth telling.

Laura hesitated and then said, almost inaudibly as she looked furtively about the room, "This is very difficult for me to discuss. It's Ben."

Their waiter reappeared with their food. "Eric? I'll have another," Missy said, pointing to her half empty glass of merlot. "Is he sick?" she asked Laura.

"No. It isn't anything like that. Well, actually, in a way it is. He's having some emotional problems."

"How so?" Missy asked, frowning at the wilted lettuce in her salad.

"Ben is confused. Sexually."

"What do you mean?"

"He thinks he might be homosexual," Laura said. "He isn't," she hastily added. "He's just mixed up. He was seeing a counselor."

"Was?"

"He isn't anymore. And the therapist told me that Ben is… involved…with your nephew. And that's why Ben stopped. Because of Stephen."

"What? That's impossible," Missy exclaimed, not bothering to lower her voice. "I don't believe it."

"It's true. The therapist said that Stephen, and this is the word he used, seduced Ben. Why would he lie?"

"Perhaps he misunderstood the situation," Missy argued. "Heavens, most counselors are fruitcakes themselves."

"No. Ben admitted it. Well, in so many words. He says Stephen is just a friend." She spat out the word *friend*, as if it had suddenly been transformed into something poisonous, something nauseating. "Maybe, technically, that is all it is for now. I pray to God for at least that. But, it is very clear as to the…nature…of the relationship."

Missy took a prolonged sip of her wine. "Why are you telling me this?"

"My son is in trouble," Laura gasped. "He is just a boy. Surely you don't think that it is okay for Stephen to..to…take advantage…"

"I didn't say it was okay, did I?" Missy interrupted. "You make too much of things. You always have."

"How would you feel if this were John?" Laura asked. "What would you do?"

"But it isn't," Missy said matter-of-factly. She recalled a moment how close Ben and John had been, almost inseparable for a while, but refused to consider anything unnatural in that relationship.

"Really? How can you be so sure?"

"I know my son. He likes girls. Probably a little too much. Remember last spring when I was scared to death that he had gotten that trampy little Morrow girl pregnant? That liked to kill me."

"Ben had girlfriends. He played football. There is nothing effeminate about him. Maybe he and John…"

Missy raised her hand and cut Laura off. "If you have a grudge against my family," she said icily, "don't take it out on my son."

"You know that is not true," Laura protested. "How can you say something like that? Have I ever been anything but grateful to you? And to Edward?"

"Oh, stop being so righteous." After so many years of higher and higher ascent, it was as if Missy had finally paused, looking back just this once, and asked the question that had been simmering between them for so long. Her eyes bored into Laura's with naked malice. "Don't you resent us? Just a little?"

"You'd like to think so, wouldn't you? You'd like to believe that. Maybe I do," Laura admitted, not really caring anymore one way or the other. "And now I need your help."

Missy remained silent, then motioned for the waiter. "Eric, I've decided against the dessert," she said. "You may bring us the check."

"I want you to talk to Stephen," Laura said, her eyes moist with tears and panic.

"I have no control over him or any other member of that crazy family," Missy replied.

"If you do not talk to him, I will. And I cannot be responsible for what Andrew might do to him. He doesn't know about this yet. But, if I tell him, I just don't know…" Laura paused, assured that if conscience would not compel Missy to act, reputation most certainly would. "You know how he can be sometimes," she added, ominously looking about the room as if her volatile husband might walk in any moment. "And you know how people talk in this town."

"I should think *that* is something you know more than I do," Missy said. "No one cared enough about my family to talk about them one way or the other. But, the Soames family. The high and mighty Soames family," Missy said, laughing mercilessly. "Well, that's another matter, isn't it? There are still people in Myers Park who knew your parents. Knew them quite well...quite *intimately*... and they still talk. Of that I can assure you."

Laura looked at Missy and said, in an eerily calm voice. "I trusted you...You said that I could trust you."

Missy did not answer. The waiter brought the check over to the table. Missy reached for her handbag and retrieved a small black leather wallet. "My treat," she said, as she placed her money on the table. "I insist."

"I want you to talk to Stephen," Laura repeated, in a strangely detached tone, with an assertiveness Missy would not have thought her capable. "I want him to stay away from my son. I don't want Andrew to…"

Missy looked at Laura, who seemed so exhausted now by this brief defiance, hunched over in her chair, trying not to cry. "All right. I will talk to Stephen. Keep that loose cannon you married out of it."

"Thank you," Laura said quietly.

Missy rose from the table. "It's funny, really," she said, her intense eyes contemptuous and dismissive. "I used to think that you were so impressive, that you were *somebody*." Then, she turned her back and walked out, with a chilly and unmistakable air of conclusion.

Laura said a silent prayer, asking God to help her forgive her friend. Asking God for understanding. But, what she remembered, as lately her memories so often were, was more for regret than forgiveness. She recalled something Andrew had said to her on their honeymoon, one morning as they were having breakfast on the terrace at the Grove Park Inn.

"Missy's all right, I guess," he said. "I mean, she's your best friend and all. But, I noticed at the wedding reception something about her. She never looks at people. She's always looking up, or looking down, depending on who the person is, how he rates, but she never looks *at* you. *Never.*"

CHAPTER FORTY-NINE
AUGUST RECESS

J ohn Harrison yawned as he rifled through the pages scattered on his kitchen table. It was his final week in Washington, and he had been assigned to help Tricia draft a memo to prepare the congresswoman for a hearing later in September to address legislation on illegal immigrants. Toller, with the fervor of a zealot unimpeded by practical concerns, was demanding mass deportations.

"This isn't going to affect our cook, Juanita, is it? Because my mom will be really pissed," he said to Tricia, grinning.

Tricia methodically made notes in the margins of the draft. "The main thing is to keep the congresswoman on message. Under peril of death, she can't be distracted by the finer points of the bill. That way lies disaster."

"Okay, got it," John said, sliding his chair closer to her. "I have a few fine points of my own to talk to you about. But, they still need a little finessing." He put his arm on her shoulder and began rubbing it. "A little massaging."

"Not now," she said, unconvincingly, as he leaned back and then reached for her hand and began pulling it down toward his lap.

Suddenly, the phone rang. "Oh, jeez, who the hell is that?" he moaned. He reluctantly picked up the receiver.

"John?"

"Mom? Hey," he said, keeping Tricia's hand firmly in place.

"How are you?" Missy asked. "Did I get you at a good time?"

"Yeah, sure, just working with one of the staffers on the immigration bill." John winked at Tricia, who responded by licking her lips. He closed his eyes and leaned back in his chair.

"Oh? That sounds interesting."

"Yeah. It's okay. I still don't see the congresswoman much. She's usually traveling now, since Congress is in recess." He felt Tricia's caressing hand under his shirt.

"Well, it's still a good experience for you. We're looking forward to seeing you next week. And the congresswoman called me again yesterday and said she would love to come to our party for you."

"That's cool. Making amends for blowing you off at lunch, huh? So, what else is going on?" he asked, somewhat breathlessly, stretching out further and running his free hand through Tricia's silky hair.

He could hear his mother clicking her teeth. "Well, I'll just come right out with it. I wanted to let you know about Ben, his being your friend and all, I think you should know this," she said. "He's gay, and he has, ahm, well, he's been spending time with Stephen."

John arched his back. "Oh...wow...really?" he gasped. "*Cousin* Stephen? When did this happen?"

"Well, according to his mother, who is very torn up about all this, it has been going on now since they met at the Rolling Stones thing at the new Bobcats arena. You remember, I told you about that."

"Does Dad know about this? Remember that guy he fired? The one who, ahm...liked antiques?" John suppressed a moan, caressed by Tricia's slippery tongue.

"I haven't spoken to your father about it, no. I just don't want half of Charlotte gossiping about our family."

"*You* don't? Ben used to hang with me all the time," he offered, sitting up now, his hand violently pressing against Tricia's head. "So, what are they saying about *me*?"

"Nothing. No one is saying anything about you. But, did you ever think Ben might be gay?"

"No, never, at least not until just this summer." For an instant, he recalled the night by the lake with Ben.

"What happened this summer?"

"There were a couple times. The way he looked at me sometimes. And then once...well, whatever." He put his hand over his mouth as Tricia's fingers made a feathery progression up his naked thighs.

"Is that why you don't see much of him anymore?"

"What? Oh, well, sure. Anyway, I guess he can't help it, being queer or whatever. But, it creeps me out."

"Oh, I know, honey, of course."

"Listen, Mom, I gotta go. I'm meeting some of the folks from work at the Monocle. Hey, did I mention I met a nice Carolina girl here on the staff?"

"No. Who is she?"

"Her name is Tricia," he said, winking at her and running his tongue along his lips. "She's a legislative aide, real smart. Anyway, tell Dad hi."

"I will, but let's just keep this conversation between us. And be careful driving home next week."

John put the phone down. "Well, that was interesting," Tricia said, looking up at him and smiling. "Listen, if mommy has any doubts about her Johnny, I can clear them up for her."

CHAPTER FIFTY
SOFT CHORDS

Edward watched Missy's intermittent scowl as she read the morning paper. If her mood was clear, the basis for it was not. This was a frequent occurrence of late in the Harrison household, and one that Edward Harrison preferred not to think about too much. He had found that civility with Missy depended on striking the softest possible chords.

During the two weeks that Missy and Andrea were at Pawleys Island, Edward had given much consideration to his wife's character, particularly her varied faults that conveniently cast himself in the role of the unappreciated husband. This methodical consideration of his wife's shortcomings served to mediate his own growing sense of moral tension. In contrast, he noticed that Alice had on no occasion spoken disparagingly of Bill. Since she did not believe her behavior was wrong, she lacked any compunction to excuse it. Alice implicitly condoned what Edward still struggled to justify. It was not exactly guilt that he felt, but rather a feeling of inequity. If he was happy now, and his wife was not, it had to be *her* fault, not his.

"Would you ever consider leaving Bill?" he asked Alice one day after making love. "Because I would leave Missy. There is just nothing left there between us. I don't know how that happened, but there it is."

"No. I'm sorry. But, no." she replied, as gently as she could, softly touching his forehead the way a mother would check for fever. "I would never be a party to breaking up a marriage. Even a bad marriage. I would never want to be the last nail on the coffin. That may seem strange for me to say, but it's the truth. And, I know it is hard for you to understand this, but I love my husband. I would feel lost without Bill. I don't expect him to fill my plate, but he will always be the entree."

"What am I? An appetizer?"

"No, you are dessert," she laughed.

"You're right. I don't understand," he said morosely. "How can you be with me, like this, and still say you love your husband? How do you manage that? Is that how they do it out in San Francisco?"

She took his hand. "Edward, I know my limitations. That may be my only real virtue, but I'm holding onto it." She slowly kissed his fingers, lingering deliciously on each one. "I know my limitations," she continued. "I guess, for me, love and sex, they are like the flowers in the garden. I love lilies, but I like roses too. One doesn't negate the other."

"You're lucky," he said. "It's more like a desert for me. I'm just glad that I found you there. I guess that makes you my desert rose. That's what you are, Alice. My desert rose."

"Well, that's okay," she said. "Desert roses bloom for quite some time. They're very hearty." He recalled how she curved her body into his, her hand caressing his face.

His thoughts of Alice were disrupted as Missy continued to violently plow through the morning paper. While probing inquiries were no longer in the best interest of their marriage, even minimal attention compelled him to address her evident distress.

"What is it?" he asked, annoyed. "Why are you destroying the paper?"

She put the newspaper down, almost pushing it over the cool marble table onto the floor. "I realize you've been very *distracted* lately, but haven't you heard?" she asked, her voice rumbling with incredulity. "Your nephew Stephen is making our family the laughingstock of Charlotte."

"You mean the UNCC thing? It will blow over."

"Maybe," she said doubtfully. "But, I have other news. His new boyfriend is Ben Caldwell."

"I beg your pardon?"

"No need to beg. My pardons are freely given," she said ominously. "You of all people should know that by now. Stephen is seeing Ben, John's moody little friend. Or, rather, ex-friend."

"How do you know this?"

"Laura told me, and then she insisted that I try and talk some sense into Stephen. And she all but threatened to have Andrew come after Stephen with a shot gun." She poured herself another cup of coffee, and then added, "I don't know who has me more upset, Stephen or Laura. Why, the gall to…"

Edward shrugged nonchalantly. "Stay out of it, Missy. I don't like it either, but it's not my problem. And it won't be," he said, looking at Missy with disapproving eyes, "unless you make it one."

"Well, I hope you are right," she sighed, placing another almond croissant on her plate. "For Christ's sake, Ben is barely eighteen! I guarantee you this is already being discussed over breakfast at a lot of tables in this neighborhood. What are you going to *say* to people?"

Edward looked at his wife, not for the first time, as a petulant, naive child. For all her Italianate pretensions, she was still just a hick from Rock Hill. "I'm not going to say anything, because no one will bring it up. The Caldwell boy is of legal age. And Stephen is old enough to act like a goddamned fool if he chooses to. Okay, fine, I get it. He's homosexual and he has a young friend, but there's nothing we can do about it."

"When did you become so liberal? I think maybe you have been spending too much time with Alice Owens," she said, then added, with portentous delay, "and Bill."

"Don't be ridiculous. I just believe in dealing with what is." he said, looking intently at her. "I've had lots of practice." Edward got up to leave, and gave Missy an obligatory kiss goodbye.

"Oh, one other thing before I forget," Missy said, as Edward was walking toward the door. "Your mother called yesterday. She wanted to tell you that Evelyn Peck needs to talk to you. Evelyn wouldn't tell

Myrtle what it was about, only that she was having some problem
with her plumbing."

Edward shrugged. "I'll have my secretary give her a call."

"You do that," Missy replied, smiling now. "Only, knowing
Evelyn, I imagine you might want to handle it yourself."

CHAPTER FIFTY-ONE
WE ARE FAMILY

Stephen settled into the soft leather chair in the library and made a closer study of the Harrison's books. It was an interesting collection, as if his aunt had instructed her decorator, "Get me the classics. I want the best." Aside from the insistent coordination of color and size, there was no order to their arrangement. Ancient Greek poets were side by side with Emerson, the Bronte sisters next to *The Interpretation of Dreams*. Proust coexisted with *The Wealth of Nations*. Neither of the Harrisons had any apparent interest in contemporary fiction, though there were liberal doses of recent biographies and histories, but only of a sedate variety, eminently respectable and almost certainly unread. Stephen found this cavalcade of learning especially ironic given the general Harrison antipathy to all things literary.

Once his grandmother was visiting his mother in New York with Uncle Edward. They were walking with Lynn down Fifth Avenue and passed Brentano's. "Well, I know where Stephen would be if he were with us now," Lynn said, pointing to the bookstore.

Both Myrtle and Edward laughed at the notion. "Don't get *me* no book!" Myrtle said.

Curiously, one entire shelf was filled with back issues of *Charlotte Now* magazine, carefully ordered by date. Stephen realized that, given the periodic appearances of his aunt and uncle in that magazine, it was a veritable catalogue of their social and philanthropic history, and of far more interest to them than, say, the collected works of Jane Austen.

Then, with regal cohesion, Missy and Edward entered the room together. Stephen nervously wondered again if he was making the right decision. Edward carried a tray of cocktails. "Here you go, pardner, one apple martini," Edward said, handing him the drink.

Missy hugged him effusively. "Stephen! You get better looking every day."

They sat down on the leather sofa opposite him and were, Stephen noted, as sartorially incompatible as ever. Edward wore faded tan Dockers, with frayed cuffs, and an old UNC sweatshirt, while Missy asserted her usual elegance in a silver Armani pantsuit and black pumps. Her one concession to informality was the pink flamingo margarita glass she held in her manicured hand.

"Drink okay?" Edward asked.

"Fine, thanks," Stephen said. They sipped idly on their drinks, as a palpable silence began to fill the room.

"Okay, so…UNCC," Edward began. He paused to take another drink of his scotch. "What is going on with that goddamned race mess?"

"Edward," Missy interrupted, pointing one red taloned finger at him while she securely maintained her grip on her flamingo glass, "there is no need for that kind of talk in this house." Stephen all but expected her to point to the books, as if perhaps Homer or Gibbons, or at least the *Charlotte* society editor, were listening in.

"Oh, sorry," Edward said grudgingly, taking a sip of his scotch and affording an even more exasperated look than usual at his wife. "So, what the…what's going on out there? You know, you can't get the blacks fired up and not expect trouble. I'm no racist, but you have never seen a bunch of whiners like the so-called black leaders in this city."

"Of course," Missy concurred. "That's why I called you, Stephen. I know you don't want us to meddle, it is your affair…but, we want to help."

"I appreciate that, Aunt Missy," Stephen said. "I have never traded on my connection to you with the university. Anyway, as I mentioned when you called, I had a meeting with my department head. Dr. Williams? You probably know him. Anyway, I was ordered not to talk to the media, and they are having someone else finish my summer course." He paused a moment, then said, "That was bad enough. But, at least I thought it would be the end of it."

"And?" Edward asked.

"Well, now Dr. Williams is insisting that I go before a peer review committee."

"Those gutless wonders," Edward seethed. "The more you stir shit the more it smells."

"Is it true they are threatening not to renew your contract?" Missy asked, glaring at her husband. "That's what your mother told Edward."

"No, not in so many words," Stephen replied. "They are more subtle than that, but they have continued dropping hints that I might be a poor bet for tenure. And the word suspension has been bandied about. I hope it won't come to that."

"Hope?" Edward asked sarcastically. "*Hope*? Son, hope is for losers. Now, listen to me, you are family. And family sticks together. Period."

"Yes, sir. Thank you," Stephen said, shifting uneasily in his seat.

"We admire your independence," Missy said. "That's a Harrison for you." She absentmindedly caressed the flamingo stem of her drink, and then added, "But, an insult to you is an insult to us."

"And that ain't gonna fly," Edward said, raising his hand to brook no further interruption. "I will speak with the chancellor, Stephen. This will end here, make no mistake."

"I appreciate that," he said, "I really didn't want to bother you about this."

"No problem. Don't you give it another thought." Edward rose. "Now, if y'all will excuse me, I have got to make a couple phone calls. Stephen, finish your drink, son. You take care now, you hear?"

"I will, Uncle Edward," Stephen said. "And, again, thank you." He noticed that Edward completely ignored Missy as he left the room, as if their mission together was complete and they could now return to their separate corners. He remembered something his grandmother had recently told him. "Edward only seems to be happy when he is working. Never at home. Never. I said to Fred, 'Fred, that marriage is in big trouble.' I never liked Missy, I'll admit it, way too highfalutin' for me, but I always thought that Edward did. Now, I'm not so sure...."

He heard Missy asking him, "Would you like another drink?"

"No, thanks. I really should be getting back home. I've taken enough of your time."

"Oh, don't be silly. We're always glad to see you." She put down her drink on the ornate mahogany table next to the sofa, and leaned forward. "I didn't want to bring this up with Edward here," she said, almost whispering. "He's not as, well, sophisticated about...some things."

"What things?"

"Ben Caldwell," she said, letting the name hang in the air.

"Oh, Ben," Stephen answered. "Yes, I met him at the Rolling Stones thing. A fine young man."

"Yes. He is a fine *boy*," she said, slowly turning the emerald ring on her finger. "And, according to his mother, the two of you are more than just friends."

"That is not true." Stephen thought of the last time he had seen Ben, standing there in Stephen's darkened apartment, the two of them entwined in that tortuous, anxious embrace.

Missy smiled patiently. "He's barely eighteen. A confused *boy*."

"Aunt Missy, I understand that. That's why I have tried to be a friend, and nothing more than a friend, to Ben. He's just trying to find his way..." Stephen resolved that he would not disclose anything further, would not compound the boy's sorrow by sharing it with Missy. "Yes, Ben is young. He *is* a young man. Like Johnny, who, I understand is involved with a woman in Washington about my age."

Missy took a prolonged sip of her drink, her jeweled finger wrapped more tightly now around the flamingo stem. "We're not talking about Johnny right now. That is another kettle of fish," she said matter of factly. She regarded Stephen with a studied patience. "Look, this is Charlotte. Don't kid yourself. Scratch the surface and you will always find a redneck underneath. I'm sorry, but that is how it still is here. You're really a New Yorker. You don't understand that. But, I do."

"What do you want me to do?" Stephen asked.

"Well, this is awkward," she said, serenely confident that any such awkwardness would be more his portion than hers. "We're on your side. You know that. But, it doesn't matter whether it is true or not. You have to be *discreet* in Charlotte. I've no doubt that Ben was chasing you, not the other way around. But, people will talk, will wonder..."

"What people?"

"People who *matter*," she said slowly, as if she were tutoring a recalcitrant child. She glanced at her shelves of classics for a moment, and then said evenly, "We *want* to help you. But, there are limits. You know that."

"Yes, I do. And I would like to help Ben, by continuing to be his friend. Is that so terrible? He needs a friend."

"Stephen," she said, smiling sweetly, her oddly penetrating eyes fixed on him, "listen to me. Help yourself. My advice would be to find more friends your own age and concentrate on your *work*."

He looked away from her unflinching gaze. Her meaning was clear. Stephen stood up. "I think I understand," he said. "I know this was not an easy thing for you to discuss."

He longed to demolish that confident, expectant expression on her lofty face. He could have told her what he knew about her own precious son. If Stephen harbored an unforgiving vindictiveness for anyone, it was for the cruel luster of his cousin. Stephen could also have told her that his fragile relationship with Ben was *ephemeral* at best, if only to send this willful, arrogant woman rushing to the dictionary for the meaning of the word. But, he did not. However distasteful, he did need their help. She was right in one respect. He did not understand the way things worked in Charlotte, and they did. Stephen suddenly felt exhausted with their burdensome expectations and his own precarious need.

She hugged him goodbye, her sharp nails lightly digging into his back. "Remember," she said, "we are family. And we stick together." She smiled and kissed Stephen gently on the cheek, then whispered, "Whenever we can."

CHAPTER FIFTY-TWO
THE ART OF THE DEAL

A lice returned from the hospital, exhausted, and poured herself a glass of chardonnay. The house was deserted, with Bill at the bank and the girls on an outing to Discovery Place with Aurelia. It suddenly seemed peculiar to her that, in spite of all the people in her life, all neatly inhabiting the particular niche she had assigned them, she was so often alone. But, Alice was a firm believer that very little happened by accident, and if she sometimes felt isolated, it was mainly due to her own efficiency in opening and closing doors.

She had performed an emergency caesarean earlier that day after discovering a breech birth. No matter how many of these procedures she had done, there was still a latent fear in them. Mindful of potentially fatal complications for both mother and baby, Alice always felt like a tightrope walker, confident of her balance, calm in her focus and precision, but acutely attuned to the danger. It would always be a high wire act. She had first tried to manually reverse the position of the baby, as the young mother moaned in agony and the woman's husband, a hulking man with a red goatee, veered into hysteria. "What's wrong?" he screamed. "What is happening?"

"The baby is in the wrong position, Mr. Johnson," she said calmly. "Don't worry. It will be all right. I am going to have to operate though." His eyes were pleading. *Save my wife. Save our baby.* "It will be all right," she said again, "but you will need to wait outside." He looked at her dumbly, as his wife continued moaning incoherently. "Let me do my job," she said firmly, and he was escorted out the door.

She had often wondered if the universal story of the garden of Eden was an allegory of the birth experience, a collective memory of nightmarish beginnings. Now, as she sipped her drink, it occurred to her again that some babies refuse to leave the idyllic comfort of the womb. Either because of size or position, or just plain terror, they can only be expelled from the womb with the grip of forceps or lifted out of it by expert cutting. Perhaps the breech babies, like the one she brought into the world this morning, kicking and screaming, are the clever ones, she thought. Maybe they already sense the turmoil awaiting them. And she sometimes wondered if those babies, many years hence, would be just as tenacious in their refusal to leave a world that they were so reluctant to enter.

Her reverie was interrupted by the ringing of the telephone. "Hello?" she said, hoping that it would be Bill.

"Alice? Hi. It's Stephen."

"Well, hello."

"I'm not interrupting, am I?"

"No, you called at a good time. How are you? Tell me something that will take my mind off of emergency surgeries."

"Well," he said, "let's see. The college has decided I'm a racist firebrand and wants to get rid of me. I am completely in over my head with young Ben. And, in my spare moments, I just want to kill Aunt Missy."

"Oh, my. Let's start with auntie. What has she done now?"

"I went to see them at the palazzo. I never knew how creepy that big old house could be when there are only three people in it. Anyway, there we sit, and both of them, all hugs and kisses, wanted me to know that I could count on their support at UNCC. That's a big deal of course, since they basically take turns serving on the Board of Trustees and I have decided not to go quietly. Then Uncle Edward conveniently left the room, so Missy could bring out the quid pro quo."

"Which is?"

"Stop seeing Ben. *Discreet* was the word she used. Oh, you should have seen her. First, she says, all solemn, 'Stephen, this is awkward, but...I understand you have been seeing Ben Caldwell. Is that right?' So, I said, 'Well, as a matter of fact, I have been. He's a great guy.' And she said, more Joan Crawford imperious with each syllable, 'Don't you mean he is a great boy? Isn't that closer to the truth?'"

"How on earth would she know about you two? I thought that you had been very private about it."

"For two people with nothing to hide, yes, we have been. I'm still not sure how it came out, but somehow Mrs. Caldwell knows and is furious. You know she and Missy go all the way back to when Queens college did not pretend to be a university. Anyway, the two sorority sisters got together and Mrs. Caldwell asked Missy to persuade me, in that sweet Sherman tank way Aunt Missy has, to end the relationship."

"So, do you think she has talked about all of this with Edward?"

"Oh, of course. But, I gather they are not talking too much otherwise these days. And that has her jumpier than usual. Not that she loves him. She just wants to control his life along with everybody else's. I guess my little train wreck has brought them together in common cause. "

"So, what did she say to you?"

"Well, they both told me that they will calm the waters at the university. She said this town is full of gossips. That isn't exactly newsworthy, is it? And she is worried about what the Caldwells will do." Stephen paused, noting Alice's silence, then added, "I don't know if she believed me or not that Ben and I are just friends."

"I wonder if, really, she even cares," Alice replied. "But, clearly, the charges she is worried about are the kind that are fired over bridge tables in Morrocroft."

"Oh, you've been studying."

"Well, let's just say it is part of the curriculum for outsiders like us. Have you talked to Ben?"

"I'm going to," he said softly. "I do care about him, but I know he wants more than I can, or should, give him. Anyway, you can imagine the difficulty. It can get pretty confusing for us both."

"Yes, I suppose so," Alice said. "But, how could you do otherwise?"

"I couldn't. You don't win any points in this town for doing the right thing, do you?"

She laughed and told him, "You do with me. Definitely. I'm proud of you."

"Well, that helps. Thanks. He just seemed so lost," Stephen murmured, as if he himself were still mystified by the relationship. "I guess I have been kind of lost as well. Worst possible timing though."

"I'm sorry," Alice said. "I really am. So, what did you say to the gorgon?"

"Honestly, a feeble thank you was all I could manage. I can read between the lines. I know what she is really asking me to do. But, I'm not going to abandon Ben. I'm not going to stop being his friend. We'll just continue to be *discreet*. It's so demeaning, but we can't always say what we really think, can we?"

"No, professor, we cannot," Alice said, cognizant of her own careful steps.

"I'm sorry to be so whiny," he continued. "But, trust me when I tell you this, Aunt Missy always wins. She always comes out ahead. And she has raised my cousin John exactly the same way. If anything, he is even worse than she is. Breaking hearts is his hobby. I really think he enjoys cruelty. Missy at least has goals. Anyway, I want to keep my job, Alice, and I don't have the luxury of telling her to mind her own business."

"I will go out on a limb here and assume that she would not take kindly to that."

"No, she wouldn't. She said that we are family, and that we have to stick together. Can you believe it?"

"Yes, I can. But, I think you can trust your uncle. Edward seems like a man who keeps his word, especially when it involves his family. But, Missy strikes me as the kind of person who wraps herself in the family mantle whenever it suits her. Which, I gather, is not too often."

"I know," he said, laughing bitterly, "only, now, she and I are wrapped in it together."

CHAPTER FIFTY-THREE
MOLD

The following Saturday morning, Alice Owens, with surgical precision, clipped red and white geraniums in the terra cotta pots that lined her flagstone patio. She could see a blue jay fluttering in the tree above her as she began arranging the flowers. The bouquet was flawless, except for one dirt-stained, white bloom, which she cavalierly plucked and tossed into the yard.

Aurelia, the au pair, had taken the girls to the park. Bill would be returning from New York that afternoon. He was in New York on business quite frequently of late. At least, she reflected, that's what he *tells* me. She planned to meet Aurelia and her daughters at Patou in Dilworth later for lunch. But, first, she would steal an hour with Edward at Villa Rosa restaurant, which they deemed far enough out South Boulevard to provide adequate privacy.

Exactly one hour later, wearing a white cotton blouse over navy blue shorts, Alice arrived at Villa Rosa. She wondered for a moment if Missy Harrison, with her Italian mania, ever came there. Not likely. A woman of Missy's lofty airs would not venture into such an out of the way establishment. Alice quickly scanned the room to see if anyone she knew was there. As Edward had predicted, it was practically empty. A single elderly woman, voraciously finishing off the last crumbs of a tiramisu, ignored her as Alice walked to a table in the back.

After about five minutes, he arrived. He had meetings in Uptown, even on Saturday mornings, and was wearing a dark blue suit and a Carolina blue tie. He quickly sat down across from her. She leaned over the table and gave him a hug. "Hello, blue boy."

"Blue for you," he said, taking all of her in with one appreciative gaze, lingering on her long, tanned legs. "I've missed you so much. God, you look wonderful."

"Thank you," she said, taking his hand. "It's good to see you. I already ordered coffee and croissants for us. How are you? You sounded a little down on the phone."

"I'm better now." He took a photograph from his jacket. "I know you probably can't keep this, but I wanted to bring it to you anyway." He shyly handed her the photograph. "It was taken one summer at Centerpoint with Grandmom. I was about six then."

Alice studied the picture. Edward, a tanned and pudgy looking child, was seated on a linoleum top table in the backyard under one of the apple trees. Rose Harrison was seated behind him and hugging him. She had white hair and wore a simple plaid housedress and a white apron. Below them chickens scattered around the table. The house at Centerpoint is in the background and freshly laundered clothes, shining in sunlight, are hanging on the line. But, it is the young boy's face that catches Alice's eye. She is struck by the wondrous expression, his mouth open in a sort of joyous shout, his hands in mid-air, as if he were about to clap for sheer happiness.

"Edward, thank you for sharing this with me," she said, touched beyond any expression of words, her eyes moistening with tears. "It is just the most wonderful photograph." She paused, noticing his discomfort. "Well, enough of that. How is your work going?"

"Don't get me started," he said, his brow tensing. "The Wellington is such a mess."

"That's the new condo building down —I mean, *up* —town? The one you showed me? I remember that day very fondly."

"So do I. Very. Anyway, it's supposed to be completed by end of next month. Not gonna happen. It's also supposed to be sold out already. We have a lot of money tied up there."

"I'm sorry," she said. "I have heard Bill talking about that project. The bank also seems a little jittery about it. I'm surprised.

Isn't Uptown where everybody wants to live now?"

"Well, that is the official line. Yes. A lot of big investors have bought condos there, but it remains to be seen just how many people will actually move in at the end of the day. And Uptown is competing with SouthPark, where folks still feel safer."

"I know. I usually don't go Uptown by myself, day or night? And I am not an especially fearful person."

"This city needs a Giuliani," Edward lamented. "And what we have is a milquetoast. I mean, don't get me wrong, he's great for business. Gives us whatever we want with a wink and a nod. But, he's soft. Whatever else you can say about her, Toller is fierce. Everybody is afraid of her."

Alice laughed. "Yes. On that we can all agree. She's pretty scary. Is your son glad to be back home?"

His eyes clouded over for a moment. "John? Oh, he's great. Doing great."

"Well, good. That was a big change for him going up to the wicked capital."

"He is a very adaptable kid. Always has been, like his mother." He hesitated a moment, and then asked, "Have you heard about Ben Caldwell, Andrew and Laura's son?"

"You mean that he's gay? Yes, I have heard that."

"What else have you heard?"

"Not much. I know that he has the good fortune to have your nephew Stephen as a friend."

"Who told you?"

"Stephen. Stephen told me."

"Oh. I didn't realize you two were still so close."

"Well," she said, smiling, "what would you say are the odds of a young gay man and a woman from San Francisco becoming buddies?"

"I hate that word," he replied irritably. "Gay. It used to just mean happy. Queer or *funny*, that made more sense."

"That isn't like you," she said, again taking his hand. "You are better than that."

"Am I? What makes you so sure?" he asked, with a sarcasm that she had not seen before.

"Because I know you." She looked about the room to confirm that they were still alone and kept his hand in hers. "I know the best part of you."

"Maybe you do," he said, "I just am tired of Stephen and the homosexual thing. *That* I have a problem with. I'm sorry, but I do."

"Well, all I know is that Stephen did not choose to be gay anymore than you chose to be straight. Some people don't like that, but it really is that simple."

"I guess we will just have to disagree on this," he said, in a more placating tone now. "I don't have any ill will toward him. He's family and, frankly, one of the better ones. I've always liked Stephen. But, I think his lifestyle is wrong. It's in the Bible."

"The Bible also says 'wives submit yourselves to your husbands.' Do you believe that too? Having met Missy, I rather doubt it. Oh, and I seem to recall something in there, earlier, about adultery. And coveting your neighbor's wife. I don't believe you can cherry pick your sins, can you? In for a penny, in for a pound. Isn't that about right?"

"I don't want to argue with you. I have my wife for that." He looked at her and lightly caressed her hand. "I'm sorry. I cannot believe that it is wrong seeing you, Alice. I just can't accept that."

She softly touched his cheek. "And I can't accept that there is anything wrong with someone because he's gay." She kept her hand on his cheek, and smiled. "But, you know what? I admire you even more for helping Stephen at UNCC."

Edward signaled to their waiter for more coffee. "This croissant is pretty good," he said. "Is it almond?"

"Yes. Almond," she answered. "Edward. Look at me. You *are* going to help him? Aren't you? He believes that you will."

"You say you know the best part of me," he said, looking down at his coffee. "Maybe you do. But, never mind. To answer your question. No. These things can be handled under the radar, but there are other factors. It's business, Alice. I'm sorry. That's all I can tell you."

"That's all? That's all you can say?"

He could see the disappointment in her eyes and knew that he had failed some crucial test. He could have explained to her that

Adam Burroughs had called him earlier in the week and *encouraged* Edward to "rein in that nephew of yours." Adam Burroughs, a wealthy and powerful black man, rarely injected race into the civic affairs of Charlotte, so that it was of unique distinction when he did. But, Adam faced pressures of his own within the black community. Even he was obliged to run with the herd from time to time. Edward could have explained to Alice that Adam Burroughs controlled twenty percent of the investment on the Wellington Tower. But, he knew that she would not be persuaded by any of these concerns. He knew that, for Alice, profit margins would no more excuse betrayal than prejudice.

But, it did for Missy.

Missy had willingly called the UNCC chancellor earlier in the week to emphasize that, despite their high regard for Stephen, it should be understood that she and Edward would never, *never* interfere in personnel decisions of the university. Even if that decision was not to renew Stephen's contract. They would *understand*, in some ways even *support*, that decision.

"We cannot condone even the *appearance* of racism, Chancellor Dunn," Missy had said earnestly, "and certainly not in our own family."

Yes, Missy understood these things, Edward had to give her credit for that. Alice did not, and now he heard her asking, "Do you have any idea how degrading it was for him to come to you for your help?"

"Yes. I do. I wouldn't be sitting here today if I didn't. You don't understand Charlotte. Stephen is a good young man, but the fact is, he *is* an embarrassment. Too many people are talking." He was about to say something else, but then just said, "You live in a neat little world where you only see what you want to see."

"Edward, he has been unfairly accused of things that aren't true, and you are willing to let him twist in the wind."

"Again, I like Stephen," Edward retorted, "but he has poor judgment. He needs to stay away from the Caldwell boy."

"He has befriended a confused young man. Why can't people accept that it is an innocent friendship?"

"Is it?" he asked. "The boy's mother doesn't seem to think so."

"Yes, it is," she replied, then added, "unlike *ours*. And your son is with a woman just as old as Stephen. That doesn't seem to upset anyone, does it?"

"That's different," he said, struggling to maintain his composure.

"Really? And you think I only see what I want to see? What I see is that a lot of people in this town always seem to be throwing stones, tearing down anyone who is different. Why is that?"

"Business," he said again dumbly, realizing the cold, hollow core of that word. And he could see, just as clearly, the love, dying now, in the woman across from him who would never accept that brutal justification. "Business," he repeated.

"No, it's not that simple," she said. "The real reason is that, as bad as we are, we need to believe that someone else is worse. So, I may be a terrible person, but at least I'm not as bad as *him*."

"What are you saying?"

"I'm only saying that judging others is what seems to get most of us through the night, and you, you of all people..." She looked again at the photograph on the table and handed it to him. "I'm sorry, Edward," she said with a steely and unshakeable resolve. "I can't keep this."

L ater that day, Alice sat on her terrace, sipping a glass of merlot in the late afternoon sunlight, waiting for Bill, while her daughters were reading inside the house. She could see them through the floor-to-ceiling window of the sunroom, engrossed in their books.

She thought of Edward Harrison. Why did he tell her? Perhaps it was a test. *If you really knew me, would you still love me?* But, the larger truth was that the affair would have perished under its own weight in any event. Alice had long understood that her love was ample but not enduring, and she knew that there was a selfish generosity in that simple fact of her nature. The only exception was, and would remain, her husband. And in that one fundamental capacity, her bond with Bill was singular and unsurpassed.

The terrace and surrounding garden were meticulously arranged. Neatly trimmed boxwoods bordered the iron railing of the terrace, echoing the sumptuous green cushions on her chairs, giving way to an artful cluster of azaleas and beds of roses.

As she sipped her merlot, she marveled at the orderly, tidy life that she and Bill had managed. Without the noisy encumbrances of maladjusted children and financial strains, or the smothering resentments of a confining fidelity, they reveled in a leisurely freedom. And yet, this very perfection was a source of some anxiety, to the extent that she realized its fragility. She understood that decay was the final, irrevocable reality, just as treacherously as minute fungi ate away at the perfect blossoms of crape myrtles, just as intrusively as errant weeds invaded her emerald lawn.

If her life was spared the tumult of jealousy and petty grievances, it was also bereft of a certain spontaneity and clutter, those warmer elements of living for which there was little room in her temperate, elegantly designed existence. And, in some quiet corner, like the encroaching mold that seeped into the crevices of her spotless basement, there was a gnawing uneasiness. If her principles had served to illuminate her own life, she was not unaware of their darkening effect on the lives of others. While she would never steal another woman's husband, she was all too agreeable to borrowing him for a while. Her sense of decency, while heartily flexible, was no less bewildering than more rigid varieties.

A place for everything and everything in its place, her mother used to caution her. As she sat there in her pristine yard, she felt an unsettling doubt. And it occurred to her that, in fact, her mother was wrong. Apart from the surface of things, there is not a place for everything.

You live in a neat little world and you only see what you want to see, Edward Harrison had told her. Maybe he was right. She and Bill maintained a conspiracy of tranquility, just as surely as their more conventional friends and family adhered to a conspiracy of conformity. Both regimens, she knew, were burdensome. She shivered, gazing at a perfect rose petal, at its peak bloom before plunging to the regenerating earth.

With an easy and assured competence, she brought new life into the world every week at the hospital. And each time she did so, she was reminded how, at its most primitive, and possibly its most meaningful, life was not orderly, was not calm, was not unfettered. And was not without pain. The most profound experience was in its clutter and messiness, and, for an instant, there in her perfect garden, she acknowledged the unique loneliness of her calibrated life.

CHAPTER FIFTY-FOUR
COMING OUT PARTY

Missy stood on the balcony of her bedroom and was pleased to see that the afternoon sun was fighting off the ominous storm clouds that had earlier shadowed the sky. The day had become a brilliant blue flash of August sun. It would be perfect for John's birthday party. More important, it would be perfect for her and Edward. She was conscious of the increased whispers about her family, and she resolved to drown them out with one hell of a party.

When she walked back inside, however, seeing her husband, her mood immediately darkened. "You cannot wear that suit!" Missy thundered. He had selected his blue pinstripe. "It makes you look like Al Capone. Besides, I told you, this is a casual party."

He ignored her, as he was inclined to do of late, and pulled out a faded blue polo shirt and tan slacks.

"Much better, but you'll want to put on your blazer. It's not *that* casual. Thank you." She cast a disapproving glance at the drink in his hand. "Isn't it a little early for another whiskey?"

As the Harrisons were getting dressed for the party, the guest of honor was nowhere to be seen. John had returned home a week earlier and, for most of the interim, seemed to be on a constant round of engagements. Usually, by his side, was Tricia White, the young woman he had met in Washington and who, by way of Biloxi, Mississippi, lived in Davidson.

While Missy did not approve of Miss White on grounds of age—she was, after all, in her late twenties—or of background, she knew that there was no cause for alarm. For all her devotion to her only son, she had no illusions as to his emotional commitments or, more accurately, the lack thereof. He had not come home the night before, but she and Edward, in unspoken agreement, decided not to interfere. Indeed, Missy, after the outrageous insinuations of Laura Caldwell, secretly was relieved that her son was enjoying the obviously satisfactory attentions of a mature, discriminating woman.

"Wild oats," Edward had commented. "Lucky bastard."

It occurred to Missy that Edward's particular oats continued to be distinctly tame. For her, at least. She lingered in the bathroom, applying her moisturizer, and was unpleasantly aware of the slight intrusion of bags under her eyes. Her face was otherwise glacially smooth, an alabaster tribute to a recent influx of botox. But, the eyes worried her. She would need to see Dr. Womack about that soon. Otherwise, she was satisfied with the enduring precision of her body, if still uneasy as to her husband's lack of interest in it.

Later, when Missy allowed herself to recall the events of the evening, it was odd that one of the remarks that crowded her thoughts was the comment that John's girlfriend, Tricia, made as she was leaving. "Well, Johnny," she said, in that drowsy Mississippi drawl, "it was kind of like a debutante ball...and with such *interesting* debs." That was *not* the effect for which Missy had been hoping.

Tall, surprisingly flat-chested, with slightly crooked teeth and straight hair that went halfway down her back, it was hard to imagine how such an angular, bony concoction as Tricia White could make such willowy, feathery sounds. "I'm so happy to meet you, Mrs. Harrison," she had said breathlessly when she and John finally arrived, fifteen minutes before the party in his honor was to begin. The wispy drawl was punctuated by the girl's enormous lips. Missy wondered if they were real. It was her considered judgment that they were not.

Missy just smiled. "Aren't you sweet," she replied, although whether that was in the form of an affirmation or question was open to debate.

"Where is Dad?" John asked, more out of curiosity than any real interest.

"He'll be down in a minute. I declare that man takes more time to get ready than I do."

"Johnny is the same way," Tricia said, smiling and hugging John with a clinging assertiveness. "He combs his hair more than I do, and I have a whole lot more hair." Her laughter was muted, a minor accompaniment to the blazing spectacle of those crowded teeth cushioned by the chemically ripened lips.

"Well, John, why don't you show Tricia around the house? I just need to check a few things with the caterer before our guests arrive."

The tables assembled on the terrace and around the pool were ablaze with candles, illuminating the blue water of the pool and the white linens of the tables. The boxwoods were wrapped in blue lights. Missy had selected party favors to be placed at each seat. These included wrapped Belgian chocolates in silver boxes. Each table would also have its own silver dish of the finest caviar. She realized, with devious satisfaction, that a number of her guests would carp, enviously, that she had once again overstepped.

With all preparations in place, the catering staff stood quietly at their stations. Missy surveyed the buffet table. The menu included smoked salmon, asparagus tips, and potatoes au gratin, all of which lay protected under gleaming silver covered trays. She noticed that one of the covers had a slight scratch just above the side rim.

Missy impatiently waved the supervisor over. "Yes, Mrs. Harrison? Is everything satisfactory?" The young woman had a practiced and determined serenity.

"No, everything is not," Missy glowered, pointing at the offending scratch. "That is not staying on my table."

"Oh, well, yes of course, I see what you mean," she said, now as one with Missy in the outrage. "Don't worry, we can fix that." She looked around the pool, and motioned for a young man to come over. "Philip, bring a new cover, would you please? Right away," she said urgently.

"Thank you," Missy grudgingly offered. "Now, remember, I want the caviar to be kept fully stocked at all times. I do not want to walk by anyone's table and see a half empty dish. I want to be very clear about that. And, again, when I signal to you, I want the cake to be brought out for my son. And every candle on the cake should be brightly lit. No small candles. Got it? *Big!* Big candles!"

The young woman smiled patiently. "Yes, ma'am. Big candles. It is all taken care of. Don't worry about a thing."

"If I didn't worry, I would have scratched silver on my table, wouldn't I?" She regarded the beleaguered young woman, then added, "And remember, tell the bartender that Congresswoman Toller is to be served the single malt scotch."

John and Tricia and all their friends segregated themselves at tables on one side of the pool. The congresswoman and her husband were on the terrace with Missy and Edward, along with Janey and Adam Burroughs. It was an evening about which John had profound ambivalence. While he fully appreciated the glamour of the moment, he realized that it was a reflected glory. Even though it was *his* celebration, the evening's spotlight was decidedly more on Congresswoman Toller than on him, and her sole purpose for being there was to placate his mother. It did not improve his mood when the congresswoman, after her effusive greeting —"John! The best darn intern I ever had. Bar none!" —had completely ignored him thereafter. Even at the tender age of nineteen, John's tolerance for insincerity was primarily confined to dispensing it.

The rest of the guests, older people who had known him for much of his life, were dispersed among the other tables surrounding the pool. Like supplicants at the twin thrones of youth and power, they alternated between paying homage to John and to Congresswoman Toller, creating a processional of sorts between his table at one end of the pool and hers at the other. Nonetheless, he consoled himself, the party was in his honor and at least he was *one* of the centers of attention. And if the slightly boyish, but tantalizingly withholding, girl seated beside him did not entirely indulge him, that was only a minor, and oddly delicious, frustration.

He grimaced as Mr. and Mrs. Edwin Parks slowly approached his table. The Parks were both in their eighties. Mr. Parks walked with a cane, and Mrs. Parks walked with his support. To see the two of them in tandem, the very picture of ambulatory suspense, was to observe a wobbly blend of increasing impairment and enduring affection. John Harrison, of course, saw none of this. They were just one more ancient pair associated in some vague, longstanding way with his parents. The old couple's chief purpose this evening seemed to be to remind him that he was already bored out of his mind.

"John, we are so proud of you, son," Mr. Parks said.

"Yes, so proud," Mrs. Parks echoed. "And to think that you are going off to college. Why I remember when you were just..." At this point, John let his thoughts drift elsewhere. He focused his vision on the two sparse white heads bobbing up and down. Mrs. Parks had only recently stopped coloring her meager hair, and now she and her husband looked like twin melting snowcaps.

John glanced at Tricia, who was being hugged now by the Parks. God, he thought, is that what we will look like someday? Old and wrinkled, wheezing for breath, hobbling around on canes? It suddenly occurred to him why so many of his father's friends were on their second and third wives. Who can blame them? How could anyone still feel attracted to a woman with such sagging, withered flesh? And that was with her clothes *on*.

Finally, they wandered away from the table. "Jeez, what a creepy pair," he whispered contemptuously to Tricia.

"Oh," she protested, squeezing his arm, "they're sweet as can be. And they love you."

Whatever, he thought. He would have told her not to be such a sap, but was still hopeful that she would finally sleep with him later that evening. He was quite willing to humor her with that goal uppermost in his mind. He felt the Trojan in his pocket, like a talisman, and felt aroused, as always, by the enticing prospect of crossing a boundary.

Most of the party had arrived and was dining contentedly. Missy sat quietly, listening to the laughter erupting from the tables, watching the catering staff glide smoothly about with drinks and caviar, and began to relax. Edward chatted with Adam Burroughs, who was pontificating on the latest acquisition of the Bobcats, much like a rancher might refer to a prize bull. Missy noticed that Edward seemed uneasy, shifting in his seat, his eyes darting about the pool.

Missy walked over to the buffet, where Alice Owens was liberally filling her plate with more asparagus tips and potatoes. "Goodness, Alice, where do you put it?" Missy asked, glancing at her appraisingly.

"Oh, this isn't for me," Alice said, adding some salmon for good measure. "It's for Bill. He's still pretty much a growing boy."

"Aren't they all?" Missy asked acidly. Then, noticing Alice's subdued expression, Missy said, "You're awfully quiet tonight. Cat got your tongue?"

Alice, at first seemed not to hear her, then replied, "I never understood that expression. 'Cat got your tongue.' Where does it come from?"

"Where? I have no idea."

"Oh. Well, I find sayings like that interesting, don't you? All the old sayings that we all use and have no idea why."

"Alice," Missy said, with a venomous laugh, "sometimes, especially in this neck of the woods, it's best to just take things as they are and not wonder why."

"Thank you for that advice," Alice said, in a sweet and melodious whisper, "I will certainly put it to use as much as I can. By the way, fabulous salad. Did you make it yourself?"

"Oh, now *that* is amusing. You must keep Bill in stitches at home. But, no, these marvelous caterers made the salad. I will take credit for the dressing though. It is from a wonderful little restaurant in Bologna, where I persuaded the manager to give me the recipe."

"Well, good choice," Alice said.

What's up with her tonight, Missy wondered. She's even odder than usual. She wondered if Edward had said something to offend her. Missy had surprised the two of them talking earlier in the library and both had appeared startled. And now, they seemed to purposefully avoid each other.

Just then, Missy looked up toward the terrace and saw Stephen emerge from the French doors. To her horror, she saw a flash of red in the form of Evelyn Peck trailing behind him, followed by Evelyn's oafish son, Keith.

Evelyn was synched into a red polyester dress with a button down top, tightly encased around her ample belly by a wide black belt. She had undone the top two buttons for optimal exposure of what she considered, still, to be her major assets. Her hulking son, who strangely seemed to fade into whatever corner was available, wore a brown leisure suit, no doubt plundered from a very dusty closet.

Missy watched Edward, as if in surprised slow motion, rise from his seat and greet them, and heard Alice say, "Look, there's Stephen. But, who are those people with him?"

Missy, transfixed by this unexpected intrusion, ignored her, and walked over to greet her new guests. Alice followed. Congresswoman Toller, looking wary and amused, was already accosted by Evelyn. "Oh, absolutely," the congresswoman said, taking a subtle step back, "I will look into the matter. I am so sorry for your trouble with your claim. Why, it's just plain common sense."

In her long and varied career as a hostess in Charlotte, Missy was not unfamiliar with greeting unwanted guests. She had encountered a long line of bores and buffoons. And yet, the garish presence of Evelyn and Keith was akin to seeing ghosts at a white trash house party. The one mercy was that most of the guests had sat down to dinner and were distracted by each other. But, she could see the curious glances of a few of the more attentive heads, and resolved to absorb these two familial horrors into the room as unobtrusively as possible.

"Well, hello," she said evenly, with just a slight touch of sarcasm in her tone. "What a nice surprise."

Edward seemed too stunned to speak, and silently nodded his head in greeting. Good Lord, Missy thought, say something. They are your hideous family, not mine. Finally, he mustered a lame, "Yes, we've been wanting to get you out here for the longest time, and so, yes...Glad you could join us."

"Well, thanks," Evelyn said, adjusting her belt. "I can't believe we ain't never seen your home before, and it is so nice. Lord, Edward, you done good, hon, you done really good!"

Suddenly, Evelyn turned to Alice. "Hi. Good to see you. You look awful familiar to me. Ever been to Gastonia?"

"No, I hear it is a lovely town."

"Hah! If you say so, honey!" Evelyn continued looking at Alice. "Anyway, you must got a twin there."

Stephen winked at Alice and then gave her a hug. "Thank you," he whispered to her.

"My pleasure," she murmured, sighing against his shoulder. "Are you having fun yet?"

"The fun is just starting," he answered. Alice smiled and walked back to her table. Then, directing himself again to his hostess, who appeared more mystified than ever, he asked "Where's cousin Johnny?"

Missy regarded Stephen and Evelyn and Keith as if they had just jumped over the fence of the state penitentiary, reserving a special venom for Stephen, the obvious ringleader. "Oh, yes, well...John is over by the pool with his friends. But, first, please, have a drink, make yourselves at home. The bar is right over there," she said, pointing toward the lower terrace.

Evelyn eagerly headed toward the bar, with Keith and Edward in tow. Missy held Stephen's arm. "May I speak with you for a moment, please?"

He looked at her, smiling. "Sure."

"What in the world were you thinking?" she hissed. "I do not recall inviting them."

"No?" he inquired, still smiling. "Well, they are family. And, like you always say, family needs to stick together. Except, well, except I guess when we don't. Have I told you I will be leaving UNCC? But, you already knew that, didn't you?"

"What do you mean?"

"I mean you were right about one thing. People in this town do talk. And *some* of them talk to me."

"Stephen, I cannot believe that you, of all people, would listen to trashy people who hate our family, who..." She was suddenly startled by Evelyn's raucous laughter coming from the direction of the bar.

Stephen walked over to the bar, feasting on the contrast between Missy's sedate friends, the artful flower arrangements, the string quartet, the caviar in silver dishes, and the vulgar, bulging red vision of Evelyn Peck. If it were possible for him to feel any real affection for that crude woman, and, in truth, it was not, surely it would be on the occasion of John Harrison's party. Nevertheless, he was certain that, in this one alliance, Evelyn would not disappoint.

"Now, don't be stingy with the bourbon, hon," she bellowed to the young bartender. "Give it to me straight." Stephen noticed that both Edward and Missy had retreated to a far corner of the terrace.

"Stephen," Evelyn said, grabbing his arm and pointing at the bartender, "this boy don't know nothin' 'bout bourbon!" The bartender looked past Evelyn and Stephen to Keith.

"What can I get you, sir?"

"I'll have a beer," Keith said. "You got any Bud?"

Stephen savored each awkward moment, the only drawback being that Missy and Edward were not in immediate proximity to see it. However, he knew that they, along with a growing number of their guests, were observing every garish eruption.

"Well, shall we go say hello to John?" he asked them.

"Hell, yes. Reckon we should say hi to the guest of honor," Evelyn said, tugging at the tight folds of her dress to further accentuate her breasts. "Let me just get myself situated here. Okay, let's go. Come on, Keith. Don't be such a stump!"

She took Stephen's arm, as Keith trailed behind. "Damn, what a place. Thanks for bringing both of us," she said conspiratorially, tilting her head knowingly toward her son.

"My pleasure," Stephen laughed. "Believe me, this party would be so boring without you to liven it up a little." More convinced than ever of her singular vivacity, Evelyn confidently squeezed his arm.

They slowly made their way toward John at the far end of the pool. This had the added bonus of requiring Stephen and the Pecks to walk the entire length of the assembled party, allowing each guest to appraise the glorious red glare of Evelyn Peck. Out of the corner of his eye, Stephen could glimpse Missy, struggling to mask her outrage and horror, smiling gamely as she spoke with old Mr. and Mrs. Parks.

By now, John could see their approach. Only as they arrived at the table did he appear to realize it was Evelyn and Keith with Stephen, and his sly grin seemed frozen in either surprise or amusement, Stephen was not sure which.

"John," Stephen greeted him. "Nothing like a going away party to celebrate, well, your going away. Having a good night?"

"Yeah, great," he replied, rising woodenly from his chair. "Thanks for coming to my *birthday* party."

"Right. Birthday. I wouldn't miss it for the world. Oh, and here's Evelyn and Keith." Evelyn bound forward and engulfed John in her fleshy arms, smothering him in a mass of breasts and hair.

"Johnny!" she shrieked. "Lord, when did you get so big? And so good-looking." She looked doubtfully at the skinny girl beside him. "Who's your little friend?"

"Hi, I'm Tricia. Pleased to meet you," she said, pulling John back to his seat.

Evelyn continued staring at her, as if confused by the girl's presence. "Uh huh," she said vacantly. "Back at ya."

"Oh, before I forget," Stephen said, "your friend Ben asked me to give this to you." Stephen handed John a birthday card.

John opened the card and briefly read it, then casually placed it on the table. The note from Ben read:

John, as Oscar Wilde said, "To love oneself is a lifelong romance. Lucky you."

"Aren't you going to read it to us?" Stephen asked.

"Oh, yeah, sure I will. Later."

Tricia had also glanced at the note. "Oscar Wilde?" she laughed. "Well, that says a lot."

"More than you will ever know," Stephen said to her, "more than you will ever know." He took Evelyn and Keith by the arms. "Well, guys, shall we repair to the bar?"

"Yeah, okay," Keith mumbled.

"You bet," Evelyn said. "Who the hell is this Oscar fella?"

While a social evening at the Harrison home was well beyond Evelyn's scope, her acute awareness of any possible slight or insult was undiminished. She was as attuned to the behavior of Missy's guests as she would be to any gathering at the Hometown Inn. This social antenna was unimpaired, indeed was perhaps even heightened, by alcoholic lubrication. And with the passing of each awkward moment, her inclination was toward an even noisier defiance.

Initially, bound by an unyielding etiquette, a few of the more gracious guests, particularly the elderly couple, Mr. and Mrs. Parks, attempted conversation. But, they quickly realized that neither Emily Post nor their own adaptable grandmothers had ever adequately prepared them for the voluptuous tackiness of Evelyn Peck and the pained reticence of her gangly son.

Stephen, having ushered Evelyn and Keith through the door, now confidently left them to their own disruptive capacities. Alice Owens waved him over to her table. Given that the other guests had concluded that he was the host for the virus that was Evelyn, there appeared to be no other competition for his company.

Bill and Alice were holding hands, enjoying the spectacle unfolding at the Harrison home. "Stephen," Bill said affectionately, catching the angry glare of Missy Harrison on the terrace, "you sure know how to get a party hopping."

"I had a little help," he said genially, casually taking a seat as if he were not at present the Typhoid Mary of Charlotte society.

Alice smiled and then, in unspoken support, gave him a thumbs up. She had called him only two days ago. *Stephen, I'm sorry to be the one to tell you this...I think there is something you need to know about what's going on at UNCC...about your aunt and uncle.*

The other occupants of the table, Frances Bulwark, the textile heiress, and her considerably younger husband, Sam, looked over Stephen's shoulder toward Evelyn Peck. Evelyn had propped herself up at the bar, breasts almost spilling out, and was impatiently ordering yet another drink.

"Mrs. Bulwark, it is good to see you again," Stephen said. "We met earlier this summer here at dinner."

"Yes, I remember," she said, nudging her husband, who remained distracted by Evelyn Peck's bountiful breasts. "So good to see you again. How have you been?"

Certain that Mrs. Bulwark watched the news like any other mortal, Stephen dived right in and said, "Well, fine, except for my unfortunate appearances on local television. And you?"

"Still anonymous," she said, smiling sweetly.

Evelyn and Keith sat at a depopulated table glaring at each other. No other guests deemed it prudent to join them. Evelyn yawned, then stood up and walked sluggishly back to the bar.

Adam and Janey Burroughs, more out of fascination than politeness, deigned to say hello while Evelyn ordered yet another bourbon. "Put a little high test in it, baby," she cooed to the bartender.

"Yeah, that's the stuff," Adam said approvingly. "I don't believe we have met. I am Adam Burroughs and this is my wife, Janey."

"Hey," Evelyn mumbled. "I'm Evelyn Harrison Peck." She was not so drunk as not to remember to reference her former married name. "Good to meet you."

"How are you acquainted with the birthday boy?" Janey Burroughs asked. Evelyn studied her, and wanted to say, 'You're what my daddy used to call a high yella,' but instead answered, rather chilly, "His daddy is my cousin."

"Do you live here in Charlotte?" Adam asked.

"Yeah. Me and my son, he's that lump sitting over there," she said, pointing at Keith, half-asleep at the table. "We got a home over on Tryon Street."

"Oh, do you live in Uptown?" Janey Burroughs enthused. "I love the new condos. And all the great new restaurants. We have actually thought about moving there."

"That right?" Evelyn asked, gulping down her bourbon. "Don't you all like, you know, the East side better?"

Adam Burroughs smiled. It was so rare to encounter such clumsy bigotry in the politely calculating world they lived in. Evelyn was, for all her offensiveness, like a blast of bracing salt air. "Oh, why not at all, Mrs. *Peck*," he said, emphasizing her last, lowly name. "Most of *us all* live here in the SouthPark area."

"Goodness, yes," Janey, always up for a little fun, added. "And our home is right here in Morrocroft. Otherwise, you just don't know *who* they will let in, right Adam? Lord knows, the East side scares me half to death."

"So, where exactly do you live on Tryon?" her husband asked.

"Well, we are around the corner from...near all them new artsy fartsy galleries. You know, where all the homos go to see art and stuff on Friday nights. Our house ain't nothing fancy, but it suits us."

"Oh, well, yes. I'm sure it does," Adam said. He looked about the terrace and then said, "Janey, there's Nancy and Bart, we should go say hello. Nice meeting you."

"Uh huh," Evelyn said, then shouted, "Barkeep! Fill me up!"

With each shot of bourbon, she became louder and more flirtatious, while noting every upturned nose and veiled smirk. And noting, most tellingly, how she was politely and vigorously ignored.

Her resentful perceptions were rivaled by the vigilant observations of Missy, who grimly endured the averted eyes, the whispered asides, that followed Evelyn. Missy watched as the bulbous red figure drunkenly made her way back and forth from the poolside table, where Evelyn sat in irritated isolation with Keith, to the bar, where she issued seductive orders to the embarrassed bartender.

Seething and helpless, Missy appealed to her husband. "You have got to do something. Oh, I could kill Stephen for this. You have *got* to get them out of here."

"And how exactly am I to do that?" he asked, frowning. "Get the bartender to run away with her? I don't think we are paying him enough for that, are we?"

"For God's sake, don't be so glib about it," she said. "Take them on a tour of the house. Just get them away from everyone."

Observing his wife's snarling expression, it occurred to Edward that, for all their obvious differences, Missy and Evelyn shared one vital trait, and that was their complete self-absorption. One may have been cloaked in silks, and one in polyester, but each was fully shrouded nonetheless. Edward had also discovered one other fatal realization about his wife, namely that she had become superfluous to him.

He felt that, for all her noise and demands, he was living with a shadow, no more consequential to him than an *haute couture* mannequin propped up in Macy's window. Such an observation would have saddened him at one time, but now it was more in the nature of an afterthought. A lonely afterthought. He had not been looking forward to the party, anticipating as he was the presence of Congresswoman Toller, a woman whom he could not stand, and Alice, a woman whom he could not forget. And now he had to contend with Evelyn.

Realizing that Evelyn would pounce on any hint of weakness—her drowsy son was certainly evidence of that —Edward approached her with an assertiveness that fell just shy of confrontation. "Evelyn, bring your drink with you," he said, "I want to show you and Keith the rest of the house."

Weary of her son's flaccid company, and in fact eager to see the glories of the Harrison mansion, Evelyn agreed. "Come on Keith. Get your ass in gear. We're gonna take the tour. Come on!"

Once Edward had securely escorted Evelyn and Keith beyond the French doors and into the house, Missy decided that it would now be an opportune time to propose a toast and try to salvage whatever dignity might still be left at the party. She cued the band to stop playing, and commandeered the microphone from the singer.

"Everyone," she said, "may I have your attention for a moment? Thank you. Thank you all for being here tonight with us. I particularly want to thank Congresswoman Toller and Ken for sharing this evening with us."

The congresswoman and her husband stood as the crowd applauded. "Smile honey," she whispered to Ken, who proceeded to dislocate her tenuous pile of hair as he was waving to the guests. Missy handed the microphone to the congresswoman.

"Ken and I are so glad that we could be here with you," she said, adjusting her hair with her other hand. "You know, sometimes I get so discouraged, with all the problems up in Washington and all. Course no need to go down that old road tonight. But, I am always happy to be with my fellow Charlotteans. It is just so wonderful to be back home." She paused for a moment, looking out at the crowd, putting her arm around her husband. "Home," she repeated, as if she had to take just a moment and ponder the treasure contained in that word. Her eyes became moist. She smiled wistfully. Knowingly. "Home."

Across the pool sat the languid form of John Harrison, effecting a petulant yet inevitably seductive pose. "Tonight is for John," Congresswoman Toller continued, "one of the finest young men I have ever known. A future leader! I look at John and think, well, it is because of individuals like this remarkable young man that our country is still the greatest country in the world, and always will be. Happy birthday, John. You make all of us proud."

Finally, to Missy's impatient relief, Toller sat down as the crowd applauded the potential greatness of Johnny Harrison. "Thank you, congresswoman. We are honored that you and Ken could be here with us tonight for Johnny's birthday," Missy said, glancing nervously toward the door to the library. "Thank you for your kind words about our son. And for taking him off our hands this summer," she said, laughing, as the waiters circulated among the guests, pouring champagne. "In just a few more days, John will be going off to college. We are going to miss him terribly. But, he casts light wherever he goes, and he leaves a glow in our hearts. He really is our golden boy." She lifted her champagne glass. "So, to John."

The guests dutifully raised their glasses, while at the same time wondering about Edward Harrison's absence, and watching the French doors for the return of the evening's chief entertainment. From his own table, sitting with Alice and Bill, Stephen waited as well. Alice nudged his arm and asked, "Do you think they can keep her at bay?" Stephen smiled nervously and looked straight ahead.

"She is truly the most ghastly woman I have ever met," Alice whispered. "Well done."

They watched as John walked over and hugged his mother. The group began singing 'Happy Birthday' as one of the waiters approached the terrace with a cake, a tremulous, petite bonfire of nineteen *small* candles.

Missy watched John blow out the bitterly small candles, as the sound of applause and laughter wafted across the terrace. Suddenly, the doors behind them opened and the grating, drunken voice of Evelyn Peck shrieked, "What'd we miss? What'd we miss?"

Edward tried to steer Evelyn back toward the bar. "Let me freshen your drink, Evelyn."

"No!" she protested. "I wanna make a toast. I wanna say something to Johnny."

Seeing the stumbling, corseted approach of Evelyn Peck, her thin lips contorted into a snarling grin, John began moving back toward his table, where Tricia and his friends were rapt with the sort of attention more typically reserved for a train that was about to jump the track.

"Johnny," he heard the slurred voice call after him. "Wait! I got to tell you somethin' baby."

He stopped, frozen in humiliating and paralyzing disgust. "Yeah?" he asked impatiently. "Okay, what?"

"Now, listen. Listen to old Evvie. I may not be worth a sack of shit, but I got to tell you something."

"I'm listening," he said, glaring at her behind a forced smile.

"You prob'ly don't remember her. And I ain't goin' to rub it in. Grandma Rose was before your time, weren't she? But, Grandma Rose, if she was here... and she ain't. Naw, she's in heaven." Evelyn paused, teary-eyed, as if trying to fix in her mind the exact location as to where heaven might be. "Yeah, she's in heaven for sure. Anyway, if she was here, she would be proud of you. Seeing how growed up and all you are. Course, she never thought much of me. But, that's all right. At least she let you know where you stood with her. Unlike some folks I know."

Evelyn looked to her side for a moment, her gaze boring into Missy. "Naw, some folks just pretend to be nice, when they don't really give a good goddam—oops, darn—about you! You remember that Johnny. Most folks are just pretending. You don't forget that, you hear? Or old Evelyn will have to come to Vanderwherever and whup your ass! You are a good boy, even if...even if..." She hesitated for an interminable few seconds, as every guest leaned forward, waiting, and then she bellowed, "even if you are queer!"

At that, enraged, Edward Harrison began pushing her toward the French doors. "Evelyn. Get a hold of yourself. You are acting like a damn fool."

"A fool? Hah!" she mocked him, adroitly twisting out of his grasp. "How 'bout you? How 'bout you and *her* at the Carolina Court? Huh? How 'bout that?" Evelyn woozily surveyed the crowd, her puffy eyes squinted intently, searching for the face of Alice Owens, who had by then realized just where Evelyn might have seen her in Gastonia and discreetly disappeared into the house. *Her* would be the evening's one enduring mystery.

The other guests were transfixed, silent and unmoving, as if they were on one of those carnival rides that spin so fast it is impossible to move, where the floor collapses and the riders are suspended in a paralytic whirl. Among these mute observers, Keith Harrison shifted his gaze between his mother, staggering about in search of *her*, and the smirking faces at the tables around him. And then he saw the kindly Mrs. Parks, sitting nearby with her husband, her head downcast. She briefly glanced at Keith with an expression of shock and, most unbearably, pity.

Keith leaped from his chair and got hold of his mother, shrieking at her, "Shut up! Shut up!" He continued this outraged litany as he bodily lifted Evelyn, who was for once too shocked to speak, if not to flail her body about in a bewildered rage. "Shut up, you stupid cow!" he screamed, dragging her away from the terrace, until they disappeared around the side of the house.

Watching, along with everyone else, this violent exit, Missy frantically waved to the band. "Play something! Anything! And make it loud!"

CHAPTER FIFTY-FIVE
FOR THE BEST

W hat did he say when you gave him the birthday card?" Ben asked, as he crumbled the remains of a cookie at the Starbucks in Dilworth. His face was unshaven, more rugged and older looking, affording a glimpse of what he might become in later years.

"Not much. He tried to ignore it," Stephen answered sleepily, still groggy from the party. "He looked at it for a second and then put it away."

Ben glanced about the room. "That's it?" he asked, disappointed. "Nothing else?"

"Oh, well his girlfriend, Tricia—the one he met in Washington— she said, 'Oscar Wilde? That says a lot.'"

"He must have hated that," Ben said, scratching the stubble on his face. He was curious about John, but more urgently his focus was on *Stephen*. He hung on Stephen's every look, every gesture, the tone of his voice, searching for some fault line in this wall of friendship. Ben felt trapped behind that wall, forced in to some lonely, inaccessible, barren space.

"Not as much as what happened later," Stephen continued. "Evelyn got roaring drunk, to no one's surprise, of course. But, then, just as John was getting his birthday cake, she rushed back out to the terrace. Uncle Edward was giving her and Keith some tour inside the house. Anyway, she rushes out and wants to make a toast to John. I mean, he had barely blown out the candles on his cake. And she starts babbling to John about Grandmom Rose—which is ironic, since I'm told that Rose knew Evelyn just long enough to thoroughly disapprove of her. Anyway, by now Evelyn's just rambling and sobbing. And she goes on about how John is a good boy and then says, 'even if you are queer.'"

Ben was silent for a moment and, despite himself, felt an unexpected sympathy for Johnny Harrison. "Why did she say that?"

"I've been asking myself that question ever since last night," Stephen answered. "She also accused my Uncle Edward of having an affair. Then I remembered my phone conversation with her when I invited her and Keith to John's party. She said she had only met John once or twice and she asked me 'Is he like you? You know, *funny?*' For Evelyn, 'funny' means gay. So, I just laughed and said, 'Well, kind of. He *is* amusing'. And I left it at that. I never dreamed that she would go off the way she did."

"What *did* you expect?" Ben asked, his tone an odd mix of curiosity and resentment. Ben hated himself, maybe even hated Stephen, for allowing someone to have such power over him. First John. Now Stephen. He kept returning to the night at Stephen's apartment, which haunted him now even more than the night by the lake with John. *Are you sure?* Ben had pleaded. *I am...For now.* That's what Stephen had given him. *For now.* Two feeble, hopeless little words.

"Well, she's a drunk and a tramp," Stephen was saying, "so I knew that, even sober, Evelyn would be a huge embarrassment to Uncle Edward and Aunt Missy. That much I expected. I'll admit it, that much I hoped for. But, then when she..." He paused, as Ben frowned slightly. "Hey, everything okay?"

"Me? Sure, fine." Ben neatly swept up the cookie crumbs on the table, enclosing them in a napkin, clenching it in his fist. He glanced about the room, unable or unwilling to look at Stephen. Ben was, once again, struggling in the old nether world of longing. Each day of their awkward friendship brought him closer not to the intimacy he craved, but rather the emerging distance he feared. "How did John react?"

"He just stood there, just as amazed as the rest of us, but he had this strange grin on his face. Nothing fazes that guy, does it?"

"No, I guess not," Ben said, then added, "I will never figure him out."

"Well, let's just say he takes after his mother. He was lucky every day that he knew you." Stephen put his hand on Ben's shoulder, "Just like I have been."

"What do you mean *been*?" Ben asked. He could see the impending collision implicit in that word, and was resolved not to look away from the wreckage.

"This is so hard for me to say to you," Stephen answered. "But, I am leaving UNCC."

"Why? You don't have to leave. They can't make you."

"Well, maybe not. But, I don't have a future there, that's clear. And, honestly, I don't have a future in Charlotte either. The one great thing about coming here was meeting you, and Alice. And not much else."

"How can you just give up like this?" Ben asked. "So easily?"

"I can't fight for what I don't really want...or need."

"Where will you go?"

"I'm not sure. I think I will go back to New York, stay with my mother a while. I have a lot to think about. There's an opening at George Mason University in Virginia. I might try to get an interview there."

"That's near Washington, isn't it? Where your friend Dylan lives," Ben said accusingly. "I'm not going to see you anymore, am I?"

"Ben, I would do anything for you. You are an amazing young man. But..."

"But we can't be together. Right?"

"I'm sorry. Someday you will understand..."

Ben, not caring now if anyone saw them or not, grasped Stephen's hand. "I don't care. If it weren't for you, I don't know what would happen to me. The other night...if you had just said okay..."

Stephen looked at Ben, perhaps hoping to afford a compassion in silence that he could not find in words. "This is all just a prelude for you, just a beginning. You will be going to Duke next week, and—I know you don't see this now—it's going to be the best time of your life."

"You're saying goodbye to me, aren't you?" Ben muttered, withdrawing his hand.

"I'm saying that I am going to miss you."

Ben rose from the table. "I'm nothing to you. I'm nothing to anybody."

"That isn't true," Stephen said. "Do you want me to say it? Okay, I love you. I do, but...It has to *not* be about sex. Ben, listen. We are each at wrong points on the road. Can't you see that?"

Ben did not answer, but stood there silently, looking away from Stephen, waiting for a solace that would not come.

Finally, Stephen said, "I want you to know one thing, if nothing else. I don't regret for one second what happened. There are plenty of people who would probably say I should, or who would call it something shameful. I don't. But, I would regret it if I took advantage of your youth. Your sweetness. Ben, I have too many regrets as it is."

Ben smiled, a quivering, bitter smile. He tried to hear what Stephen was saying, tried to focus on the kind, resonant voice, but it was like capturing just a sliver of light in a darkening room. "I have to go," Ben finally said. "It's okay. I'll miss you, Stephen."

He walked out the door. Once he was outside, Ben stopped and allowed himself one parting glance, one last moment to carry with him. Stephen was standing in the doorway, looking at him, and slowly mouthed the words, "I'm sorry." They were just words though. For the first time in his life, Ben understood the bitter tyranny of hope.

"I'm sorry," Stephen again said, waving goodbye. Just words, as sincere as they were futile.

CHAPTER FIFTY-SIX
DOWN FOR THE COUNT

Edward Harrison, only slightly drunk, sat on one of the thickly cushioned rattan recliners on his terrace and took in the twilight sky. He had waited patiently for that moment, that brief instant, when the sun disappeared over the trees at the far end of his property. He sipped his scotch, and resigned himself to a stealthy, approaching darkness on this quiet Sunday night.

He remembered the sunsets from his grandmother's back porch at Centerpoint, golden clouds towering over the flat landscape. After supper, they would move to the front porch, quietly listening to crickets, looking for the infrequent headlights of an approaching car. After so many years, it was the quietness, the stillness there that he remembered so clearly. Sometimes, in the Boys Room, before he fell asleep, and the old house was slumbering with various relatives, the lights from a passing car would flicker across the wall, a sort of fleeting, luminous mystery.

He drowsily finished the scotch and closed his eyes. There, in the darkness of his expansive lawn, in the quiet of twilight, he could almost clear his mind and retrieve his memories of Alice Owens. Her mischievous eyes challenging him to recall the colors of a room. The blasphemous caress of her hand as she offered him the communion tray. Her laughter as she tossed a red blanket to the floor of the Carolina Court. For just an instant, he could see her marveling at the green horizon from the Wellington Tower, just as Edward found solace in gazing up at her. And then, too soon, that last conversation in the library, the night of John's party.

They were alone, standing beside the fireplace. Looming above the mantel, he could see the portrait of Missy, serenely oblivious, with her steely grip on the bouquet of roses. "I'm sorry I disappointed you," he told Alice. "I seem to do that to the people I care about the most." He tried to embrace her, but she moved away, stepping further back from the fireplace.

"You were right," she said, glancing nervously at the door. "I do see things as I want them to be." She had looked at him then with such regret, and perhaps an unbidden resentment as well, then added, "Until I *don't.*"

He opened his eyes. A dog barked in a nearby yard, its yelping joined by the sudden croaking of a solitary frog. He heard the sound of a car. A door slamming. And then he heard his own doorbell ringing, an artificial, though melodious, accompaniment to these natural sounds. Edward got up and walked inside. Missy, who had been stonily aloof since the events of the previous night, was not yet home from a shopping expedition to Via Veneto. She planned to meet Janey Burroughs for dinner afterward at the Palm.

Missy had insisted that she could not possibly show her face in Venice without armoring herself in the newest designs. Edward frankly did not care whether she showed up in Italy in a sackcloth or a mink, so long as she did indeed go. He wanted nothing more than to be left alone. He found that, as he approached the insistent doorbell, all he really wanted anymore was silence.

He could hear the faint sound of music, some clanging synthetic noise, from Andrea's room. He called up to her. "Andrea, are you expecting someone? How many times have I told you to tell your friends not to come over after nine o'clock?"

"No, Daddy, no one," she said, somewhat regretfully.

Edward looked through the peephole and saw the earnest, nervous face of Ben Caldwell. He opened the door. "Ben? Hello," he said, in a questioning and not at all welcome tone. "It's kind of late, isn't it son?"

"I know. I'm sorry, Mr. Harrison. But I heard that Johnny was home. I really need to see him. If that's okay." Edward noticed that Ben's upper lip trembled just like Laura's.

He regarded the boy with hesitation. Ben's khaki shorts were wrinkled and a coffee stain spotted his baggy white shirt. It appeared as if he had not shaved for several days, although the whiskers afforded him a more mature, if disheveled, demeanor. "I'm sorry, Ben, but I believe John has turned in for the night."

Matters would have ended there. Even in his agitated state, Ben Caldwell would not be so bold as to challenge the will of Edward Harrison, who was never so formidable as when he was saying *no* in his own house. But, Andrea, with a gleeful if vague sense of some pending disturbance, called down from the landing, "Oh, he's up. I'll get him."

She rushed down the hall with surprising agility to the closed door of her brother. Since last night's party, he had spent most of the day and now the waning evening in his room. She had heard him call his girlfriend, that older woman from Washington, several times, and each time he had asked, with mounting anger, "Well, will you tell her I called?" Someone had actually rejected her golden brother. Andrea had delighted in every second of her relative ascendance. After all, that awful Evelyn Peck had not called *her* a pervert.

Andrea knocked on the door and, not waiting for a response, walked into the room. John lay on his side in bed, listening to music on his iPod. He turned over and, through squinting and reddish eyes, looked at Andrea as if she were some obese hobbit, concluding, not for the first time, that she was. "What?" he asked irritably, removing the earphones.

"Ben's downstairs to see you."

He rolled back over onto his side and mumbled, "Tell him I'm sleeping. Jesus."

"Okay, I'll tell him you said you were sleeping."

"Not *said*, you retard. *Am!*"

The murmurs of John's and Andrea's conversation drifted down to the foyer. As Andrea walked back into the hallway, she could hear the sound of footsteps coming up the stairs. And the slightly slurred voice of their father. "Ben," this unfamiliar, offended voice said, "I told you. John is asleep."

But, then they heard an even less familiar voice that belonged to the plaintive, but insistent person of Ben Caldwell. "What? Oh, I'm sorry, Mr. Harrison. I thought I heard John talking."

John called out to the two alien voices. "It's okay, I'm awake." And then he saw Ben standing in the doorway, with John's annoyed father and his anticipatory sister hovering on either side. "Ben," John said, sociably waving him into the room as if there were nothing out of the ordinary for Ben to come charging up the Harrison stairs unannounced. "What's new?"

Suddenly, Ben seemed more like the shy, hesitant boy of old. John was now sitting up in bed, naked from the waist up. "Sorry it's so late," Ben mumbled. "Maybe I should come back another time."

"Yes, that probably would be better," Edward Harrison said, casting a commanding glance toward the stairs.

"No, stay." John smiled, enjoying as ever his dominating allure. "Not a problem. What's up?" he asked, clearly signaling to his father and sister that they should leave him to visit with his friend.

Edward looked doubtfully at Ben, but then said, "All right, then. You boys have your visit, but, Ben, do not ever come to this house again without calling first. Am I clear?"

"Yes, sir. I'm sorry," Ben said. "It won't happen again."

Edward slowly closed the door, leaving it just slightly ajar.

"Close it," John said softly, looking quizzically at Ben. "So we can have some privacy." John leaned back a little onto his pillows, and put his arms behind his head. "So talk to me, Benjie. Talk to me."

Ben closed the door. John sat up further in bed. He was tanned from the summer, and the padded curves of his chest seemed thicker, harder. He had let his blond hair grow and its silky strands almost reached his shoulders.

"Have a seat," John said, motioning Ben to a place at the foot of the bed.

"I just want you to know," Ben said haltingly, "I just want you to know that…"

"Know what?" John asked, his half-grin enticingly in place.

"I want you to know how much I hate you."

"No, no you don't, Ben," John purred, stringing out the words. "You *want* to hate me, but you can't." He smiled, and again stretched back out on the bed, his arms behind his head, the pale blue sheet sliding further down the tawny, sharp ridges of his stomach.

"No, maybe I don't. You want to know the truth? I don't really know what I think about much of anything any more. You. Me. All of it. Tell me one thing," Ben said, trying not to look at him. "What happened? Was it because of that night? Was that night so awful?"

"*What* night? Ben, come on," he said, his voice tinged now with sarcasm. "You make such a big deal about everything. Just like your mom. Jeez, you're turning into an old lady. It was *nothing*. But, you kept pulling at me." He moved one hand slowly, caressingly down his naked waist, then murmured softly, "I don't like that."

"I don't know why I came here," Ben replied, desperate to pull away from the pulsing, insinuating presence of John Harrison. He stood up and walked toward the door. Then, remembering, he added, "Sorry I missed your party. Oh, wait, but I wasn't invited, was I?"

John yawned. "Mom made out the list. She always thought you were kind of strange. Sorry."

"Don't worry about it. I wouldn't have come anyway. Must have been interesting for you though."

"Yeah?" he asked nonchalantly, his voice taking on a studied, deeper resonance.

"That woman, Evelyn...pretty embarrassing, huh? I mean, your own family calling you a..."

"She's *not* my family," John interrupted, his smirk briefly vanquished. "She's nobody. She only was here because that fag cousin of mine brought her. Anyway, no biggie. Don't be such a putz."

"How did your girlfriend...Tricia, right?...How did she take all this?"

Once again, for just an instant, Ben could see an odd, thrilling discomfort in John Harrison's eyes. "She was there with me, wasn't she? Trust me, Benjie, she can't get enough of me. Just like you."

"You'd like to think so, wouldn't you?" Ben asked. "One thing I'm curious about though. What makes Stephen a, as you say, a fag, and you're not?"

"Ben, you are so innocent." John laughed, his lip curling into a knowing desire. "It makes me miss you, just a little. You're wasting your time with that geeky cousin of mine." He raised up one massive, browned leg, causing the sheet to hang precariously over the whiteness of his thigh.

"He's a better person than you'll ever be on your best day."

John threw the sheet off of his body. "Really? That right?"

Ben began walking toward the door. Suddenly, he felt John behind him, one arm around his chest, the other lower around his waist, pulling him closer. "Come on, Ben. For old time's sake. Come on," he whispered. "You know you want to."

CHAPTER FIFTY-SEVEN
VENETIAN VASE

Monday morning, Missy huddled under her silk comforter, trying to assure herself that the party on Saturday night had been a dream. Edward was up early. "I have to meet Adam Burroughs," he had said, as he hurriedly dressed, eager to lose himself in the one thing that he could count on. His work.

"Really?" she said. "Awfully early for the office. Goodness, I just don't know how you keep up with such a hectic schedule." She paused, and then lethally inquired, "What did Evelyn mean when she said she could tell a few things about you? Something about a motel?"

He carefully adjusted the knot in his tie. "How on earth should I know? I don't think I need to tell you what a nut she is."

"No, I guess not," she said, unconvinced. "Nice tie. It suits you. You should wear it more often."

He did not bother to kiss her goodbye. She heard the front door close, and was suddenly aware of the vast quietness of her home. Missy lay in her bed, and thought of each room in the grand house. Each quiet, empty room. Maybe we should move to one of those new condos Uptown, she sighed. Low maintenance. Uncluttered. But, no. There was more and more talk, more nervousness about gangs, hordes of black and Hispanic thugs gathering, massing, threatening on Uptown street corners. They would as soon cut your throat as look at you, she thought.

We have our wall. We have our gate.

"How 'bout you at the Carolina Court?" The accusing voice of Evelyn Peck came unbidden into the Italian refuge of Missy Harrison's bedroom. She lay there, thinking about the grotesque gathering the night before. *You and her at the Carolina Court.*

If Edward had, against all odds, strayed, then who accompanied him on that forbidden path? She was fairly certain that there was a motel by that name in Gastonia...*You and her...You must have a twin in Gastonia.*

While she could confront him with her suspicions, she would not do so. Missy sensed that to acknowledge infidelity was to empower it. She wondered what disturbed her the most, that Edward may have been with another woman, or that he had needed to be? In either case, she had to consider that she had not been paying attention. Her husband had become a fixture in her life, as ornamental as the Venetian vase, a Murano creation of a perfect burgundy tint, on the mantel in their bedroom, and about as intimate. And perhaps she had become a similarly decorative, and not at all essential, artifact to Edward.

She assured herself that, in the end, she and Edward were most comfortable on the surface of things, and disinclined to explore any darker waters. Secure the surface, she believed, and the depth can manage on its own. Evelyn Peck's words at that awful party had ushered Missy into the unfamiliar and inhospitable territory of ambivalence. It was not a realm in which she was comfortable, and she did not intend to remain there for long.

Dad always took the long view, she decided. I can do the same.

Missy heard her phone ringing on the gilt table next to her bed. She hesitated to answer, unwilling to face the inquiring calls of gossips who would be all too eager to linger over the rotting corpse of the party. She would let the vultures circle a while longer. She glanced at the phone, and then noticed that the number on call waiting was Laura Caldwell's. Impulsively, Missy answered.

"Hello." There was silence. "Laura? Hello?"

"Hi," Laura said. "How are you?"

Jack Gardner

"I'm fine. Why are you calling so early?" Missy asked.

"Well, I just wanted to check on you," Laura said nervously. Her voice sounded faint. "About Saturday night."

"What about it?" Missy asked warily. "Now, Laur, you know I had nothing to do with who was invited. That was up to John, and since he and Ben don't...well..."

"Oh, of course, I understand all that. That's not why I'm calling." She paused, searching for the right words. "You don't have to pretend with me. I know what happened. That cousin of Edward's? Evelyn somebody?"

"News travels fast. It's really no big deal," Missy replied, brittle as ever to the tenuous border between sympathy and condescension.

"I just wanted to call and tell you I was thinking of you," Laura said with gentle futility, echoing some last remnant of the former closeness between them. "It must have been awful, for someone to come in to your home and to behave that way."

Missy felt a growing fury. *She's just loving this*, Missy thought. *She wants me to wallow in it.* "Thank you for your concern," Missy said. "Is there anything else?"

"Oh, well, I don't want to bother you with this now..."

"I'm wide awake. Go ahead," Missy said.

"I feel terrible about our lunch, Missy. You seemed so upset, and..."

"I'll get over it," Missy replied curtly. "Don't worry about it."

"Well, I appreciate that. Thanks." Laura hesitated, and then asked, "Did you talk to Stephen? I have just been worried sick about this. Ben seems so depressed. He just sits in his room. Missy, I don't know what to do anymore..."

"I talked to him," Missy said. *So that's why she's calling. She doesn't give a damn about me.* "You needn't worry any more about it. Stephen is not seeing Ben. They are just friends."

"That's all? What else did he say?" Laura asked doubtfully.

"Do you really want to know?" Missy got out of bed and walked over to the mantel and slightly moved the Venetian vase so that it was perfectly centered. "Stephen felt sorry for Ben, tried to befriend him, but this only egged Ben on."

"I don't understand," Laura said. "Why did the therapist tell me they were involved?"

"Well, I don't claim to read the minds of every half-baked counselor in Charlotte, but I guess in Ben's mind there was a...what?... romance?...with Stephen. But, as far as Stephen was concerned, I suppose Ben was like a stalker. Obsessed. And, well, never mind..." *She has always thought she was better than me. Always.*

"And what?" Laura asked anxiously.

"Well, isn't it obvious? Ben is the one who wanted sex...begging for it...I think Ben practically raped him...tried to force Stephen to...to...well, it is just so disgusting..."

"Ben would never do such a thing. He is not capable of such a thing. Stephen is lying. He is a predator, taking advantage of...an innocent boy."

"You never thought Ben was gay either," Missy said, taunting her. "You might ask yourself how well you really know your son." She paused, letting the cruelty of those words sink in, and then said, "Look, I did what you asked me to do. There's really nothing more to say."

She could hear Laura sobbing over the phone. "No, no I guess not," she said, struggling to say the words. "I tried to be a good mother, you know that." She began crying again, unable to speak.

Missy felt nothing but contempt. *You used to be somebody*, she thought again to herself. "I'm sorry it had to come to this, really I am," she said, her rumbling words as hard and distant as mountain stones. "But, life is full of things that you cannot control."

"I wanted to do my best," Laura said in a feeble, diminishing voice. "I mean...*my* mother.... But, it isn't enough sometimes, is it?"

"I have to go. I'm leaving for Italy next week. I need a break. From *everybody*." She waited impatiently for a reply, but only heard the futile sobs of Laura Caldwell. Then, like a tiny explosion, she heard a click, and the line was silent.

Missy put the phone back on the table. That hypocrite, she thought. So pathetic. A loser. Perhaps I do cast my lot with winners, Missy conceded. In that merciless calculation, Edward had currency. Laura did not.

If the party for John was a skirmish that Missy had lost —and she had to admit that, indeed, it was a mortifying evening —she would not entertain the notion that anything of more significance had been surrendered. I'm still the diamond girl, Missy decided. She pulled back the heavy drapes of her window and smiled with renewed contentment as a ray of morning sunlight drifted lazily across the room.

Laura Caldwell would continue to fade into the nonentity she was destined to become. Missy imagined they would see each other at occasional events, smile politely, gush the obligatory, "Oh, we really have got to get together some time. Yes, it has been so long..." But, they would gaze across an increasing distance, with Missy acknowledging her former friend, her friend who dared to think she was better than Missy Gilmore of Rock Hill, South Carolina, from an ever more rarified height.

And Evelyn Peck's wild accusations would remain in the sewer from which they were uttered. It was as if the night had never occurred. And while it would be the occasion of frenzied gossip and speculation for a time, it would pass, filed away, if not entirely forgotten, in some rarely opened drawer of bad form. Most of their acquaintances had an Evelyn Peck of their own, roosting on some lower branch of the family tree. Indeed, even Tough Toller, as she and Ken were leaving the party, hugged Missy and consoled her, with perfect compassionate malice, "Don't worry. We *all* have an Evelyn too."

It was amusing, Missy assured herself. Exotic even. She looked at her gleaming vase, its burgundy richness shimmering in the morning sunlight. Venice. That's where she would soon return. Check in to the Gritti Palace, sleep under a lace canopy as the Venetian light glittered on the Grand Canal, and leave all the litter and garbage of this abortive summer behind.

Take the long view. That was it. Just like Dad.

Missy lay back down on her bed, finding a sensual comfort in the smoothness of those 600-thread count Egyptian cotton sheets. She looked out the palladian window at the neat rows of purple and yellow chrysanthemums just recently planted. All that vibrant color.

The precision and order. It reassured Missy, as material things always did. She studied the circle of flowers carefully placed around the large fountain, which was gushing spouts of water. So beautiful, she thought. Then she noticed a divot in her smooth green lawn, where clods of dirt were left by the gardeners, like some garish fecal insult, smudging the pristine buds. Those stupid Mexicans, she seethed. They don't understand beauty.

CHAPTER FIFTY-EIGHT
MYERS PARK

Laura could feel light beads of perspiration coursing down her face, warm from the late afternoon sun. She was crouched over, planting mums on the back lawn. Mums were her favorite flowers. She waited patiently for them through most of the summer, not planting until well into August. Mums rewarded patience and they would bloom well into fall. She had arrayed a long arc of them this morning, creating a lustrous burgundy and white curve all along the green border of boxwoods that lined the terrace.

At first, she did not realize that Ben had walked outside and was standing above her on the terrace. "Mom," she heard him say. "Those look really nice."

She looked up. The afternoon sun was shining behind him, creating a slight glare. Laura shielded her eyes with her hand and said, "Oh, thank you, honey. Are you feeling better?"

He walked down the steps and stood there quietly. His hair was brilliantly dark against the cloudless blue sky. He hesitated for a moment, and then said, "I'm sorry I let you down."

"It's okay, honey. Don't you worry," she reassured him. Laura stood up and hugged her son. "You are just confused. You *can* change. But, you cannot go against God. We all make sacrifices in life. You have to have faith."

"Mom, God made me too, didn't he?" he asked uncertainly, somehow both emphatic and regretful in his realization.

"Yes, he did," she said, hugging him more tightly. "God is testing you. Can't you see that, honey? We are just journeying through this life, just in passing. God gave you the will to choose."

"Well, then I guess I have made my choice..." Ben sat down on the steps and silently looked at her, his eyes calm and steady, glinting with a reluctant, but tenacious truth.

"You don't mean that," she said, dropping the spade that she held in her hand, watching it plunge to the ground. "You're upset. We will go see Reverend Dunlap tomorrow." She crouched down again, picked up the spade, and resumed planting the mums, as if to signal that the matter was settled.

"No," she heard him say. "I know how disappointed you are in me. I tried. Really, I did. No one, except Deb, was willing to tell me that it was okay." He paused. "And Stephen. He..."

"Stephen!" She spat out the contemptible name. "I don't want to ever hear that name again. Ever," she said, furiously plunging the spade into the black soil. "He's just toying with you. He's taking advantage of you, of your sweet nature. I'm sorry, Benny, but he is. And when he's done, then what? What will you do when he has no further use for you?"

Ben smiled bitterly. "What I'm doing now. Stephen is moving away. And he really did just try to be my friend. I was the one who wanted it to be more than that, not him. He wouldn't..."

Laura shuddered at this admission. She looked up at the sky, searching, but all she could hear now was Missy's cruel taunt. *Ben practically raped him...he tried to force Stephen to...*

"Hon, don't you see?" she asked, "Whatever you have done, whatever mistakes you have made, God is giving you a second chance."

He stood up and then, looming above her, said, "Mama, I don't want a second chance. And, if anyone used me, it was not Stephen. It was John Harrison."

"What?" she asked. "How did Johnny use you?"

"How? Well, for starters, he gets his kicks from other people, guys or girls, wanting him. Then he shoves them out of the way.

That's what he did to me. You didn't want to know, so I never told you."

She sat there, mute, almost unable to comprehend what he was saying.

"Mom, please don't worry so much. I can make my own choices. Last night, I said no to John Harrison. This time he wanted me. And I said no. I never thought I could do that. But, I did."

"You can go back into therapy," she said, unwilling to hear any more.

"Go back into therapy?" he asked, incredulous. "Would you like to know about therapy, Mom? Mr. Douglas made me watch gay porn. He gave me medicine so I would throw up." Ben waited, as his mother comprehended the disgust in his eyes, and then continued. "That's right. He had me watch two guys having sex, and then had me vomit. Other times, I sat beside him half naked while he hugged me. This was supposed to make me all right? This is supposed to be normal?"

"Oh, Ben," she said. "I'm so sorry. I had no idea." Laura wanted to console him, to take her wounded son in her arms as she had so many times before, but she feared that any further comfort would imply an acceptance of his sin, a concession to his fall. And so, in somber determination, she only said, "You can still learn to live a *good* life."

"A good life? You mean pretending. You expect me to go through life that way?"

"I expect you to marry and have a family the way God intended you to. Life is more than pleasure. Sometimes that is the price you pay."

"Is that the price you paid? Was it worth it?" he asked, his gentle face contorted now by grim certainties. It was a face that she realized with a shock that she had never seen and did not recognize.

Stricken, as if he had slapped her, Laura began walking into the house, leaving the unplanted flowers recumbent and forgotten on the freshly tilled soil. She turned and looked at her son. "I am not going to discuss this any further. I will pray to God to forgive me."

"You don't need forgiveness for who I am," he said, his voice a constricted, agitated cry. "And neither do I. Okay, I'm not perfect. But, does that mean that I'm not good?"

"You cannot go against God," she repeated.

"Don't you get it, Mom?" he asked desperately. "We're *all* bad. All of us. But we need to believe, somehow we have to believe that we're good too. I just wish that you and Dad could have helped me, helped me even just a little bit, to do that." Then he said, in a brutal assertion that she could never have imagined, "I can't stay here anymore."

"Ben, this is your home. We love you. You know that. Please don't go." She moved to hug him, but he backed away.

"I'm sorry," he said, and then repeated, "I just can't stay here."

Laura felt something within her breaking, something solid and hard drifting away. "Go then, go!" she screamed. "After all your father and I have done for you, all we sacrificed. Go, get out!"

Laura walked inside, into the kitchen, and then collapsed on the floor. She heard the front door close, heard her son driving away. To where? Stephen's? To some awful bar? In a stupor of exhaustion and grief, she lay there on the cool tile floor powerless to move or speak.

She spied a cricket, moving slowly underneath the cabinet. The cricket stopped, jerking its body left to right, as if fascinated by this new and potent creature sprawled on the floor, and then hopped beyond the cabinet and scurried across the room. Eventually, she got up off the floor. There was someplace she needed to go, someplace where she would find her son, but she was not yet certain where that place might be.

I have to tell him. He will understand then. He will know I tried to do my best. I can still help him, she thought, as she got into her Lexus and backed out of the driveway. The palatial homes of Piper Glen grew smaller and smaller in her rearview mirror. Ahead, the towering spires of Calvary Church looked like jagged bolts of lightning, a pinkish glow against a darkening blue canvas. She turned right onto Highway 51, the 'highway to heaven'. This used to be nothing but empty fields, she thought. This used to be the highway to nowhere.

Nowhere. That was the chilly wilderness she now lived in. Nowhere. Nothing. And in that void, in that empty place, all she could see was the wounded and accusing face of her son.

She drove slowly, as the lingering rush hour traffic surged by her, horns honking. A man in a silver gray Mercedes passed her, shaking his fist as he went alongside her, and then giving her the finger, a sort of obscene benediction, as he pulled in front. She approached the intersection of 51 and Providence Road and the stream of cars widened into a clamorous herd into six lanes of traffic. She turned onto Providence Road. Who named it Providence anyway? Was it for fortune or faith? Many of the neighborhoods she passed also made claims to providence. Providence Commons. Providence Landing. Providence Square. Trust to providence. That's what people always told her. Trust to providence. But, which was it? Fortune or faith?

She felt a vague nausea, an indefinable disgust, weighed down by a blur of homes and cars and trees. The city of trees. That's what they started calling Charlotte some years ago, in yet another effort to give it some kind of distinction. So phony. All of it. So false. So desperate.

Laura glanced wearily at the brick walls, those illusory defenses facing the highway, behind which sat endless rows of colonial style homes. More walls. More red brick. Above those walls, the upper windows, shadowed by pitched roofs, looked out like eyes, unseeing, lifeless eyes.

In her youth, there were the grand homes of Myers Park, the wide front-lawned estates along Sharon Amity. Those homes were special. Imposing. Now, the whole city was just drowning under this avalanche of luxe Levittowns, just a pile of cheap brick and vinyl siding. It occurred to her that all those people in Providence Plantation and Challis Farms and Ballantyne, even in Piper Glen, all of those poor souls knew that. Those 4000 square foot mini-mansions were only special to those who hadn't yet moved in to one. For the rest, they were a repetitive, mundane shock. No wonder they looked back so uneasily at the Wal-Mart at the Arboretum, or the Hampton Inn next door to the Palm.

You haven't come so far, after all, those places screamed. You're not special, and you know it. Even with their Ethan Allen sofas, their fox hunt prints hanging above the family room mantel, their burglar alarms promising protection that could not be delivered, they still knew it was a farce. And every time they drove by the Wal-Mart, they shuddered that what once seemed such a leap up was no more than a temporary exhilaration.

The newer neighborhoods gave way to older ones as she headed in the direction of Uptown, eventually passing the gothic solidity of Myers Park Presbyterian. Her earliest memories were of sitting with her parents in that beautiful sanctuary, secure between the ramrod straight, starched collar bearing of her father, his white hair neatly trimmed and parted, and the satiny, tailored glamour of her mother. The age difference of her parents never troubled her. It was as if, between the two of them, she lived in a secure world of maturity and beauty. It was an illusion, of course—she found that out eventually— but, as illusions go, it remained intact longer than most. That was something, she supposed.

Suddenly, a red light. She hit her brakes, barely coming to a stop at the eerie intersection of Providence Road and Queens Road, where both roads continued in two directions. She glanced at the gold statue of crazy old Hugh McManahan, the 'mayor' of Myers Park, that long forgotten, eccentric figure who used to direct traffic with a white linen cloth. There he stood, a silent, mischievous guard. Oblivious drivers ignored him and raced on by. Bits of fading sunlight glistened on his golden cap. Hugh McManahan. Roller skating through Myers Park on just one skate.

Can't find the other one! Can't find the other one!

Laura turned left on Queens Road and gave herself up to its canopied, serpentine splendor, winding its reptilian way through the treacherous Eden of her blighted childhood. She instinctively turned left on Sherwood Street, and stopped the car in front of a white, two-story colonial home with an expansive lawn and perfect symmetry. *Their* home, she thought. Not mine. Never mine.

Now, as she gazed at that home, it seemed as empty as a tomb. She looked up at the room at the end of the house on the second floor. The maple tree out front, which had barely reached the window when Laura lived there, now towered above it. That had been the guest room. Laura turned the car off and slumped back into her seat. She sat there, waiting to see if the curtain would be drawn back.

For so long, she had believed her parents hung the moon. He was so dignified and sturdy. And her mother possessed an incandescent beauty, stunning and somehow comforting in her self-contained distance. Laura thought they were perfect. She never heard them argue. Never really even saw them cross. But, buried somewhere within her, there was an uneasiness, the kind of foreboding one feels just before a light is turned on in a shadowy room.

One night, when she was a senior at Country Day, her parents were having the Bakers, their best friends, over for dinner. Their families had taken trips together, to Pawleys Island and once even to Europe. Their two sons were her age. Horrible little hellions. But, she had loved Mr. and Mrs. Baker. She was staying over at her friend Allison's that evening. Allison lived just down the street. Around ten o'clock that night, Laura realized that she had left her overnight bag in her room.

"Allison, I need to run over to my house to get my bag," she had said.

There were exactly two lights on upstairs in her house. The light in her parents' room, and the light in the guest room. It was windy that night, and she could see the top limbs of the maple tree brushing against the guest room window. That's odd, she thought. Who would be in the guest room? She walked inside to the foyer, very quietly, and crept up the stairs. As she approached her parents' room, she could hear noises. The sounds of a couple making love. But, the woman's voice was not her mother's. It was Mrs. Baker. The lilting, feathery voice that she had heard at the beach and in Paris was now, purring, unhurried, in her parents' bed. The other voice, in a rushed gasping for breath, was her father's.

She continued down the hallway, toward the light coming from the guest room. The door was slightly ajar, and she could not see the people inside. But, it was her mother and Mr. Baker. And her mother was saying the most awful things. Sexual things. Laura had tiptoed to her room, hoping they would not hear her. She quickly grabbed her bag, and was going back down the stairs, when she heard her mother call out, "Who's there?"

She hurried out the door and down the sidewalk. For an instant, she glanced back at the white-columned house, and thought she saw the curtain pulled back from the window of the guest room. Laura never told anyone except Missy years later. Not a word was said to her parents, then or later, but she would always wonder if her mother knew.

After Mr. Soames had died, Mrs. Soames had moved first to the Carlton. The house had been sold after Laura, with unusual ferocity, had told her mother that she had no intention of living there. Ever.

"But, Laura, this is our home. It is part of our family's history, who we are," her mother had protested.

And in the closest moment to the truth that they would ever have, Laura said, "I will have my own traditions, Mother, and I hope they will be better than what our family has had here." Not for the first time, as Laura sat in her car, unsure where to go next, unsure of anything, really, it occurred to her that once again, as always, her mother would have the last laugh.

She drove back toward Providence, and she could see the new and imposing skyline of Uptown in the distance. Those distant towers of Uptown, gleaming in steel and glass, cold as glaciers, seemed to be mocking her. Laughing at her. Relic, they hissed. Go back to Myers Park or Piper Glen, or to God, wherever it is that relics and failures live. You do not belong here. You are past. We want the young, the hip, the different. Take your sagging breasts and flaccid ideals, your gelatinous flesh and collapsing values, take the detritus of your slippery life and go home.

Home? she laughed. And where exactly would that be?

Reverend Dunlap said that God was always present, that God would never forsake her. God was mysterious, and it was arrogance to demand answers. The mystery of God. Faith must suffice.

Once, when Debra was a little girl, she asked Laura where did Adam and Eve's son find his wife. "Who was she, Mommy? Where did she come from?"

"The Bible doesn't tell us, honey," Laura had assured her, "but, don't you fret about that. You can be sure that God took care of it. He just didn't tell us how he did it."

"Why didn't he want us to know?"

"Because if he told us everything, then he would ask nothing of us to believe. That is what faith is, honey. It is believing what you can't always see."

And what of believing what you *can* see? Wasn't that just as demanding?

Speeding now, hurtling toward some kind of resolution, she felt the exhilaration of flight. The crape myrtles seemed almost crimson now under the twilight blue sky. Laura Caldwell felt the confining boundaries of her life falling away, but the signposts of her life were fading as well. The traffic was getting heavier, the roads full now of Uptown commuters making their way back to the green and isolated lushness of their perfect homes. She searched the faces in the cars speeding by, wondering if one of them might be her son. And as each car passed her, they became nothing more than mocking lights and metallic flashes signaling her that her son was gone.

She was finally back on Highway 51 and again saw the spires of Calvary Church. Those grasping towers, somehow promising so much, the portent of answers, of understanding. Ascending the heights. Reaching for God. But God was too far off now. Like her son. Like Andrew. Even Missy. All of them had drifted away from her clinging and rigid embrace.

As she approached the intersection at Rea Road, Laura could see a truck barreling down toward her, pushing to get through the yellow light. Good luck, she thought. She suddenly felt so weary. Caution lights. Endless and exhausting. Not what she had hoped for. What was it again? She had studied it in college. Got an A. Her mother had professed amazement.

The green light. That was it. The green light.

You don't get many of them in this life, Ben. It will elude you too, sweet boy. The roar of the approaching truck grew louder. She felt transfixed by its blinding solidity. And then the horrible sound of screeching brakes, and her own muffled scream. "One fine morning... one fine morning..." Laura smiled briefly, for one unbearable instant, and then closed her eyes, waiting for a light yet to come.

EPILOGUE
CENTERPOINT

October, 2005

This highway is just terrible," Myrtle muttered, as she and her grandson drove along Highway 601. The two-lane road, as usual, was crowded with enormous trucks, all on their way to the Wal-Mart distribution center. The state of South Carolina, salivating at the prospect of Wal-Mart jobs, had agreed to the construction of the distribution center. Unfortunately, the monolithic building and its invading trucks arrived years in advance of any widening of the congested road.

"Somebody ought to sue Wal-Mart or the damned state for this," she said. "It just burns me up." The huge trucks flew past, separated only by a thin yellow line. She looked somberly at the crosses and bouquets of flowers along the side of the narrow shoulder of the road, in memoriam to those unfortunate souls who happened to encounter one of those trucks at the wrong time.

Stephen nodded his head in agreement. He had been quiet for most of the drive, staring straight ahead as they rode along the gently rolling hills toward Chesterfield, South Carolina. The autumn sun sparkled in between an intricate lace of red and gold leaves.

Several years ago, Myrtle and Edward had driven over to Centerpoint and were shocked to see the condition of the old house. After Rose Harrison had died, the home had been sold to Jack Lilly, a longtime family acquaintance, who then proceeded to allow the property to fall apart under the tenancy of a succession of impoverished, elderly men. When she and Edward had visited, a recent slapdash coat of white paint had done nothing to obscure the ruin. A portion of the roof over the back porch had collapsed. They did not go inside. Myrtle wondered if there had been any improvement since, but doubted it.

When she and Stephen got to the area called Hilltop, from which one could see the countryside below for miles ahead, Myrtle asked him, "How is your young friend doing?"

"Ben? Not good," Stephen answered, his voice halting and raspy. "He's at Duke now. He has had a terrible time."

"Poor fellow," she said. "I met his mom once. She seemed like such a nice lady. To tell you the truth, she seemed so sweet, I wondered how she could be friends with a snob like Missy."

"Friends?" he asked bitterly. "That word is so easily tossed around nowadays. I don't think Aunt Missy is friends with anyone outside her own reflection. Now she has latched onto Janey Burroughs. I guess she figures it wouldn't hurt her reputation at this point to have a best friend who is rich *and* black. You know she is back in Italy?"

"I heard," Myrtle said. "Edward told me she's there for a few months. That she is just sick with grief over Laura Caldwell's death. My tail! She's just spa-ing away her troubles and, just between you and me, I think Edward was glad for her to go. All by herself over there. And with those scary eyes of hers, she will probably stay that way. I bet you those Italians don't give a flip for her. I'd be so lonesome if it was me."

"You know she would not even speak to me at the funeral," Stephen said. "And the funeral was bad enough on its own. Andrew Caldwell had the preacher talk for thirty minutes about how we were all going to hell if we didn't 'get right' with Jesus. Right now! He actually asked us to raise our hands if we were saved."

"Did you talk to Ben at the funeral?"

"Yes. Just for a few minutes. I've never seen a human being so wounded looking. I think he blames himself for his mother's death, even though they insist it was just a horrible accident."

Myrtle looked doubtfully at another cross beside the road and sighed, "Well, guess we'll never know. I feel sorry for him though. You know, some people in this world are just sad creatures, and I am afraid he is one of them." She glanced at her grandson, and left unspoken her fear that he might also be among that unfortunate group. He would be moving to Fairfax, Virginia, at the end of the year, starting over at George Mason University.

"I wish you could have seen Missy and Johnny there," Stephen said, "looking all teary eyed and reverent as that idiot preacher kept talking. And then Missy had them announce that she was making a big gift to Queens in Mrs. Caldwell's memory."

Missy's charity had also been reported in the latest *Charlotte Now…*

Charlotte philanthropist, Mrs. Edward Harrison, honors late friend with donation to Queens University. The gift will provide for the establishment of the Laura Soames Caldwell chair in religious studies. Mrs. Caldwell died in a tragic automobile accident in August.

"Good Lord," Myrtle said. "I heard about that. I remember showing Fred. I said, 'Fred, look at this. All that money and Missy never even liked that college.' Anyway, that's Missy for you, though, always comes out smelling like a rose."

"A rose with thorns," Stephen replied. "It almost made me nauseous. I remember at the funeral, at least Uncle Edward had the decency to look uncomfortable."

"So, will you see Ben again sometime?" Myrtle asked.

"I want to. I told him so. Just as a, you know, just as a friend, if nothing else. But, he said no. Not a good idea. He wants a… different…life. One that his mother would want for him. So…"

"Well, I'm really sorry to hear that," Myrtle said. "I'm just an old woman, but I think a person ought to try and live their own life, try and be happy. It took me a long time to figure that out. Not many people seem to manage to do it though, do they?"

"No," he said, as another truck roared by them. "I'm not sure I know anyone who has really managed that, except maybe you."

"Hah! Not me, honey. Rose Harrison did. Of course, for her, living her own life meant living for others. That's not a very popular thing to do anymore." She looked out the window for a moment, studying the pine-scrubbed South Carolina countryside where she grew up. "That Fred said something the other day that really made me think. You know, the man doesn't talk much. Just sits there and does his woodcarvings when he isn't writing checks to that no account grandson of his. Did I tell you he sent the boy $500 last week? Said his car wouldn't run and it would take $500 to fix it. And never a word of thanks. I tell you, it just *burns* me up...'

"What did Fred say, Grandmom?" Stephen asked.

"What? Oh, Fred, that's right. Yes, I was talking to Fred the other day about, you know, recent events, and he said, 'Myrtle, it's simple really. There are the survivors in this world, always getting ahead, and then there are the ones who get left behind.'"

"That's very interesting. And a little sad."

"Yes, it is," she agreed. "It's like life's one big train station, people getting on, getting off, and some just lost and wandering. You can bet Missy will always get on the train, no worry about that. But, who knows where it will take her, honey. Who knows?"

They turned onto Angelus Road, the street name that had been given to Highway 9, and could see in the distance the gabled white frame house with its columned front porch. As they approached the property, it was clear that the intervening years had continued its grotesque decline. There was peeling paint along the side of the house. They drove up the dirt driveway, which was full of weeds and small potholes. The current tenant, a thin and decrepit old black man, walked out onto the sagging back porch. He wore boxer shorts and a New York Mets cap.

Stephen and Myrtle got out of the car. "Afternoon," Stephen said to the man. "How are you?"

"Oh, I do all right," the old man said, "long as my arthur-ritis don't act up on me."

"I hear you," Stephen said. "Nice day though." He took Myrtle's arm in his and walked toward the screen door. "I'm Stephen Rayfield, and this is my grandmother."

Myrtle attempted to smile, as she looked wearily about the property. "Hello," she said. "Our family used to live here. Would you mind if we come in?"

The old man offered up a toothless grin. "Sure, come on in. It's a little messy," he said, without a hint of irony.

The back porch was now open to the sky. The collapsed roof had simply been hauled away. Myrtle looked at the gray, cinderblock steps to the porch. Rose Harrison had died, alone, trying to get back to those steps, back inside, on a hot, sweltering June day. Just recently turned eighty-two, her body a treachery of swelling discomfort, she had nonetheless been tending to her vegetable garden. Before she could get to the steps, she felt a sudden explosion in her heart, and fell to the ground. Annie Briggs, who lived up the road, found her, already dead. "Miss Rose looked so peaceful," she told the family later, "like she was just resting awhile."

As they walked inside, Myrtle gasped. The kitchen was dark and grimy, with the greasy smell of unwashed frying pans. There was no longer any table in the kitchen, just an old egg crate propped up in a corner and a single caneback chair beside it. The Harrisons used to sit for hours around a linoleum top kitchen table. Rose would constantly put on another pot of coffee, for both the sober and hungover members of her family. How many times had Myrtle heard her gently offer to a visiting, drunken son, including Myrtle's own husband, "Have another cup of coffee, son. It's no trouble."

That simple kitchen table, with its plain metal frame and vinyl padded chairs, was the compass of the family. It was also the well-traveled site of an unending stream of gossip and chatter. One of the in-laws once commented that he was afraid to get up and leave the room because then they would surely start talking about him. "I'll hand it to them though, if they have anything bad to say about you," he allowed, "they at least wait and say it behind your back." That wasn't such a bad plan in Myrtle's view. Better than the Oprahfied, let-it-all-hang-out world they lived in now. Gossip might bring families to the table, but sometimes it's looking the other way that keeps them there.

It had always seemed to Myrtle that the further they journeyed from that kitchen table, the messier their lives became. Was it any wonder that they all had returned year after year for as long as Rose was there to welcome them?

Half of a torn curtain hung from the window that looked out toward the side yard and the untilled fields beyond. The stove had long since ceased to work, and Jack Lilly, wily skinflint that he was, had obviously decided not to replace it. A hot plate sat on top of the sagging counter beside the sink. Newspapers and magazines were stacked three feet high along one side of the room, stopping just short of the refrigerator, allowing the door to be opened.

There was a hole in the floor in the corner near the pantry. That was the pantry where Rose kept cakes and cookies. "There's cookies in the pantry," she would whisper to Edward, her favorite grandchild. Myrtle opened the door to the pantry, causing a swirl of dust to scatter. It was empty except for discarded bottles of Jim Beam. Amazingly, the shelves, which used to hold Mrs. Harrison's Mason jars full of canned vegetables, were still there.

The old man grabbed his bottle of Jim Beam from the little wooden table and went into the adjoining den. "You all just take your time," he mumbled.

"Oh," Myrtle sighed, "I could just kill that no account Jack Lilly. He always made up to Mrs. Harrison when she was alive, just waiting to take this land. What a snake!"

The den next to the kitchen had been converted into a bedroom, furnished with a twin bed and a rocking chair. The old man rocked in the chair, Jim Beam at his side on the floor. More newspapers and magazines, along with bags stuffed with old clothes, cramped the little room. The built-in china cabinet was empty save for a couple of dusty rags. Rose Harrison used to have a miniature Statue of Liberty there, and one of those old snow balls with a likeness of the Manhattan skyline, and inexpensive figurines of Little Boy Blue and Little Bo Peep.

"Have you lived here long?" Myrtle asked the old man.

"No, ma'am. Just moved in the last month. I still got to get my things together."

"Well, yes...you know, Jack Lilly ought to fix this place up. He could start with the roof over the porch. Do you just get your social security?"

"Yes, ma'am, that all I get."

"Would you mind if we walk on through?" Stephen asked.

"No, don't mind a bit. You all go on ahead."

The rest of the house was practically uninhabitable. It was like walking through the back rooms of a flea market. Ceiling boards were sagging and, in some places, collapsed.

Rose Harrison's bedroom, which was off of the den, had two soiled mattresses on the floor. Every piece of broken, rusted, chipped, and scratched furniture was stacked in the corners. Myrtle looked in the closet of the room and was pleased to see that, in the midst of so much neglect, the varnish on the inside of the door was still shiny.

They walked silently across the hall into the Boys Room. It was a spacious room where the grandsons used to go to sleep while embers in the fireplace crackled. The men used to hide their liquor in the closet of that room. Now, light filtered through the rafters of the roof where parts of the ceiling had collapsed. Scraps of wood and debris were scattered on the floor.

They proceeded down the center hallway that led to the front porch. When the Harrisons had moved to Centerpoint in the waning days of the Great Depression, this hallway had seemed like the corridor of a palace. Now, it appeared small and dingy. Upstairs, in the loft like attic, where the girl cousins slept, Myrtle could see the outline of a floor length mirror that had been removed from the wall. Granddad Harrison used to tell them that a ghost named Peter Murphy lived behind that mirror. The names of the granddaughters, who at family reunions had turned the attic into an annual pajama party, were still scrawled on the unpainted wooden plank wall. Myrtle surveyed the wall for one in particular. *Lynn Harrison was here!* was at the top of the wall in a dramatic, loopy schoolgirl script.

Myrtle held tight to the banister as they made their way back down. "One time, when I was expecting your mother and visiting Rose, there was a huge black snake crawling down these steps. Lord, I almost went into labor right then and there. But, Mrs. Harrison, she just went to the pantry, grabbed a hoe, and killed it with one whack."

She declined to tell him about another time, when she was pregnant with Lynn. Mr. Harrison was home that weekend too, on one of his periodic returns to Centerpoint. Myrtle wondered why he bothered. Everyone knew his mistress lived with him in the apartment house they owned together in Atlanta. He was as gruff and forbidding as ever, especially after he had a couple of drinks. Myrtle had been coming down the stairs when she heard Rose run screaming down the hallway. "John! You stop right there!"

Myrtle had raced after Rose, and gotten in between them. She wheeled around, gasping for breath from running and rage, and faced her father-in-law, "You touch her, and I will kill you," she said. He looked at her menacingly, towering over her. But, he stopped and then walked back down the hall.

Myrtle and Stephen walked into the living room, which was at the very front of the house. The old mahogany mantelpiece was still remarkably intact. "Do you remember how we used to all come up here and sing?" she asked Stephen.

"No, not really. I was so young," he answered. "But Mom used to say that Aunt Sally would play boogie woogie and then Aunt Dot would play hymns. Kind of sums up the family, doesn't it?"

They walked outside to the front porch. The brick foundations of the white columns were crumbling and some of the floorboards of the porch had buckled. The yard was a barren expanse now of sand and patches of grass, punctuated by the fleshy stump of the old pecan tree. Across the road, the mailbox was dented, and sat precariously atop a faded, unpainted post. But, the red flag that they used to raise to alert the postman that they had something to mail was still there.

Myrtle was grateful that Monroe had been an easy one hour drive, and she and her husband had managed to visit Rose at least every other week. The last few years had been hard, as the old woman battled the incessant, merciless heart disease, and the children battled Rose's aversion to taking her pills. "They make me woozy," Rose would complain, and then stealthily put the pills away.

One day, during that last year of Rose Harrison's life, Myrtle remembered sitting with her in the kitchen, enjoying a breakfast of grits and eggs and biscuits. Her enjoyment of the meal was tempered by watching Rose's exhausted, insistent efforts to prepare it. "Rose, why don't you leave this place," she had asked. "It's too much to keep up. You know you could come and live with any one of us."

Mrs. Harrison gave her a bewildered look, as if to say, 'I know you mean well, but what a crazy idea.' "No, honey, I could never do that," she said. "I don't want to be a burden. And there are just too many memories here for me. Sometimes, late in the afternoon, I go sit on the front porch and I can see all the children laughing and playing. No, I could never leave my home."

"She was a great lady," Myrtle said, as she and Stephen stood there on the front porch, gazing toward the fields beyond the yard. "Mrs. Harrison was the greatest lady I ever knew, bar none. She somehow always knew just the right thing to say, to cheer you up, to encourage you. She was like that with everybody, but especially with family, young and old."

"We were a happy family then, weren't we?"

"Yes, I suppose we were," Myrtle sighed, her eyes moist with remembering and with regret. "I miss that world," she said. "It was so much calmer. Slower. I remember a conversation I had with her near the end and all. We were sitting one evening out on this porch, just as the sun was going down over that meadow across the street. She knew that I was a little depressed. Your granddad and I were going through a rough time. Of course, make no mistake, she always would take up for her sons. No matter what!

"But, she said, 'Honey, live your life and do the things you enjoy doing, because your life is just not long enough. I don't have many years left to be with the ones I love and do some of the things that I wanted to do, because my life is almost over.' Of course, I said, 'No, it is not. You've got plenty of years left'. But, she knew that she didn't. She just hated so much to leave us. I don't think she was afraid of dying, actually. She just hated so much the thought of leaving us."

Stephen and Myrtle walked around the side of the house, past the ragged, spindly shrubs, back to the car. The autumnal sky had quickened to a porcelain blue, delicate and exquisite with waning sunshine. Myrtle got in the car and, as they pulled out of the driveway, she looked back one more time at the wreck of Rose Harrison's sweet home.

They drove beyond the meadow that was across the road, up to the top of the hill that looked down at the house. In that merciful distance, the crumbling old house looked almost the same as it had so many years before. The towering maple tree, rich in autumnal colors, hovered protectively, as if in one last effort to shield the home from further decline.

"Stop here," Myrtle said, "let's stop here for just a minute." She and Stephen got out of the car and looked across the meadow. Myrtle could almost imagine Rose Harrison sitting on the front porch, could almost see children in the front yard playing kick the can on firefly evenings.

Myrtle felt a slight breeze. For just an instant, she marveled at that mysterious intersection of the past and present. She held Stephen's hand and said a silent prayer. And from the hilltop, beyond the darkening shade of red and gold leaves, the home at Centerpoint, intact now only in memory, offered its welcome and assurance.